JESSICA MACK

Guardians of Masks and Memory

Ebony Xscape Publishing

First published by Ebony Xscape Publishing 2021

This novel is entirely a work of fiction. The names, characters and incidents portrayed in it are the work of the author's imagination. Any resemblance to actual persons, living or dead, events or localities is entirely coincidental.

Jessica Mack asserts the moral right to be identified as the author of this work.

First edition

ISBN: 978-1-7364980-0-2

Cover art by Jessica Mack

This book was professionally typeset on Reedsy.
Find out more at reedsy.com

To all the black girls who have been othered and to all those seeking to find themselves.

Prologue

M: Come here, Ebony, and take a seat. Yes, right in front of the Wall of the Pages.

E: Why are they shimmering and moving, like that?

M: Well, Ebony. Words cast spells, which is why we call it spelling, and you have cast many spells, unbeknownst to you though. Spells that have leaked out of your imagination and twisted time, leading to so many variations of you on so many different worlds.

E: So, what am I, really?

M: Hmm, there are many variations of names for someone like you. Technically, some may call you a griot, a storyteller for your ancestors and *technically* since the story on Alfajiri exists in the past on the timeline of the Wall of Pages, it kinda fits. And since all of this is of your making, you are the Matriarch of the Megaverse. All in all, you are a storyteller.

E: Okay, so what story am I to tell?

M: The Book of Wonders at the center of the wall will tell you that. It's going to give you what you need now, at this very moment. But once it starts, you won't want to stop, but fear not for we will be here to help you. So, go ahead and tell yourself the story.

Ebony looked at the Wall of Pages and felt the world go black around her, as if she closed her eyes and then she was flying. She landed as if she were a fireball, but when Ebony collected herself, *she* was already waiting.

M: I know this is your first time Traveling and I wanted to make sure that you made it here without too much of a fuss. Now, my darling you've opened a portal to a universe that slightly intersects with this one. This universe, like all the others, is built upon a narrative question. Your reason for opening this one and parsing through its pages is unique. Now, take my hand and this world of prose and verse will transport you through the rich and colorful plain of the megaverse.

I

Part One

BEFORE

CHAPTER 1 - MALEDA

Contrary to popular opinion, the princess was in the tower because she wanted to be and contrary to what her family said, she was not a butterfly refusing to fly out of her cocoon, but rather a butterfly that liked her tree. That was what Maleda thought as she noted the castle guard walking on the streets below, seemingly annoyed. She was definitely out of place as the castle's peaks were part of the distant skyline above the city. Which meant that she had to prepare for the Fair, to be around the other royals. Though, Maleda ignored the guard, who had suspiciously familiar brown curls, and kept her in her periphery as she focused on her painting and the ocean in the distance. Maleda had gone to the ocean earlier at the edge of the city, unsure that she would be caught there, but thankfully she was able to stare at the waves and sketch in peace. Sunlight streamed into the large window of her tower as Maleda's paint-stained, brown fingers danced over her choice of brushes laid out on her palette. Her head danced back and forth, jostling the fluffy black twists that ran down her back and the mess of a bun atop her head. She needed more yellow, and she wasn't going to stop working on bringing the world in the canvas to life. It was a window that she merely needed to open, and she would happily do it in her quiet sanctuary, but before Maleda could get three strokes in, there was a rapid knock at her door.

"Princess, it's time to go."

Maleda tilted her head up and huffed out a curse, but none of that reached her response.

"Okay, I'm coming."

Of course, it wasn't just one of the random guards. It had to be her. She rose from her stool, brushed her hands over her stained painting clothes, and breezed down the stairs barefoot, savoring her last bits of her own little world. She opened the door to find herself looking into crossed arms and then up into a caramel face with a quirked brow.

"Hi, Mirriam." Maleda smiled, hoping it reached her eyes, and gestured for her to come into her haven. There were few people that Maleda let into the tower. Into her sacred space. She had no choice with Mirriam as she was her personal guard, but she was at least content that she trusted her. Mirriam's arms remained crossed as she surveyed the space and turned back to Maleda, brows raised.

"What?" Maleda asked innocently, palms showing.

"Why is that on the day of the Fair that you are here in the University, in your tower dorm, and not at the castle getting ready?" Mirriam challenged, amusement in her caramel face.

"Would it help if I said that I didn't know it was today?" Maleda questioned, messing with one of her twists.

"No," Mirriam hummed as she sat down at one of the stools in the center of the room nearby another unfinished work, stretched out on a massive canvas, "I'd say that's precisely the reason you got as far away from the castle as possible. All the rush and crowds of people required for the preparation. I get it."

She only half got it. Mirriam was spot on with the crowds, but Maleda also wanted to avoid the *parade* of it all and the formal means of how she would receive private and underhanded insults about being the second in line. Second best. The other one. Sneaking out of the castle and avoiding her parents and the requests of her siblings to wade into the city traffic was a blissful and exciting escapade. Maleda didn't even risk visiting the stables to see her beloved and cheeky owl griffin, Bamidele, even though Maleda wouldn't get to see her until after the Fair ended. The whole purpose was to avoid alerting castle staff, which would alert Mirriam. This was supposed to be a low-key kind of morning, where she did not have the expectations of a princess. She was just a quiet stranger on the street, absorbing the world around her. When the world became too much, everything too loud and her heart ratcheted, she would come to the tower, her own world, where she could watch her people below, but not be among them. Mirriam usually seemed to let it slide, but Maleda suspected that she always followed her. Staring Mirriam in the face in the middle of her tower proved her right. She was a hummingbird, an elegant busybody.

"Well, I've already packed, and I brought my traveling clothes here, so I'll just change and we can get going."

Mirriam reached out an arm to stop her.

"Are you alright?" Concern swam in Mirriam's light brown eyes.

No.

"Yes, I'm fine. Just give me a moment to change and we can get going."

Mirriam quirked a brow and the ghost of a smile faded from her face.

"You really think that you've shaken me off the scent with *that* as your answer?"

"I just had a dream last night. It's nothing."

"Nothing you say?"

"Yeah, I barely even remember it. I guess it made me wake up uneasy."

Mirriam's concern lightened but did not completely fade.

"Well, if you're feeling uneasy, perhaps you should visit an interpreter, a medium."

Definitely not.

"I don't think I need to do that." Maleda waved Mirriam off and went upstairs to her bedroom to change. "It'll be fine. Like you said, I get nervous, so my mind is probably playing tricks on me in my sleep."

Mirriam's mouth opened to argue further, but she was interrupted by a crystalgram call. Maleda thanked the Orisha for the intervention and she dashed up the stairs into her room shutting the door behind her. Maleda stood against the door while the image of the girl turned away in the radiant, yellow coat was at the edge of her mind, but she blinked it away and moved to her clothes that were laid out on the bed.

CHAPTER 2 - MALEDA

There was no extravagant bowing when Maleda departed the tower dorm at the university and walked through the city with Mirriam. There was a quiet sort of respect, some nods and smiles, but an otherness, nonetheless. There was no need for a wide berth as no one would dare. An average citizen may have said it was because Mirriam's face and skill were known, but Maleda simply believed there was no reason. Joy and contentment was what she usually saw on the faces that she passed and for that she was grateful. The Empire of Two Shores was a city of cities and to traverse it easily, Maleda traveled by means of the city train system, which ran both above ground and below ground, but today, Maleda felt like walking. The castle wasn't that far and she could smell the sea. They were approaching the castle gates, when Maleda spoke.

"So, how are things going with Puzo?"

"That is essentially none of your business," Mirriam scoffed.

Even though Mirriam tried to hide it, Maleda could hear the smile in her response. A grin curled on Maleda's lips, but she kept her gaze forward. She had hit her target.

"Oh, come on. You know you have my blessing."

Mirriam turned to face her fully and Maleda glimpsed the surprise and amusement from the corner of her eye, but couldn't help herself from fully turning to look at Mirriam's expression a laugh easily dancing out of her mouth.

"That's rich coming from you. An absolute child, who hasn't confessed anything of the sort."

When Maleda laughed, her heartbeat quickened, but not for mention of any potential love interest, but because she could already see the staff rushing around outside the earth-toned castle. *Just make it up to the throne room*, she told herself. Once Maleda and Mirriam passed through the grand front doors, the rushing only increased, but Maleda made sure to keep to the walls and out of the way of the staff. Arms full of cloth and ribbons were the major feature that she passed as everyone was working so hard on decoration. Even so, Maleda kept looking ahead, her gaze focused on nothing just so she could make it upstairs to the emperor and empress. Once Maleda had gotten to the familiar set of doors, Mirriam opened the door for her. Maleda almost forgot that Mirriam was there. Mirriam looked down at her knowingly and gave a small smile and Maleda nodded her head, grateful that she was there.

"There you are!" Maleda turned to the raspy, honeyed voice and the empress squeezed her into a hug. Her mother's black hair was in waist-length braids and her brown skin was radiant. She donned a gold, simple floor-length dress, perfect for traveling. "Maleda, we've been getting everything together so that we can go meet everyone on the other shore." The empress breezed through her next words, and it was only years of listening that allowed Maleda to grasp everything she said. "Selene and Folu were butting heads again, so Apara had to briefly referee. You were already gone by the time the little ones had breakfast and I should have guessed sooner that you were at the tower, but you do have several other places that you frequent. Your father was being difficult this morning and I've barely seen him all day. Speaking of the university, how is your research project going? Is there anything I can do to help you?"

Before Maleda could answer, her father walked into the room next to Puzo, one of the high-ranking castle guards and his head was bowed over a pile of papers that Puzo held. He muttered his okays as well as his disagreements and then looked up through his sheet of black hair at the empress with a tight smile, but his face relaxed a bit more when he looked at Maleda. His copper skin was in danger of going wan. He loved this time of year, but he barely admitted how much it took out of him. Maleda couldn't help but feel like a buffer between her parents, one where her mother gave her status reports on everyone, including how she was feeling about her father spending so much time in the lab lately. She wished Berenice took more of her mother's crystalgram calls. It was all so much to handle, another reason for her to seek refuge in her tower and dream about traveling to the other territories and kingdoms on the continent. The emperor finished his exchange with Puzo, who inclined his head to the empress and emperor and looked in Mirriam's direction with a sparkle in his eye, before he turned to leave the room. The slight brightening in her eyes was almost imperceptible. Puzo was to remain at the castle heading up the guard, while Mirriam was gone. Maleda couldn't even enjoy the romance that was clearly unfolding in front of her.

"Maleda, dear," her father started, "are you not bringing a project to present this year?"

"Like I was going to say to mom, no. And before you can ask why, it's because it's not done yet. There are still improvements that I'm trying to make." Bringing something unfinished would render eye rolls and dramatic exasperation from her least favorite instructor and the Whitland King's brother would join the chorus. Before her parents could protest, Folu, Apara, and Selene sprinted into the room, up to their usual antics. Usually, it was a mix of chasing each other around or a battle of wits that typically reduced to name calling. Selene assumed the position and grabbed onto Maleda's leg as she gave her brothers her best scrunched up face.

"What are you all on about this time?" Maleda sighed and looked down at Selene who now donned a devilishly sweet smile and blinked up at her. The picture of innocence. "But Maleda. They were bothering me." Selene dragged out Maleda's name, her usual tactic for trying to get her way.

"See, I would believe that." Maleda bowed over Selene and gave an equally sinister smile. "But you and I both know that you were just as likely to have been bothering them." Folu and Apara opened their mouths to start arguing, but the last sibling sauntered in.

"See, if you were here," her oldest brother Akande declared, "then, they wouldn't have come running to me with their bickering. I'm busy learning to be emperor y'know." And therein lied the problem. Her brother just expected her to take on everything. Don't get it wrong. The empress and the emperor never did anything to make her doubt that their love for Maleda and her siblings was equal and Maleda would always love her brother, but he relished all the compliments that he received that seemed to go to his head. He never bullied her, but he didn't exactly lift her up either. She didn't want to be next in line for the throne and she wanted to still figure out what she wanted, so she was fine that her parents chose Akande. At his heart, Akande was good, but he needed to be humbled. Maleda rolled her eyes. "Well, you'll shape up to be a sorry emperor if you can't *at least* multitask."

"Alright, now. Don't start on that." The empress looked between her two eldest children with raised brows.

"Yes," the emperor continued, "let's put that energy into diplomatic greetings once we get to the other shore, Akande." He clapped Akande on the back, just enough to make Akande's eyes widen a bit. Yet, he smiled at the challenge and declared, "Well, I've got this. First impression is everything." Akande was the one to clap a hand to his father's back and usher him out the doors, likely to the boat. The emperor just looked back to his wife and eldest daughter, shaking his head and rolling his eyes. As Maleda watched them go, they almost looked like twins with their long sheets of black hair, but slightly different brown skin tones. Maleda knew that Akande wanted nothing more than for father to be proud of him. She shrugged and walked with her family to the docks.

The ride over to the northern shore of the empire was brief, but Selene usually liked to go up the coastline and Maleda's parents usually obliged her. It brought them closer to their destination anyway and it allowed everyone to glimpse the part of the shore that crawled to the north, beyond their lands. The evening sun danced on the waves as it greedily swept over the beaches. Docking was quick and Maleda had no need to rush back to her cabin quarters. She had everything she needed in her satchel: a sketchbook encased in leather, a little pouch with various writing and drawing utensils, and even a vial of ink. Gaiety and crowds were gathering and milling by for the Fair, but once the boat's platform lowered and Maleda and her family started their descent, that's when she saw the King of the Whitlands standing next to his son, Zuvan, and Zuvan's guard Berach.

***

Heat radiated from Maleda's skin, but that was to be expected. What with all the people, even if those people included her friends. Maleda made to descend from the boat, but her youngest siblings ran for it first, nearly tripping her in the process. She looked at them scurrying away in disbelief and smiled apologetically at Zuvan. He half-smiled back.

"Welcome to the other side of the shore, my friends," the Whitland King smiled widely, and a hearty laugh burst out of him. Maleda always felt like his voice belonged in a bigger body, not someone tall and lithe like him. Though his son Zuvan possessed a similar frame, his voice was lighter, gentler. On top of that, where the king was fair, Zuvan was brown and while they both had shoulder-length, dark hair, the king had loose waves while his son had tight coils. The King visited the northern shore of the empire every year for the Fair. He and Maleda's father loved to nerd out over over potential inventions and prototypes. During some of their most animated conversations, Maleda found herself rolling her eyes, but also laughing because of course she loved it too. When she wasn't painting or doing whatever other hobby she experimented with, she found herself musing on new ideas for inventions, as well.

The king and emperor clapped each other on the back and Maleda found her mother approaching her side and putting a hand on her shoulder, rolling her eyes and smiling knowingly as the two men walked away. Zuvan and Berach remained in their spots waiting for Maleda and her family to go through the remainder of the welcome parade.

"I'm sorry I wasn't with them to greet you."

Maleda and her mother looked towards the silky voice and saw the Queen of the Whitlands approaching with a cheeky smile on her brown face. She gave both Maleda and her mother a warm hug. She released them enough to look into their faces.

"I've just been doing some research and I think you'll be very interested."

10

Her eyes darted between Maleda and her mother. The adults were going to continue their conversation in a great hall in one of the mansions on the sea. The idea of all the new eyes that would be on her and all the looks made her blood go cold, but she kept the smile on her face. As she was about to muster up the words for her exit, Zuvan intervened.

"Mother, Maleda and I were going to join the others down by the beach." He said it in way of parting with an open smile on his face, already turning Maleda away from everyone to start their walk.

"Oh, of course! Have fun!" Zuvan's mother waved them off and continued speaking to the empress, eyes wide with excitement. Maleda turned to wave to her mom as they walked down the windy, beach away from the thick of the crowds and looked back at Zuvan to find a light dancing in his eyes, like he knew a secret she didn't. Berach stood next to him muscled and serious, but a slight smile graced his bronze face. How could he help it, what with his ginger, brown curls blowing across his face? Maleda smiled back at them and said, "Hi Zuvan, Berach. It's nice to see you both."

"Likewise, Princess Maleda," Berach inclined his head and then looked to Mirriam, silently hovering behind Maleda, "Mirriam, always a pleasure."

"Equally so, Berach," Mirriam nodded her head to him as well and they continued their walk with Berach and Mirriam trailing silently behind, ever vigilant.

Maleda looked to Zuvan, raised a brow, and asked, "What are you hiding?" His brows lowered as he shook his head and said, "I'm just glad to see you. What have you been doing at the university? Daydreaming or have you actually been doing your assignments?"

"Listen, I do my assignments and still have plenty of time to *think*. Besides, I have no desire to get on any of my professor's hit lists, especially Buru. He thinks he's the best thing on the continent, maybe the planet," Maleda scoffed. It was Zuvan's turn to roll his eyes and laugh. As they sauntered down the beach, their friends came within earshot. It was in the courtyard of a red-stone, beach-side mansion where Maleda could glimpse them sitting on wicker furniture through a curved archway. Even with the lapping of the waves, she could hear Cherika's delighted cackling. Maleda and Zuvan walked through the archway to find the courtyard filled with fronds of different sizes and colors all over, while the rest of the teenage royals sat in its center. Maleda waved and smiled at them all, the next generation of leaders for the continent of Alfajiri. She hesitated when she saw Girani's large, barrel-chested frame on the ground laughing into the dirt, but of course antics were to be expected. The question is how the saga would continue this time. Mirriam and Berach took positions on one of the walls, always watching out for them. Maleda settled between Zuvan and Cherika, who was too overtaken by laughter to speak. She could only wrap her arms around Maleda, laughing into her shoulder. Where Maleda was tall and skinny, Cherika was tall and full-figured. While Maleda usually tried to shrink, Cherika gladly and unabashedly took up her own space. Maleda wished she could borrow some of her sparkle.

"What's got you cracking up like a hyena and Girani why are you burrowed like a turtle under that chair?" Maleda stared at Cherika astonished as her fuzzy, coily, blonde hair draped over her.

"Oh, Gods!" In between laughs she said, "Girani here suggested that Dunia couldn't hold her own in a fight, so she just knocked him to the floor, chair tumbling over him and she didn't even need to get up. He was just bug-eyed staring at her." Cherika went back to her laughing fit, leaving Maleda helpless to only use her arms from the elbows down. If Cherika's brown skin were any lighter, she'd be an alarming shade of red. Maleda quirked a brow at Girani and asked, "Is this true?"

"Well, to tell you the truth, I was so surprised that I just started laughing," Girani shrugged as he got from under the chair, sat down, and righted himself. Jassiem merely looked on through his brown dreads, shaking his head and threw up his hands. Dunia was lounging back in her chair admiring her handiwork with a bored expression and Jasmine sat next to her with a satisfied smile, twisting one of her cornrows in her fingers.

"Was that one of those times when you wanted me to protect your delicate emotions? Flutter my eyelashes and pout?" Dunia crooned as she inclined her head toward Girani, sending her thick, fluffy black hair jostling over her shoulders.

"Of course not," Girani countered with that easy smile on his dark-brown face, "I have no doubt that you can hold your own in a fight. I just wanted to see how your temper was holding up these days."

"Bold of you to assume that my temper needs helping," Dunia retorted with raised brows and an equally easy smile. This was the game they played. Easy going Girani teasing the impenetrable fortress that was Dunia. Maleda guessed that it was because of some of the pig-headed males in the Ardhi kingdom that liked to challenge Dunia, despite her short fuse and muscled frame. She would mention it occasionally and offhandedly, but Maleda thought more of it. She didn't know what to say to Dunia, other than silently feel for her.

"Well, other than checking in on our tempers, how's everyone been?" Maleda looked over her friends faces as Cherika deigned to stop squeezing her. "Jasmine?" She was usually quiet, but Maleda didn't want her to feel like she was hovering in the background.

"To be honest, I was wondering about the presentation tomorrow and if there would be anything worthwhile or absolute drivel. Speaking of that, are you still presenting tomorrow?" There was a soft kind of challenge in her dark brown eyes. *Drivel. You are the drivel, Maleda.* She felt a sharp pain in her chest, but she shoved it down and just pulled her messenger bag onto her lap. Between Dunia's temper and Jasmine's cold flame, Maleda didn't know why she bothered, yet she kept bothering and even so, Jasmine kept bothering to hang around them. Maybe she too didn't cope well with being a royal sibling and she sprayed her venom on unintended targets. Sometimes, Dunia's and Jasmine's moods were as mysterious as how their rich, dark skin shined like it was laced with stars, as if they were made of the great beyond itself. It didn't help to have the dream of the woman in the yellow coat hovering at the fringes of Maleda's mind either. "Now you know that I was never going to present. The project I'm working on now is taking longer than expected and I'd rather not rush it and have drivel, like you said. I'm perfectly happy listening to what others are bringing to the table. It may be so thought-provoking that it'll inspire changes for my work." Jasmine merely pursed her lips and looked down at her hands.

"I, honestly, think you'd be a lot better off if you just showed us your stuff," Zuvan broke into the iciness with that easy tone. Maleda screwed her face and shook her head, ready to rebut but Zuvan continued. "Well, could you do it for me at least? The Whitlands is much closer than everybody else's homeland and I am dying to see what you've been agonizing over. We could—"

"I've told you multiple times that I need to work on it alone." Maleda grinned as she threw a fist into Zuvan's knee for emphasis. "It'll be ready when its ready." Jassiem just watched silently and so did Cherika. Maleda turned and looked at the confusing expressions on all her friends' faces, showed her palms, and exclaimed, "What?"

It was Jassiem's turn to show his palms and he shrugged. A flicker of thought passed over his light-brown face. "Nothing, I was just thinking that the other presenters would probably benefit from seeing Girani knocked on his ass."

Girani blinked and threw his head back laughing. "Well, if I'm to get my ass kicked, then you must fight your sister. Unlike you, I'm not crazy."

Jasmine interjected on behalf of her brother, "I'd beg to differ and most definitely diagnose you with some form of crazy."

"Well, I'd like a second opinion." Girani taunted with a smug smile.

"Okay," Dunia started, "You're ugly too. I suppose I should knock you down again, so you can keep crawling around like Sundiata and no one will have to look at your face. I mean, you can't be weak and ugly. You gotta pick a struggle." That set everyone laughing and Girani dramatically shook out his mane of a black afro as he narrowed his eyes readying his comeback. Even as Maleda playfully chastised everyone, she and Cherika giggled. Yes, there was always the antics.

CHAPTER 3 - MALEDA

The presentations and exhibitions took place all over the northern shore. People from many countries and other continents altogether came to present their research, artwork, and artisanship. There were artists in the markets on the streets, shielding themselves under tents of many colors, some solid and some patterned. They were also in the arena of the northern shore's university campus. Maleda rose from her seat and left one of the university's lecture halls. She made sure to sit in the back, near the door, so she could beat the crowd that would surge out. The less people she had to filter through, the better. She walked towards a quieter part of the corridor and looked over her itinerary, determining where she would like to go next, but then she heard the Whitland King's brother.

"Are you just going to ignore me?!"

After looking up at the ceiling in exasperation, she plastered a smile on her face as she turned to greet him, but he was not there.

"It would surely be beneficial for you to give it at least a *first* thought, brother."

His voice came from a door left ajar. She didn't wish to be seen so she kept to the wall away from the view between the hinges.

"How could you even think about doing this...And how would you even accomplish such a thing?"

Maleda's face tightened, and she backed away. She couldn't hear everything, but whatever this was, it wasn't good, and she needed to get away. It wasn't her business anyway. When she turned around, Maleda was face to face with the queen of the Whitlands.

"There you are!" Her caramel face held a warm, open smile. She unknowingly and promptly led Maleda away from her husband and his brother. "I wanted to talk to you about your art project."

"Oh, okay. I was just trying—" The Whitland queen waved off Maleda's flustered disposition.

"Oh, I know. You were trying to find the next presentation or exhibition to go to. Well, there's no need to worry about that right now. Everyone's on break at this hour. How about you and I go have lunch together?"

Maleda knew that this wasn't up for debate, so she just smiled and nodded at the queen. The queen was always bubbly and bright, like the flame of her home country. She came from the Moto nation along with her sister, who married the Whitland king's brother, Lucien. Maleda entered the banquet hall in the university with the queen and she felt her body stiffen. She tried to stare ahead at nothing, avoiding gazes. Yet, she felt the queen's hand on her back, a soft, quiet encouragement. They gathered their plates and Maleda walked with the queen to a quiet balcony. There was a view of the northern shore around them and the southern shore in front of them with the sparkling river in between. When they had both started on their meals, the queen asked about Maleda's project again. "So how is that project of yours going?"

"It's going all right." Maleda answered, looking between her plate and the queen. "It's just that as I keep doing more work on it, I'm finding that it's more complex. I don't want to stop doing it though. I just want to be able to take my time."

"So, I take it that it's frustrating when we all keep going on about it."

"Uh, well…I wouldn't say that." Maleda stuttered, but the queen tilted her head knowingly. "Oh, come on, you don't have to protect my feelings or anything like that. Tell the truth. If it's annoying, then it's annoying. Come now, say it with me."

"It's annoying." Maleda hesitated, but was met with that same warm smile, eyes gleaming and the queen looked back down at her plate.

"Beautiful. I know your mother probably already tells you this, but I want you to be bold enough to speak your mind. How you feel is important, y'know."

"I'll work on that." Maleda assured the queen and smiled to herself.

"Remember." The queen started and paused, so Maleda looked to see the queen look serious. She was rarely this intense, so Maleda beared that look and waited for the queen to continue. "It may feel like all you're doing is chipping away at something that's too much for you, too big even. Even with that frustration, you need to remember that is how masterpieces are made. Everything is happening as it should be."

"Thank you for that." Maleda felt her shoulders sink. She was readying to be told to hurry up or that she was missing things by taking so much time. What good was it to present something if she didn't give it her all and make it the best that she could?

After Maleda and the queen of the Whitlands finished their lunch, they proceeded to another presentation. Maleda whirled in her seat to take in the room, but she paused when she saw Berach perched against a wall and sure enough, Zuvan was seated in the lecture hall, as well. On the same row. He was sitting next to his father. When the Queen of the Whitlands took notice, she simply smiled at her son and husband. She waved them over, but before either father or son could seat themselves, an excited squeal sounded over the gathering audience.

"Maleda!" Cherika scrambled over and plopped herself down in the seat next to Maleda with a contagious grin on her face. Maleda found that all her friends had arrived to this presentation, alongside their parents. Her parents took up the seats behind her, meaning that Akande was likely with Folu and the twins. Surely, he was annoyed and that made Maleda smile to herself.

At this particular lecture, there was a woman in a yellow coat sitting at the front of the room waiting for everyone to filter in. The same radiant yellow coat that the girl wore in her dream. Except now, Maleda could see that she was a woman who seemed to be in her twenties. Her skin was sepia colored and her coily hair was black, with a portion of it cornrowed back. Maleda had never seen anyone like her, except in that dream. She was positively otherworldly.

"I understand that Emperor Olmec and Empress Clementina are not just the rulers of an esteemed nation, but that they are both scholars and scientists. Creators. Today, I specifically wanted to show off Emperor Olmec's skills with creating the initial designs of his living paints. While written word is important among the people here and across the sea, the tradition of storytelling through dance will never lose its place." She turned away as she spoke, running her hands over her face. When she turned back around, her face was covered in intricate white markings, like a painted mask. There was surely no way that she created those markings without some kind of blessing from Olodumare, some kind of magic. Then, she started to dance. Maleda was already trying to get over her awe at the intricacy of strokes on her face, but as she danced, the *paints* danced. The paints had risen out of their individual bottles and pooled in front of the woman. As she moved her arms, she manifested—a word for using magical power—and the paint moved in time with her hands, simulating the words she spoke:

A phoenix first must burn, so set fire to the skies black butterfly.
While you sleep the promise will not remain, but your faith is sure
And you are now free, and the world will witness how proud and beautiful you are.
Sail the waters and tell the descendants what the struggle brings.

As Maleda listened to the woman's words, she heard something *different*, something else. It didn't make any sense. One set of words left the woman's mouth, but Maleda felt a different voice entirely reverberate through her and she could not declare what that voice said out loud. Maleda had the feeling that she was forbidden from doing it, but she was honestly too scared to try. It was like the woman in the yellow coat knew. She addressed the whole audience, but there were occasional moments when she looked in Maleda's direction. And just as quickly as the dance started, it was over. The woman inclined her head thanking the audience for their attention and turned to assemble her paints and supplies into a bag. Maleda just blinked, watching as everyone started to speak and rise out of their chairs. It was like they had all been in a trance. No one even asked for her name and Maleda had never seen her in the labs as her father developed the prototype. Maleda found herself rising and walking over to the woman, while her heart ratcheted, and her stomach clenched. Of course, she was curious and wanted to learn just who this woman was, but it was so against her nature. Maleda fumbled for words, but she just made herself ask.

"Where did you get those paints?"

The woman simply looked up at Maleda and smiled, still squatting in front of her bag. There was something cheeky at play with that smile. "Oh, from Emperor Olmec. I thought I said that." She quirked a brow and tilted her head, as if contemplating.

"How do you know my father?"

"The same way you know me. From a dream."

"Wait. How did you—"

"Can't answer that."

"Well, why—"

"Well, in this timeline, I can sort of answer that."

Maleda's eyes widened. "This timeline?"

The woman winced and adjusted her coat. "Somehow, everything works out in this version even though I said that." She picked up her bag and put a hand on Maleda's shoulder. "Please, come with me and I'll tell you."

"She's not going anywhere." Maleda and the woman turned to see that Dunia was standing there, sizing the woman up. Alongside her was Zuvan, Cherika, Jassiem, Jasmine, and Girani with Berach at the doorway behind them.

"What did you do?" Zuvan asked the woman as he took Maleda's hand and pulled her back.

The woman in the yellow coat looked out among them and let out a breath between her teeth.

"Wait, did she get in your head too?" Maleda asked looking between her friends and the woman.

"Yeah, but I literally can't speak what I've seen." Girani looked between

Maleda and the woman in yellow.

"What's going on?" Maleda asked.

"We should see about our parents." Jasmine suggested.

"No need, they are frozen in time."

Maleda let go of Zuvan's hand and ran past Berach to almost crash face-first with an official who was frozen in front of her, suspended in time. Her friends had already followed and she saw the quiet terror on their faces. She was stunned into silence, her jaw hanging.

"It will only last for a minute." They all turned back to the woman in yellow, grounding themselves into fighting positions except for Maleda. She just waited for what she had to say next. "I'm not here to bring you harm, only to prepare you. I've watched your world and I know that it can descend into chaos. You know what I speak of." She looked at Maleda then. The world Maleda saw looked so alien, so enraged and broken and sad. The woman in yellow looked over them all and declared, "Do not speak of what I showed you until after the Forgotten War and please, all of you, find each other again."

Everyone turned round on themselves looking for her, but she had simply vanished. There was no poof, no smoke. Just gone. The guests of the festival began to move again, and they were no longer suspended in time. Not all of Maleda's questions were answered. Actually, none of them were, but she had a bad feeling.

CHAPTER 4 - MALEDA

While the moon was high, Maleda was awake, sitting up in her bed. She let her twists cascade around her like a protective curtain. She and her family stayed in a cozy mansion on the northern side of the shore. Maleda could hear the ocean whispering to her through the open balcony doors and she took comfort in its song. She stared past her moonlit room into nothing in particular, unsure if she should sleep at all. She saw the woman in yellow from her dreams along with a completely different woman in yellow, yet she was forbidden from discussing the matter and so were her friends. Maleda had tried to keep her face placid throughout the rest of the day, focusing on Selene's antics and verbal swordplay with Akande. She drew up her knees and pressed a hand to her chest, trying to claw into her rib cage and alleviate the pressure on her heart.

Aaah!

It was a sharp and sudden cry that made Maleda jump. Before she could convince herself that she was just hearing things—

Ghhh! What are you—

That was Mirriam's voice. Maleda was on her feet and through the door. A wounded cry sounded then. Her heart sped up in a way that had nothing to do with the run she broke into and a sickening cold coiled in her gut. Again, so against her nature. When Maleda reached Mirriam's quarters, the door was barely ajar and the sounds of struggle stopped instantly.

Maybe she should have stayed in her room.

The door opened soundlessly at the push of Maleda's hand and there was

Mirriam crumpled on the floor. She wasn't moving. Maleda rushed over and squatted in front of her to see if she was breathing, but a gasp escaped her when she was yanked back before she could touch Mirriam. She was pulled back onto her feet and a black, leather clad arm pulled her against a stranger's body. She strained to get free, growling at the attacker, but a small gasp escaped her when there was a sharp prick in her neck. The arm released her, and a heaviness blanketed her, a heaviness that slammed her into the floor behind Mirriam. Maleda's limbs were too heavy to move, and her vision was betraying her, as well. It was sharpening and blurring as she fought to stay awake, but she was dragged into inky blackness just after she saw the perpetrator disappear through the window.

* * *

Sound was warped and stretched in the inky blackness, the volume constantly rising and falling. The world looked so misshapen, writhing and in pain. No, it wasn't the world. It was her friends writhing and in pain. She heard someone say *poison* and she felt her own body twisting against the pain. Yes, she remembered the prick in her neck. The arm that held her hostage. New sets of arms held her down. Was that her father's voice above the wailing, crying out for help and guidance? Maleda's eyes kept betraying her. Her vision blurred and sharpened, but then she saw something past all of them.

A woman in yellow, a different one, whose eyes glowed white. She was the last thing Maleda saw before Maleda succumbed to the blackness again. When she came to, she gasped for breath. This process of fading in and out was exhausting and nauseating, or maybe that was the stinging in her back. Maleda was laying on her stomach and she felt heat in her back and pricks on her skin. Each new stroke of pain drew shallow breath from her, but she felt a hand stroking her head and she heard her mother's voice.

It's alright Maleda. She will watch over you.

***

Before Maleda's eyes opened, she felt her back ache. The pain radiated to her extremities. Her arms and legs were too heavy, and she could barely move her hands and feet. The effort it took to twitch her fingers drew a groan from her throat, but a hand already curled around hers. She opened her eyes to find the room full of sunlight and Zuvan looking down at her hand. He was seated in a chair close to the bed and he looked worse for wear himself. His eyes were sunken, and eyelids were half open. Did he get any sleep last night? Maleda struggled to speak, and her voice came out as a croak. "Zuvan? What happened? Where is everyone?"

Alarm ran across his face at the sound of her voice, as if he was asleep with his eyes open and she woke him up. Zuvan looked at her with worry across his features. "Your mother and father stepped out for a minute." He paused then as if he were unsure if he should continue. "I'm not sure how much you remember, but we were attacked last night. Somebody poisoned you and Mirriam. Poisoned me, Cherika, and everybody else except for our parents. No one else was hurt and no one else saw anything." Maleda gaped at Zuvan as he spoke. "I didn't see who attacked. I just woke up looking in your father's face. They're alive though."

"By Olodumare." Maleda exhaled. Her heart ratcheted.

"There's something else, though."

"What?"

"No one can find Queen Anya or…" Zuvan dipped his head as if words were too hard and he needed to rally himself. "Or my mother." Maleda was beyond words, and she just took in the twisted expression on Zuvan's face as he continued on. "I couldn't believe it, can't believe it. They wouldn't let me into the emergency meetings. They kept saying I was too weak, and I needed to rest, but I snuck out of my bed and listened in. They think it was an assassination attempt on my parents. Someone else said that Queen Anya and my mother had some secret plot and disappeared with ulterior motives."

Maleda pulled him in, wrapping her arms around him. She didn't need to think about it. Zuvan let himself be pressed into her, his arms by his sides. His shoulders sank and he finally wrapped his arms around her. He shuddered. "My father. I tried to speak to him, but after the meeting he just went into their room and looked out the window. He wouldn't say anything, but his shoulders were trembling."

Maleda still had no words, nothing to properly comfort him, so she just kept holding him and he continued to hold her. She wasn't sure if the woman in yellow was a hallucination as her father treated her, but what had been revealed to her…the idea of her having some sort of power. It was too much. She refused to dive into it, learn it, or unfurl it. She wanted to be distracted from that tidal wave of self-indulgent worry, but not like this. *Why? Why here? Why now? Why him? Why us?*

CHAPTER 5 - MALEDA

Some days after the attack, the usual time of departure came and passed. Instead of everyone going home, they simply crossed the river bridge to Maleda's family's home, their castle. The royal parents and their children decided that they should meet, albeit the parents were having their own meeting and their heirs had their own. As Maleda waited, she looked out of the window in her room and down at the beach remembering how she and her friends would run wild on the shore. Little children with sand flying up behind them, all with the rainbow colors of the empire at one side and the river at the other side. Everything was so different now and even though she did her best to prepare for it, she couldn't shake the fear that gripped her. She turned from the view and went back to pacing her quarters, watching the chiffon curtains lightly billow in the breeze. The knock at the door came as promised and Zuvan was there waiting for her. He offered a smile and a bow.

"Don't tell me you've been pacing this room all by yourself?" he questioned with a raised brow.

Maleda rolled her eyes.

"Is it a crime if I am? There are dark forces at hand, and I have the right to worry. How are you feeling?" There was a long pause as Zuvan looked at the floor.

"Life's not fair, is it?"

Zuvan's face was haunted, and his brown skin was somehow wan. Maleda's face grew tight and she wanted to take him in her arms and keep him there, but she wasn't brave enough. Immediately after embracing him days ago, she broke into a sweat everywhere but her face, totally warding her off from doing anything similar. Strange.

"Well, hopefully we can figure out some of this at this meeting," Maleda offered. Zuvan smiled at her effort, offered her an arm, and she took it. They strolled down the halls until they reached the castle library and they ascended into a private reading room. One wall was made of glass to let in the view of the city and sunlight for the plants filling the space. Everyone was already there waiting. They were all so full of information, but there was nothing that they were allowed to say, courtesy of the woman in the yellow coat.

In the days leading up to this final meeting, the earth king Onire was much like Zuvan's father. His wails of rage could be heard throughout the castle on the north shore, but he kept to himself, shunning even Dunia. With shaking hands, Maleda tried to seek out Dunia, but she was either hard to find or shut out Maleda and the others entirely. She did come to the meeting, but she was stony as ever. She had every right to be. She had every right to be parsing over how she would find the perpetrator and end them. Maleda wrung her hands as she addressed her friends.

"I'm sorry that we have to have our final meeting like this and I'm sorry about the circumstances that led to it, but we've got to figure this out somehow."

"And how do you suggest we do that." Dunia interjected with venom in her voice. Not a question, but a statement of their obvious deficit. "We've been banned from speaking to each other about the knowledge that damn woman gave us."

"Maybe it's for a reason." Maleda tried, but Dunia barked a laugh. "This isn't one of your little stories that you can analyze in class. This is real." Those last three words broke her voice, but she looked like she would start an earthquake and although Girani was silent he looked like he would see her through that earthquake.

Cherika started, "Dunia, we know—"

A boom sounded. The castle shuddered around them and then silence. They all looked at each other and even the other room with their parents had gone silent.

Another boom, and the castle convulsed. Maleda and Cherika clutched onto each other while Zuvan bowed over them. Zuvan looked at Maleda, giving her a silent message, and sprinted out of the room. Maleda looked over her friends and their expressions turned blank, like they were asleep with their eyes open, and their bodies were suspended in time. Mirriam ran in along with the royal parents. Maleda and Cherika were torn apart by Mirriam and Cherika's mother, respectively. But Cherika's mother slowed until she was frozen as well, along with the other parents. This was a spell. By the lady in yellow? Even with Cherika's name on her lips, Maleda realized that Zuvan must have gone to look for his father and get everyone's parents. Was he frozen as well? Maleda took one last look at her friends and as the castle shook again, she fell to the ground and when she looked up her friends had disappeared. When Mirriam dragged her from the room, she could only take in the abundant smoke and the shouts of war. Whether Mirriam noted the disappearance of the rulers and their heirs, she didn't say.

"We're under attack!" Mirriam informed Maleda. She drew her sword and Maleda's stomach dropped. Maleda followed Mirriam through the chaos, holding on to her cape, unable to see anyone else through the smoke. A hand pulled Maleda back and she let out a yelp alerting Mirriam, but when Mirriam turned to face the attacker, the empress's voice came through.

"Come this way!" She urged as she tugged them both away from the chaos. Maleda stayed under her mother's arm, while her mother held her own sword.

"Who's the enemy?" Mirriam asked as they got away from the smoke.

"Don't know." The empress's eyes flitted around, and she looked to Maleda. "I need to get you out of here."

"Where? What about father? Akande, Selene, Apara, and Folu?" Maleda panicked. There had never been an attack in Maleda's lifetime. Was it a continuation of the attack from days ago?

"Maji nation." Maleda's heart skipped a beat. Would she be able to say goodbye to her father, her brothers, and her sister? She'd already lost that chance with her friends. "Your brothers and sister are hidden away with Puzo. Your father has gone to find out what's attacking, and I must join him." The empress squeezed Maleda into an embrace and Maleda reciprocated. She fought to hold on longer as her vision clouded, but her mother pulled away enough to look into her face. "We love you and everything's going to be alright." Another boom cut their goodbye short and it seemed to be closer this time, too close. The empress pushed Maleda in Mirriam's direction. "Go! Through the passage Mirriam!" Maleda just stood staring after her mother, until she rounded a corner and was gone. Maleda knew she had to keep quiet, knew she had to live, but she tried to run after her mom only for Mirriam to pull her back. They got to Maleda's quarters and Mirriam rushed them both into the room, shutting the door behind them. Mirriam's shoulders sank a fraction, but she still kept out her sword.

"I don't think we were followed. I'll send you through the passage, but you need to go alone."

Mirriam started investigating the wall closest to the window, surely looking for the secret passage that Maleda's mother spoke of. This was all happening so fast. Too fast.

"By Olodumare, Mirriam! There has to be something we can do, something here! I can't do this by myself!"

"You have too! Something happened to me and even the emperor doesn't know what it was."

"Why is it that you didn't freeze like the others back there?" Mirriam paused her searching and turned to face Maleda.

"Why didn't you?" Mirriam could never—

Bang! The door reverberated. *Bang!* Maleda jumped behind Mirriam, to get further away from the door and closer to the hidden passage. *Bang!* Mirriam dropped into her fighting stance, sword drawn. Maleda turned to the wall seeking the passage with her fingers and just as she felt a promising give under her hands, the door exploded open.

Maleda spun around to see Zuvan standing there, two swords in hand. His chest was heaving and his face was simultaneously burning with rage and flooded with pain. Was it his father? Was he missing? Dead? He stepped forward with his swords still raised. For all the summer heat around them, Maleda's blood went cold at the thought that raised fear in her mind. *No.*

"Choose wisely prince." Mirriam warned him. *No. It couldn't be.*

The anger on his face turned wholly into pain. Something was wrong, but when Zuvan opened his mouth as if to confirm Maleda's suspicions, a loud explosion rocked the castle. Zuvan was so focused on recovering his footing that Mirriam took the opportunity to grab Maleda and pull her into the secret passage and just as the door shut behind them, Maleda glimpsed Zuvan's horrified, ashen face.

They careened down a set of stairs and through a long winding hall. They dodged rocks and they were just short of getting crushed as evidenced by the accumulating scrapes on their clothes and skin. Yet, they needed to go faster, but their legs could only do so much and even Mirriam seemed like she was getting winded. They were halted by a large piece of falling rubble and found themselves in an open space with an array of tunnels before them. Which one did they need? *Screech!* The call sliced through the air and cut through the rubble, but Bamidele emerged from one of the tunnels shortly thereafter. The trusty owl griffin screeched again and she made a motion with her head, as if urging them to mount her back. They obliged and as soon as they were seated, Bamidele shot off into another tunnel.

CHAPTER 6 - MALEDA

Minutes could have been seconds for all Maleda knew. Time was warped as the sounds of war continued to rumble around them and her thighs burned from gripping Bami's sides. She kept her arms wrapped around Mirriam's waist, for fear of falling off at Bami's top speed. The rumbling and booming quieted and became distant. Mirriam's growl brought Maleda out of her stupor and she witnessed the blocked passage that rendered their escape route impassable.

"Do we have another route?" Maleda asked.

"Yes, but it means that we won't be able to head directly to the Maji. We'll need to lie low somewhere else for a bit." Mirriam was already nudging Bami in a new direction and they were off riding again. As time stretched out further, Maleda could only think of the woman in yellow and the information she had given her and her friends. Did she tell all of them the same thing? Or did they each get something different? Maleda's mind wandered back to Mirriam.

"Mirriam, how did you keep yourself from freezing?"

"I tried to protect myself, likely same as you."

"You put marks on yourself?" Maleda asked. Mirriam turned her head and nodded in confirmation. "Why didn't you say anything?"

"Like you, I was hoping that I was wrong. Hoped that I was just a little too paranoid."

This new truth resonated between the two, like a plucked string and Maleda silently concentrated on that. But before Maleda could lose herself to that invisible string fully, they had apparently arrived at their destination.

Still astride Bami's back, Maleda watched as Mirriam dismounted, ascended some stairs, and unlocked something in the ceiling of the tunnel. A door. Mirriam flipped it open and laid a hand on Bami, coaxing her up the stairs to access the exit. They were just outside one of the many desert oases surrounding the empire, but now they were in a watchtower perched above the surrounding buildings on the outskirts of the oasis, beyond the wall. There were already guards waiting for them, none that she recognized. They all bowed their heads and one stepped forward.

"General," he addressed Mirriam, "We're glad to see that you and the princess have arrived safely."

Mirriam nodded and helped Maleda down off Bami. "Thank you and have you seen any updates around here, anyone suspicious?"

"No, General. We started—" The earth rocked and a close boom sounded, silencing the guard and a bright, scarlet glow lit up everyone's faces. Bami's feathers rose and she hissed in the direction of the threat. When Maleda recovered her footing, she saw the fire then, heard shouting from below, and saw soldiers rush towards the walls of the oasis. Where was the attack coming from? She looked to the skies but couldn't see a source. Maleda's breathing quickened and she spun her head between the guards leaving through the secret exit and the flames rising in the oasis. She gasped when a pair of hands grasped her shoulders and alarm flared through her skin, like a light trying to shine from her core. Mirriam's voice was far away, but Maleda could hear her alarm. Bami sprinted up the stairs that let out at the roof of the tower and Maleda shouted after Bami, but Mirriam covered her mouth. Maleda turned to the window again and saw something, perhaps someone *flying* over the oasis.

* * *

Maleda barely got a look before Mirriam whisked her away back into the secret exit in the floor and back into the tunnel. She could tell that it was a body, but it was swathed in light. Had Olodumare turned against them? Was this punishment? Something pulsed through the air as they ran and it made Maleda's stomach turn. Whatever or whoever it was called to her power. It made her stomach turn and a wave of oily nausea coursed through her body. It threatened to bring her to her knees while also making her want to explode out of her skin. The tunnel was the only unseen path and it took them back underneath the oasis. The rumbling in the tunnel started anew and Maleda's heartbeat thundered in her ears. Surely, they were under the city at that point. At one moment, Mirriam was leading them on and in the next, Maleda was on the ground.

The world kept going out of focus around her and her vision kept fading to black and coming back to the frenzied scene around her. Part of the tunnel had caved in and the scorching, angry light from above poured in. Black. Someone was hauling Maleda upwards into the smoke-filled air. Black. Maleda felt the shifting of the ground beneath her back and someone stood above her, with worry creasing their face and then they were gone. As Maleda treaded the inky blackness, she tried to remember the person's face. The woman. And as Mirriam's name and face became clear in her mind, Maleda pushed through the surface and found herself awake and alone. She was in a wrecked portion of a building, with the ceiling and timbers caving in over her, close enough to reach up and touch. She rolled onto her side and beyond the wreckage she sheltered in, Maleda saw Mirriam. She was sprawled on the ground and her face was turned away from her. Maleda could have sworn that she saw Mirriam twitch. Maleda's muscles quaked as she attempted to rise from the ground. She didn't care. She would crawl for her, but her blood went cold when a shadow swept over Mirriam's body. An enormous shadow, like a cloud. At one moment, Mirriam was on the ground and in the next people in black had swept her up and carried her off. Once she was out of sight, the shadow disappeared. In that moment, Maleda felt the power thrum through her again and through the ground itself. With hot tears streaming down her face, she closed her eyes and bowed her head to make a bargain.

* * *

32

After Maleda lifted her head and let the tears dry, an uncontrollable tremor coursed through her body. Whoever this was had killed everyone, taken Mirriam and was doing who knows what to her. Now, they were going to kill her. Maleda always feared death, even if she was raised to believe that it was not the end. No one could really tell you about it—not like she had actually tried asking someone on the other side about it anyway—and she thought that she would be a long way off from knowing, but in that moment Maleda knew she could not escape this fate. She could not escape this fate, bargain or no, and somehow it was that undeniable fact that allowed her to close her eyes, take in a breath and remind herself *it's okay to be afraid*. She exhaled with the same thought radiating through her body along with the addition of *courage means to do it scared*. She wasn't sure if it was her own acceptance that helped her or if the bargain empowered her body. Maybe it was a little bit of both, but no matter the source Maleda crawled out from under the wreckage and stood amongst the flames and smoke to look her opponent in the eye.

The being who stood yards in front of her wore a mask crafted of iron and fire framed the edges of the mask. They wore black as well, with no skin showing, no evidence of who they were. They tilted their head up, like in satisfaction that their prey was alone and conclusively defeated. But they only made it one step before Maleda's eyes started to glow white and they wisely stopped advancing. Although no one stood with her, Maleda felt Olodumare's presence and swore that Olodumare's children were at her back.

Maleda took a breath and kept her voice even, "I've come to bargain."

"Oh?" the being questioned. Their voice was a distorted, blood-curdling, layer of voices.

"If you take me now, my powers will be rescinded, and I will die as soon as I am in your custody. You won't be able to get any information or use out of me. However, if you send my spirit through the universe, effectively wiping my memory, and wait for the designated year, we will duel then."

Maleda did not know why Olodumare requested the specific number of years, but she knew she would have to find her way back through some sort of griot. The masked figure tilted their head to the side, considering her offer as flames licked the edge of the mask. They made a show of drawing their fingers across their chin and crossing an arm over their body, but they let out a dark chuckle.

"Well, I accept," the masked figure declared. Maleda shoulders nearly sank, yet something was off and she could feel it as she stared the being down. "But. you should have considered what you said more *carefully* princess."

The masked figure rose in the air on a pillar of flame. Maleda staggered back, but the new power in her veins, allowed her to match his new height on a pillar of water. Two of Olodumare's children used it to extinguish the flames around the city oasis, allowing her to focus on the masked figure. Yet, after the masked figure finished humming to himself and choreographing the spell with his hands, he turned *away* from Maleda and not toward her. It was in the direction of the empire! A wide ribbon of light shot towards the distant empire like a feral rainbow and Maleda could barely see a glittering dome settle over it and then effectively become invisible. He was wiping the memories of the empire! And he was going to shoot Maleda's spirit across space, then take her body! She could feel the outrage of Olodumare's children and she begged them to intercede and manifest in her further. *Please. Please help me.* The masked figure thrust their power at Maleda and Olodumare's children helped her match it, like two beams of starlight shooting at each other. Maleda could feel her spirit trying to part with her physical body, but she fought to hold on. She couldn't kill the masked figure now. That's not what she promised. *Please, somehow make him honor it!* Maleda shouted in her mind. It seemed that the more she begged, the harder her spirit was working to leave her physical body. Tears streamed down her cheeks in the effort to hold on, but a small gasp escaped her when she heard a collection of voices speak in unison. *Trust us.* The only way she could move forward was to let go, so Maleda nodded as she stared down her aggressor. Time seemed to slow as Maleda steeled herself. *It's okay to be afraid. Courage means to do it scared.* She didn't understand the magic that poured out of her. It was like trying to grasp lightning or trying to hold a stream of water with your hands, somehow barely tangible and dangerous at the same time. When Maleda spoke, her voice was layered as well, but her voice was layered with the children of Olodumare.

"In your attempt, to dishonor the bargain, we will force the years and send you back to your kingdom."

The sensation was that of silk being pulled off her as she rose above her limp physical body that still hovered before the masked figure. Somehow, Olodumare's children filled her body, and her body was instantly alert, power restored anew. A sphere of white light expanded around her body, kicking up a windstorm, but as debris flew past, Maleda's spirit remained unaffected. It was only until the expanding sphere reached her, that she felt her spirit being shot away.

Her body and the masked figure had become ants, as well as the planet itself. Stars stretched into long lines as she shot through the great beyond and she heard voices overlapping each other. Maleda found herself flying through so many colors, pluming and streaming around her.

She arrived in front of a world that looked very much like her own, at least from the maps and drawings. Yet, as she hovered, looking at the turning sphere in front of her, her eyes had traveled a far distance, down to the planet itself. What she witnessed for those years, was pain, suffering, shackles, people being tossed off boats. Yet, she also witnessed a bridge made by someone from this world to her own. Maleda witnessed amnesiac generations do their best to reclaim themselves after the worst had already happened. She knew why Olodumare and their children sent her here to watch. One kind of apocalypse had happened, with another quickly underway and it was up to her to stop it from happening on her planet. Then, a voice seemed to whisper. *Black Butterfly, awaken.* She was instantly pulled back the way she came, barely able to register all she saw as she was pulled backwards through the universe as if by an invisible hand. The planet she just left no longer held the strength of the magic of Dziko. Yet, the magic on the planet she just left held its power unwaveringly in its music. It was as if somehow, the music-makers knew what she needed, knowing that she would forget as soon as she returned to her body. The music laced itself into her soul like spells. Two in particular weaved themselves around each other, around her. The first told her to always believe in herself and the latter told her that she was a Black Butterfly with a destiny.

It wasn't long before Maleda felt herself entering the atmosphere and in seconds the blackness of the great beyond transformed into a blue sky. She barely got enough time to twist her body around to see the unconscious girl laying in the sand amongst rubble and ruin. She wished she could—

Black. All was black.

The sun was too bright and its red light filtered through her eyelids. Someone had surely wrapped a metal band around her head and struggling to move was just too much. Her fingers curled and met sand? She felt around more registering more sand and possibly rocks. Where was she? She placed a hand over her brow as she opened her eyes to see utter wreckage around her and sat up on her elbow. A world trying to claw its way out of sand dunes. What was this place? It felt other, but like she should know it somehow. The girl stilled as the vague familiarity of this ruin settled over her. It was something she could not place, could not name. Name. Name? What was her name? She was jolted out of thought when shuffling sounded nearby. She whipped her head about frantically and her eyes landed on a figure approaching. They leaned on a crumbling wall as they advanced forward and something glinted in their other hand. A sword! The girl's breath turned ragged as she tried to scoot away, but the figure quickened their pace and as they approached, she could see that it was a woman. A woman with brown skin and a mess of curly hair. She put up a hand and sheathed her sword.

"You're all right," she said gently. "It's okay." The girl looked the woman over. She wore dingy armor, but some parts still gleamed. One of her sleeves looked like it had been torn off. Her curly brown hair was haggard as if she'd been through an ordeal.

"I'm going to protect you," she offered while kneeling in front of Maleda. She put a hand to the girl's back and eased her into sitting up as she said, "What's your name?"

In a moment of alien clarity, the girl responded, "Maleda."

II

Part Two

AFTER

CHAPTER 7 - MIRRIAM

"Blasted thing!"

It's all Mirriam could do not to give up on her trek into the oasis. She and Maleda needed some more supplies and Maleda always appreciated the books and scraps of paper she brought back. The trouble was hauling the rickety cart they constructed out of scraps that laid around. When she awoke in the abandoned oasis, her body was like lead. Having no idea who she was, or how she got there, she immediately suspected foul play and a sword was in her hand. A sword? She drew it from her belt as if on instinct and light nearly blinded her as she lifted her hand to inspect it. The reflection of the armor she wore. For all the raw confusion that buzzed in her body, there were two words that ricocheted in her mind. *Protect her.* Somehow, it urged her on. In her heart, it felt like she was looking for something far away. Another variation of the demand started to crop up in her head. *Find her.* It didn't occur to her who she could possibly be looking for, but from the looks of her own clothes she had been in a bad way. An attack? Travel with no resources? Heatstroke? By the sands, it could have been all three. When she came across that girl, Maleda, it was like a string was plucked in her. Something between them resonated and she knew she was the one she had to protect. Why? The why barely bothered her, no matter if it was because of some attack or other general misfortune, she couldn't just leave her there. She knew that her wearing armor and Maleda not having any could not have been coincidence and neither was the fact that they were the only people around.

Mirriam passed through the crumbling walls that bordered the oasis and went to her usual fallen building. Maleda was at the tower outside the oasis just a couple dunes over. A tree had grown up through it and it was somehow carved out to make a couple levels of rooms. It still seemed alive though, regardless of so much of its innards missing. Once Mirriam entered the building, she pulled down her hood and shook out her hair, minding the caved in portions of the ceiling. Gods, it was hot! She leaned her back up against a shadowed part of the wall and closed her eyes to let her breathing even out. The trek to the oasis had gotten easier and she could always manage, but that sun was criminal. All she wanted was to rid herself of her protective layers, but she knew better than to try her luck with sunburn. A gentle breeze blew across her brow, but she didn't feel it anywhere else. Wait. Mirriam's eyes flew open. Something wasn't right. She quieted her breathing and willed the air into her lungs as she tried to seek out the cause of the shift in the air. She could have sworn that she felt something. Her hand was already on the hilt of her sword, itching to draw it out. Yet, there was nothing. She silently ground her teeth, frustrated at her own jumpiness. Mirriam kept her hand on her sword and continued to proceed. There was a new room she wanted to investigate. She had made sure to at least poke her head into most spaces to check that they were clear, but she knew better than to try and haul rooms' worth of resources to the tower all in one day. She dragged the cart into the new room to assess its *wares and wonders*. Hmm. Some bundles of fabric tattered at the edges (useful), a warped chalice (probably a bit ostentatious in its prime), and a book…in fairly good condition.

With a swift inhale, Mirriam rolled her trick shoulder and had turned around only for her sword to meet another. It was a battle of wills as she tried to hold the stranger there so she could see their face. Yet, there was no such luck as the stranger pushed back and jumped away. Mirriam staggered only a moment from the force and was coming at the stranger again.

Mirriam lunged forward with sword outstretched, but the stranger simply turned out of her sword's reach and as Mirriam continued to fall forward, the stranger grabbed Mirriam from behind. The sensation was sickeningly familiar, but for reasons she could not place. It was like her body knew, but her mind didn't. Her eyes widened at the recognition, and she twisted around to strike their side, but the stranger was already there blocking her blow. Mirriam gritted her teeth as they continued with swords striking each other. She just couldn't find an opening. The stranger tried to end it by striking down from above and Mirriam raised her sword above her head to block it, but the stranger grabbed the end of her blade and used their sword to force her down and rend the sword out of Mirriam's hand.

"We don't have time for this." The stranger exhaled.

Mirriam tried to rush the stranger already pulling out a dagger, but they knocked her down against a wall. The swift impact knocked the wind out of her, but she did her best to force her eyes to stay open.

"Somehow, I knew the only way to talk to you would be to disarm you first." Amusement played on the stranger's voice, but then they sheathed their sword beneath their robes and pulled the hood down, revealing their face. Three other strangers filed into the room, as if they had been off waiting for their fight to end. Mirriam looked back at the man in front of her, he knelt to become eye-level with her, and he offered her a hand.

"Come now, we have much to discuss, Mirriam." And discuss they did, for days and days. Somehow, those faces conjured up alien images. Perhaps memories, but she couldn't be sure. At first, she kept her sword out when she talked to the strangers, but as time passed and trust built, she kept her weapons sheathed. All she knew was that she had to keep Maleda in the tree tower until she could figure out what was going on.

CHAPTER 8 - ZUVAN

Ragged breaths escaped Zuvan's lungs as he looked down at his ballroom attire. He didn't want to have to do this again. In the mirror, he could see shining black boots, his black velvet jacket and pants, and the red sash across his chest. Each time there was a ball or party to be held, Zuvan had to will himself to attend unless he decided to face the wrath of his father and he didn't pick the latter often. He instinctively held his gloved hands behind his back. Courtly. Formal. Yet, he knew that even though he hid as much skin as possible, the vipers would come at him all the same. He finally looked up to see his face in the mirror, dark eyes sullen and pale skin just like how everyone liked it. Just like Alusamae had been born with. He had trained himself enough to make his face reflect different things. Bored, aloof, and detached to withstand the taunting eyes. A quiet menace and a smile that didn't meet his eyes for those that needed to remember they were beneath him, under his command. Once he had mastered himself, he ran a hand over his wavy black hair, keeping some of it tied behind his head, and turned on his heel to make his way to the ballroom.

* * *

He did not want to be announced so he slipped in quietly by hidden doors next to the throne. The party had already begun with the dancers at the whim of the orchestra. Zuvan stood dutifully by his father's throne and waited, observing the crowd until his father spoke.

"So, you finally deign to make an appearance?" The king questioned.

Zuvan had specifically waited for the dancing to start as everyone would be preoccupied.

"There was a matter I needed to attend to."

"Oh, did you miss a spot on your face?" the king quietly taunted.

Zuvan let his eyes glaze over and let his face become bored as he felt his father's eyes boring into him, could see his inspection from the corner of his eye.

"Well, it seems that you're alright for the moment, but you could have covered yourself better."

The only sign of the sting was an easy inhale as Zuvan looked out over the spinning bodies.

"Where's Alusamae? I thought she would be down here already."

"My pride excused herself for a moment but should be back shortly."

Zuvan let this sting wash over him too.

"Don't let me keep you. Why don't you see *if* you can find a girl to dance with?"

Zuvan bowed and quietly descended the steps from the throne. He supposed that was his embarrassment for the evening. He could feel the smile blooming on his father's face, watching him retreat into the crowd. Berach wasn't going to be around, what with commanding the castle guard and all. He was probably pacing outside the ballroom if he was lucky. If he wasn't so lucky, then he'd be stock still somewhere in this room, helmeted—courtesy of his king—so Zuvan couldn't pick him out and likely reigning in his own eye rolls. Zuvan stuck to the walls, avoiding the gazes or any people that bowed in his direction, save for one woman who was trying to hold his stare. Ignoring her, he soundlessly walked out onto a lonely balcony with the sound of music and gaiety following him, but it didn't reach him. It did not matter what he did, his honor was so hard to achieve in his father's eyes. Hell, basic respect was not attainable. He came to the railing at the balcony's edge considering the height from which he stood. Why? Why continue with this existence in this desolate capitol? It did not matter that he was the king's son and lived in the king's palace. For all the gold and ivory walls, he had no one. Zuvan considered the books he had read, fictional and real, that spoke of places that were away from anything he had ever known. He eyed an oblivion over that balcony that could bring him peace. Yet, he just stared, with his expression wan. Could he even get there? What mattered? He couldn't remember. He wanted the night air, wanted the moon, wanted the view of the kingdom. Most of all, he wanted *her*, but she was gone.

"Good evening, your grace."

The voice dripping with an easy poise woke something in him and he turned around to see one of the musicians standing there. She was uniformed and half-masked like the others that were still playing behind the nearly closed glass doors. Zuvan's thoughts almost ran away from him, afraid that somehow, she saw what he was thinking. Yet, A smile, broad and open was on her face. He nearly balked at it, so different from the cold indifference that he was used to confronting, but he decided to master himself and something in him further decided to be *easy* with her. He was surprised at himself, chest clenching when he gave her a ghost of a smile back and a nod in her direction.

"May I stand with you, your grace?"

Still stunned, he realized he had not spoken yet.

"Yes, please," he offered with a hand. As she approached, Zuvan saw that she was one of the older musicians, but time was graceful to what he could see of her brown face. It was rare that the king let in anyone of color in the castle other than those that entertained him or performed some utility.

"May I ask you what you are thinking about, your grace?"

Her voice itself was a comforting melody and Zuvan barely hesitated.

"First, can you swear that you would not tell a soul, not even your colleagues about our conversation?"

A pause and then she nodded.

"I swear, your majesty," she smiled.

"You do not have to call me your majesty. Zuvan is fine." He smiled at her, fuller this time and looked out over the kingdom, "There are people special to me that I miss. They are beyond the kingdom."

"Well, Zuvan, are you going to visit them?" She put a playful emphasis on his name that made him chuckle. He did not know why speaking with her was so effortless, but he continued whether this conversation damned him or not.

"I'm afraid that they are beyond the land of the living, as well."

"Oh, I see. I am so sorry to hear that."

"Thank you, it just seems like a part of me is lost with them and I don't know how to get it back. I heard that there are people beyond our lands who know how to communicate with their passed on and part of me wants to do that too, but I'm not sure if I should seek it out or if it even works."

"Why is that Zuvan?"

The music rose behind them, drum beats prominent.

"Well, for one thing the king will only tolerate so many foreign inclusions in his kingdom. I'm sure he would be furious to even hear of me trying something like that."

"Well, he doesn't have to know," a mischievous tone took over the woman's voice, "I take it that your friends are from beyond these borders, correct? And that your father does not like foreigners very much?"

Zuvan nodded, eyes narrowing.

"Well, I suggest that you forge your own path, a path beyond these borders even. You're not as different from us *foreigners* as you think."

"What you're suggesting is going directly in opposition of the king. That would be world upending, dishonorable."

"It sounds more like you're trying to convince yourself of that. Listen, the world has ended for me many times and every time I start again in the morning. Surely, you can decide what you want your world to be like and create it, maybe even help stop the ending of worlds."

"This sounds like a lot more than considering a ritual and I believe you should mind your words about the king."

Duty, even when honor would never be bestowed upon him. He looked back out over the kingdom, lights flickering below.

"Of course, Zuvan," she paused on his name and continued, "Yet, I ask that you consider everything we've discussed tonight. You know what will happen when you step back into this ballroom, back into this ivory tower. If you do not want to continue with more of the same, I suggest you follow the path that others cannot see."

A beat of silence passed and when Zuvan turned to look back at the woman, he saw that she had already gone, disappeared into the crowd to go back to the orchestra. He considered what the woman said as the music of the orchestra swelled behind him.

Screams halted the music and Zuvan spun around to see that the room was filled with smoke.

One of the players, still masked and uniformed, barreled at him through the gray puffs, knocking him into the railing. Zuvan watched as the player had scaled the side of the castle, trying to make her way onto the roof. Zuvan decided to put his skills to use and scaled after her. The musician hopped between roofs and Zuvan followed after her as well. He was gaining on her and reached out a hand to grasp her shoulder. He bit out a grunt as he landed on his back. She had been one step ahead and grabbed his outstretch arm and whipped him over her head, like a rag doll. With a hidden strength like that, she could have very well incapacitated him, but it felt like she tried to slow his body down as he fell. How maddeningly curious. He furrowed his brows as he rose up to pursue her again, but she just stood before him. The sounds of alarm continued to echo through the grounds of the castle, but no one seemed to realize the perpetrator was on the roof with him.

"Nowhere to run." Zuvan said through gritted teeth as he stared down the masked musician. "Surrender now."

The musician just tilted her head and smiled. "But we had such a lovely conversation, young prince." Zuvan just grounded himself into a fighting stance, patience wearing thin as he recognized that smile from minutes ago. Why did he have to be a fool and talk to someone? On top of that, he divulged more than he should have. He should have just kept it to basic pleasantries or maybe haughtiness would have been better. He did not have his sword, but he wasn't bad at hand to hand. Still, she just stared with that placid smile on her face. He wasn't about to try and advance on her again.

"So, what was all that talk?" Zuvan questioned and raised his chin at her.

She simply shrugged and the wind carried her wisps of her black and silver hair, "It was just talk, Zuvan. A talk I think you needed to have. I saw the look on your face." She almost sounded empathetic, like she was sorry for him. Confusion and rage tangled up inside him.

"Enough games. What do you want?"

"To free my family," she said simply.

Consequences be damned, he advanced on her. She was just going to keep toying with him, baiting him so he had to make the first move. She blocked every one of his hits and Zuvan worked to keep the alarm out of his face, replacing it with fury. She wanted him close, wanted him to make the first move, but why? As he parsed through the questions and kept an eye on her limbs, she blocked him again and, in an instant, reached under their stagnated arms to draw a circle on his chest and *lightly* push Zuvan away with a fist. Zuvan stumbled as a clamminess claimed his skin. Yet, she kept him in reach when she held onto his wrist, twisted him around so that his back was to her, and he felt her drawing lines across his back. Just like that, his body was heavy, and his vision blurred. He caught himself as he tumbled to the ground, holding himself up on quaking arms threatening to give way. He stared at the stranger as best as he could through bleary eyes.

"What did you do?" Zuvan asked with gasping breaths.

She had been mocking him in their conversation earlier, knowing full well that the rituals he hinted at worked, knowing that other magic worked too. She had been eyeing her prey before she went in for the kill. No one was going to find him up here. He was going to rot on this roof, probably to the indifference or pleasure of his father. Yet, he felt his body roll over onto his back and his eyes found the inky sky strewn with stars. Zuvan pulled at his jacket as heat continued to build up under his skin. He wanted it out. Now! Right now! His skin was too tight, and he groaned against it, closing his eyes against the night sky, wanting oblivion. His opponent, the musician, lifted him with ease and draped one of his arms across her shoulders, but she grunted, "Ooof, you've gotten heavy." She dragged him along and Zuvan could barely make his feet comply. The world around him was tilting at impossible angles. He was going to be sick. His vision kept betraying him, fading in and out.

Black.

Somehow, the stranger had half-carried Zuvan across the roof.

Black.

She had made it to a more familiar rooftop, with him strewn across her back and shoulders.

Black.

There was a series of drops and sudden stops until they were at the balcony of his room. His stomach was lurching, and he said as much through the mumbling groans. The musician laid him down on the bed, but he fought his placement. He had to get away. Had to get away from this impossible heat in his stomach. He lurched off the bed, the stranger attempting to pull him back, but Zuvan pushed her off. He just kept crawling, unable to stand until he was grasping the side of the fireplace. The churning suddenly stopped, and he felt it coming. He wished he could keep it down, but there was no other means of relief. Yet, when his mouth opened *fire* flew from his lips in a golden fury, crisping the logs there. Zuvan was a living contradiction as his body fought to sag with relief, yet fear tried to drag him upright. He scooted back until he had hit the bed frame. His damp hair clung to his face and the taste of sulfur and ash remained on his lips. He laid a hand over his chest as his lungs chased ragged breaths and little stings tormented his fingers. His eyes widened as he fought for more air and his heart was going to leap out of his chest. He turned his head to see the musician was still there and she stood watching over him. Something like worry seemed to cross her eyes and she knelt to Zuvan's side, cupping a hand over his mouth. He was too weak to fight her off, so he just stared at her. *Just kill me already,* he thought. *I'm dead anyway.* Yet, all she said was, "Breathe, slowly." Unable to nod, Zuvan simply obeyed. She could have had poison coating her hands, some kind of powdered concoction to send him to his demise, but no such thing happened. She just kept one hand over his mouth, inhaled and exhaled in time with him, and rubbed his back. His body relaxed with each deeper breath and the relief from the burning drew tears down his cheeks.

"What did you do? I can't wield elements. I shouldn't! Who are you?"

"You've been able to for a while yet. I just cracked the door open a little."

"What do you want from me? Why did you do this to me?"

"What you need to know is in your mother's note in the catacombs."

The mention of Zuvan's mother made him tense and he stared at the masked musician.

"What do you know about it?" but the rage wasn't built up behind his words like he wanted. Rather, they were laden with exhaustion.

"She wants you to remember everything you've been told to forget."

Somehow, those words made him more exhausted, and his head listed to the side as he watched the musician retreat onto the balcony and disappear into the night air. Zuvan dragged his eyes away from the spot and staggered to his feet, went for the pitcher on a nearby table, and doused the fire.

* * *

"I'm sorry," the words were a choked whisper from Zuvan's mouth. "I wish I could have…done something." Zuvan stood before his friends that he barely remembered—seeming to only cling onto their faces—and confessed, yet he lingered a little longer before *her*. Day after day, year after year he had minimized his words to her. He could only speak to her in death, admitting things to her grave. Zuvan stood in the cemetery surrounding the entrance to the catacombs. He couldn't pass by without saying something, but he also knew that he couldn't stall going to see his mother. After the musician had disappeared and he doused the fire, he had successfully mastered himself. Zuvan opened the doors to find Berach inches from his face. Berach clasped an arm around Zuvan's shoulders.

"I wanted to make sure that you hadn't disappeared too or worse." Berach pulled back to survey Zuvan, who reassured Berach that he was fine. Once he was satisfied, they both joined the fray of looking for any sign of the musician. He didn't know exactly what he would have done if he came across her. He ventured off by himself and didn't go with any of the guards that were searching the grounds and the castle itself. Before a horde of them broke off into groups, Zuvan brought them up to speed, explaining that he chased the musician onto the roof, but she eluded him. No further explanation given and certainly none that they needed if he wished to keep his head. They just listened, stone-faced and ready to obey. Zuvan barely had room to wonder what they thought of him, not for letting the musician get away as they believed, but rather for who he was, at least in the eyes of his father. The contemplation was a ghost of a thought in comparison to this unwanted thing inside him and what he could possibly find at his mother's grave. Zuvan took a breath and walked past the rest of the gravestones, surrounded by manicured grass. He was cloaked and hooded, sneaking out of his room by way of his balcony and moving on the roofs out of sight to any castle servants. The entrance to the catacombs themselves lay at the center of the graveyard, which was an arrangement of pillars surrounding a courtyard. In the center of the courtyard, there was a fountain with stairs in front of it that led down into torch-lit darkness. Zuvan listened to the stairwell and when he was satisfied with the silence, he descended the steps.

The torches provided the halls of the catacombs with an amber glow and the place was devoid of sound, save for Zuvan's own footsteps and the rustling of his cloak. The guards for the grounds of the dead were at the edge of the graveyard, pacing its borders, making note of whoever entered. When there weren't hallowed parades for funerals, it was usually small clusters and solo travelers that came. Still, Zuvan didn't want to take any chances with regards to last night, so he snuck in. No one save for the mages and the occasional royal would come to visit the catacombs. He came upon the doorway that led to his mother's room in the catacombs and opened the door easily. No locks needed for this place. There were no torches lit in her room and Zuvan's breath caught as he looked down at his hands, but instead of pondering that possibility, he decided to grab one of the torches in the hall and light the sparse candles in the room. Once he had returned the torch, he quietly shut the door behind him and looked at her coffin, with a sculpture on top that captured her likeness, as if she were just simply sleeping atop the box, frozen in stone. Zuvan's hands trembled. Yet, something was missing. Zuvan clenched his hands into fists as he approached his mother's coffin. Her hands rested in fists atop her abdomen, but when he looked closer there was a hole formed by her fingers, like something should have been there. Zuvan grabbed a candle and lifted it over his mother's sculpted form and saw a darkened spot over her torso in the shape of a sword. Zuvan barely remembered the sword. He had tried to keep the door to memories of his mother shut, as they often brought him to his knees. As he pried that door open and paced around his mother's form, his foot tapped something light. When he looked down, he saw that it was a rolled-up piece of paper. He briefly looked to the door checking that no one was approaching and once he was satisfied, he sat and examined the paper. He unfurled the paper and something new dropped into his hand from the bundled page as he read the note. The trembling in his hands returned anew and he had to steady his breathing. She was out there, actually out there and this would show the way to her. He had to go to his father and ask to take an airship beyond the borders of the kingdom, give him what he wanted to hear so he could go on this mission. This was not the end.

CHAPTER 9 - MALEDA

Maleda swore that she saw the sands move. Maleda blinked with her brush still aloft and turned back to her painting. Perhaps, she'd just been staring too long, and she was hallucinating. That wasn't exactly a comforting thought. Still, wouldn't it be interesting to be surrounded by a sea of golden yellow, constantly bobbing and cresting? Surely, things could travel to her on those waves, like ships. Hell, she'd take an abandoned ship at this point. Or maybe, with the bobbing of the golden yellow ocean, she'd be able to see what it had buried. Perhaps, if the waves stilled and flattened, she'd be able to see something on the horizon, other than the abandoned city. Maybe someone. The thought coaxed her to rest her cheek in her hand as she leaned out of the baobab tree tower, and it was only then that she remembered the wet yellow paint in her palm and made to keep her fingers away from her hair. Maleda had taken a break from her painting and leaned out of her carved window to look at the abandoned oasis below and the abandoned city a few dunes away. The light from the water of the oasis danced against the tree bark and against her paint-smeared brown skin.

"One day, I'm gonna go to a place with lots of water, a whole ocean. It'll be beautiful and I'll just look out over those never-ending waves."

A familiar loneliness silently came over her soul and she did not want to give in to it, so she turned away from the empty outside to the world she had built for herself in her room. Her black fluffy knee-length, hair wrapped around her as she admired the years of paintings that she created over the tree's walls. Thank goodness that her hair had shrunken from its true length, else it would have been stained by the palettes of paint she had on the floor. She puffed her chest out and told herself the story again.

"Once upon a time, legend has it that across the universe there was a planet lush with green and blue much like this one with a special continent called Africa. Africa was a land of varying warriors, travelers, rulers, and adventure. This world also contained a goddess whose ancestors were from Africa. Through the power of her ancestors' roots in Africa, she created the megaverse."

Maleda spun around going through her imagined visual history.

"At first, she didn't know that she had breathed life into it and thought it was only paper schematics and musings of dreams never to come alive. On her home planet, her people had forgotten how to use their gifts to help and most only used their gifts to destroy. Yet, she wanted more. She dreamed a dream where technology and magic were indistinguishable, a dream where the broken could heal, and where she could heal. So, she spread herself across the megaverse and created narratives of worlds where she could heal herself and others. This place is just one of them."

Maleda ran her hands across the wall of her drawings and paintings, remembering each dream that conjured each stroke. Even the story she just recited, was something that came to her in a dream and she used it as her purpose. With bright onyx eyes, she turned to her audience, a collection of professors of her own making at her imaginary presentation.

"I know that we are not in a position to explore the entire fabric of the megaverse, but we are here on this planet of Dziko living in the shadows of a civilization of the past that thrived on the elements of water, earth, air, and fire, right at our doorstep. I have learned that this place possessed fascinating technology beyond our own capabilities and due to an unknown catastrophic event, their civilization is nothing more than ruins.

Now, you probably find yourselves asking, why are we delving into the mystery of some past civilization? Well, according to the texts, there is evidence that this civilization was a sister civilization, or even a smaller portion to a greater territory. The texts show references to different customs and cultures, but all circulated in one populous location, like a city.

These people came together. They all brought different advancements to places like the location outside. There are references to machines capable of flight and power sources. There are also advancements in what appears to be medicine through botanical research and symbolic value in the civilization through catalogs of art.

I propose that if we pursue a field study of these sites then we can learn more about who they were and who we can be..."

Maleda's voice faded as she saw a dark speck out of the corner of her eye. Mirriam had returned home and from the looks of her load, there were probably new books for Maleda to look through. Maleda climbed down the inner column of the tree and ran outside towards Mirriam, leaving the illusion of her presentation behind.

CHAPTER 10 - MIRRIAM

Mirriam pulled down the hood of her cloak and shook dust from her dark brown curly hair. Maleda was a brown blur with thick black twists flying behind her back, so Mirriam picked up her pace so that Maleda didn't have to stray too far from the edge of the oasis. That girl seemed to be getting quicker every day. Mirriam took the full impact of Maleda as she ran in for a hug.

"You speeding gazelle, do you even feel your legs?"

"How was the trip? Did you find anything interesting?" Maleda was already poking through the things, but Mirriam lightly swatted her wrist.

"I see, I'm just slave to an 18-year-old, here to fetch things for you! Well, I found some foodstuffs, supplies, and for you I have brought some more books." Mirriam laughed as Maleda bounced on the balls of her feet and the smile radiated off her face. "Calm down and wait until we get inside."

The two headed into the shady oasis and passed by palms and ancient ruins of buildings. The clay-based buildings were colors that varied based on the sand of the desert. Most were missing their roofs and light entered them by way of rectangular carved windows. They reached a clay wall split by a crevice as if a giant hand pushed it inwards and in front of it was their home, the baobab tree. The tallest tower and only tower in the desert, carved inside so that she and Maleda could live there. Even though the books that Mirriam brought back were damaged to the point of fragments of illustrations surviving, she was still careful about which ones she decided to bring to Maleda. This time, she had three new books for Maleda and a short scroll.

"Oh, thank you!"

Mirriam gave a half smile and a mocking bow as Maleda took the reading material.

"So how are things here?"

"Well, we have had some radical changes around here since you've been gone."

Maleda made a show of gesturing to the place and sarcasm danced off her tone while unloading some foodstuffs from the sled. "You may want to take notes."

"Oh really? Do tell." Mirriam said with mock intrigue. She removed her dark green cloak to reveal skin tanned to the color of cinnamon.

"Well, on second thought, all the details may overwhelm you," Maleda quipped.

Mirriam laughed and rolled her eyes, turning to the materials as she unpacked. She could sense Maleda wringing her hands as she decided to try approaching her again.

"Umm, Mirriam? Wasn't it hard bringing all of this back by yourself?"

"Well, you know it's nothing that I can't manage."

"But wouldn't it be better if I were there to help you bring these things back, even look through what's in the city?"

"Whatever caused this city to become abandoned could still be out there and—"

"Well, it hasn't come for you yet, even with all your journeys between the abandoned city and the tree."

"Even so, I would rather you be here and be safe. I've been fortunate so far."

"So, what am I supposed to do if you don't come back?"

"Maleda, you know we've talked about this—"

"Yeah, I know. I know."

Mirriam saw the light in Maleda's face dim, and she walked over and took her hands. "Please, just stay…for me."

Maleda sighed, "You know I will."

Mirriam embraced her and Maleda hugged her back.

"You know I hate telling you no." Mirriam pulled back to look into Maleda's face.

"Could've fooled me."

Mirriam raised a brow and rained in a snort.

"And I know that the last thing you want to do is stew around me, so why don't you take these books upstairs?"

"You sure?" Maleda barely hid the glint in her eye.

"I know all you want to do is read those books to connect with the world of the past, so get out and bury your nose in them," Mirriam said with a full-on smile.

"Okay," Maleda gave Mirriam one last hug and went back up to her room at the top of the tower.

Maleda ran up the stairs clutching the reading material. Then, that smile faded into worried, furrowed brows as Mirriam contemplated what she found and did not bring back from the abandoned city. Given what she learned, there was no telling who was out on the dunes.

CHAPTER 11 - MALEDA

s Maleda traveled back up to her room, she chastised herself for not getting further with Mirriam. Mirriam always seemed to worry so much and Maleda didn't want to disappoint her, but she still wanted to go to the abandoned city. Maybe there wasn't anything for Maleda there. She just wished that she had a way to know for sure. She wanted to dismiss her thoughts, so Maleda ran up the spiral of stairs carved into the tree, past Mirriam's room all the way to her room. Her room had the looks of that of an unorganized professor with books stacked by her lofted bed and everywhere else. Some were in makeshift shelves on the wall. Sketch-filled parchment, wooden carvings, and parchment models of little figures were scattered about. She paused to admire the mural that covered her wall, covered in vibrant images from her dreams. She was at her musing again, hoping to find some semblance of an answer to the question of her past. She opened the first book, which had an impressive amount of water damage, leaving dripping images of a city on a few pages, but the forms were so muddy. There was no readable text as it was all incredibly faded. The second book was no better, but it had barely-there drafts of what looked like schematics. However, the images were so distorted and faded that Maleda could not tell what the schematics were for.

Staring at all those books gave way to a building headache, but she wouldn't stop until she got to the last piece of parchment. The sun was on its way to dipping behind the dunes and once again she had not found a shred of useful knowledge. Giving into her exhaustion, she fell back on her bed with limbs splayed out and eyes closed. Maleda briefly winced when she felt one of her books hit the floor with a thump.

"Well, it'll be okay," Maleda shrugged. It was only when she heard a drum beat hum through her bones that her eyes sprang open. Shadows were cast across the ceiling against a golden light and she heard voices echoing around her. It sounded like they were singing a song. Maleda's heartbeat ratcheted, and she looked over the side of her bed to see the source of the light, which was the book that fell to the floor of her bedroom. Maleda abandoned the ladder and jumped from her bed to make sure that the book wasn't on fire. It was upon closer examination with hands in front of squinted eyes that she saw that it was not the book that was glowing. It was a beam of light underneath it, from the floor itself. It was almost like the light would not stand to be contained as its brightness grew, but the light dimmed just as quickly as it intensified.

Maleda's eyes widened, and her arms fell as she looked up to see streams of glowing blue falling from the ceiling, like streams of water coming from an invisible and otherworldly source. Caught up in her awe, she was too slow to move as one of the streams of light hit her hand. Her first fear was that it would somehow burn her. Rather, it pooled over her hand like cool water, and continued to fall. The light collected on the floor like puddles after rain and Maleda scooted back until she felt the wall, yet she couldn't get away from the sparkling, flowing light as it enveloped her feet and the rest of the floor.

Maleda was afraid that her books would be lost forever to the light, but as she scrambled to place them on higher ground, she found that they were perfectly unharmed. The light pooled around her, not touching her. Hopefully, it was only contained to the room. If it weren't Mirriam would have been banging on her door by then. Maleda found herself drawn towards the waterfalls of light and she approached one in the center of the room.

"What are you?" Maleda inquired in a whisper and just as she brushed her fingers over the column it split open to reveal another blinding light, which sent her tumbling back to clutch a leg of her bed and after the light, two figures appeared. Their faces and the rest of their bodies were hidden by hooded cloaks. She had to get out of there. Maleda let a toe touch the ground and neither of the two figures flinched. She let her body down and the items in her satchel shifted and the shorter figure casually looked in her direction. Maleda scurried and hid on the other side of the bed. The taller figure was already there and walking towards her. Maleda's eyes shown the whites all around them and she was frozen in place. The figure extended out a hand and she shut her eyes. Yet, she felt nothing. Nothing. Maleda opened her eyes and saw that the cloaked figure was very much in front of her, and the hand had gone through her shoulder. He was looking past her as if she wasn't there. She decided to reach for him, but her hand simply went through him. She waved a hand in front of his face, but he didn't respond.

Maleda moved aside and fought the crawling of her skin as she saw that the man's hand was left behind. *They can't see me?* She stalked around the figure, a little less afraid and she strode over to the shorter figure. Neither of their faces were discernible. The shorter figure reached out a brown hand to stroke the interior of the trunk. It seemed like they were both studying Maleda's work. If they were speaking, Maleda could not hear them and their footsteps were silent, as well. The taller one seemed to call out to the shorter and the shorter strode over to the central column of the tree. Something had alarmed the two figures and they disappeared.

Before Maleda could catch her breath, another hooded figure immediately followed. *By the sands! Who else is coming in here?!* As she watched the figure stroll around the interior of the tree, this one didn't see her either. Upon less dumbfounded study, the figure seemed to have the build of a man. This one was in nondescript black clothing and his hands were covered by shiny black gloves and his face was shrouded in shadow. He seemed to be looking for something, maybe the other two hooded figures. Wherever the stranger stepped, they were encircled by dried floor, as if there was a barrier keeping the water from touching them. Maleda stumbled back eyes wide at the appearance of this person, but the cloaked stranger looked around the room, as if bewildered, but they stood still as their eyes were fixed on the murals on the wall. Maleda crept towards the stranger and waved a hand in front of their shadowed face, but the stranger didn't flinch.

"You can't see me?" Maleda questioned aloud and tilted her head. The stranger started to walk towards the murals and passed through Maleda's hand. A chill went through her at the sensation. When the stranger reached the wall, they ran their hand over Maleda's strokes and colors.

"Hello?" Maleda inquired, but the stranger didn't turn back to her. "Can you hear me?" Maleda didn't know whether to be grateful or frustrated. The first time she meets a person other than Mirriam and she can't communicate with them. *This must be crystalgram,* she thought. She'd read about them in the recovered texts that Mirriam brought back. A crystalgram projected an image of a person that was in another location, so that they could see and talk to each other. It seemed that the stranger's crystalgram was damaged somehow, since he could neither see her nor hear her. Or maybe *hers* was damaged. Had she possessed one all along and just didn't know that she had a way back?

He stopped at the one Maleda had drawn yesterday of the figures in a room with light by their feet. The drawings! He could see those. She needed to send a message. If she wrote on the trunk, he would see it! But did she dare? Upon their first meeting, Maleda had assumed that Mirriam could be the source of danger, but this man could equally be to blame. She did know that if she did not act in that instant, he would be likely to disappear and there was probably a slim chance that he would return. He was beyond the sand and with that in mind, she pulled out a striking stone and a fresh stick. She had blackened the tip and started to write, but even as she quickly scrawled on the wood the hooded man did not seem to hear her. He seemed lost in thought while staring at the drawing until he turned and saw the image appearing on the ground. He swiftly came over and got on hands and knees as he watched her finish the message. *Who are you?* He ran a hand over it and Maleda could see through it to the message below. She stared at him, and he looked up slightly as if he was trying to see her there, and he moved to adjust something in his world that she couldn't see from hers. He pulled something from under his cloak and held a book. He placed it in the center of the room and something about it shifted in the space. The water also stayed away from it. A crackle sounded as his voice tried to find a way through the static, "I don't see you. I'm not sure if this is a delayed broadcast or if this is really happening, but we've been looking for you. I've been looking for you."

Something had caught his attention just like the other two figures and he vanished as he looked back at the message. A rapid and sickening heat ran through her and her heart thumped in her ears. What had gotten into her to start beckoning to the images of strangers? She reminded herself that Mirriam was just as much of a stranger and aside from the worn state of Mirriam's cloak, hers was like those of the visitors. Could they have put her in exile and if they did, then what had she done? Was she kidnapped?!

"Wait, slow down," Maleda muttered with her palms pressed to her head. Maleda stayed on the ground looking around the room, the only world she had made for herself, the only room she'd ever known.

"Let's weigh it out," she whispered with arms wrapped around herself, "Mirriam will never let me go to the abandoned city with her. She says it's because it's not safe. There could be someone out there, someone dangerous. If I stay here, I'm safe. I'm sa—" Maleda paused as a glare of light shined into her eyes from the book that the stranger placed on the floor. Something was buried in the seam.

"By the sands of the desert." She hesitated as she crawled toward the book and flipped back the cover to reveal what was stitched underneath. When she held the object up for examination, she could see that it was a metal sphere, etched with hairline grooves in a symmetrical design and it fit between her index finger and thumb. After wiping off the dust, she could see that her name was engraved on it, but it faded right into the sphere after a few seconds of laying her eyes on it. She could easily chalk it up to her mind playing tricks on her, but she saw her name. Someone was looking for her. Her heart skipped a beat at the idea of being found. Maleda squinted at the sphere and her eyes widened as it floated outside of her fingertips by a will of its own, but then light danced from it. Little figures of light of different colors gliding about in the air. Blue, green, silver, and red. It was somehow different than the strangers that showed themselves earlier and there was music thrumming from it! It was impossible, yet undeniable. Voices, strings, and drums lilting through the air. Yet, the vocalizing and humming was quiet as if it were only meant for her to hear. Thank goodness as Maleda didn't Mirriam to come rushing up the stairs. It was so beautiful and enchanting, but the figures vanished, and the music faded only for the sphere to shift into different patterns, turning inside of itself. The way it altered seemed wrong to Maleda's eyes and she pulled her face away from it.

"Oh, I'm sorry," a small voice uttered, and the sphere smoothed itself out, no longer changing. Maleda let out a gasp and backed herself into her bedpost with eyes tightly shut. When she felt a squeeze on her finger, she opened her eyes to see that the floating sphere was gone and was replaced by a ring on her finger. She was afraid that she was losing her mind. She was certainly not going to try talking to it, for fear that it talked back, or was it worse if it didn't? Instead, she focused on its new form. The bottom part was made of wood that transitioned into glass at the top. Maybe it was resin. The glass seemed to hold a world inside it, a world she had seen once before. Her eyes widened and she scrambled up the ladder to grab an assortment of books and parchment. She spread them out on the floor and flipped to the corresponding pages. The place in the ring looked like the city she constantly dreamed about. It was there in all those washed-out images and muddy sketches that she had made. They all looked like pieces of this city. Someone had survived the conflict. They were alive. There was someone out there trying to get her attention. But what did that mean for Mirriam? She could not have hidden the ring in the book. She would have just given it to her. By the looks of the stitching, she would not have even noticed it.

So why was she lying to her?

All those times that Maleda had told her about her dreams and asked questions, Mirriam never said anything beyond the world of the past being killed by war. She had never revealed anything about herself. If Mirriam did not hide the ring in the book, then that meant that the abandoned city, was not lifeless and someone was looking for her.

Maleda's nerves had become frayed in that instant and she rose to her feet and began to pace turning around on herself. She had to leave. She had to see. She would not die in that desert at the edge of a world she had never seen. She couldn't leave that night. For all she knew, Mirriam was suspicious of her. Mirriam would probably go to the abandoned city in the morning and if she didn't, Maleda would fight her way out.

Sleep seemed out of the question as Maleda grabbed her satchel and stuffed it with small containers of pigment and writing utensils. She couldn't take all her books, so she opened her sketchbook and nearly filled it halfway with the muddy sketches she had seen in the books. She even grabbed her scraps of parchment and folded them between the pages. The paper and wooden models she created would slow her down, so she made sketches of them at various angles before ascending to her loft with satchel in hand. She scrambled through which papers to take, and she fought exhaustion as she made the last few sketches from the books gathered on her bed. She wouldn't stand a chance trying to get away if she was in this state. She had to rest. She let herself lay down on top of the mess of covers, while clutching the ring in her hand and staring at that far off city. She would wake up before the sun was high. She had to if she were to make it past Mirriam and see what was beyond the sand.

CHAPTER 12 - ZUVAN

A crackle sounded as his voice tried to find a way through the static, "I don't see you. I'm not sure if this is a delayed broadcast or if this is really happening, but we've been looking for you. I've been looking for you. Stay away from the empire. Something's wrong."

He did not notice the shadow encroaching him from behind. He was entirely focused on the frail possibility that he could be talking to her. He did not know they would cut the signal, send stars across his vision when they struck him across the head, and in his unconscious state lock him in a cell with a monster.

He just knew he had to find the brown-skinned girl with the long, thick twists of hair. It was his last thought before he fell, his last thought, before he was locked away.

CHAPTER 13 - MALEDA

Maleda's brain was in a fog and her head was slightly pounding as she awoke to the sound of parchment crumpling under her. Then, she popped upright as she felt the warmth of the sun and remembered last night. *So much for waking up before the sun.* She was still clutching that ring. She made quick work of gathering her satchel and bounded down from the loft. She changed from her previous day's attire and now donned a cloak similar to Mirriam's. Maleda did not have a weapon to speak of. Her best chance was her ability to run with the wind and pray that Mirriam did not catch her. When Maleda was satisfied with her attire and preparations, she descended from her room, passed Mirriam's empty room, and made it to the first level. It was quiet and she was not there. No note had been left and Maleda knew that she had gone out to the abandoned city.

The question was how she would make it to the abandoned city without Mirriam catching her on the way back. She didn't have any choice except to run for it, but as she attempted to bolt, she found herself being dragged back. She was dragged so hard that she fell onto her back, and she looked to the ring on her finger.

"Please, don't go that way," said the ring. Maleda's eyes widened as she realized that she had not imagined that voice from yesterday. She stumbled to her feet and quickly made her way into the tree.

"Are you telling me that you can speak? Like really speak?" Maleda questioned the ring.

"Obviously," the ring said in a cheery tone.

"Well, why shouldn't I go that way?"

"Because she will catch you, but I know another way you can go."

"Really, well—" Before Maleda said the question, the ring pulled her to the side of the tree farthest from the abandoned city. There were various neat piles of supplies and the ring pulled her forward until her finger gestured towards a pile of fabric.

"Move that pile of fabric aside." Maleda followed the ring's instructions and she found that the floor was uneven. She was able to lift it up like a hatch and she found a tunnel. Maleda was able to see a torch inside and retrieved striking stones from her bag. Yet, she was afraid to make her way down into the darkness.

"It's all right. I'll be with you." The ring encouraged her. Maleda looked to the ring on her finger and squeezed the stones as she made her way down the steps. She quickly lit the torch before closing the hatch above her sealing them both in the tunnel.

"From the drawings that I've seen, you are eager to learn much about the ruins of this place," the ring said while they continued down the tunnel, "but I bet you didn't know that this place has underground tunnels. Back when this place was alive, it was a means to split up travel above ground and below ground, not to mention that it's a lot cooler down here."

As Maleda carried her torch through the tunnel, she observed that the tunnel did not have any remarkable features other than torches appearing every so often on the walls.

"How do you know all this and what are you? Where did you come from?"

"I am a helper, here to make sure that you have guidance as you find your way. You can call me Cham."

"Um, you didn't really answer all of my questions. Look, Cham, can you at least tell me who sent—"

Maleda was cut off by the creature as it seamlessly transformed back into its sphere state, floating in front of Maleda's face.

"Listen girly, I would love nothing more than to tell you everything, but when I entered your world, I became bound to its curse."

"Curse?" Maleda questioned, "What curse?"

"A curse that I can only mention and not exactly discuss my dear."

"Okay, what can you tell me?" Maleda sighed.

"It's all muddled together actually. Well, I know that I can transform from this form into the ring, but they've limited what I can actually say, and I don't know until I attempt to say it."

"Ugh." Maleda looked to the ceiling frustrated with the creature and she saw that they came upon a blockage in the tunnel, as if it had fallen in some time long ago, but there were rays of sunlight coming from above. "Well, it looks like we've got to climb out now." After a quick and faint glow in Maleda's peripheral vision, she looked down to see the sphere become a ring on her finger again. As Maleda climbed fallen timber and rock, she wondered what could have caused the cave in. She doubted that the sphere would be able to tell her. She squinted as wisps of sand fell on a phantom wind, but she kept climbing towards the light. Her arms and legs were burning by the time she made it up to the sliver of light, but when she reached up, her skin warmed at the presence of the sun. Maleda crawled out of the tunnel, looking back at the way she had come, shivering at the height that she had climbed. Everything was white around her, but as the light gave away to edges, forms, and shadows she could see that she was in the abandoned city.

CHAPTER 14 - MIRRIAM

They hid in the shadows of the abandoned city and the cover of the ruins would have been a comfort, but Mirriam knew that if she could hide then so could her enemies. She sat in the company of four other figures that were cloaked in darkness breathing in the dusty air. The only evidence of light filtered in through cracks from above, covered up now and then by fabric blowing in the rafters.

"You can't possibly be serious?!" A seething voice hissed.

"Buru, I'm telling you that I didn't send for a call." Mirriam said calmly. Even in the darkness, she tried to uncoil the tension in her body.

"Well, we got a signal," Buru started, "and we weren't the only ones to sense it. Don't get me wrong, it wasn't anything magnificent, more like a phantom whisper. Still, how long do you think it's going to be before people start recognizing a change in the air, before *the evil one* senses it?"

"Don't you think I've considered that?" Mirriam's voice rose. She took a silent breath and emphasized each word. "I understand what you've told me, been telling me. I know that the princess died and Maleda was her friend. My last promise to the princess was to protect Maleda. Maleda doesn't know anything of the old world. She fancies it, but there would be no way for her to activate a signal. Besides—"

Mirriam was cut off by a metallic creak and shadow that temporarily swathed the room in complete blackness. *Maleda.*

"Look, a decision has to be made now. Either we let her perish to them or we take her back and I've already made my decision. I'm following my word to the princess to whatever end." Mirriam sprang to the surface, still covered in shadow and she hissed to the four figures in the forgotten pit below. "I'll recover her alone and we'll meet you in the central building."

With that, Mirriam darted from shadow to shadow readying herself for Maleda's rescue.

* * *

Maleda

The city was beautiful, even in its forgotten state. Maleda's mind danced with questions as she walked by old pillars, some fallen and some standing. *What is your name?* Maleda asked the city in her mind. Sand had swept itself up in between the building making every effort to build its own dunes with time, regardless of the remnants of structures standing defiantly in the way. Maleda looked further ahead and could see that she was in the outskirts of the city. A few dunes away, there was still a great wall before her with a chunk missing, wide open, as if it was waiting for her.

Several dunes later, Maleda reached another peak and she saw jagged forms protruding from the sand and the beaten wall had encapsulated it all. She was nearly there, and she was about to make her way down to the flatter expanse between her and the city, but something like furious thunder roared in her ears and the force of it sent her tumbling down the slope of the dune. She struggled to stand as she faced something giant.

CHAPTER 15 - MALEDA

achine. Something like the muddied illustrations of tech from the old world that she had seen, and it was flying in front of her. It was a magnificent and terrifying display of metal and smoke. Whorls of decorative gilding ran along its sides, and it hovered. Maleda didn't know if running would do her any good, but she suddenly felt that it was foolish for her to hope that the person she contacted was on her side. Was this the work of Mirriam or someone above her? Then, she heard a voice.

Zuvan

For weeks, he had been looking through that machine, trying to locate her and for weeks he had planned what he would do when he found her. He did not want to think of his temporary imprisonment, courtesy of the ship's Second. A Second who was loyal to his father before anything else. That imprisonment was a warning for what he could expect back at the kingdom, but he had to chance it. For her. She had tried to forget him and maybe she had succeeded, but after this day, he knew she never would.

"Who's out there among the dunes?" His voice was amplified by the machine.

She seemed to have gone dumb as she stared up at the machine. The whites around her eyes were ever-present as she said, "I am but a humble traveler. I wanted to see the city and—"

"I would not suggest that in these dunes. This airship would help fix that problem. All you have to do is come onboard." He had to get her into the machine and from the looks of her barely blanketed terror, he considered that it might be better to run her out and capture her, rather than coax her in.

"Where would you take me?" Where? She did not ask for a specific drop off. He scoffed a little, so she really was clueless or amazing at acting.

"Beyond the dunes, to the Atlas Mountains if you wish." Sense would tell that girl that she had nowhere to run. Even if it was her destruction, she had to go with him. She made a look as if to consider his offer, but as she opened her mouth to respond, the roar of machinery sounded from behind. It was the pirates! Those showoffs couldn't listen to his patrol orders, and they were going to ruin the snare he had laid out. Before he could shout an order, they were already firing warning shots of cannons around her. By this time, the girl had gotten to her feet, but still cowered. As if from the air itself, another body appeared in front of her, fully armed, and there was a primal sound so fearsome that it threatened to shatter the desert sky.

Maleda

Maleda didn't know how the person had gotten there and she didn't have time to consider it as she kept well away from the projectiles. The person was decked in a dark cloak and their head was covered by a turban while their face was veiled by fabric. A shadow passed over them all and there was an animalistic screech that tore through the sky. It drew the attention of the two machines, and both started to fire at it. The smaller of the two directed another volley of projectiles, but before they were halfway to their target, the person had thrown something that exploded smoke. Maleda's eyes burned, and she couldn't get air to pass to her lungs as she coughed. The person grabbed Maleda's hand and yanked her along as they repeatedly yelled, "Run!" They made it further into the ruins of the abandoned city as the cloud behind them began to fade. The stranger ran with an assurance and Maleda couldn't shake their grip, but her heart flew into her throat as they dropped into what felt like an endless darkness.

Zuvan

Once the dust had settled and that beast was gone, he seethed as he looked across the sand for the girl and her savior, but they had disappeared. They couldn't have gotten far. All he had to do was figure out a plan and wait.

CHAPTER 16 - MALEDA

Maleda's heart pounded at the darkness that surrounded her below, so she focused on the light above. The stranger had dropped into the darkness below, while Maleda grasped at a frayed rope that dangled from the ceiling and she swung from shadow to light. Her hands burned, but she wasn't about to let go. Just as the ship passed over, Maleda had swung into shadow, but she kept her cry of relief buried in her chest.

"I think they're gone for now."

Maleda yelped at the voice, forgetting her new shapeshifting companion which was still a ring wrapped around her finger.

"If you want to get anywhere, you're gonna have to let go," Cham urged.

Maleda's heart seized at the thought.

"Are you crazy? I can't see anything down there!" Maleda hissed, panic edging at her tone.

"Well, you certainly can't climb back up and I'm pretty sure that person down there will help you."

Person. And as is if by Cham's narrative command, Maleda heard a voice.

"Maleda, it's me. It's Mirriam," her voice echoed from below.

Cham chimed in, "See? Told ya."

"Maleda, you must let go," Mirriam called again, "Just drop!"

Maleda stayed silent for the simultaneous panic of dropping and for having to face Mirriam after defying her wishes.

"Oh, by the Sky Father, let go," Cham whispered as it squeezed Maleda's finger and *dragged her hand down.* Remarkably, it was enough to loosen

Maleda's grip and she fell into the darkness with a yelp on her lips. She bounced onto what felt like a giant canopy of fabric and she slid down it, her speed increasing. Her body found the end of the fabric and she ramped into the black air. As she fell, Maleda spread her arms trying to find something to catch her fall and she was greeted with a gust of air from below slowing her descent, as well as a pair of arms that caught her.

"There you are," a light voice whispered, "We've been looking for you."

Maleda jumped at the realization that it was not Mirriam's voice that she heard, and it was not Mirriam's arms that were holding her in the air. They were wearing a hood and their face was cloaked in shadow. Maleda fought in the stranger's grasp as they backed themselves away from the light shining from above. Amidst the struggle, they let down Maleda's legs, but held a grip on her hand.

"Please, stay quiet. I'm with Mirriam," the stranger said.

"Zaddae!" Mirriam hissed from a cracked doorway, "What are you doing?"

"I thought that you might need some assistance," he gestured between Mirriam and Maleda, "You don't seriously think I was going to let you deal with all of that and not come along as back up. It looks like a good thing that I did come after all."

"Oh, by the sand!" Mirriam hissed and gestured into the doorway, "The both of you—get in here."

Maleda and *Zaddae* hurried past Mirriam and stood in a passageway dimly lit with torches. In the light, Maleda could just see his eyes, topaz like the flames in the torches, and dark fabric shielded the bottom half of his face from view. Maleda looked over Mirriam's shoulder to try and get a hint of what old treasures she had stumbled past, but before Maleda could get a good look, Mirriam had shut the door. Apparently satisfied with her inspection, Mirriam led Maleda and Zaddae through the dusty passage.

"You just couldn't wait. Could you?"

"Wait for what?!" Maleda questioned, arms outstretched. "What was that out there? Who were they? Is this what you have been protecting me from?"

"Maleda," Mirriam halted her flurry of questions, "those things are the reason why this city is abandoned, the reason why it's dead. All of this time,

I have been trying to make sure that things like those had gone away, but somehow they picked up our location."

The man in the tree.

They were coming closer to a greater source of light and Maleda had caught up with Mirriam's stride. Zaddae kept his distance behind them.

"That may have been my doing."

"How could you have done it?" Mirriam seemed to be calculating the problem herself. "You have nothing to signal with."

Signal? She'd find out about that later. As for her answer, lying was the best bet.

"I think one of the books you brought back had some hidden stitching and I found a ring in it and—" Mirriam looked at Maleda and her nostrils flared, and her eyes seemed to burn. The fierceness in her eyes almost tempted Maleda to keep her distance. Mirriam shook her head back and forth with fury and looked back to Zaddae.

"Did you have anything to do with this?" Mirriam asked him.

"I have no idea how that could have gotten in there, no idea how anything could survive this place," Zaddae promised.

Mirriam turned back around continuing her march and muttered to herself, "Buru. When I get my hands on him! Giving you some of the old technology. By the sand of the desert, I'll massacre him when—"

Mirriam had cut off her bloodlust imagination and just muttered to herself. Maleda turned to Zaddae who only winked back at her and gestured out a hand for her to continue forward. "I want to make sure that I stay behind you to keep you safe, so please keep after Mirriam."

Maleda simply blinked at him, still astonished that this stranger was present and caught up with Mirriam.

"Buru?" Maleda interrupted. "Who's Buru?" She tried to stop Mirriam by grabbing her shoulder, but Mirriam simply kept walking with a stone stare.

"Buru is going to be dead in a minute, but you'll meet him before I slaughter him for endangering you." Maleda didn't have time to ask any other questions as she practically ran to catch up with Mirriam while they proceeded down the dim hallway. Mirriam came across a hidden door that

Maleda almost didn't see and forced it open. When Mirriam walked through it Maleda and Zaddae followed finding themselves in a giant corridor that had to have once been grand. Windows as tall as trees had glass shattered from their panes. The stones in the wall and floor were chipped, some missing entirely. How could anyone be in this city? It looked ancient from the sand caked in window gaps and the faded state of the stones, but how could she possibly know? She couldn't even clearly remember the state of the world that she left.

"Look," Mirriam started, "I know that this is all suspicious."

"Clearly." Maleda cut her off. Maleda sounded like she demanded an immediate explanation, hiding her shaking hands in her cloak.

"It's not going to make it any better when I tell you that I can't explain much about what just happened out there."

"And why not?"

"Because it is a curse of masks and memory."

"Right! That's what it is!" Cham chirped happily.

Mirriam immediately drew a sword and gritted out, "Who's there?" She only got to circle Maleda like a mother lioness for a second before Maleda's ring shifted off her finger and morphed back into its original spherical, floating state.

Mirriam stepped in front of Maleda assessing the new target.

"Oh, I come in peace. I promise." Cham assured her new audience.

"Please don't hurt it Mirriam," Maleda urged moving between Mirriam and Cham, "It actually—"

"It's from the times before," Zaddae spoke attracting the attention of everyone, "It is said that this is an organism from beyond our land, something that came down from the sky around the early years of our world."

"Sent by the goddess of the megaverse." Maleda realized looking at Cham with a new fascination.

"Well, that's what some may say," Zaddae responded, crossing his arms.

"Is that it? Did the goddess of the megaverse send you?"

Although faceless, little beads of light pulsated through Cham's intricate designs as if she were thinking.

"No." Cham finally spoke. "No, she didn't send me. I don't remember who did. I just know that I'm here to help you, help guide you."

"Look." Mirriam started, with a finger pointed at Cham. "I don't know what sick joke you and Buru are playing, and you won't leave my sight."

"All right." Cham conceded. "I understand, but I will stay with Maleda. I won't be separate from her."

Mirriam looked between Cham and Maleda and simply responded, "Fine. Come on, we've lingered too long already."

As they continued down the hall, Maleda decided to ask Mirriam more questions while she cradled Cham in her hand. "What do you mean by a curse of masks and memory?"

"Something bad happened a long time ago. I'm sure of it, but my memory only goes up to a certain point and the rest of it is hidden away from me."

"What about the war that tore apart this place?"

Mirriam gestured to the walls around her. "It never ended, and it is a bit more complicated than a war. What you saw out there was likely a series of scouts, and they don't want anyone near this place."

"If they have been roaming the desert all this time, then how did they not see the oasis?"

"That's the thing. They haven't been scouting, which is why it was *safe* for me to come here, but the signal must have alarmed them to come check out the area."

Throughout all this, Maleda didn't notice that they were approaching an impressive set of colossal wooden doors.

"Is the person who gave me this ring behind this door? Will they tell me what it is?"

"If I don't wallop them first." Mirriam growled. She shoved the doors aside and Maleda followed her in as she gazed upon what seemed to be a beaten-up throne room. At the end of the room, was an empty set of two white and gold thrones surrounded by four men who did not care to hide their faces. They were all cocooned in fabric, each of them donning a unique set of colors. Maleda also thought that she saw glimpses of metal shining underneath all that fabric.

Armor. But who were they fighting? They all straightened slightly when they caught sight of Maleda and Mirriam. The man in green attire greeted them with a particularly, stony expression.

"Mirriam." She simply nodded and looked like she was restraining herself from rolling her eyes. "And who is this?"

"The girl that you nearly killed." Mirriam started.

"Pardon?" The man in green smirked. "I don't believe I was the cause of the show by the wall."

"Well, if you didn't do it, I would be surprised." Maleda may have thought of something to say post-conversation, but she stood by like a ghost as they were discussing her. Her fear was at the back of her throat, but just before she dared to cut in, the man in green had started again.

"Girl, do you even know who we are?" Mirriam seemed especially irked at the way he addressed her.

Maleda was reigning in the surprise and anxiety of suddenly being confronted with so many physical people and conversation, as savage as it was.

"You are very convincing, you know," he said approaching her.

"What?" Maleda was more confused than anything as the man in green prowled around her.

"You look like her. You sound like her. Stars, you even give off her air."

"Who?"

"Well, evidently since *you* cannot even remember that, perhaps I am mistaken." The man in green retorted while looking her up and down. The look in his eyes suggested how unimpressed he was. She was tempted to keep her eyes on the floor, but some ancient instinct kept her staring at him.

Something from *before* was telling her to keep him thinking that she would not back down from his stare, even though her internals were churning.

"So," Maleda started, "you're saying that you're not the one who sent me this." Maleda held Cham up in front of her face letting the sphere levitate in front of Buru, whose brows furrowed.

"Y'know," Cham raised her voice pulsating with light, making Buru jump to Maleda's pleasure, "I don't appreciate how you're looking down at my girl here. I am sworn to protect her, and you don't want to push me."

"Oh," Buru challenged, "And just who sent you to protect her?"

"Well," Cham fumbled, "I'm not exactly sure of that, but that's beside the point."

"There is no time to discuss *this*." Buru said pinching his brow. "It seems that the ships are gone, which means that we can prepare to travel at first light."

Travel? Maleda did not notice how much time had passed until she looked outside and saw afternoon crawling away and turning into evening. Everyone seemed ready to part into different directions, but Maleda could not sit on all that had happened that day in silence.

"Wait, I would like some answers. What happened out there just can't happen." Maleda looked at Mirriam. "I never believed that another human could exist after you described the severity of the war, but here I am staring at you all and you didn't tell me."

The man in green looked like he was ready to verbally strike, but Mirriam interjected as the man in silver held him back.

"Are people still out there in spite of the war?" Maleda asked amongst the silence.

The strangers briefly looked at each other and the man in silver armor nodded. Since he seemed the most civil, Maleda focused on him.

"You don't have to tell me your names. I doubt you will anyway, but could you tell me who you were before?" The man in green rolled his eyes, but the man in silver's eyes became warm and he extended a hand out of the throne room to invite Maleda to follow him, so she did.

"Before the war uprooted our lives, we were professors. However, there was some event that came over us all at once, a sort of amnesia which we call the curse of masks and memory. There was a war from before, but whoever we were fighting with didn't want us to remember something from the time, something that could have probably saved this city, protected the people living in fear now."

Professors. They were men of history, literature, and science torn away from their crafts and forced to fight to survive. Maybe they were the source of the sullied books that Maleda had received. Strange, indeed. The group walked until they came to a set of worn wooden doors. Upon opening them, Maleda saw that the doors hid a well-kept secret of colorful tapestries, a plush bed, a well-kept fireplace, various pieces of furniture, and a balcony with open doors with panes of glass and chiffon-like curtains. It was like the war had not touched this room.

"This is where you and Mirriam will stay for the time being," the man in silver said, "and I would advise you to get some rest as we'll have to travel a trying distance tomorrow." Before Maleda could form a proper question, the professors had already started down the hall. Zaddae had briefly lingered, but he followed the others until only Mirriam remained.

Maleda had forgotten that she still held onto her ridiculous supplies, and she dropped them onto the bed, trying hard to find the sister in Mirriam's face and not the feral bodyguard.

"I'm sorry that I can't tell you more, but we've all lost our memories."

"Oh really? It sounds like you all can at least remember a portion of your lives, while I can't recall anything. So, if they can't tell me and you can't tell me AND there are machines out there waiting to stain the sand with my blood, then will anyone even have the chance to tell me? You can't just expect me to accept this and not have questions about everything." Maleda's eyes were big and daring, but fear lurked behind that mask.

"You've got to understand that it kills me not to tell you and I know that this doesn't make sense at all, but I promise that you will find out who you were before."

"How can you be sure?" Maleda sat on the bed, head hanging.

"Well, you shouldn't sound so defeated for a girl that made it past my nose to the abandoned city and encountered a piece of old-world technology." Mirriam knelt down and took Maleda's hands, "I just happened upon you. I didn't know who you were before. That's for you to figure out. I just took in a girl that was lost in the sand and it pained me to see you pining after what once was, especially when I couldn't tell you how you fit into it."

"Buru kept referring to me as *her*, a *specific her*. If you don't know who I was, then don't they?"

"They might," Mirriam dragged her hands down her face, "but I don't want you to get your hopes up. Once we leave tomorrow, we'll be able to find someone that could help us confirm your identity." Mirriam crossed the room and closed the balcony doors. "You, however, need to rest. I may not be able to tell you everything, but I don't think that I have to tell you that the machines out there are more dangerous than the men in here. That is not a lie. You have to trust me."

Maleda peeled her eyes from the floor and studied Mirriam's.

"I trust you." Mirriam's eyes shuttered and she nodded before she left the room.

Somehow, Maleda could feel that Mirriam was not there to harm her. There was nothing she could have gained from Maleda's presence other than a stand-in family. Still, the plan could have been to bait her into comfort for the past few years, so she would be caught unawares by the charade. She could not turn back to the sands, but she would not sleep like a helpless child while these strangers discussed matters that she should know about, a world she should know about, and a self that was unbelievably foreign. She decided to wait until the sun had edged closer to the dunes and she put the satchel across her shoulder again. Maleda urged Cham to transform back into her ring state, and Cham slipped over her finger before Maleda crept into the hallway to follow Mirriam.

* * *

All Maleda had to do was follow the dusty footprints lit by modest candles in the hallways. There were some that parted into other directions, probably to throw her off, so she wouldn't listen in on their conversations. She decided to follow the more crowded footprints. The sky was glowing with the orange of approaching evening as she found a door that was slightly ajar with candlelight and shadows pouring out of it. Maleda stayed close to the wall and peered in through the cracks in the hinges. Only Mirriam and the man in silver were in her view. They were sitting before an empty table, save for the weapons that looked like they had just been cleaned. How often had those weapons been used to subdue, to kill?

"How can we trust anything she says? She could be lying to us to keep playing runaway." The man in green sounded like he was pacing the room given the steady rise and fall of volume of his voice accompanied by the rhythm of footsteps.

"You and I both know that if she is whom you speak of, she would not have left dishonorably under any circumstances." Mirriam stepped in to defend her. "Even though she cannot remember, this has to be part of something bigger that went wrong." From the sounds of it, Maleda didn't know if she would trust her former self either, but then a pain seized her right behind the eyeballs, but she tried her best to ignore it as she listened.

"Either way, we will know to truly trust her by bringing her to the empire." The man in blue offered. "They will decide if she is some sick illusion, or the real thing."

"She's able to work with tech from the old world." Mirriam interjected. "That isn't just some coincidence."

"Mirriam," the man in blue countered solemnly, "She could look like her, sound like her, and appear as if she is clueless. We've got to be ready if that's the case."

"Well, I'm not the one who gave her the ring," seethed Buru, "and if she is a copy somehow concocted by whoever, then you two will have to pay for your foolish dreaming and hoping that she could survive."

A copy? A copy of her? She didn't know what happened to her before and for all she knew, this body wasn't her own if she was made to be someone else. Maleda strained to listen, but could hear nothing, so she peered through the door hinge cracks to see an empty room. Before she could turn on her heel to creep back to her assigned quarters, a hand smothered her mouth, and an arm was bound over her middle. Zaddae leaned forward to face Maleda and removed his arm from around her waist to lift a finger to his lips.

The man in red pointed down the hallway and Maleda saw the figures casting shadows across the floor as they silently crept through the roof.

The other professors and Mirriam were on them in an instant, encircling Maleda. She held onto the satchel and gripped Cham, still in ring form on her finger.

They were backing away soundlessly until the pain from before seized Maleda again and she barely let out a cry. The figures in black were on the ground, with faces unseen and they were facing the group. Mirriam grabbed Maleda by the arm and ushered her to run. It had to be Cham that they wanted, and they probably wanted its new owner. The light from the evening sky flashed overhead as Mirriam led Maleda careening through the halls. The sounds of war were echoing behind them and the pain in Maleda's head persisted.

"Don't look back and keep running!" Mirriam ordered.

Maleda gritted her teeth against the steady pulsing in her head and in her body as she ran. The professors had caught up with them looking wild-eyed and feral with weapons drawn. After a turn, the group came upon a space that opened to a harbor. The only vessels that were there were long canoes.

The boats looked like they were starting to rot, but they would have to do. Mirriam and Maleda jumped into the first one that they saw. Maleda had to adjust to the bobbing of the boat under her feet but steadied herself into an upright sitting position as they rocketed forward.

Maleda heard and felt the whoosh of some projectile go past her cheek and disappear into the waters. To keep her head, she lowered herself at the front of the canoe until she was almost crouching. She could see that they were in the middle of a lake with the abandoned city surrounding it and were approaching a small island. Atop the island were lush trees and stone, like that of a small castle. Once they hit the pebbly land, Mirriam jumped out and pulled Maleda out by a hand. The pain remained at a steady beat but grew in intensity.

Maleda tried to swallow it down and clutched the satchel, with Cham wrapped tightly around her finger. They bolted into the forest and continued until they reached broken steps that were overgrown with greenery. The doors to the castle were hanging loosely from their hinges and there was enough space between them for the company to make their way through the old halls. After twists and turns, they arrived at an impressive set of wooden doors that still shone intricate carvings despite the obvious lack of care. Mirriam pushed the doors inward and revealed an exact copy of their home tree back at the oasis.

Everything was there, even the same branches. When Maleda turned back around, the professors had done their best to blockade the door. Despite death biting at her heals, Maleda still had the gall to speak.

"How is this possible?" Her answer was the banging against the doors. Instantly, Mirriam was in front of her and backing up onto the tree root bridge. The professors were arranged in front of them, ready to duel with weapons drawn.

"I don't have time to explain, but if we are smiled upon in this place, then you will see me again."

Another bang sounded at the doors and it looked like the figures in black would be inside at any second. Mirriam backed Maleda up into the tree, but Maleda found that there was no floor. As she fell, the last thing she saw was Mirriam spin around to face the entering captors with two swords in hand.

* * *

When Mirriam spun around the men in black were hurtling through the barricade and she was ready. There was one for each of them. Mirriam's opponent leapt onto the tree branch trying to follow after Maleda, but Mirriam swiped her swords this way and that until they were at the start of the root bridge.

She didn't have time to tell her where to go, but Maleda had to have some sort of good sense to lead her away from that chamber below. The men in black were armed with swords, but they were not armed with any old-world tech. That was a merciful thing to note. They were not supposed to kill, but if it came down to it, they would.

With every swing of her sword, she believed that meant that it was Maleda that Mirriam had cared for in the oasis. If she was a copy, then Mirriam would be brokenhearted, but she staunched that thought as she slammed her sword's hilt into the back of her opponent's head. When he was falling to the ground, the professors were already climbing the tree, headed for the hole in the glass ceiling. Mirriam scurried past them and made a grand sum of three leaps from the tree trunk to branch, and through the hole in the ceiling helping each of the professors out.

* * *

Maleda had fallen into pitch blackness but hit a dusty floor. Stinging bit into her palms, her joints, but she looked up and saw that the light from above was still far enough away that the figures in black could lose her. She started crawling for some sign of exit and she felt it before her eyes adjusted to the darkness. There were distant sounds of war from behind and above, but it came to a sudden stop, which encouraged her to crawl faster.

Just as her arms seemed like they were at the peak of burning, she made it to a curve with light hitting the bend. A way out. Maleda gritted her teeth against the fire and when she reached the lip of the tunnel, she dragged herself out.

Without sure intel on the enemies in pursuit, she stayed low to the ground and was as quiet as possible. She was surrounded by trees and was at the back of the castle. The gentle lapping of the water told her that the shore was nearby. She voted against hovering in one spot and stayed low as she crept toward the shore looking for a way off the island. By the sand, there was nothing at the immediate shore. Of course, there wasn't. She decided to make her way back to the rocks that towered upwards behind the castle to monitor the shore without being seen. They had to have sent more soldiers after them.

Maleda's thighs began to burn and her back felt strained by the restricted range of movement, but she saw fabric billowing in the sky. It was attached to some upright wooden...*thing*. A ship? She crept from behind the rock blocking her view and indeed saw a ship that looked like it could fly. For her to escape with Mirriam and the professors, the vessel had plenty of room.

It had the masts, but some of them jutted outwards like wings and there was a silver contraption that seemed to power it in the middle. It looked like its fuel was fire. She didn't have time to decide if she should wait to see if it was truly relieved of its crew and she started towards it clutching the satchel. Even as she faced this monster of a machine and potential ambush, she still thought about how she could do with something that didn't get in the way as much as her satchel slapping against her side. The plank to the ship was already lowered and there didn't seem to be any activity aboard, so she crept forward onto the ship. She silently made her way around like a cat, until she turned to hear running footsteps shifting the pebbles on the shore and she ducked behind the railing. She couldn't fight, so she would learn if she could swim. The footsteps sounded up the plank and she made ready to swing over the edge, but Mirriam was there and one of the professors was yanking her up by the shirt.

It was Buru. Of course, the loveliest of the bunch.

"And where do you think that was going to get you?" Maleda didn't have a response due to the shock coursing through her body, so she just looked at him with resentful gratefulness. She would probably think up the perfect snarky response later. The man in red was already at the fire chamber with a fire started and Mirriam was at the helm. The ship lurched forward, and they were rushing the sand shore before them. They were going to run onto the sand. Shouldn't they have pulled up by now? Yet, all doubt faded and Maleda had no words as the ship lurched itself into the air and she gripped the railing so as not to go sliding around the main deck. Miraculously, they leveled out and Maleda could stand with no support as the wind brushed past her face. She turned to see that they were clearing the abandoned city as well as the oasis.

She looked back at the oasis in silence, trying to memorize it as it was likely that she wouldn't see it again anytime soon. She swallowed her fear, but it almost got caught in her throat. While she tried to muster some sort of calculation into her face, she made her way over to Mirriam. They would not listen to some whining girl who lost her memory. She dreamed out in the desert, but her dreams were right next to scraps of research made up of ruined books, hopelessly foreign images, and schematics as well as dreams that she knew had to be memories. She didn't have a sword, but she had her brain, no matter how clueless she felt.

"This ship has the ability to navigate the waters and the skies." Mirriam offered. "It requires that metal chamber to have a fire going, which generates heat, and the heat helps keep this ship bound to the air. This is a modest one. There were far grander ships than this before." Fascinating. Yet, the more fascinating idea was that even though those figures in black most likely wanted them dead, they had still come from *somewhere*. For all that Maleda knew, the world was nothing but that desert. She had no idea what could lay beyond it. Even her dreams seemed to be censored as she could not clearly see a location or a place. Her hope was built on those dreams being real. They couldn't have been some desperate, unconscious desire to create something that never was. She grasped onto Cham, still wrapped around her finger.

"Mirriam," she inquired while turning the ring over in her hand, "is there a world still out there to go back to?" After a beat of silence, Mirriam took one hand from the helm and held Maleda's.

"I want you to believe there is," she whispered, "because it helps me believe too."

CHAPTER 17 - ZUVAN

Zuvan had long abandoned monitoring the sands for her and had retreated to his office aboard the ship. That beast in the sky may have been the *other* thing that they were looking for. In their great flying machine, they had left the desert, but their retreat left him unsatisfied. Did that monster truly shred their bodies and take what was left over to whatever den it made in that abandoned city? Possible. Still, he was unconvinced as he looked upon the sea that they flew over to go back to the kingdom. Despite the sun sparkling off it, he stared out of his cabin with a cold, calculating expression. Perhaps, it was because he could see his pale reflection, sullen dark eyes, and shining black hair brushed from his face. The face of the one who lost her, a failure. He had a meeting in a few minutes as his father wished to speak to him and he had no choice, but to oblige him.

Already dressed in fighting leathers of red and black, Zuvan turned from the glass between him and the sea to stride out of his cabin.

His footsteps were a steady thud underneath his boots, and he moved with lethal grace to the communications room. Several soldiers were milling about the room, which was centered around the raised platform. Light started to build from it and the head of the room dutifully declared, "Ready to begin communications, sir." Zuvan gave a curt nod and ascended the steps to the platform with hands laced together behind his back. Barely a hum and then the glass in front of him that beheld the sea had turned black with the shadowed figure of a man on the other side. Zuvan bowed at that shadowy figure, his father.

"Empty-handed, I see." That was his uncle who spoke first monitoring from nearby and then appearing at the side of the king. His father waved a hand for his uncle to stop and for the prince to proceed.

"With all due respect," Zuvan began, "how would you know if I do not already have the prisoner stowed away? Maybe I am not the kind to flaunt my prizes and I just put them out of sight where they belong."

"Hmm...," His uncle crooned. "You still don't have her though, do you?"

"On the contrary, the only thing I would have likely been able to obtain is bloody robes. Some creature attacked us, and some sort of guard came to her aid, but not before the sand was kicked up and we saw what was left."

"You didn't take the robes to let us assess them?" His uncle continued. "How negligent."

"We couldn't take the robes because we were under attack by some beast that we could not see, but seemed like one of the creatures you were interested in. We barely made it out with our lives."

"Not important," His father started. "The point here is that you failed your objective."

"Well, not entirely." Zuvan began. "We took our ships away but left some special operatives behind to check the ruins. None of them reported back and with our strict protocol, that can only mean that they have perished. So, I believe that someone may have survived with some special talents. Whether that is the knowledge to handle a weapon or the manifestation of the elements, I don't know. Given that all of them are gone means that it is more than just the one guard with her or that there were at least survivors. We decided that we should return to the kingdom to give them a little reprieve and safe travels."

"If she survived, some news would have to spread about some strange girl from the sands."

Zuvan confirmed his father's conclusions with a nod and said, "And she may just lead you to what you're looking for."

"Report back here swiftly and hope that what you believe is true." The screen went black and Zuvan's chest fell a little, but his hardened expression of cunning did not let up. It was one of the more pleasant conversations he had with his family. He left the room, allowing his soldiers to continue their milling and did not stop until he reached his chambers and shut the door behind him. Miraculously, the second on the ship, Calhoon, said nothing during that curt and brief meeting. He probably enjoyed watching him being made to feel like his efforts were insignificant and the results were brought on by luck. He observed his reflection instead of the ocean below with his fist to the glass. Still in this prison. He grimaced as a chill overtook him, radiating from his heart. Zuvan soundlessly strode over to his bed which was carved into the wall and sat on its edge. He held his head in his hands. He was trying his best to execute this mission smoothly and he felt cursed to not have been better. A second more and she would have been aboard.

While a heavy sigh left him, Zuvan peeled his boots off with his feet and discarded his leather jacket to reveal the tunic underneath. As he drifted off to sleep surrounded by shelves of books above, Zuvan pondered how that girl would fare as this venture continued.

When he awoke, he arrived back at his circle of nightmares and raised his cunning once again, preparing to watch the girl from afar.

CHAPTER 18 - MALEDA

Maleda woke up in a cabin on the ship and almost panicked at her surroundings until she remembered the events of yesterday. Professors with weapons. Figures in black. A flying ship. She rose onto her knees to look out of her window to see the sand passing by like a golden ocean below and the sun at its midday position. Then, the secrets hit her. Maleda had said nothing to Mirriam about the man that had somehow traversed through the tree. She had almost forgotten about them given the ravaging events of yesterday. A fair chance that she would not see them again, but she decided to keep that to herself.

For all she knew, speaking that secret aloud would bring them misfortune and she was entitled to her secrets too. Maybe there was a way she could reach out to who she saw and find out what they were looking for. She was completely unaware of their intentions, but at least they were the only people who hadn't tried to kill her, but who knows? *He* could have sent those ships to the desert after she laid that message out. She was so desperate for interaction beyond Mirriam, desperate for a world that she thought had been destroyed long ago from a war that she didn't even remember—a life she didn't even remember. She could have doomed them all by her message, but would it be so bad to choose to risk a sedentary life in the sand especially when there was a chance that the people were still out there—her past was still out there? Maleda may not have felt prepared, but Mirriam and the professors knew how to fight well enough. Hopefully, she wouldn't need to witness their talents again, at least for a while. Her satchel was sulking against the wall, only standing because of the supplies that were in it. She ruffled through, not putting it past her *companions* to take away anything. That was the other thing. What was the curse of masks and memory? She had to find out these things for herself Mirriam said. Completely nonsensical. Maleda shook her head at the nonsense of it all and pulled out her sketchbook to write in it. She recounted the people she saw in the tree, the message she left for the lone male figure, the machine with that smooth voice from the desert, and each of the professors, particularly trying her best to recall images of that machine. Although a voice came out of it, it seemed to be a vessel like the one they currently rode in, but wildly different as if it were from another world. Maleda walked through the ship and thought on it as she got to the main deck. People had to be inside that thing unless metal itself had been taught to speak. Mirriam and the professor in silver were up at the helm quietly discussing something, pretending not to tense up at Maleda's presence. Maleda stretched her lips thin into a mockery of a smile and strode over to the railing. Let them keep their secrets from her for now. She would have to find out about things at some point. Maleda was convinced that they were not there to take her prisoner, but they all made strange allies. Mirriam finally strode over to her and took up a place leaning on the railing.

"So," Maleda began, "are we any closer to the part of the world that hasn't been reduced to sand?"

"Yes, surprisingly this thing has been holding up against our need to hurry." Mirriam smiled, "Actually, we're just getting there."

Mirriam pointed towards where the ship was traveling. Maleda had never seen so much green. The desert had possessed its dunes that turned to rocky hills, but this was a forest with mountains. Even though shy bits of shrubbery started the transition, it was still so sudden and stunning. There had to be life in this place, human or no. Maleda didn't know how long she stood there appreciating the approaching landscape, but they were almost upon it when she spoke again.

"And how much closer am I to hearing you tell me what this is all about?" Maleda tried to keep her voice cool as she asked, but she knew that her desperate curiosity was betrayed by her open face. Mirriam sighed and in that moment of calm, she sounded sympathetic.

"I've told you that I am not the one to tell you. Maybe the knowledge would do more harm than good."

"To who?" Maleda challenged quietly.

"You." Mirriam turned to face her fully. "It would be harmful to you and I'm not saying that just to save my own hide. If the truth comes from any of us before we get there, you could very well be hurt, and I don't know if I could help you out of it."

"I see no sense in your argument. How could me hearing something, namely the truth, hurt me?"

"You won't understand until you feel the pain of it," Mirriam sighed, "Besides, she made me promise that no one would tell you and that only you could find out for yourself."

"What—"

The ship was starting to shake, and that silver contraption sounded like it was choking. Fire started to creep from its corners like water in a boiling pot. Mirriam swore and Maleda backed away even though she was a healthy distance from the thing. Fire. Fire on this wooden ship. Why couldn't it have been made of metal and fly away spectacularly like the other that had attempted to attack her first. Maleda heard Mirriam roar at the others to help get the fire under control—with what she did not know— as she ran to her cabin to retrieve her satchel. She fell to her knees as the ship somehow felt like it had jettisoned forward. Luckily, her satchel had remained untouched with all contents remaining, including Cham. She swiped it and ran back out onto the deck welcomed by the sounds of shouting. The fire was creeping its way over to them and the boat started to buck from side to side. Maleda barely kept herself upright, but she managed to make her way up the stairs to the helm with the others quickly following suit. Her breath hitched and her heart was beating in her ears. They were over the forest now, somehow leaving that golden ocean of sand behind them. The fire was overwhelming the main deck.

"We have to jump," Maleda realized. They weren't going to make it. They would be speared by the trees only to be burned at their backs, but there was a small chance. There was a quiet, wide river winding some distance away. If they could just hold a little longer, they could hope that the water was deep enough to receive them.

Maleda braced herself against the railing, while the rest were balancing on the railing and grasping the ropes strung to the masts above. She couldn't even out her breathing. They all kept an eye on the fire at their backs and the river approaching. Still, the fire had crept up faster than they wanted. Maleda was cursing herself for writing a message to that figure, not telling Mirriam about it, and for the fact that this would-be adventure was now going to be the cause of her death.

"Get ready!" One of them shouted, but the boat would not wait. A small explosion erupted. They were not quite over the river yet. Maleda tried to haul herself onto the rail, but the boat was already turning onto its side. Maleda made it onto the hull due to Mirriam shoving her, but the others were scrambling when the ship exploded and Maleda was thrown away from the sky wreckage and towards the river.

* * *

Mirriam

Mirriam and the professors landed in the woods and could barely hear the river from their position, especially considering the sounds of falling debris in that disturbed forest. It was like landing in this place, closer to their goal had restored some sense of knowledge to her. Sound was muffled to Mirriam's ear and its slow returning was accompanied by a ringing. Mirriam called out Maleda's name, but she was nowhere around, probably on the other side of the river. She was remembering, just a kernel of something useful, but she would use it. If anyone caught her, they should be aware of who she was soon as they saw her and judging by the awakening of what crawled underneath her skin, they will know that she was indeed real. Soldiers had probably caught up to her by now. There was no use trying to catch up with them to try and explain, but she prayed that they stayed their hands long enough to consider who their intruder was without being blinded by the curse of masks and memory. The professors all looked around and then to Mirriam with a combination of fear and purpose in their eyes as if they too regained kernels of their memories. Mirriam rose off the ground and started to feel the stinging in her shoulder as the adrenaline began to wear off. She was supposed to escort Maleda back, but it had all gone so terribly wrong. Without Mirriam's presence they would take her for some enemy, but she would not fail her.

"Let's go." Mirriam commanded, and the professors shook off their injuries as they all ran to save Maleda.

CHAPTER 19 - AKANDE

The only sound was the unhurried trotting of the three horses through that sunlight-filtered forest. Three soldiers were each atop their assigned steeds and they were moving forth in a straight line decked with armor of metal and cloth that gleamed in the sun. The one out front felt some sense of urgency, probably from the nightmare he had last night, and he wanted to get beyond the walls to see the forest, just to make sure that it had not come to pass. Despite their stately manner, the leader was very much annoyed with the other two. Why did Akande have to get stuck with these two for rounds of training? Folu and Apara were abundantly irritating. With Folu's cheap calls for glory and Apara's smart remarks, it was a wonder that Akande hadn't gone against the crown and offed them right there, but he would never do that as the crown would surely have his head and he liked it very much on top of his neck.

"My opponent wouldn't know what's coming for them." Akande rolled his eyes and looked back at Folu. "Why I'd have my spear through them before they could start a battle cry." Folu puffed out his chest.

"First of all, you're barely twelve and second you don't want to have to tell the stories of spearing someone. It's more haunting than it is glorious." Akande was an able young man who had the fortune of not seeing war, but with the mysterious origins of the assassination, it could come at any time, especially since they didn't have what they wanted. Folu had his mother's coily dark hair and her clever brown eyes, a softer looking child, while Apara's dark hair was cornrowed backwards and his spectacles kept sliding down his nose with each trot, forcing him to push them back up to frame his lighter brown eyes. Apara was ten.

"The goal is that you don't have to fight. Remember?" Apara glanced back over his glasses. It was a fight for Akande to keep Apara from bringing any books along. What a combination. One that would not know how foul it would be to have blood on his hands and another that usually didn't see past the books in his hands.

"The crown demands our protection." Akande turned to face the forest ahead of him, "which means that you two will have to learn how to defend it and yourselves sooner rather than later."

"What do you think I was doing when you interrupted my reading this morning?" Apara protested. "I have read about battle strategies to know how to execute them properly. He picks up a wooden sword and starts jumping around like some valor-drunk idiot."

"At least I am moving from theory to practice. All you would be good for is shouting vocabulary."

Akande moved his thumb and forefinger across his forehead, ready to wallop them, when he heard the explosion. At least that's what it sounded like.

"Wha—" Akande put up a hand to shush them. He made a motion with his hand to signal them to cover their faces and the rustling meant that they obliged. It came from the river behind them. They were close enough for Akande to peer through the trees and see a girl on the shore downriver.

She looked helpless strewn across the ground, but that is probably what the creators of the curse would do. They would lay out bait to operate as some sort of spy or foot-soldier that looked like one of the people they had lost from years ago. Akande had enough training to take someone like her and he would not let them get away with this smug reminder. Akande motioned for them to follow him so as not to be seen by the girl as they stayed hidden in the woods and began their hunt.

CHAPTER 20 - MALEDA

Maleda was blown upwards by a blast of heat before she started to fall. She couldn't tell what had hit her, but it made its mark and briefly made her vision go black before she came to. The wind was whipping her face.

Too fast.

This was too fast to be falling.

It was a struggle to keep her eyes from blurring and she couldn't blink it away fast enough, but she could tell that she was not headed for the river, but the bank beside it. She didn't have time to aim herself in another direction or contemplate the permanent blackness coming for her. The wind tore the panicked scream from her throat. That pain in her head racked her entire body then, but she didn't have time to reckon with it as she screamed and crossed her arms over her face to blind herself from that forever blackness. Maleda did not want to die then, but she was grateful to know and see a world of green beyond the desert.

Something should have happened by now.

She opened her eyes to see a blade of grass right between her eyes and bent slightly at the touch of her nose. She couldn't hear anything past her heartbeat pounding in her ears. Without warning, her hovering died off and she thudded face first into the dirt, groaning and wincing at the soreness in her back. Her eyes were burning then. Before it was all in her head, but her eyes were on fire. The river was only yards away, so she dragged herself over to the water's edge to wash out her eyes.

Mirriam had to be alright.

The professors had to be alright.

They could not have sacrificed themselves in that blast, just so that she could survive. They must have been on the other side, blown the other way by the blast. At least that's what she hoped for. At the water's edge, Maleda grabbed a few handfuls of water before she paused to peer at the girl staring back at her.

So strange.

Maleda had never had a proper mirror out in the desert and the water was rushing just enough to make her reflection warped, but she did see the red eyes staring back at her. Before she could make sense of it, a raucous sound came from the forest behind her, and three horses burst out with riders atop them. She shifted to wariness as she saw that these armored riders had their weapons drawn for her. They were dressed similar to the professors, but perhaps these were not their allies. The desert had taught her quite enough about strangers bursting out of nowhere, so Maleda grabbed hold of the satchel strung across her body—surprised that it was still there—and bolted, but one of those riders already had a whip around her ankle. She had no weapon to cut it with, but it was loose enough for her to pull her foot out of it. They were almost upon her when she ducked into the forest. She called on those days in the desert when it was easy to run, when she had flown swiftly through the sand of the oasis, but exhaustion gnawed on her bones, and she was starting to feel lightheaded. Still, that didn't stop her from swatting away branches and jumping over fallen trees. She dodged left and right, trying to vary her path as much as possible, but they knew these woods and she didn't. Her only guide was the fact that the river was to her right, beyond the forest. She tried to keep that in mind. An arrow shot past as she dodged once more and the warmth seeping down her arm was her only signal that she had barely been hit. She had to get away. There was a steep incline blocked by bramble and bush. She decided to dive through it and shut her eyes against the snagging and scratching. She had made it through, and they couldn't, not without going on foot. Maleda was still surprised to hear their galloping die away, but she didn't dare slow herself down and she didn't dare look back. It was only when she passed a considerably wide tree that she stopped to hide behind it all while her chest was heaving. She did her best to quiet her breathing and strained to hear anything past her pounding heart.

There was nothing, but they were on horseback. It was only a matter of time before they found a way around. From the sounds of it, the river was close, but to check she decided to ascend one of the trees. She had climbed the tree tower in the desert, but this was a little more difficult given that it was not carved out with man-made pieces to save her from a fall. Yet, she still had the strength to haul herself up. She kept an eye on the canopy approaching and the forest floor departing, but there was no sign of the riders. Deciding it was best to stay off the ground, Maleda followed the sound of the river by carefully moving from branch to branch and tree to tree. She was close enough to see the river between the trees and the mountains from earlier. It was an impressive chain going into the distance, peeling away from the river. She had no hope of finding Mirriam now. In all her panic, she couldn't tell how far away she had gotten from where she fell, and the wreckage was blown so far away that she couldn't see any sign of a sail pierced by the tops of trees. She gasped while her arms tightened to her sides as the rope from before found its way around her torso and this time it was too tight to come loose. They were on the bank and the one holding the rope was the tallest of them. As he ripped his arm back, Maleda sailed through branches and toward the shore. The other two caught her, quick to pin her to the ground despite how small they appeared to be. Panic was fighting reason as Maleda sought a way to best her opponents, but there were three of them and she was caught. Their faces were covered with fabric, save for their narrowed eyes. The tallest of them stood before her with hate brimming in them.

"Who sent you here?" he demanded. *No one.* That was what she wanted to say, but Maleda could tell that they would not take that for an answer. Were these the people that Mirriam and the professors warned her about? Maleda shook her head.

"Answer me." He seethed "And don't even think of lying."

Maleda's eyes were wide and the only sound that escaped her mouth were shudders. She didn't have time to think on crafting an answer or pulling up the courage to say something as the tallest nodded, which signaled one of the two that had her pinned down to tie a cloth around her mouth. She pleaded with her eyes, but the tallest just knelt shaking his head in disgust.

"You're not real," he said too quietly as he made work of tying ropes to bind her arms at her sides and tying a knot to twist her wrists together, "and the empire will make quick work of eliminating a threat like you."

Maleda was too stunned to move as she took in his words. Empire? There was an empire beyond these woods…and they were going to kill her there. She was yanked to her feet and a rope was strung through the ones already on her wrists. He tied her to his horse as the others mounted theirs. If she could just tell them that she had no idea what her life even was and that she had known nothing but the desert, maybe they would understand. Maleda tried working the fabric and pulled on the ropes in desperate protest. He looked like he would strike her, but he pulled the cloth down from her mouth.

"Ready to talk, are you?" He said while raising a brow.

"I don't know what you speak of. I have lived—" The fabric was blocking her speech before she could finish, but this time it was fashioned into a gag. Another piece was pulled round her eyes. Maleda could see a slip of the ground beneath the fabric, but she gave no indication as he seethed at her.

"I'm not interested in the story you crafted for yourself and since you seem unwilling to truthfully admit who sent you, your end will not be pleasant." The horse grunted as it started marching and Maleda followed the pull. There was no getting out this time and since Mirriam had not come for her by now, she and the others were surely dead. As they trudged up the shore of that river, Maleda racked her brain for a way to escape, but she had no ideas. By the sands. What was she going to do?

CHAPTER 21 - MALEDA

Maleda didn't know how long they had been walking, but her feet felt leaden underneath her as she dragged them. Exhaustion and hunger were biting at her body, at her mind. Her terror mixed with numbness. She had led herself to her own end when she didn't tell Mirriam about the figures that had appeared in the tree. Even though she wanted to trust Mirriam, the fact that the men parading her around were wearing outfits like the professors had her questioning if they were all in allegiance to have her killed. Eventually, they reached a spot where the river's voice had died down to a burble. The sand shifted mercilessly underneath her feet until she felt the first splash of the river beneath her. She briefly dipped her head to see that they were crossing the river. The horses let out a small sign of protest, but the loudest sound was their sloshing through the water. Maleda rolled her shoulder in an attempt to keep her satchel on her arm. Just as she was noting her thanks that they did not take it, a set of hooves clopped closer, and she barely had a chance to wince as the strap was severed and the weight of the satchel dissipated. She barely saw a clip of those hooves clop further ahead, surely to hand it over to the one that led them. Maybe, if they thought she was so dangerous, they would inspect its contents or maybe that was what would keep them out of it. Why wasn't Cham speaking now?! Was her silence part of the curse too? Maleda's head bowed truly this time and she barely cared as she stared at the river shifting into forest floor. The warmth of the sun had shifted to one side of her body for all the time that she had been walking. As her feet crunched sticks over the forest floor, Maleda concluded that she was horrible in her previous life. This *new her* was guilty of crimes from a life that she did not remember. All she wanted was to know a life beyond the sand and what her life had been before the sand, but maybe that life was what truly sealed her demise. If one look at her—a defenseless traveler armed with nothing but a satchel—meant danger, then perhaps she was dangerous.

Her attention shifted and her head tilted up like prey in a field when her foot made contact with metal. The warm kiss of sunlight was replaced by a stagnant sort of air, where the warmth was muted. Somehow, the light that leeched from in front of her was not a comfort and it made a shiver run through her spine. There were hushed voices all around her and for all she knew they were discussing how her butchering should be carried out. A rough yank on the ropes had her grit her teeth and stagger forward. The skin had been irritated and surely rubbed raw, but the rope had been pulled from a lower position, so he had dismounted his horse.

"We will quietly dispose of you where no one will remember you." Maleda's head dipped at that, "How loud your screams are, will be up to you." Maleda's attention snapped at that. Maleda did not want her life to end, but if it was quiet, she could try to find some solace in the forsaken silence, but what he threatened was gruesome, torture. She backed away and shook her head trying to scream through her bindings that she did not know anything, but a different set of hands stopped, stronger than the two shorter pursuers from before. The tears came then as she was awestruck with terror. They would listen to nothing that she said and marvel at her screams when they did whatever they wanted. They had brought her up onto a platform and shoved her shoulders down until she was on her knees. Her hands were cut loose of their ties and her arms were strung out to either side, but she was bound with chains this time. There was barely any give, and she could not maneuver enough to relieve the burning in her thighs, knees, and back. The blindfold was removed, and it provided little assistance. She was in a dark room, almost black save for the far away spotlight of sun above her. On either side of her were two circular tunnels filled with nothing but consuming blackness. In front of her was a small gathering of people. All of them were unmasked and they all had hatred brimming in their eyes. One of them strode up the platform. The taut chains didn't give her room to cower, but her heart galloped.

"You are a lie." That's all she heard from the man in front of her who possessed the voice of the leading pursuer in the forest. His long black hair shadowed either side of his face and his dark skin almost challenged the darkness around her.

Maleda did not have the courage to protest anymore, so she just took in what he said with the eyes of a spooked doe.

"You think that you can come into our lands and mock our loss with a face that looks like hers," he bent over and was inches from her face ", Well, for her name and the unyielding will of the empire, we will make you regret it." He merely turned and stalked away. Maleda didn't want to end this way, so she writhed and yanked against the chains as a hum started to build. A white light was building in both of those tunnels, and it was careening for her. She didn't have time to scream before it hit, and she had no way to collect herself against the power.

She had nearly forgotten who she was against it. The chains slackened but her arms remained outstretched as if the tunnels were holding the chains in a tug of war. She couldn't hear anything beyond the crackling of that light, that power. Maleda had nearly forgotten who she was and was almost defined by the essence of that awakening. Her eyes were pinned on the sunlight that shone from above. She had a feeble hope that she would return to it, see it again somehow. Her mouth was open in a silent scream as it overwhelmed her. Her dreams had hit her then. All of them flashing in her mind and before her eyes all at once. There were even ones that she didn't remember scattered amongst them. Then, the voices came, starting like a whispering stream and crescendoing into nonsense again, but it all meant nothing to her. She felt the power collecting at points along her body all making pathways to shoot out of her hands and feet. It seemed to be an effort for tears to even slip past her eyes. The bright power was collecting and surging towards her upturned eyes. The pain that racked her body started to dominate her back. She had been kneeling there and ravaged for an eternity. When would she die? Her body would not let her go, but she begged the forever blackness to take her and bring her up to the sun. Her vision had gone white and then she truly forgot all, but it stopped. It all stopped. The white light that danced around and within her was receding and Maleda's muscles loosened until she fell to her knees again, but the chains were slackened so she was not saved from slamming into the uneven stone platform. Her heart *boomed* in her ears.

Let them do what they wanted with her body. She didn't care.

Boom.

Her vision was blurring and sharpening, but hope had cleared, and fear survived. Maleda had no choice, but her seething body did not seem to want to welcome darkness.

Boom.

The most alarming part was when she was surrounded by faces and someone pulled her up into their arms with heartbreaking gentleness and that act shocked her so much that her eyes closed, and she greeted darkness.

CHAPTER 22 - MALEDA

She had been moved to a different space or maybe it was the same room.

She couldn't tell. The room was so dark that she could not see the walls. Again, a spotlight shown down on her. She lifted her head to see that there were indeed no chains around her wrists, and she was free to sit up, free to walk around this room, but since she had no idea of what lay beyond her fence of light, she remained where she was. Maleda didn't have the energy to chastise herself for dreaming of going beyond the desert. Her arms were just shy of quaking as she pushed herself up onto her side. Maleda realized that there was a light that broke up that darkness and it came through the window that barred her from the next room, where a collection of figures stood. Probably the same from before. What had they done to her body with those tunnels of light? She didn't dare question them as she stared through that glass, but she was nearing insanity thinking about what they would do to her next. Maleda broke her gaze with the figures cast in black and looked around with the feeble hope of finding something to defend herself. There was nothing in the blackness around her, save for Cham in the ring form that had been stowed away in her bag placed neatly on the floor a few feet away.

"Did you steal that?"

Maleda didn't take her eyes off the ring.

"No," Maleda said hoarsely. That thing went through her so thoroughly that her voice had been ravaged.

"If you did not take it, then how did you come about having it?" Unyielding demand filled that voice.

"It was given to me." Maleda looked back at the huddled group. "Or at least that's what I think. I found it in a book—"

"And who told you to say that?" A different voice this time, but just as lethal.

"Nobody told me to say anything. All I know is that it is from the old world, and I thought that it was meant for me to find it."

If you really think it is meant for you, I dare you to touch it."

A wrongness floated around Cham as she took in the words. Cham didn't seem *alive* like before. No light pulsated in the threads of her design. Perhaps Cham was a relic from a golden time that happened to survive, and the professors had inserted her into a sick scheme. Perhaps Mirriam had too. Maleda knew that they would not let her out of the room, and she had a feeling that they would put her back against those tunnels of light if she did nothing.

"What happens if I don't?"

"We're patient."

Maleda did not like the threat that casually danced off that statement. She looked towards the ring. They had surely done something to Cham, but the question was whether she wanted to face that torture again or whatever Cham held. Maleda picked up the ring and it was almost like Cham wouldn't let her go, almost like the horrors from just before. Images flashed before her eyes. So many sounds and voices. Tears were released to balance out the pressure that kept building in her head. This wasn't possible, unless somehow Cham had let her see memories. Her memories. But how? A tone was ringing in her ears threatening to drown out everything else and her limbs shook.

Her body had enough. By some miracle, she let go of the ring or was it pried from her fingers? She fell over again, senses too overwhelmed and body too exhausted to care if she slammed into the hard floor, but those arms caught her again.

She couldn't think past the heartbeat and tone in her ears. Maleda knew that death was coming for her swift and true this time, even as she sensed light in the darkness.

CHAPTER 23 - MIRRIAM

Mirriam's breathing was the only thing she could hear, but she saw the fire, felt the heat at her back, and remembered Maleda falling out of sight. Once she and the professors were able to collect themselves and run, they tried to seek out where Maleda was. Once they found the river, they traveled alongside it and looked for Maleda. Mirriam believed they just needed to keep looking, but then she skidded to a stop mid-run. She saw where the dirt along the bank had been disturbed. She trudged through the waters while the other professors shouted and splashed after her, but then Mirriam was there on the bank, and she saw the smudged footprints and hoofprints. Maybe it was a patrol of guards who didn't know who she was or what if it wasn't and they were strangers to the empire sneaking around as they were. Either way, it looked like Maleda fought and made a run for it. *Please let her get away.* Mirriam gritted her teeth, and her breath was starting to get away from her. She was off and running with the professors following close behind, but when they got to the hidden entrance, she yelled at the professors to open the door. Once they obliged, she ran inside and the one in blue tried to keep up with her constantly calling her name. He kept telling her to wait and tried to slow her down, but she saw Maleda and the white light coming from her eyes. The wave of power that pulsated from her stopped her in her tracks, made her fall to her knees, as well as everyone else in the room. Mirriam's breathing just got louder and it competed with the volume of her own heartbeat pounding in her ears. The last thing she remembered was charging for Maleda. Wait! This wasn't happening again. She was asleep. She had to be right? Her body slowed down, and her limbs wouldn't obey her. Was she drugged? Everything faded to black, but she kept slicing through the darkness until there was light again.

She fought for breath as her fears for Maleda rose and she reached up clawing at the air. Her hands met something hard and clear. Everywhere she reached, her hands met a barrier. Fatigue threatened to drag her back under. Or was that the drugs? She couldn't hear herself shouting over her own thundering heartbeat. Her own terror was going to knock her out and it distracted her from noticing the person who entered the room and frantically pushed an array of buttons. The glass above Mirriam finally gave way and lifted with the push of her palms. She swung her legs over the side of the thing she was laying inside of and took in huge gulps of breath as she faced her attacker. Yet, Mirriam could only get a glimpse as the churning of her stomach forced her to stare at her feet. Four sets of feet? Well, that was it. She was going to have her head lopped off amid a drugged induced stupor. Yet, as she leaned forward to fall someone caught her and she leaned into the crook of their neck.

"Mirriam?" Whoever it was, said her name like a question, but that didn't matter, she needed to find Maleda. Mirriam pushed the stranger away and stumbled out of the room until she made it to a balcony where she grasped on tight to the railing, knees threatening to buckle. Her vision was still blurred and staggered, but she was able to make out the streaks of orange and purple that indicated the twilight.

"Mirriam. It's alright." The stranger kept trying to reassure her, but she refused to believe it. "You don't have to keep running."

Yes, she did. What were they talking about? The heavy truth threatened to drag her to the floor, but before she could descend all the way down the stranger caught her.

"Please, put your arm about my shoulder." Mirriam had no choice but to obey. "I suspect the adrenaline has run dry." The stranger chuckled. She growled in response. Mirriam had not faced an enemy in so long. The professors didn't count. The stranger lowered her onto the edge of something softer that had some give to it. A bed, perhaps.

"Mirriam, drink this." Mirriam hesitated, eyeing the pristine glass. "It's just water. I promise you." She couldn't hold herself back any longer and let the stranger tip the glass to her lips. She fought to hold back a moan at the coolness that surged down the dry riverbed of her throat. Some soldier she must have been. Her instincts of caution and hesitation were there, but those things were secondary. Surely, before whatever happened, she would not have been this sloppy, this careless. No matter her current state.

"She fell," Mirriam started. Her voice rose, not quite a shout, but enough to let this stranger know she would go there, "I tried to find her. Where is she? Where's Maleda?" Mirriam looked from the glass to the stranger who sat beside her. It was a man. Skin like umber and sympathetic eyes like night under dark brows, knit in *concern*. She wasn't helpless. She was a soldier but judging by his expression she must have been worse off than she wanted to believe. Once Mirriam's vision ceased doubling, she focused on sizing him up. Muscular build and he seemed to be her height. One of his hands retracted the water he held for her and the other pressed into his thigh.

"Mirriam, Maleda is here, but she's resting as you should be. She's safe now."

"I must go to her. I am to guard her." Mirriam attempted to rise, but swayed, leaning into the stranger again.

"Whoa, General. And what makes you think you're in any fit state?"

Mirriam's brows knitted together as she repeated him, "General?"

"Oh Gods!" The declaration made Mirriam's head turn, and she could barely get a look at the regal woman who wrapped her arms around her. "Oh, Mirriam! I'm so sorry."

"Careful, she is still weak."

"Puzo, you know as well as I do that there's no stopping her now." That voice came from the doorway, with a light timbre. Mirriam could only glimpse that there was a man leaning against the doorway and the name Puzo wrapped around something inside her.

The woman leaned back enough for Mirriam to see dark brown eyes framed by brown skin. The woman's voice trembled as she said, "Oh, Mirriam. We've done something horrible."

III

Part Three

ESTABLISHMENT OF SAFETY

CHAPTER 24 - MALEDA

The warmth of the setting sun kissed her arms first and then a pounding in her head introduced itself. The forward nature of it kept her from daring to open her eyes. She was dead and whatever hope she had believed in had swept her away to an in-between torture where she felt pleasure and pain. She shifted and was surprised to feel her body, as well as the fine cloth that surrounded it. After repeated attempts, her eyelids stuttered open. She felt the phantom control of her limbs. This was a dream, but it was so much clearer this time. Maleda's body was leaden, but she didn't have to be able to move her head around to take in the grandeur before her. A river of silk was above her, but so far away. The canopy was a waterfall that let out at either side of her face. She pushed herself up onto her elbows and dared to run her fingers across it as her arms quaked beneath her. Maleda pushed past her curtains of night and swung her legs over the side of the bed without bothering to move the covers, which shifted onto the floor. The sun had warmed the floor beneath her feet, coaxing her to step forward and she moved towards the balcony side of the room. The light assaulted her eyes and tightened her head, so she steered away from it to the walls. To call them walls was an insult to their relief-sculpture glory. There were scenes that she could not fathom chiseled and smoothed with expertise. Then, there were smooth panels of pattern and paint that alternated with sculptured panels. Scenes of mountains, travelers, cities, all in wooden ebony glory with some fully painted. Maleda didn't have the breath to scoff as she was too busy gawking at these precious creations.

So, she was to die and have one of the most beautiful hallucinations, or whatever this was, without the time to remember it? How cruel to know something like this and forget? Who made these? She traced her hands feather-light across the walls, marveling. The tightening in her head was her only indication that she approached that sunlight-filled balcony, so she moved around its arc to the wall on its other side and went back to running her hand over those walls. The mountains and the sea carved and painted with such skill. She didn't know if she could ever make work like that in her tree. Work that lured her into forgetting her need to sleep or move but pulled her eyes towards it. She was saddened to think that this was her last dream and that she didn't have her whole life to savor it and remember it.

One moved with her as she passed it.

Maleda kept her eyes on the floor and backed up until she saw her feet padding backwards in that intricate golden frame. Strange. It seemed like the sun shone differently across her feet, like its golden light crept underneath her skin. The hem of her nightgown was simple with no embroidery and a golden-white as if it were baked by the sand. Her hair had shrunk to her waist, and it was in thick, puffy twists. It was alarming to see her freckled brown face. Okay, so those were faded acne marks, but they could pass as freckles. Still, the pouty pink lips and wide-curvy nose, but her eyes seemed to spark with something *other*. They were dark brown and the glint of the sunlight on the mirror helped her differentiate the iris from the pupils, but something seemed to dance underneath and through that brown, like other slips of color she could barely see. It seemed to dance throughout her face, like the light that pulsed through Cham's designs, but these threads of light were somehow more organic. She moved a hand to her face to inspect the eye, but that suspicious light at her feet had crept into her hands like it was a network of veins.

As she backed away with eyes darting between her hands and the mirror, she could see the color in her eyes and skin dancing wildly now keeping up with her panicking heart. When she turned her head away, her only indication of the colors swimming in her eyes was a dizzying sensation in her head. She was completely aware of her body and her phantom control was there. Why hadn't she woken up? The pain then concentrated on her back and her body threatened to sink to the floor. Her gut sank as Maleda realized that for as impossible as it was, she was awake and that was when her head snapped to the wooden door silently opening at the entrance of a man and woman.

They had tried to kill her and then they did this to her body. Maleda's knees began to quake, and the man and woman rushed to her catching her as she fell down the side of the bed. She did not face them as they held her and kept her from crashing into the floor.

"Please, stop," she begged as her voice threatened to break, "I know that you were there in the desert, but I don't know anything that they're asking of me."

Maleda felt a sickening chill run through her, quickly followed by a heat all while her heart galloped in her chest. What was this sick game? The man and woman said nothing as they moved her back to her spot in the bed. They tucked the sheets around her as Maleda silently wept with an occasional choked sob as they knelt by her bedside. She did her best to observe them through her heavy eyelids.

"Why are you helping me?"

It was the man who bowed over and clutched one of her hands—still fiercely glowing— in his, bringing it to his forehead as he shuddered with what might have been a sob. Maleda was bewildered by the...mourning nature of the gesture. The woman laid a hand on her head and stroked Maleda's hair.

"You don't remember anything do you?"

Maleda's silence was the answer as a tear slipped down her face and the woman swiped it away with her thumb.

"This place is called the Empire of Two Shores," the woman started gently, "There was an attack here, long ago. Many lives were lost and for a while we thought that included yours."

"Do you know who I am?" Maleda pleaded quietly.

The woman nodded and said, "You are my sister's daughter, Maleda."

"Is she alive?" Maleda asked.

The woman shook her head and said, "I'm sorry, but she perished in the attack along with your father. They sent you away before it was too late with Mirriam."

Maleda was silent, but the tears were a torrent.

"I felt what you're feeling right now all that time ago, when I thought we lost you and your mother. It's how I felt when I lost my own daughter to the attack. I can't express how grateful I am that you have come back to us, and I want you to know that I am here for you. We are all here for you. And we are so sorry." The woman promised as her voice faded with the onset of tears.

The man finally spoke, "We are so sorry that we put you through that. Ever since the attack imposters have come through pretending to be you, only to try and attack us and sometimes just taunt us. We never knew their origins. We have been suspicious of strangers in the land ever since but your reaction to the light caught us off guard, and we knew it was you when you reacted to the ring."

Maleda's mind drifted to Cham and the others.

"Mirriam, what about Mirriam and the others?" Maleda pleaded weakly.

As if she waited in the wind, Mirriam was there and strode through the open door over to the other side of the bed. She remained standing, but tears sparkled in her eyes. Narrowly escaping that explosion had roughed up her clothes and Maleda could see the tiredness in her stance.

"She was the one who ran with you," the woman said, "when you were trying to get away. We have to thank her for your being alive."

Mirriam spoke then, "Maleda, I'm so sorry that we got separated. I'm glad that you're alright and now that we have returned, there is so much to tell you."

So, this wasn't some cruel dream. She had not died, and these people were trying to protect themselves. They were her *family*. Still, there was so much more that she needed to know.

"There's so much I don't understand." Maleda looked at each of them. "So much I want to know."

"There will be time for that," the man's face was streaked with tears, "but you have been through too much already. You should rest."

As if the words themselves held sway, Maleda's brain felt muddier.

The man shifted the pillows beneath her head as he helped her lay back. The glow in her skin dimmed to nothing as he did so.

"I promise that we will be here tomorrow."

Maleda didn't have the energy to say anything as she watched the three of them silently exit the room, save for the shift of fabric across the floor, and she drifted off to sleep.

* * *

As Maleda's body recovered with rest, she floated between sleep and a lethargic sensation. Through the closed glass doors and gossamer-like curtains, she could see a figure had dropped onto the balcony, smooth and efficient. Surely, she was dreaming. Fighting her droopy lids, she saw the door open and shut silently, but Maleda was too weak to protest. In such a daze, it was an effort to turn her head towards him, so she mostly had her eyes swim across the ceiling of the canopy, which was wreathed with glowing white flecks, a tribute to the stars almost as breathtaking as the true ones sewn into the sky.

"I didn't mean to frighten you and I'm so sorry for sneaking in like this, but this was the only way I could come. They don't really want you to have any visitors, but my favorite person is ill, and I just had to see that you were okay."

Whatever he was going on about, Maleda didn't care. She had gone through a fresh round of torture, where not only her body was ravaged, but she felt like with the little she learned that she was a walking phantom. The girl from before was alive, the girl from the life that she did not remember. The girl in the desert was hopelessly naive and the girl in the bed recovering was a moving shell.

"May I stay?" The stranger asked quietly and Maleda hesitated. "You just say the word and I'll go." Maleda considered it and found her answer.

"Yes, and who are you?" Her voice came out hoarse and drowsy.

"I caught you in the desert after you snuck after Mirriam. I am Zaddae and I am an old friend."

Maleda glanced in the direction of the figure silhouetted by moonlight. She could barely make out the planes of his face.

Maleda closed her eyes, exhaustion coaxing her back to sleep.

"I don't want to overwhelm you, "he continued softly, "and I don't want to cause you anymore pain, but I truly missed you, Maleda." Maleda looked at him with no recognition, but he was quick to see and amend. "Even if you don't remember me. We have been looking for you and at one point thought it was hopeless, but you miraculously and unbelievably proved us wrong."

"They told me my parents died to save me, but I don't even remember them."

Though Maleda's voice was even, tears slipped past her eyes and down her cheeks. The stranger's shoulders seemed to sink at her pain.

"I'm so sorry, Maleda," he whispered as he sat next to her on the edge of the bed and gathered her into his arms.

A harrowing emptiness filled her, and she did not know what to make of anything anymore, but she was soundless in his warmth.

"I will never hurt you. I beg you to believe that. I did not mean to masquerade here into the night and scare you, but I couldn't stand not seeing you okay."

"Will you help me along the way...to remember?" Maleda asked.

"I promise I will."

She decided to trust him, and she remained gathered in his arms. He was there as the stars glittered in the sky and she fell asleep.

CHAPTER 25 - MALEDA

The clicking of the door handle woke Maleda up and she felt for Zaddae, but he had already vanished. She struggled to sit up, but the effort roused the soreness in her body, and she winced at the ripple of it. The man and woman from the previous day finally entered the room dressed in finery, but they looked regal not flashy. They managed small smiles, but their features seemed to be laced with pain as if their guilt at Maleda's condition still ate at them.

"Hello, child. Are you feeling any better today?" The woman spoke first and took up her position from yesterday, but the man had brought her a chair. He went to his knees and put the back of his hand to her head. Maleda watched his face, tight in concentration.

"I don't know," she answered. Maleda's brain was still muddy, but she thought it was better to not mention her *friend* from last night who had comforted the chasm that she thought she knew but had only grown bigger.

"That's understandable," the man nodded withdrawing his hand from her face, "I take it you have never seen the light before then?"

Maleda shook her head as much as she could manage as it was still throbbing.

"Before we go any further, there's so much more I want to know, like your names and who you are."

The man and woman exchanged looks.

"I'm sorry," the woman apologized ", We have come poking and prodding you out of care, but we forgot ourselves. I am Clementina, empress of the Empire of Two Shores."

"And I am Olmec, the emperor."

Maleda may not have remembered her past, but she stiffened at their titles. The emperor and empress were fussing over her? As if they sensed her seizing insides, the emperor laid a comforting hand on her shoulder while the empress took her hand.

"Don't let our titles scare you child." The woman smiled. "I don't know how much you remember of yesterday, but I meant it when I said that I want to treat you as my daughter."

The man smiled sheepishly at her, an apology for her overzealous fussing, but even though it overwhelmed Maleda she did not entirely mind it.

"We want to give you an official assessment to make sure that you are physically healing…and we want to explain everything to you. Does that sound alright?" The emperor asked.

Maleda nodded and as if on cue, a woman walked into the room. If Maleda's aunt and uncle were emperor and empress, then the way this woman carried herself made her a queen in her own right. Her angled eyes were near pitch black, hair covered by a black headdress, brown skin glistening, a ghost of a smile lingering on her lips. The emperor backed away to give the woman room.

"Hello, Maleda. It's nice to see you again. My name is Ramonda." Her voice was rich and calming as she talked through her actions. "I'm going to pull back the covers so that I can do a full body scan."

Ramonda had a flask strapped to a leather strip that crossed her body. She unfastened its top and waved her hand over the lip and with a pulling motion, drew water out of the flask. Maleda watched stunned as the water hovered as a sphere in midair, inches from Ramonda's hand. It was like she had charmed the water to do her bidding. With another elegant and fluid motion, the water encased her hands like gloves and Ramonda's hands hovered inches above Maleda as she drew them across her body.

"How did you do that?" Maleda asked.

"It is through the manifestation of magic," Ramonda said as she focused on the scan, "You will be able to learn about it someday soon."

Braver this time, she looked down to see those veins of light dance through her skin. They were fainter than before, but they gently pulsed brighter and fainter again. She did not feel the pain this time, only a sense of being awakened as if she were walking around in her sleep before, dull to the sensations around her. It was unfathomable. She felt impossible.

"The reason why you lived through the machine's work yesterday with minimal injury was because your old-world tech was protecting you, your body." Ramonda clarified.

"Was I born this way?" Maleda stared at her hands and her arms as those vines of light curled through her skin.

"No," the emperor answered, "it was implanted inside you. You see, the old-world tech that we made originated from special minerals here in Alfajiri. "They are naturally occurring in the continent, and they go by many names, but I like to call them heaven stones." He held up a raw jagged crystal that covered up his palm.

"Yes, there will be plenty of time to talk about that," Ramonda started, "and it looks like you are healing well. The machine has made your old-world tech implants 'activate' in a sense. Right now, you will feel sore and disoriented because it's like a new means of sensation has opened up to you."

"But why was it implanted?" Maleda blurted. A sadness crept into the emperor's eyes.

"Because dear Maleda, you and our daughter were attacked." The emperor said. "This was before the war and you had been poisoned, debilitated in some way. Your body was shutting down and the only way to save you was to implant the terratech. I had the most experience experimenting with it, so I did it myself. We were able to save you and when the war came you got out, but our daughter did not survive. The poison was too much for her."

The emperor faded at mention of his child, so the empress laid a hand on his shoulder and continued.

"Your parents perished in the attack, but we promised them to always protect you. Your mother's name was Berenice and your father's name was Mshindi. We asked Mirriam to take you away, to keep you safe and that meant hiding you outside of the empire, so we would not know if you perished or not. There was to be no communication, no signal, nothing. We were kindred spirits, your mother and me. It was like losing a part of myself, but I promised her that we would let you go and not pursue you, lest it be dangerous for your survival. I promised her that if you miraculously returned that I would look at you as my own."

"Why don't I remember?"

"The implants were placed around various parts of the body in hopes of quicker healing, one of the spots being near your brain. So, while it healed, it likely also erased or maybe even caused trauma. It was the only way you and our daughter could have lived, so we took the chance. It doesn't help that there's a period that it seems none of us can properly recall." The emperor looked at the floor and his brows furrowed. Maybe it was to do with the curse, his frustration with it. Still, Maleda decided that the look on his face was reason to veer away from the topic, at least for now.

"Were your daughter and I close?"

"You were so close that sometimes I could not tell you two apart." The empress answered.

The painful hollowness enveloped Maleda's heart then and she truly started to carry the burden of being the girl who lived, while her apparent beloved *best friend* had died. She did not know what to put in that hollowness given that her pool of memory was so foggy and practically empty.

"But she believed fervently in Olodumare and in his charge to care for this earth, so I know that she rests in a place where she is at peace."

Strange. It was all so strange. If what Maleda felt was only a whisper of what terratech and heaven stones, as the emperor called them, could do, then she would hate to encounter someone who had full control over it and could manipulate the elements with ill intent. She tried to run from the thought, but it hounded her. She wished that she knew this cousin of hers and she wished that she had the pleasure to remember her. She did not know how to ask it, but she said it anyway.

"How do you care for your passed on?"

Everyone seemed to stiffen at that, despite their best efforts to hide it. "I'm sorry if I'm being too forward. I just—"

"It is quite alright," the empress said with something like guilt and pain written across her face, "We understand. Everyone in this continent handles the remains of someone differently, but we chose to dedicate a place to her, both of you considering that we were unaware that you were still alive. After we finish your assessment, we will take you there and Mirriam will accompany us."

Maleda managed a small smile and nod. Her eyes moved from the floor to her reflection, and between the emperor and the empress as she tried to prepare herself for what she was to see.

***

Maleda insisted that she wanted to start walking and she was given a pair of crutches. Mirriam pursed her lips and raised a brow but agreed and kept a wheelchair in her possession. When they finished with Maleda's exam, she was ushered along to a closet connected to the ruler's rooms where they still kept Maleda and the princess's clothes. Mirriam helped her change into some casual day wear. It consisted of brown pants that were cuffed from mid-calf to the ankles and a loose yellow tunic. Once Maleda was ready, Mirriam guided her to meet the emperor and empress outside of her door. They walked along in the palace through halls that had truly been loved by an artist, or maybe hundreds of them. The ceilings were filled with paintings of various scenes: skies, silhouettes of people overhead, canopies. It was so bright as if no one would dare leave the place without color. Busts and sculptures lined the halls. Some were colored ebony or variations of it. Some had their own color schemes, so strange and wonderful. She wished she could believe that she was just refamiliarizing herself with her old home or learning about the glorious art that was the palace as well as everything in it, but she was here to visit a grave of sorts, a grave of her kindred spirit.

Her heart trembled as they finally approached a set of giant doors, intricately carved in relief to look like tree branches twisting about each other along with a lush landscape. When the doors were pushed inward, Maleda was welcomed into a bright sunlit room with panes of glass at the ceiling. Some panes were open, and she could hear someone singing and a bird chimed as it perched in an open window. The light glistened off the leaves of the tree that looked exactly like hers. It was like it picked itself up by its roots and followed them here. Her arms trembled as she came closer. As alive as it was, Maleda saw some ghost that claimed her, but she could not fairly claim it back. The difference was that there were lights on the inside, strung along like cheery decorations. It was because of that light that she saw the drawings, her drawings. They were scrawled across the wall in the exact collage that she laid out. It was those drawings that sent her to her knees as they approached the tree. She did not know if she could look at it, should look at it. Maleda did not really cry often out in the desert. There was longing and some sadness for what she did not know, but Maleda miraculously shook with sobs and covered her face as she remembered that she hated crying. Some part of her remembered that she was easy to be moved and the quarreling of heart and head were easy to spill from her eyes. There was no way to recover from the vulnerable and embarrassing display, so she whispered a question through her tears.

"What was her name?"

A pause. Maybe she should have thought before she asked that. They had never said her name, likely because the idea of saying that name would resurrect the pain all over again, fresh as—

"She was named after her mother, Clementina." The emperor spoke with pride as he looked at his empress.

"Don't forget Kianira Layla Lesedi." The empress finished.

Maleda had barely noticed that they had knelt beside her and covered her with their arms. They both took a hand of hers and gently peeled it away from her face. She cracked a sound that was like a broken laugh as she said, "She had quite a name." They squeezed her tighter at that.

"Well, we couldn't pick one," the emperor laughed as he shifted his glasses to swipe tears from his eyes, "so we used them all."

Maleda laughed despite the tears slipping down her cheeks and the empress laughed through her tears, as well. Mirriam was still standing behind them, a look of melancholy on her face, but the empress extended a hand to her. Mirriam took it and was fitfully yanked down with them into their group embrace.

"We may have lost *our* daughter," the empress began, "but we still have you both. I am grateful that you were able to save Maleda and yourself. I have missed you both and since we thought you were gone, this tree was put up to remember your life, as well as Clementina's, and how the essence of you goes on. Your drawings are in there because when this tree was erected it was meant to be a receiver, a signal of sorts, so that we could communicate with others and receive messages. The signal on this tree is connected with a network of many others and as a last hope, we visited this tree not only in mourning, but looking for any signal, any sign. The one that you had back in the desert was faulty, damaged and we could not receive anything from it. For all we knew, you, our daughter, and Mirriam were gone, but one day we got a signal and all your drawings loaded themselves onto the walls. The crystalgram function was faulty so you probably saw us walking through like ghosts, but we could not see you. We knew then that you lived. Whether you were still alive or not, we could not say, but you lived long enough to try and remember and draw. We held onto that in spite of everything, but when you came and we realized it was you, Maleda there were no words and there are no words. Everything is wrong and broken but we will be a family, different from before, but stronger and no matter what has happened and what we all have lost, we will love you as our daughter."

"You can come here anytime you like," the emperor continued trying to keep his voice even, despite the tears, "We put this tree here in memory, but you are free to use it as you did in the desert. Draw here. Stack books inside. Climb to the top and look at the city with sunlight or starlight. We will get you back on your feet and we will do our best to help you remember who you were and even if we cannot reach *that* Maleda, we will help discover someone new. I don't believe that we need to explain again how much we love you, but we will tell you anyway."

Maleda's shaking became less violent and she let herself rest in the arms of the rulers and Mirriam. By the sands, she was loved and even in her broken return she was still loved.

CHAPTER 26 - MALEDA

After they had all picked themselves up out of their renewed grief and joy, Maleda was escorted back through the palace halls by twilight to her room. When the empress offered to help Maleda change, the emperor waited outside and returned when the empress called him to let him know they were done. The empress helped her put on a white, airy nightgown with a rising and dipping hem to accommodate the heat. The empress and Mirriam helped her into bed. The sun was still clinging on to its last shreds of visibility as Maleda looked between everyone sitting on the edge of her bed and the sheets.

"When will I see the city?"

They all looked at each other. Perhaps they did not think she was strong enough to go traversing about it and they had said that someone had tried to poison her and Clementina before. It was probably best to keep her cooped up, but she was surprised to see the smiles on their faces.

"We'd be happy for you to see the city," the emperor started and then he gained a more thoughtful look, "as soon as you are able to walk with more steadiness on those crutches."

The empress spoke this time, "That attempt to get you both was on foreign shores, not in this city. You should be able to walk without fear, caution maybe, but not fear."

She held the side of Maleda's face.

"Besides, it would be absolutely cruel to keep you locked up in here, especially from a city that you loved so fiercely. I believe that with fresh eyes you will fall for it again."

Maleda was overwhelmed at this caring that ran so deep within them.

They should have looked at her with spite and anger at her survival and not their daughter's. Her eyes caught onto something that briefly shimmered in the balcony, but she drew her eyes back to the empress.

"Don't you ever blame yourself for living. Be thankful that you did. Be thankful that Olodumare kept you walking Dziko."

She would be thankful, but it would be hard to harbor that feeling of other: hollowness, unrecognizable grief.

"Besides, we are not the only ones happy to see you up and walking and here and alive," the empress smiled.

Maleda's chest tightened a little at the vague suggestion. Someone else or some other people were happy to see her alive. Guards had brought in a trunk that she was told contained her things, namely her satchel and its contents. She did not know how everything worked, how recognizable she was. If she walked among the city, would people balk at her? Was she one of the girls that stood in the shadows? She had to consider this whether she was best friends with the daughter of these rulers or not, but that hand moved from her face to her shoulder. The emperor took her hand, as well.

"But don't worry," the emperor said with light striking across his glasses from the moon, "we will help you along the way so that you are not so frightened."

Again, Maleda was overwhelmed at the sheer bounty of kindness that these people possessed. She did her best to stow away her tears and nodded. The emperor handed her a glass of water and urged her to drink it. She finished it and he placed it on a nearby nightstand. All of the toil of her emotions and struggling through the repair of her body ushered her into tiredness and she struggled to keep her lids fully open. The empress kissed her head and the emperor kissed her hand. Mirriam simply patted her leg, but before they could all move to go Maleda pulled them back to her so she could embrace them again. She felt like a child when doing so, but she had a feeling that no one minded.

* * *

Several minutes after they left, and silence enveloped the room—save for the sounds of the city outside—he came again. He dropped from somewhere above the balcony and slowly rose to standing as if it were nothing.

"Hello there," he said simply.

"Hello," Maleda's voice shrank into something quieter but at a slightly higher pitch.

"Do I have your permission to enter your room and come closer?" the stranger asked.

"Yes," Maleda said while shaking her head. She found herself drawing in her knees, but she did not quake as he approached the bed. "Everyone else has been honest with me so far," she began. She had to give herself credit. Although her voice sounded wary and her body sent off alarms, she did not shrink from him. There was nowhere to go with the pillow behind her anyhow, so she rambled. "I am still in pain knowing that my parents are dead, but the emperor and empress keep telling me that they already think of me as their own, even with the loss of their own daughter."

He remained silent and just sat on the edge of the bed, careful of touching her it seemed, and he was messing with something on her nightstand.

"I visited her burying place today. At least that is what I understand it to be. It's a tree, beautiful, wide, and towering. I believe that she was my best friend. Still, she isn't here, but you are and as I said everyone else has been honest. You didn't get a chance to explain yourself."

Still silent and still fiddling.

"Unless you're going to keep me guessing at who you are. I don't even know why I let you console me or why I didn't call for anyone. Still, you didn't—"

Before Maleda could get out a question or something useful to say, his brown skin was cast in the scarlet glow of the lamp. For a moment, Maleda did not say anything as she drank in his features. She was so used to darkness enveloping this figure. That was how she understood him to exist. It was a whole other reality to see his topaz and brown flecked eyes, curly-near-frizzy brown hair enveloping his shoulders beneath his hood. Those same eyes from the desert.

"Zaddae"

She was struck dumb. Wouldn't she remember a face like his?

"Zaddae?" She questioned.

"Yes, that's my name."

"Oh."

"As this is the second time I've broken into your room, I thought that I should at least do better than speaking to you from the dark."

The words that left Maleda's mouth seemed to be independent of her gaping, "Are you really a professor?" He just smiled at her, gentle and open.

"Not yet, I was training to be one around the same time that you were. The universities here in the empire are bounties of opportunity. We were friends, studied together and all that. We even plotted and schemed to get into the parts of the library with the restricted books. Are you alright?"

She just stared.

"I'm sorry. I shouldn't be stalking around, but when the emperor and empress said that you were all right, they said that they would reintroduce us, but I just couldn't wait. I thought you were gone like everybody else did, at first. But then, you were there in the desert, but then the ship exploded, and I was so afraid. They may have decided to treat you like their own, but they would smack me around for putting you under this stress and confusion—"

Maleda barely lifted a hand and he stopped talking, half covering his face with his hands. A rambler too, she saw.

"I'll keep your secret and when we *meet*, they will know nothing of this. I still can't believe what I am doing here and given the circumstances, I can't believe that I have allowed you to traipse into my room—twice now—without a well-deserved hit and scream."

His body convulsed once and then over and over. Was he crying? What did she say that—

He tipped his head back and he let out a low cackle. Laughter. He was laughing at her. In spite of their renewed meeting, she shoved him at that as if he were an old friend, as if it were instinctual. It was like her body remembered him, but not her own mind. He put a hand up in defeat.

"That sounds exactly like something you would have said before. Always quick with words and a brush you were."

She let out a breath and it came out like a laugh too, in spite of her frazzled state.

"It's so strange," she began, and his face turned thoughtful, "because I feel like I know you, but since I have forgotten my past self, it feels familiar but clouded somehow."

He eyed the starred canopy while he spoke as if he could find the words there and he looked back at her.

"Well, you've been through the unimaginable."

Maleda didn't want to get lost in the abyss again, so she asked another question.

"Tell me, what did you mean when you said that I was quick with a brush?"

"Well, you were studying as an artist, and it was hard to find you without a journal to sketch in."

Maleda had missed so much and even though she did not have a memory harbored, she felt a tinge of something pulling at her. Zaddae seemed to observe the thoughts that traveled across her face as she was silent.

"I don't want to think about what I missed in a way of regret," she started quietly, "but I would like to think that the time away could make me more grateful. When are we supposed to be *reintroduced*?"

Maleda started to play with one of her long twists.

"Tomorrow, I believe," Zaddae stated, "though I am not exactly sure of where. The empress had not decided on a meeting place yet."

Maleda nodded and brought her eyes back up to his.

"The emperor and empress told me they will help me recover my memory of my family, my life, of Clementina," his jaw flickered at that, as if trying to contain that grief, "but I wonder if you would help me remember our friendship. Things we did. All the stuff we talked about."

She unwrapped the twist in her hand and began retwisting it.

"I mean I don't know how close we were. They told me Clementina was my best friend, but I don't know about us as you could probably guess."

He gently pulled Maleda's quick hands from her twisting work.

"I would like to think that we were close," Zaddae gave a small smile, "and that was a habit of yours."

She quirked a brow in question, "What?"

"Constantly untwisting and twisting your hair when you're thinking or nervous."

She chuckled in spite of herself. Then, his eyes flicked to the door, and he perked up.

"What's wrong?" Maleda's eyes went to the door as well.

"Someone's coming, likely to check on you, but I think it's best if I disappear if it's all the same to you."

Maleda nodded and he rose with a dip of his head and turned to walk back to his acrobatic escape route.

"Zaddae," she grabbed him by the wrist and with him not expecting the gesture, her hand slipped into his as she held him back, "Thank you."

Again, that childlike smile danced on his lips but more open this time. "Until tomorrow, Maleda."

Maleda smiled right back at him. She watched him as he made his way to the balcony and scaled up the side, waving goodbye as he did so. She returned the gesture and he disappeared into the night. Some professor-in-training indeed. Maleda barely chastised herself. Still, she felt as though she could trust him. With all her years in the desert, being around people had made her slightly spooked, but Zaddae did not scare her, and she held onto that kernel of hope as a reason to trust him. The door silently and slowly opened inward. She didn't bother with the light. She decided to let them think she was…thinking and restless in this unfamiliar place, but it was not either of the rulers that walked into the room to stare at her, mere yards away from the bed.

CHAPTER 27 - MALEDA

y the lamp that he held, Maleda could clearly see his face. It was something like the emperor's with brown, near copper, skin and jet black hair. His eyes were like obsidian and it was those eyes that she remembered, from the explosion. The river with those three guards, or were they soldiers? The mask of coolness that she tried to keep up with Zaddae had dissolved. He closed the door without a sound. Did he not believe her *performance* and so he decided to come here in the night to interrogate her again or to finish the job? A small fearful gasp escaped Maleda, even though given her past habits, she should have just welcomed this stranger in, but that small sound she made had an effect because he showed his palms to her and got on both knees as if *she* were a threat or as if he was showing he meant no harm.

"Please, don't be afraid," he quietly said as he still held the lamp up to one side of his face, "I promise you that I am not going to hurt you."

He stood and quickly crossed the room with a labored look on his face. He stopped right where Zaddae had been and whatever control he had over his composure had vanished as he sunk to his knees and wept into his hands. The lamp was discarded on the floor next to him. She could barely make out words through his tears, but she gathered 'sorry' and 'mistake.' Before she could even think of how to respond, he had swiped the tears from his face and looked up at her with a faint glistening around his eyes as he tried to gather his composure, his breath.

"I am so sorry. I didn't know it was you Maleda. You looked like the people that had been sent before, so I did not think it was truly you. I was trying to protect your good name and memory, but I was wrong. So wrong," he wrapped his arms around her, near crushing her, "I have missed you cousin." She had gone dumb again and merely repeated what he said.

"Cousin?"

"Yes, I am your cousin Akande."

It was like nothing existed anymore, like all of this had been intricately woven into a dream. She feared that if she breathed the wrong way, everything would melt or slip away like paint sliding down the tree when she added too much water. Between Zaddae and this man she was overwhelmed by who she had left behind and who she had found again.

"I have a cousin," she said distantly as her eyes started to burn.

He finally let her out of his embrace and his face was slick with tears still. For as haggard and guilt-ridden as his features were through her tears, knowing who he was and seeing his face was like a dream.

"You truly don't remember anything?" He asked with begging eyes and Maleda shook her head.

"What do you mean about the people sent before?" She inquired through her tears. She had a foggy recollection of what the emperor had said when she first woke up in the room, but she wanted to hear it again. He started to shake his head, but she continued, "Please don't try to protect me. The emperor and empress told me that there was a war and that I was poisoned, but no one is saying anything more than that. At least tell me what caused you to mistake me for an enemy." He looked at his hands and back at her, but before she could badger him again, he spoke.

"Even though your parents risked their lives so that you could run away, we still were not sure or even hopeful that you made it. It was possible that the *other side* had access to your body if you were dead. Even if they didn't, they developed some sort of scheme where they would send crystalgrams of girls that looked like you. Then, the crystalgrams began to materialize somehow and these girls tried to attack and taunt us. You would think that it was some hallucination or culmination of extreme guilt, but they were real. There are guards that have encountered her with enough remnants of fear to prove it."

"I've seen something like that before," Maleda searched for her thoughts in the sheets and looked back to him, "When I was in the desert, I saw the emperor and empress, but they could not see me."

"They probably already told you that your signal was likely broken or there was some sort of damage. They would only be able to see marks that you left in the space, but the ones we faced were just so different."

Maleda nodded and looked past him as the thoughts swam in her head, but she closed her eyes against them.

"There will be plenty of time to learn about everything I guess." She looked back at him. "But thank you for telling me that. I can't imagine what it was like to see...my ghost."

"It was unspeakable." He deflated, and his shoulders sank. "To see you and my sister's image dancing around in mockery. I'm glad that I got you back at least."

"It's getting late, and I don't want you to let my reappearance ruin your rest. I'll be here tomorrow." Maleda smiled to reassure him. His brows were blocks of stone over his eyes.

"Are you crazy?" Maleda almost shrunk away. "You've been gone for years, and I thought you were truly passed on. Then, I find you and almost slay you, only to learn that it is really you. No, I believe that I have a life debt and as your stubborn cousin I am not letting you out of my sight, at least not for this night."

There was no use arguing against the hard determination in his face and before she could ask about where he would sleep, he plopped onto the floor next to her bedside.

"I feel that I should probably say something about my crazy cousin sleeping on the floor, shouldn't I?"

"It doesn't matter if you do because I'm not budging."

"Even if I tell you to just take that long chair and scoot it over here?"

He flicked his head to the chair and awkwardly rose. "For your information, it is a lounge chair," he said as he sheepishly tried to redeem himself. She put up her hands and let her smug smile be her response as he dragged the chair next to the bed. Akande did not bother removing his shoes as he put them up in front of him. There was even a sword on the floor, as if someone would charge in. Well, Zaddae did sneak into her room, and she let him, so maybe she should be wary or maybe *he* was just that good. She looked over him as he tried to get comfortable in that absurd chair and the words escaped her lips.

"I think I missed you." He stilled at that.

"I thought you couldn't remember anything." His voice was hesitant.

"I don't, but I feel like I missed you anyway. Isn't that strange?"

"Yes, considering that we butted heads often." He flourished with his hands. She laughed and stared back at the constellations, and it smacked her in the face.

"So, my parents were your aunt and uncle, and I am your parents' niece?"
He nodded, "Yes."

"I don't know why it took me so long to think about it, put a label to it. It's all so overwhelming I guess," she said as she caught the tear that slipped out of her eye. She looked at Akande and it looked like words were buzzing through his head as his brows lowered over his eyes.

"I'm sorry," he said as he swung his legs onto the floor and strode over to the balcony. His long legs had eaten up the distance, but Maleda did not give a kernel of sand as she swung her legs out of the bed—much to the chagrin of her side and everything else—and secured her crutches underneath her as she strode over to him, the click of her crutches the only sound as he sank to the floor. She was surprised to see him silently weeping with a hand at his chin and the other arm wrapped around his middle. It was so alarming to see this hard-looking soldier—her cousin—be so frank with how broken he was. They had told her not to feel guilty for living so she tried to fight it off as she comforted her cousin.

"No." She put a hand on his shoulder. "Please, don't be sorry. I was afraid of you when you came in this room, but both of us were mistaken before. I learned that I have a cousin and one who fights so fiercely that he fought off my ghosts for so long that he could not tell that I was...real."

The pain ratcheted up her side and she had no choice, but to find the floor next to him. She tried her best to conceal her hiss of pain as she leaned her head onto his shoulder and wrapped an arm around his back. Maleda could not explain how she knew it was safe to be this close to him. She silently cursed the memories that she could not retrieve that kept the truth from her. Maleda tried to focus on the lights between the rail of the balconies and she became enraptured by the blur of the city, even as she winced through the pain. He seemed to remember her state at that moment and scooped her up before her vision focused enough to see the starlight city properly. There was no room to protest.

"Why did you get out of the bed?" He fussed over her like some nursemaid.

"Well, excuse me, you were crying, and I wanted to console you." She retorted.

"Well, I thank you for that, but you are in no condition to move about as if your body's not damaged." He gently placed her back onto the bed and found his own seat. "Crying in front of anyone was not something that I ever did." Maleda tried to cheer him back up.

"What? Did I make fun of you or something?"

"No, I just wasn't that type of person. Tears seemed like they were weakness and pointless."

"I'd like to think they are cleansing, but you shouldn't upset yourself any further. I'm here and you're here." She looked from him to the balcony. "The city is out there, and we'll figure this out together, right?" She tried to reassure herself as much as she wanted to reassure him. He nodded.

"Promise me." She hoped her eyes weren't desperate as she asked him.

She found herself being pulled until her chin was resting on his shoulder and she was embraced in a hug.

"I promise."

He released Maleda and reclined into his chair while she settled back into the pillows and stared up at the constellations.

"In spite of our estrangement, I'm glad I met you again…, saw you again." He was silent for a moment as he faced the back of the chair.

"So am I."

CHAPTER 28 - THE PRISONER

From a faraway window, the prisoner could see someone smiling to themself on the roof, listening to the lost girl and her brother before they bounded away. That smile was true and warm, but the prisoner could barely glimpse those feelings.

Dark, it was so dark in this secret room, wherever it was. It didn't matter how much he told himself that there was nothing there. As he gathered himself in, exhaustion gnawing at his consciousness, he meditated on the hope that nothing would grab him in the inky blackness.

CHAPTER 29 - MALEDA

The warmth of early sunlight woke Maleda first and with a healthier state she instinctually thought about drawing her surroundings. She flinched when she remembered that she had nothing to sketch with, but she saw the trunk in the mirror at the edge of the bed. Maybe her sketchbook was inside it as well. Maleda kept an eye on Akande who was still soundly sleeping on that chair, chest rising and falling, while she slithered from between the sheets and slunk across the bed until she was staring down at the trunk. She reached over and felt for the clasp at its center, unhinged it and pulled the lid back towards her. Her sketchbook was there along with her satchel, but there were beautifully crafted vials of different colors, all the same size. Maleda heard rustling and her eyes widened as she turned back to see Akande still sleeping, only rolled over. Guard or not, it was probably the best sleep he had gotten in ages considering that Maleda was finally…home. A soundless exhale escaped her mouth, and she retrieved the sketchbook and placed it next to her on the bed. Curiosity got the better of her and she rushed through the sketch of the room—she would go back over it later— and picked up a vial. The vial was a sparkling golden yellow that blushed with glitter in the light of the sun. She braced her fingers around its top, unsure of how it would open and if she would make a fool of herself spilling the contents on the bed, but it released its bond with the lid easily as if it had never been used or as if it was new. It was then that she realized that the illustrations on the vial were the only colored parts of the glass as the pigment inside gave it color. So as not to spill it, she quickly corked it and placed it back into the trunk. A slight tension built in the back of her head and Cham seemed to slightly squeeze her finger in ring form. *What?* She asked Cham with her eyes, as if they could speak mind to mind. She silently winced against the tension and the ache truly faded as the vial rattled and the paint gently pushed aside the top and flowed out, followed by the others.

Was it shock or terror that kept her quiet? Maleda did not or could not disturb Akande who was still asleep without a twitch to be seen. The paint defied gravity and flowed up the trunk and slithered across the bed as Maleda backed away to the head of the bed. Maleda released a fraction of the tension that kept her muscles taut, and shoulders drawn up towards her ears, just as the paint formed itself into a little world, a microcosm of people like the ones she had painted in her room in the tree—faceless and graceful—but their forms were clothed in different colors. It showed a girl running through a forest of newly arisen paint, golden light haloing the scene.

Her? It was her, but how—

The paint melted down and reformed into a wall and other strands of paint crawled up its side creating illustrations…similar to the room where she presently sat. The form of some hooded figure appeared, but Maleda could not see their face. It seemed like the hooded figure looked up, right at Maleda.

Then, another hooded figure appeared with a feline grace. Maleda imagined that the two figures met each other in the night, but for what? Both figures moved about each other giving various hand gestures, as if they were conversing and hurriedly. Their heads snapped toward the door and one of them turned towards a wall, while the other sank into a stance as if ready to fight.

Tap tap.

Footsteps! Someone was coming, but just as Maleda's alarm rose, the paint fell into puddles of color and raced back over the bed and into the vials in the trunk with no trace left behind, as if it was conscious of the secrecy it was supposed to keep. She silently scooted backwards in disbelief at the idea that Akande was still asleep and made sure the sheets were over her legs. There was a little bit of racket, as if people were arguing beyond the door, but it suddenly ceased when the door clicked open, silently swung wide, and in stepped a lovely little girl. She had to be half Maleda's height and age, but her brown skin seemed to have a radiance of its own along with her jet-black hair secured into an impressive curly puff on top of her head. She cocked her head and dark brown eyes stared at Maleda.

"Hi," she said softly.

"Hello there." Maleda responded with a smile.

"Did I wake you up?" She inquired while twisting from side to side.

"No, I was just thinking. What's your name?" Maleda asked, but the girl merely walked over with eyes darting from the floor to Maleda's face, climbed onto Maleda's lap, and hugged her. Who was this enchanting child? She pulled back and looked into Maleda's face.

"Do you remember me? I'm your cousin Selene." She asked in a small voice.

"No, Selene." Her name was lovely, but strange on Maleda's mouth. "And I'm sorry that I don't."

Someone shouted from the hall, "No, I believe that you will take that back shortly."

Maleda frowned as the shy, enchanting girl disappeared as she turned her head and bellowed, "Shock me and say something intelligent!" That was what sent Akande nearly tumbling out of his chair as he fumbled for the sword on the floor, mumbling nonsense all the while. An instant connection formed as Selene and Maleda looked from Akande to each other and shrieked with laughter. A guard indeed. Maybe her presence was making him too comfortable. As they recovered from their laughter and Akande tried to recover his dignity, two boys strode into the room looking very much like Akande. If the three males stood in a line, their heights would surely descend on a diagonal.

"I did say something intelligent," the perpetrator muttered. The taller one—the perpetrator—had short coily hair, while the shorter one had a head decked in neat cornrows and rounded glasses slid down his nose. Selene merely moved to sit next to Maleda, legs straight out in front of her.

Maleda decided to speak as she shoved away her laughter.

"What are your names?"

"I am Apara and this is Folu." The taller one gestured to the shorter boy. "We're sorry." His head dipped and the laughter on Maleda's face melted away. "Akande, Folu and I ambushed you. We thought that you were an enemy and—"

"No," Maleda stopped him, "I understand. Akande explained it to me. You were only trying to protect your home, but I'm here."

That snapped the serious demeanor the young men tried to strap to themselves, and their shoulders caved in a little as they quickly walked over and crushed Maleda in a hug. She didn't give the soreness in her body the satisfaction as she hugged them back. From the weight added on, she could tell that Selene and Akande joined in the hug. By the sand, she could not stop the burning that began in her eyes, and she barely swiped the tears from her face.

Maleda's voice was muffled under all the bodies "So, are we somehow related?"

"Yeah." It sounded like Apara was holding back his own tears. "We're your cousins." Maleda was swept up in the warmth of it all. She had left behind so much, missed so much.

"I'm sorry to interrupt." A voice came from the door. "But we haven't been properly introduced." Her cousins parted enough for her to see the topaz eyes framed by the frizzy curly brown hair in all its glory. Zaddae gave a small smile and remained at the head of the bed cloaked in red armor and cape as Mirriam and Ramonda entered the room.

"What is your name?" Maleda asked. Half her feigned curiosity was genuine.

"My name is Zaddae—professor in training and an old study partner of yours."

Maleda meekly nodded at him, trying hard not to make her gaze casual.

"I was part of the operation that helped save you from the desert. When the ship exploded, we feared the worst, but it is good to see you alive and I apologize for not being able to properly escort you into the city."

"Well, I think it was all worth it for it to lead up to this moment." She emphasized her words by squeezing Selene.

Zaddae nodded and continued, "In addition to welcoming you, we want to help you get back on your feet as soon as possible."

"Indeed," Ramonda grinned, "Well, I'm glad that you all got to see each other, but we must borrow Maleda for a meeting so she must get ready."

Maleda's cousins begrudgingly abandoned their group hug, but Selene lingered the longest squeezing Maleda once more. Her small frame still managed to squeeze the air out of Maleda's lungs. Maleda decided that she really liked that girl, and they were going to be great friends. Zaddae waited by the door as the cousins filed out with Selene bringing up the rear. He followed Selene out while secretively giving Maleda a small smile outside of the view of Ramonda and Mirriam. Ramonda patted the bed and gently said, "Take your time. Zaddae and I will be waiting outside."

Ramonda winked, turned on her heel to leave the room, and Mirriam took her place at the foot of the bed. Ramonda shut the door behind her, and Mirriam rose a brow while she crossed her arms. Those intense brown eyes were focused on Maleda, and she struggled to not shrink in Mirriam's gaze. She only spoke when she came to Maleda's side to help her out of the bed.

"What was that?"

"What?" Maleda asked, genuinely confused.

"Oh, don't play games," Mirriam retorted.

It was only then that Maleda realized that Mirriam picked up on the act between Zaddae and her.

"Aaah…I don't know what you're talking about." Maleda smiled.

"Mhm." Mirriam smirked. "You insult my intelligence. All right, get up."

Even though Mirriam commanded her, she still gently helped Maleda to stand and dress. Maleda emerged in a wheelchair pushed by Mirriam. They all silently escorted her through the palace and Maleda continued admiring the walls and ceilings for all their splendor. Some ceilings were just fantastic works of crossing beams. She noticed that they were coming upon an impressive set of doors down the corridor with relief sculptures of trees with branches turning into flying papers. There were also two impressive carvings on either side of the doors of a creature she could not name. The head of an owl, yet it sat proudly on two hind legs with two muscled front legs. The sculptor had somehow made the stone simulate feathers.

Then, they made a sudden turn and Maleda found herself craning her neck to look back at the sculptures.

"Wait, what were those sculptures?"

"Oh, the owl griffins," Ramonda responded.

"Yes, I'd love to look at them more. The sculptor was truly gifted."

"Well, that will have to wait until another day."

They came upon a set of tall doors that were less ornate, but when they went through them, Maleda was greeted by a gentle breeze. She was faced with a large dining room and a lounge area with various seating. A mix of understated patterns on the wall and green plants sprinkled about the room. Once she looked past the room, she saw the balcony beyond with the view of the empire blurry behind the chiffon curtains blowing into the room. Once her eyes gobbled up the room, she was able to focus on the professors sprinkled about the space, as well as the emperor and empress sitting at the head of the table side by side.

"Oh good, you're awake," the empress smiled, "Did you sleep well?"

"Yes, I did." Maleda nodded and silently recounted her eventful morning.

Mirriam helped her out of the wheelchair and Maleda seated herself on the side of the table closest to the empress. Mirriam took up a seat by Maleda's side and Ramonda sat opposite of Maleda.

"Very good, my dear." The empress gestured towards the professors to usher them over. "We're going to go ahead and get started." The empress introduced each of the professors. "These are Professors Busara, Buru, Auni, and Ramonda." Since they were no longer on the run, it was easier to sit and just look at the men from the desert. Busara wore deep blue robes and kept his dark, coily hair cut short, but Auni's hair was long and fluffy against his silver robes. Maybe he braided it up every night and took it down in the morning. If so, that was intense dedication. It took Maleda days to parse through her twists, not to mention that her long tresses were even longer as she stretched them out. Thank goodness that they shrunk, or she would be stepping on them. As opposed to his peaceful colleagues, Buru lounged in his green robes with a permanent furrow in his strong brows and his shoulder-length dreads were a curtain to reveal the spectacle that was his scowl. Of all the brown-skinned men, Auni's skin was darkest and therefore loved more by the sun.

The professors took the remaining seats at the table, including Zaddae.

"Ah, I trust that you are doing better today?" The one named Busara asked.

"Yes, I am." Maleda smiled.

"Well, thank you all for assembling here today." The emperor looked around the table. "In spite of all that we have gone through, I am happy that we are able to welcome our niece Maleda back to the empire. We wanted to be clear about the conditions that you are coming back to and the conditions in which you left."

The emperor paused and lowered his eyes as if he wanted to take care with what he said next.

"Around the time you disappeared there was a war, and the city was cursed with amnesia so we can all remember fighting in it, but the face of our enemy is wiped from our minds."

"What happened? Where were my cousins?" Maleda asked in the silence.

"They had their own guards assigned to them and they were hidden away." The empress continued. "By that time, our eldest daughter had already died from poisoning and Mirriam worked between guarding you and I per my instruction. I was trying to go with you both to guide you to safety. It got to the point where I needed to join the fighting and I instructed Mirriam to take you without me."

The empress looked to Mirriam to continue.

"I remember that I was with you in these hallways, creeping along with hands ready to draw my blades. But it's like the empress said, it gets patchy after that. Something happened and somehow in our getaway, we made it all the way out to the desert, but I don't remember how. I just looked over and saw you unconscious. I was confused, but I knew I had to protect you, so I weaved some lies so as not to scare you further and I'm sorry for that."

"Part of me wishes you didn't." A shadow of hurt passed over Mirriam's eyes but Maleda quickly continued. "But I understand why, and I don't blame you. This place is cursed, and we are cursed. Yet, there were things I remembered somehow, and I don't know why. All those drawings I made were connected to this place, but I still don't know what it all means."

"Well, I would like to help with that," Cham's voice chirped.

Everyone flinched, looking around the room, weapons drawn.

"Who is that?" Buru barked. "Show yourself!"

Cham was resting on Maleda's finger in the form of the ring, but she unfolded herself and reformed into her own sacred geometry, shifting into different patterns, turning inside of herself. Yet, as Maleda looked on her brain still itched, but she found herself in awe of Cham's form.

"Ah, you've decided to show yourself." The empress grinned at Cham.

"You again?" Buru made to grab for Cham, but she danced backwards in the air, out of his reach.

Maleda caught her and looked at Cham, "You know you have a habit of waking up at really inopportune times."

Cham stayed perched over Maleda's hand and made her announcement, "I understand that you all have been affected by the curse as well and I wanted to assure you that I am here to help Maleda as a guide. I might as well make my presence known for this conversation."

"Okay, so as a *clueless* guide, how are you going to help?" Buru countered with a raised brow.

"Everyone keeps saying that," Cham huffed, "Look, I will do what I can just as you are. Now, please continue."

"Actually Buru," the empress continued, "We've already looked into Cham, and she seems like an otherwise harmless piece of old-world tech. Rare too. Besides she's the one who led Maleda here and knows she needs to help Maleda, so I trust her." The empress turned her attention to Maleda and laid a hand on her arm. "The key thing that we wanted to tell you is that we're a little lost, just like you are. We don't know if we've somehow angered a being from the Spirit World or what's going on, but we don't want this to stop you from living. We still want you to enjoy the fruits of the empire, like going to university, taking your time to paint, be an apprentice, even explore the city."

"With caution of course." The emperor cut in. "The Royal Painters guild would be happy to have you and I would be lying if I said that I didn't want you to be my apprentice, but it's your choice. It's all your choice,"

"That sounds amazing, but I still have some questions." Maleda started. "Like, what exactly is the light that shows underneath my skin?"

Ramonda answered, "That light is a residual affect from the terra stones. The terra stones helped to keep you alive all that time ago, but they have a power that, naturally, wants to be released."

"But it hasn't been bothering me until recently, just before I set out to the abandoned city."

"Interesting…well, even though the trigger is late, it indicates that the power wants out, but we would be hesitant to aggravate it since this is a unique situation what with it being triggered so late and with a faceless enemy."

"Right," Maleda said with her brows furrowing.

"And don't worry too much," the empress expressed, "we'll go at a pace that you're comfortable with regarding everything."

"Do I have permission to speak your majesties?"

Everyone's head turned to Zaddae and Maleda saw an earnest warmth in his eyes. Even though he looked at the emperor and the empress, she felt like that warmth was meant for her too. Thank goodness, her skin was dark enough to hide the heat in her cheeks.

"Of course." The empress smiled.

"If I may offer my services, I would be honored to principally work with Maleda on her reintroduction to the empire, even to be her personal guard."

"Well, I think that would be a lovely idea. You two did work closely together before. Maleda, what would you say to that?"

Maleda looked between Zaddae and the empress and nodded.

"I think that would work well."

"Well, then it's settled," the empress stated, "Of course, we want you to rest, and there will be plenty of time to talk about this."

With that, the meeting concluded.

Once Maleda was back in her wheelchair, she asked for Mirriam to help her over to the balcony.

"So, when are we going to start?"

"Well, I think that you should rest for a few more days."

Maleda tried not to resign herself at the thought of being stuck in that room to pass out from pain and boredom.

They had to be on a mountainside as they were so high up, but even at that altitude Maleda could see the grace and might of the empire. It was different that night because she was high on pain and sorrow, so her eyes did not bother capturing this glory. It was not just a city, but a city of cities, like its own world. Buildings towered in the distance marked with symbols and shaped so organically, as if it was formed out of Dziko like a range of mountains and plains. The people were no more than dots of color, but she could feel their energy as the city buzzed around. There was no way that this place could go quietly into any night. There was no way it could ever sleep. Turning her neck and shifting her eyes was not enough to take in the land before her. At the edges of her vision, she could see that the castle wrapped around with the mountain, like an arc and it blended so well with the mountain that it jeweled. She could barely catch the full wonder of its sunshine glow as she was so caught up by the city and beyond that, the sea.

"Why did I have to miss this?" A gentle hand stroked her shoulder, and the tears pricked her eyes, but Maleda fought to hold them back. Her heart broke at the idea that she departed a place like this not knowing if she would see it again, but her pain was dimmed by the thought that she could rediscover it. Something told Maleda that she never knew all its secrets in the first place.

"Trust me," Mirriam said quietly as if she were in awe of the sight too, "if I could have kept you safe here, I would." Part of Maleda wanted to protest at that notion. She could have died in the desert with that band of machines, and she could die here in this place anyway. At least she would have been in a beautiful place.At least Maleda would be where she came from, but she held her tongue.

Professor Buru came over and spoke to Mirriam, "The emperor and empress wanted to briefly speak with you."

"Thank you," Mirriam began and then she gestured to Zaddae, "You can start your duties right now. Stay with Maleda while I speak to the emperor and empress."

"Of course." Zaddae nodded.

"When you start to get a stitch in your side or anywhere else, let me know and we'll head back to the room," Mirriam said as her footsteps receded along with Buru's. Maleda scoffed quietly because she would not let the state of her body keep her from—

"Mmm," Maleda restrained the full force of her pained grunt and scooted her chair closer to the railing of the balcony.

"I can't believe that I was away from all of this. I can't understand how this can exist when it seemed like Mirriam, and I were the only people alive. The professors. You all were one thing, but this…" Maleda trailed off and looked at Zaddae who was crouched at her side looking at her.

"If you were my friend—are my friend—I want you to show me this." She gestured to the city of cities that surrounded them, to the sea before them.

A breath of silence passed before Zaddae responded. He seemed to be studying her eyes.

"Of course. They are trying to protect you from an unknown enemy." Zaddae began in a hushed tone, "Yes, they want you to know about your powers, but they would rather you not need to defend yourself in the face of an enemy, with the hope that the enemy won't come back. It's no coincidence that you were almost captured and that your powers are igniting. They could attack you again and I will not have it. I'm not a master of any element and there are no teachers in the city, but I will help to connect you to older traditions that stoke that power. To keep their suspicions at bay, we will go through books, some rudimentary but still useful and some that hold the knowledge that you really need."

"I honestly thought I was going to have to convince you to help me, but you've taken the suspicions and words from my mouth. So, can we make a pact to figure out who this enemy is while I'm also figuring out who I am?"

"It's already done." Zaddae assured her.

"I do think that you will be ready for our *training* tomorrow."

"Truly? You're not just saying that to stop me from asking about the empire?"

"Honestly, I do, and we will both need to go beyond the walls of the palace at some point." He laid a hand on her shoulder. "Now you should get some rest Maleda. We start tomorrow."

Mirriam

Throughout the whole meeting, Mirriam tried to maintain a cool and aloof composure as she was internally burning with annoyance. Suffice it to say, she was not pleased with the idea of Zaddae spending so much time around Maleda. He seemed like a decent enough person, he helped Maleda escape in the desert, and he was Maleda's friend, but Mirriam was always the one to watch over her. She could barely stand the idea of Maleda being out of her sight when she had to travel to the abandoned city for supplies back at the oasis. Yet, after Mirriam arrived at the castle and woke up, the empress and the emperor explained that she would be a better protective asset to Maleda from afar. That Puzo even agreed with them. Strange. There was something familiar about him that she couldn't quite place. The empress had visited a medium and they provided her guidance on the matter, but the empress never said exactly what the medium told her, which only annoyed Mirriam more.

"Are you sure this is a good idea?" Mirriam asked with arms crossed. Even though she was seething, that was the only displeasure she would allow to show in the presence of her empress. "I've been the one guarding Maleda all this time. And now he is?"

"Mirriam, I trust what the medium said. It's not like it doesn't rattle me too."

"Well, what exactly did the medium say?" Mirriam's brows raised. As the empress hesitated, Mirriam looked around the room exasperated and saw that Buru hovered close by and Maleda was still talking to that Zaddae who was crouched by her. Mirriam looked back to her majesty and was about to protest again, but the empress spoke.

"The medium specifically said 'I'm suspicious of Mirriam. Mirriam should not be Maleda's guard. Zaddae should. They will uncover the past.'" The empress was completely calm, hands lightly steepled. However, Mirriam was about to start, and it was only the otherworldly muscle memory of maintaining soldier composure that kept her together. They believed she had an ulterior motive, or at least the medium did.

"Suspicious of me?" Mirriam whispered and kept her face neutral. "I've done nothing but protect Maleda and did my best to make sure no harm comes to her."

"I understand. Believe me, I do." *And it worries me too. I couldn't possibly believe that,* was what Mirriam hoped the empress was thinking. "I'd just rather be cautious and listen to someone who's in communication with the spirit world. But, I don't want you to believe that Maleda has no need of you, and that we have no use of you. I want you to guard her still, only from afar. Split your time between observing where she goes in the city, look into anything suspicious that you think has to do with her, and accompany Olmec and I when we need you. I know you don't want to leave her, but it seems that if we're to figure out how to recover the past, she'll need to trust Zaddae."

"Empress, what do you think is going on?"

"I don't know, but it seems that we're part of something way bigger."

* * *

With the secret between Maleda and Zaddae, Mirriam returned after her talk with the emperor and empress, then escorted Maleda back to her room with Zaddae at her side. Once Maleda was truly left alone in her room, she heard the trunk begin to rattle in the night. The paint reared up again this time, but it seemed stronger, like Maleda could sense its energy in the air. She scooted into the bed frame and her breathing became ragged. This *creature* had not killed her yet. It had only been telling her things and only when she was the only one aware or present. She made no attempt to run, but she remained rigid. It rose up like a wave with its own sparkling light but barely wider and taller than she was. The colors came together to make the wave, but they did not mix. It seemed like the colors were trying to make an image atop the structure of the wave, like a person trapped inside or maybe that form was part of it. The wave gestured toward the bed, and it partially crested and rolled forward, letting some of it flow onto the covers to create a scene.

There they were again: the two hooded figures in this room, one backing away and the other getting ready to fight, but the scene wouldn't continue. It only started to melt away and skip to another time. The figures turned and ran through a newly risen door twisting and turning down a hallway until they reached another set of doors, but much grander, much larger. They barely opened and just before the scene completely disintegrated, Maleda could see the room barely start to construct itself. Towering partitions, or shelves, and a tower in a corner.

That was all she could catch before the paint rejoined the larger wave. The wave turned itself away from her, toward the mirror and glided silently across the floor, so Maleda followed until she was standing next to the creature and in front of the mirror. A portion of the wave pooled at her feet, starting that glowing color under her skin again, like a network of veins. Maleda lifted her clothes to reveal it winding up her leg, only to watch it grow faint and then disappear, as if her skin were not a plane but a chasm that it fell into.

"Can you speak?" She whispered but the wave did not respond. Instead, it quickly swashed about on itself before flowing over the floor and back into the individual bottles within the chest. Maleda stared, convinced that it would rise again and when the paint remained hidden, she turned back to the mirror.

Cham, who was a ring on her finger, had transformed into a paintbrush in her hand, but she remained silent. Maleda walked over to her bed and sat down, cradling Cham in her new form. How was this light trapped under her skin and what could she do with it?

CHAPTER 30 - THE PRISONER

The way that he was bound kept changing, though he did not know how often. He guessed that it was every day, but time was strange here too. Sometimes, it was iron cuffs chained to the wall leaving him slumped over with his arms secured above his head and other times his cuffs were chained to nothing and he was left to lean against the wall of his cell. It's not like he had the energy to try to escape anyway. He didn't even know how he could.

From the faraway window, the prisoner glimpsed those who walked in his place. An accidental villain, but a villain nonetheless and a lost boy. Some mad hope let him keep feeling for the girl beyond the window.

CHAPTER 31 - MALEDA

When Maleda woke up, she was even more itchy to do something than the previous day. The paint did not do a display for her, and it remained in its bottles, but she looked from the chest to the mirror recounting the events from yesterday. Cham had also gone back to her ring form on Maleda's finger. Somehow, she slept albeit after staring at the canopy of stars until her eyes went blurry. Mirriam did not come to wake her, so in her restlessness, Maleda rose, able to walk and a little less sore than the prior day, washed in a basin, and changed into a tunic with sleeves slit open from shoulder to wrist and slightly billowing pants cuffed loosely at the ankle. She went into the trunk and grabbed her satchel, which contained her sketchbook and writing sticks. In the midst of retwisting the sections of her hair that came undone, she only paused to sketch a bottle of the paint, draw her memory of the wave, and the gestures that it made as well as the scenes that it constructed. Her brows furrowed at the curiosity that welled in her and she cursed the knowledge that she could not recall. She asked questions on the page full of scrawled notes and images that she felt could not be answered by anyone.

Knock. Knock.

With one hand holding an unfinished twist and the other holding her writing stick, Maleda turned toward the door. With the one available hand, she shoved her work into her satchel and put it under her pillow, while throwing a light scarf onto her shoulder from the dresser. She slid it over the majority of her hair leaving some of her front twists dangling from the fabric. They couldn't know what the paint was doing, especially if it was encouraging her to discover what was working underneath her skin, possibly to fight. She strode barefoot to the door, finishing up her twist. Maleda opened the door to find Zaddae standing on the other side of the threshold along with a new set of guards posted on the walls by her room. He was a respectful few feet away with hands behind his back. Upon seeing her, a smile tugged at the corner of his mouth, and he slightly dipped his head, putting a hand over his heart and then his palm face up with fingers toward her.

"How are you feeling today?"

"A little better and a little restless," Maleda said tugging on the hem of her tunic. Zaddae just stood in the hallway smiling.

"Oh, you can come in." Maleda stepped back into the room, and he obliged her.

"Thank you. We will officially be starting our lessons today in the library."

Maleda nodded and grabbed the satchel. They were on their way down the hall when a question started to gnaw at Maleda.

"Was it scary? Me not being here I mean," Maleda started. He kept his eyes forward as they strode down the hall. Perhaps he did not want to divulge in the subject.

"It was like a room that you always visited that was filled with the stuff of memories and then one day you open the door to the room and its empty. I remember talking to the moon, talking to the tree that they planted for you. It was…overwhelming."

Maleda could tell that even though she had returned that Zaddae still had not fully recovered from her sudden emergence. Still, something about him felt so familiar even in her lack of memory, so she would fight for it.

Maleda could tell when they got to the library because the doors were guarded by those owl creatures from yesterday. The entrance was the same impossible grandeur as the rest of the palace, but something about it seemed especially sacred. When those titan doors opened, her eyes were flooded with such varied grandeur. Maleda couldn't help but be enthralled by all the books that surrounded her. It was like a whole city devoted to parchment and vellum, or even a whole world in itself. There weren't just levels to this place, but intricate sections that bowed in and out of the mountain, yet all carved with power and grace. There were lower levels that dipped into the deep part of the mountain, where the sea of black was dispelled by the lights gleaming from below. There were many tables and lounging areas to read in with rugs and daybeds. Sunlight poured in through a titan of a window and she could see fringes of the life below in the Empire of Two Shores. They strode up a set of winding steps that took them right up to the window and even more of the city of cities filled the window.

Maleda's breath caught and she had to blink away the stinging in her eyes. This was the world she had left. All this life kept buzzing while she was gone, but she did not intend to miss any more of it.

"Could we study by the window?" Her own voice sounded far away.

"Actually," he started, "I already have the materials in the tower."

Tower? She looked to where Zaddae pointed and sure enough there was something that looked like the glimpse of the tower that the paint wave showed her the day before. Maleda tried her best to school her face, but the tower alone looked fascinating. There were windows all around the top of it and stone vines in relief curled around and up the tower, along with colored relief sculptures similar to the images in the walls of her room. The patterns were so bright and vibrant. How could stone look like that? Maleda didn't put up any argument as she followed Zaddae to the tower. It had an arch-like entrance with a simple door, and it was wide, wide enough for them both to step in. The door clicked as Zaddae closed it and Maleda turned to see that the inside of it was painted. Some of it was chipped and faded, leaving only shadows of the vibrancy that was there before.

"She loved doing things like that." Zaddae snapped Maleda out of her stare. "Painting and drawing in places that she wasn't allowed." There was a glaze over his eyes as he looked at the remnants on that doorframe, a glaze for the princess. Maleda lowered her eyes to the floor, but she didn't have much time to dwell on what to say.

"Anyway, our materials are upstairs." Zaddae gestured to the grand staircase that was recessed into a lounging space that had a fireplace of its own. The two traveled up the stairs, passing all of the rooms, until they got to the top. It was even more of a getaway than the bottom floor of the tower.

Chairs of all sizes were littered everywhere, with brightly colored tapestries and rugs, another fireplace, and windows all round that showed the library and then the glass of the library beyond that showed the view of the city. It was even more appealing at this height than before. Zaddae had already spread out several books and papers on a long table, but even though Maleda had hungered to see texts in this condition ever since she lost her memory, she felt cheated every time she looked at the city below. Even though the sun had barely made its entrance, lights danced in the streets and buildings below. She wanted to see it shine from the streets. Reluctantly, she took a seat in one of the chairs and pulled it up to the table.

"So, what's the subject for today," she asked, trying to peel her eyes from the glass that kept the city from her. Zaddae smiled at her in a knowing and near-mocking way.

"Well, it's whatever you like on this table," he said gesturing towards the books. "I think training doesn't just take place in the body but in the mind."

"Whatever I like?" The glee danced in Maleda's voice.

"Of course," Zaddae smiled with a new light in his eyes.

* * *

Days had gone by like this where Zaddae labored over papers and Maleda poured through different texts, occasionally peppering Zaddae with questions or doting on the stories of the empire.

Maleda decided to get lost in a stack of books and texts that allowed her to walk into other worlds. She saw the intense imagination and theory of someone who described a planet parallel to that of Dziko. A planet where magic didn't manifest in the physical world or at least not often. She also saw through the eyes of a prince who wanted adventure in the great wide world beyond Alfajiri.

"Zaddae, have you ever heard the story of the Mariner Prince?" Maleda asked with the book pressed against her chest.

"No, I can't say I have." His brows were knit together as he was looking over his papers.

"There was a prince from far away who had a lust for adventure and wanted to know what lay on the other side of the sea that bordered his kingdom. In the text, it says that he and his crew got caught in a storm and he was separated from them, but it looks like he wound up on the shore of a faraway land."

Maleda barely noticed as the light of the sun passed over them and disappeared into twilight. She was fighting tired eyes, but she would not let go of her cozy reading spot in the plush chair in the tower.

"Maleda," a voice called her name.

Her eyes had lost their focus and the black words had become muddled on the page, but she looked up to find Zaddae looking down at her with the ghost of a smile on his face.

"It is time for me to escort you back to your room."

"Oh, I'm coming," Maleda said as she clung her current book to her chest. She didn't realize how much of her energy went into that day's reading as she swayed upon standing. A stray sliver of pain caught her side and her knees threatened to buckle, but Zaddae was already there to catch her. He did not linger on the gesture and swiftly set her upright. Maleda thanked him and long after she made it back to her room, she tried to calm the heat in her cheeks. Instead, she tried to focus on the latest story that she started as sleep took her. Maleda wished that she could meet the people she read about, draw them, write about them, pay tribute to their mighty and innumerable legacies.

CHAPTER 32 - THE MARINER PRINCE

"Sire, I must advise against this...venture."

Maleda was looking at the king as he strode on down the golden, sunlit hallways, with purple robes flowing behind him as his advisor expressed his worries. Maleda was an observer but disembodied and with no voice. At some moments it seemed like she was outside of herself, watching a golden, yellow spirit hover over the two men.

"I have already arranged for my departure. I trust my brother to rule in my stead while I am gone," the king said.

"And what if you never return, your Majesty?"

"Then, he will continue to rule and pass on the mantle to his children. Hopefully, he and you all will remember me."

He chuckled as a sad, sentimental look passed over his soft, dark eyes. A gentle breeze carried his black dreadlocks, until they fell back to his jawline. It was like the wind beckoned him to follow and he would answer her.

"But sire I—"

The king put a hand on his advisor's shoulder.

"Don't you trust my brother? Trust me too?"

"Sire, I trust your brother and he would be a fine ruler, but I don't want you to go out on those waters and suffer. There may be another land and then there may be nothing but more sea. I know that you have wanted to see more sire and I will not stop you from seeking that adventure...May the Orisha be with you."

The king had never embraced the man so hard, but they just stood there. He was more than an advisor, but also a childhood friend.

* * *

That golden afternoon seemed so far away as the king fought the waves that tried to toss his men and him across the boat. Everyone was shouting at each other and the king feebly shouted orders as the boat tossed them from side to side. The waves were colossal, threatening to turn over the boat and the rain was a volley of arrows, sharply stinging as it pelted the king and crew.

One moment, the king was speeding to help a fallen crew member that was likely to be tossed overboard, but the king had lost his footing and the next wave left an empty spot where the king was standing. The king did not have time to process his regrets as he was fighting to break the surface of the dark, stormy waters. He heard them calling his name, but he had swallowed so much seawater. In between coughing up the ocean, he tried to scream for the help of his crew, but they kept drifting further and further away.

* * *

Maleda

Maleda woke up clawing at the air and shot upright, chest heaving. She gripped the sheets, grounding her in the world and she noticed that Cham had turned into the paintbrush again and the paint was drifting back into the trunk at the foot of her bed.

IV

Part Four

REMEMBRANCE

CHAPTER 33 - MALEDA

As Maleda prepared herself for the day, she found her eyes flicking between Cham on her finger and the trunk as if they would come alive. She could still feel the golden warmth of the sunlight along with the thrashing of the sea, could still hear the prince's screams. Zaddae came to escort her to the library for their usual routine and she did her best to keep herself from fidgeting instead focusing on holding the book.

"So, what's the subject for today?" He asked once they had arrived at the top of the tower. Zaddae smiled at her in a knowing and near-mocking way, but it faded as he observed Maleda's restraint crumbling into flitting glances around the room and her voice edged into panic.

"Zaddae, I had a dream last night about the story I was reading yesterday, the story about the Mariner Prince. It felt so real. I could see them, hear their voices."

Zaddae guided Maleda to sit down and knelt in front of her, holding her hands while his calluses brushed over them.

"Maleda, look at me and breathe slowly."

She obeyed and the ratcheting of her heart lessened. Zaddae even breathed in time with her.

"When you're ready, tell me what happened."

Maleda took a breath and recited the dream to Zaddae. She even explained how her paints had come alive in prior days and how she witnessed it animate itself.

"Zaddae, this wasn't just a dream. I've had dreams about the empire before when I was out in the desert, foggy ideas of what life here was like, but I shouldn't have seen that so clearly. It felt like someone guided me there to witness the events."

Maleda waited for Zaddae to respond but when she finished, he looked at the floor, working her hands like he was thinking about what to say. Maleda was about to break the silence, but Zaddae beat her to it.

"I think there's something you need to see out in the empire. It actually makes me think of what you're describing." He looked up at her with lowered brows.

Maleda's eyes widened, and the questions came tumbling, "But what about the empress and emperor? Won't they come looking for me? Or Mirriam? The royal children? Surely, they won't like this."

Even though she voiced her doubts, she was excited at the notion to leave the walls of the palace, no matter how grand and mysterious they were. Zaddae seemed to read all of this and replied as he handed her a bundle of things that were hidden away underneath a chair.

"The emperor and the empress are locked into investigations of their own on the other shore. Their children are each bound to their duties all day and Mirriam is attending to the emperor and empress, to her reluctance. On top of all that, I will make sure, that we go in a secret way."

They were really doing this. They were going out into the city. Zaddae merely put on a pack and hid away some weapons in his boots and waistband. Maleda stood with her bundle and merely looked from it and back to Zaddae. He must have been waiting for this moment, always prepared yet never pushing the matter. He moved the pack from her hands to the table and unfurled it, revealing its contents. He wrapped a lightweight dark cloak around her shoulders held together by a chain.

"You need to raise your arms." She did and he looped a thick belt around her waist where a satchel fell to either side of her thighs. He wrapped straps from those satchels around each of her thighs. Zaddae somehow fashioned her own satchel through the loops on the bottom of the satchel on her left side of the belt. He wrapped a leather bracer over the sleeve of her tunic armed with straps holding an inkwell and another holding a strange sort of writing utensil made of intricately carved metal. It would be a lie if

Maleda denied that all the physical contact didn't heat her skin, but she could distance herself from the thought with the bigger stakes at hand. All these supplies were a new sort of weight that somehow kept her grounded. Zaddae closed the flaps of her cloak over her new hardware and tapped the chair for her to sit in front of him. He then grabbed scraps of folded leather fabric and laced his fingers through the holes.

"They're for your feet. May I?" He asked. She silently shook her head and he proceeded to kneel as he laced them over her bare feet. She was so used to walking through the world barefoot, always having contact with the world. Her toes protruded from them with the ties facing up. "You're not used to the city, so we should take precautions with how your feet will handle it." Maleda silently nodded again, excited, but bewildered. He was kneeling in front of her and tending to her feet, but no matter. There was a bigger picture, and he was right. Who knew what she could cut herself on?

"I'm not going to pretend that I can imagine what all of this is like for you, but if you want to turn back, you tell me. I will put away the cloak and undo the satchels. You just tell me and its done, but if you really want to learn about what lies under your skin, you are going to have to trust me. Do you trust me?"

Maleda considered it. The emperor and empress wanted her to suppress her powers even though her killer could come back for her. She needed to fight for herself because whether they liked it or not, her killers could come back to extinguish the ghost. She could die either way, but if she followed Zaddae out into the city, she could live. Cham had been quiet recently, but Maleda swore she could feel her energy buzzing as she took her out of her pocket and held her in her hand.

Maleda shook her head and managed a quiet but firm, "Yes."

Zaddae nodded back and dragged over a low wooden pedestal and placed an open book on top of it.

"I've been doing some reading myself. So far, I know that this ring is built to show displays and transform." He pointed to a diagram framed by some text on the page that showed a similar ring. Cham then flattened out into a thick disc with a button on the top of it. When it clicked open, it showed a three-dimensional map of the library with Maleda and Zaddae standing in it. The map itself seemed to be made of some sort of the same light display as before, but with a substance, like the paint in her trunk. She squinted her eyes at the detail until Zaddae handed her a pair of glasses similar to the ones that the emperor wore, but these were fitted into a leather pair of goggles. She took them and once she slipped the goggles around her head, the ring became more intricate. She could see well enough before but looking through the glass changed her view from standard to high definition. When she looked out of the window, the blur of motion that was the city even looked clearer in the coming daylight. She wanted to remember, and she wanted to see.

"Will this show us the way through the city?" Maleda asked.

"Some parts, but others may need to be filled in." Zaddae tilted his chin at her. "By you."

Her heart clenched at that.

"What do you mean? I don't remember anything. Why can't you just tell me?" Maleda tried to keep herself from rising into a panic. She rose from the chair and went to a wall with a map of the city on it.

"Your dreams could be a sign that you can remember even more than you think. In the desert, it was just blips, but now you're seeing things with such clarity. You said yourself that it feels different…I've only come to this side of the empire to come to the palace and ever since you've been gone you could say that I have not made many visits," Zaddae continued as Maleda looked on at the map bewildered, "I remember some secret passages in and out of the palace, but as far as the city there are holes in my memory too. It's not like we can't find our way back to the palace. I know the entrances to get in here and we can always just walk back towards the palace walls if it gets too difficult. I wanted to tell you in here rather than out there, so that you didn't get overwhelmed in the street."

"Well, is there a place that we are looking for?" Or were they just going out for a stroll, with an amnesiac leading the way?

"Yes, we are going to the Connected Path. It is the star museum of the empire, connected to one of the universities and we need to find something in collections."

"How do you know that?"

"The princess told me." Maleda's eyebrows knitted together when Zaddae approached with a role of paper that had been tucked in his cloak. "She left this."

Once unfurled, Maleda could see that there was a printed image of floor plans with many other rooms crossed out or scribbled through, but one room was circled, and a note was written next to it that said

Something with the Mariner Prince and my project? Maybe here? They may have moved it. Find it, read it, finish it.

"What *it* was she referring to?" Maleda ran her hand over the text.

"It sounds like the prince that you're talking about, but with the emperor and empress away, it may be one of the only times that we can find out what it is." Zaddae moved to one of the lush tapestries and moved aside the flourish that it made on the floor. He then grabbed a mirror that hung on the wall next to the map. Maleda watched as Zaddae positioned the mirror in a chair so that the light from the terratech lamps bounced off the mirror and onto the floor, revealing two glinting handles on the floor laid perfectly next to the wall. Zaddae abandoned the mirror and heaved the handles upward until the floor folded back on itself, revealing a dusty dark descent into an ancient stairwell.This place must have been beyond her age by at least a hundred years, maybe two. She sharply breathed in and seized the hem of her cloak.

This was not that descent in the dark in the desert when those rebels in black came to attack them. Zaddae was with her. He looked up at her from the floor and Maleda clutched Cham inside one hand, while pulling the hood over her head with the other.

"Let's go," she said with equal quiet and firmness. Zaddae's eyes brimmed with something bright as he nodded and swung himself halfway into the hole, while Maleda cautiously proceeded down the first few steps after him. Zaddae reached up finding a twin pair of handles on the inside of the secret door and pulled it closed with a whisper of a thud.

CHAPTER 34 - MALEDA

There was no light down there, only the ever-growing echo of their footsteps as they started their descent. Zaddae took hold of Maleda's hand, and she was grateful as she did not want to lose him or her footing. Maleda held the Cham in the other hand, who was still splayed out like a disc. Cham barely showed enough light, but she could see their twins mimicking their descent downwards and glimpses of their environment. They were framed by walls, and they were walking in a spiral. There seemed to be things jutting out of the wall, probably torches or old holders for terratech lights. They had surely passed the tower by now and they had descended into the lower parts of the library, as if they were tucked away in the walls. Maleda wondered what emergency meant that these passages needed to be used.

"How many passages do you think are in the palace?"

"Enough to call grounds for naming it an underground city. On this side of the shore, I believe the passages beyond the castle are much more alive than this. Maybe a little wider and definitely more crowded. Barely any space, yet people still sell goods and play music in the underground as the world rushes around them. There's even—"

Zaddae stopped short and Maleda did not need to look at the display to feel the shift from descending spiral to open space. She moved the hand holding the disc to the wall nearest them and she began to follow it, while Zaddae trailed silently behind her.

They eventually came to a corner and Maleda could feel the box that they were in, and she continued down the new wall until she saw passageways, open cavernous archways with no light coming from any of them. Maleda counted seven of them. Where did they all go?

"So, which way do we go?" Maleda turned to ask Zaddae. His face was streaked with patterns of light and shadow that made her heart briefly tighten, but he only bit his lip with furrowed brows as he stared up at the archways.

"This is actually where you come in." He nodded towards her. "I only remember up to here." It was one thing to navigate streets with those tall buildings as landmarks, but there was no telling where those seven archways would lead. To other parts of the palace, to the outside, to the other shore.

How would she know? She let go of his hand and fidgeted with her glasses, but he merely laid a hand on her shoulder, so as not to get separated. The disc was useless as it only showed the archways before them and their little avatars in a square empty room. There had to be a way to get Cham to show more, so Maleda turned Cham over. She tried running her fingers over and through the display, but her fingers just made the three-dimensional display fuzz up into a grainy and wispy substance.

"How am I supposed to remember? I don't even understand how to work this thing," She muttered. "Is there a way for me to trigger a memory, an actual memory?"

"Was there ever a dream about a door or set of pathways?" Zaddae asked.

Maleda shook her head and she paced as she thought.

"No. Maybe if I remembered my life, it would all make sense in context, but sometimes, the dreams would end abruptly or shift. There was just so much color."

Maleda continued to pace. Colors. She would take the colors she saw and make drawings out of them in the tree. She tried to etch drawings into her room back in the desert. Mirriam would try to find pigment and make awkward sticks of it for her to use. Still, the most brilliant colors she ever saw came from the Cham's display in the desert. On top of that, Cham's lines were brilliant when they pulsed with color. Cham did turn into that brush, and it seemed to be in tandem with the wave. Was she influencing it somehow? Could she tell her something? Maleda's feet stilled and she stared at the disc.

"How can I change Cham back into the ring?" She asked Zaddae.

"Like this," he beckoned her over with a hand and she knelt by his side, while he laid his hand over hers, "Just twist the nob like this and it should reconfigure itself, at least according to the books." Sure enough, the disc folded and formed its way back into a ring. Strange enough, it still had its own glow.

"Zaddae, I saw something in Cham before when I was in the desert. It made a display and I could hear voices, music. How did it get there?"

"That would require programming. Someone had to put it there. I could speculate, but I have no idea. Maybe one of the professors put it there to see if you were there? It's possible. If we manipulate the settings, maybe we can find it." Zaddae put his hand over Maleda's and began turning the nob on the side of the ring. There was no definitive click, but something flickered from the light of the ring and a column of light bloomed from the top of it, gentler than before and there was a masked girl in the display.Her face was hidden by an array of golden intricacies and her eyes were too shadowed to see their color, but she spoke.

"I am Princess Clementina and I can only speak in riddles because I do not know who will find this. The people who came to kill me and Maleda are still out there, but I still don't know who they are. Maleda, you need to look at yourself for who you are now. You may glimpse the past, but your current reflection is key to finding who you are inside. You should be able to play that over again. If you find this, it means that I, Clementina, have perished."

The display faded and a faint glow was left in its place. It was like that last sentence was an afterthought, as if she were in a rush to tag that last bit onto the message.

"Do you have any ideas?" Maleda asked as a headache started to build behind her eyes.

"I'm trying to remember." Zaddae strained with a hand on his head.

Maleda faced him fully.

"I know we've got the curse to worry about," Zaddae sighed, "but for some reason my memories around that time are hazy. Maybe the trauma made me shove it down. I don't know. Maleda—" As her sight moved from the chambers around them to somewhere else, she distantly felt Zaddae's arms holding her up. It was like her dreams, but she was wide awake and could no longer feel the world around her.

There were frames on a wall and the wall ascended feet above her and a girl with a turned head looked into one of the frames before her, but there was no reflection. Loud. It was so loud.

Zaddae was shouting her name and Maleda was gasping for breath as her sight returned, as if someone else had used her lungs.

"I saw something." Zaddae straightened as Maleda left his grasp. "A room filled with mirrors and a girl looking into it with no reflection."

"At the museum, there used to be a display of mirrors that showed things that some could see, and others could not. It was taken down though. Maybe we can look in collections for it, but which path should we take?"

Maleda pointed out the correct hall and they were on their way.

* * *

The passageway was dusty with times' passing and the ring illuminated the space so that they could see a few feet in front of them. Their footsteps made quiet echoes as if afraid to tempt what was in the darkness. They reached a set of stairs descending and had to turn about themselves many times. Then, they climbed up another set of stairs to be greeted by a door in the ceiling, like back at the tower. Maleda's breathing was a little labored as she pushed against the door. How far had they walked? It barely creaked and she pushed it again, but it barely gave. Zaddae was a few steps behind, as Maleda had run ahead at the first signs of light filtering through the cracks.

When he caught up with her, Maleda was half spent, sitting on the steps, but she rose to help him push the door.

"I think something's on top of it," Zaddae said through his teeth. A slight sudden shift.

Maleda tried putting her hands out to either side and pushing at the wood, while Zaddae moved to do the same.

"Why would something be blocking it?" Maleda strained. "Maybe the museum is closed? You said you don't come to this side of the shore often."

"Yes," Zaddae countered, "but I'm holding out here. I choose—"

"I already can't ask my parents about what happened before. If this was erased in the time I have been gone, then I don't—"

"Maleda," Zaddae interrupted, "Trust me."

Something groaned and they could hear something sliding on the wood. "I choose—"

Zaddae was interrupted when they half fell into warm light, their torsos laid out on the wooden floor around them. The now open door was laid against a crate, the culprit that almost kept them from the room. Shelves upon shelves of artwork were around from painted canvas, wooden relief sculpture, free-standing sculpture, busts, drawings, so much that Maleda could not take it all in. Silent and full of grandeur. They must have been above the museum. She almost didn't notice Zaddae as she was slowly turning around, eyes gobbling up the strokes of history and expression. Zaddae put a hand on her shoulder stopping her from turning.

"I was going to say that I choose to believe. Now, the princess's note said that it was something in here that we must find and read. It could be a piece that hints at who may have assassinated her, like an enemy to the empire. Who knows? Maybe it's near the mirrors."

"But what about 'reading' it?" Maleda's brows furrowed. "Is there going to be some writing attached?"

"Not necessarily," Zaddae gestured towards a free-standing sculpture of a woman, "It looks like they are just cleaning this one up, but I'll tell you what I see. I see a woman staring into the eyes of a place or a person with quiet and fierce determination. Her hair is in twists and knotted on top of her head, like her own crown. One hand grips her billowing swimsuit wrap, while the other cups the wind in her hand, as if she could take it for her own or become a part of it. That's how you read a piece, whether it be word, sculpture, or paint. There are words and stories hidden in them."

Understanding felt its way into Maleda's heart as she looked at the unfulfilled longing in Zaddae's eyes. She quietly asked what she already knew.

"Is this Princess Clementina?" It didn't take Zaddae's nod to understand the grandeur of this piece and how well kept it was. A youthful girl, around Maleda's age stared out above them, a titan that only wanted to enjoy the breeze. The sculptor had created a mask of white dots and lines that slightly obscured the princess's face. A peaceful young royal, who looked so at odds with the buzzing empire around her. Zaddae remained quiet, so Maleda suggested, "Since it seems like we're the only ones up here, we can probably split up to look."

Zaddae only nodded again before silently heading in one direction and Maleda turned and started walking the opposite way down an aisle of two-dimensional works that suddenly became haunting.

* * *

There was no way they could go through half of what was in collections that day. Each piece was paired with a terratech plaque that displayed the place of origin in relation to the continent. Books with illustrations so detailed that you could stare at the script for minutes without having read a word, vertical rows of panels with rugs imported from some country in the east, weaved baskets, and ornate wooden staffs stringed with beads and hollowed rinds from the west were only grains of sand compared to the levels to be explored. All the pieces had been given, a peaceful collaboration between nations, the world. Maleda had to remind herself not to linger too long in front of these works. She made her way down an aisle into a dimmer part of the collections room, until she reached a wall where there was a yellow glint in the darkness, ornate with carvings. The corner of a frame. Maleda reached a hand towards it and felt her way across the frame. It was at least twice wider than her hand. She followed the line of the frame and was halted by something smooth and cool in her path. Removing her hands from the frame, she felt her way around her obstacle's form. There was a window, too high above for her to reach so she grabbed the terratech ring and turned its dial until she felt the light bloom from the top. This time a display, like the one in the desert, showed itself with people of many colors dancing, barely illuminating the sculptures around her and the canvas before her. The little dancing figures led her along the side of the painting, where she caught wild glimpses of color, but then the painting ended with the frame and all she saw were mirrors.

Some were hanging on what seemed to be an infinitely tall wall. Others were leaning against each other, like forgotten relics. Her body stiffened at the girl facing away from her, but she kept on moving towards the mirrors because she wasn't there. She could see so many angles of the room around her, but not her. These were the mirrors that showed things other than the self. They had to be, but Maleda saw nothing in them. She chose one to look into, curious. Why didn't it see her? Some faraway feeling tugged at the tightness in her chest. Yet, she heard footsteps and turned to see Zaddae behind her. He approached her staring at the mirrors that bejeweled the wall, "Well, you found the wall of mirrors."

"Yeah, I don't know what we're supposed to be looking for here. I've read that sometimes they show our true selves and even what we aren't but even the texts aren't clear about what that means. Some think that the mirrors have their own consciousness, but no one knows for sure. No one can really nail down the true nature of them because they are either infused with or made totally from terratech minerals. All I can see is me. What led me here was the light from—"

Maleda was cut short as she looked into the mirror and saw spears pointed at her and Zaddae.

CHAPTER 35 - MALEDA

They were surrounded by masked, uniformed guards all pointing spears at them. Eclipsed by shadow, they looked like they were wearing black. The agents in the desert. Somehow, they found her again. Maleda's breathing picked up and she grabbed at Zaddae's arm. They stepped in closer securing their circle and Maleda could see that they were all women. A woman broke the circle and stepped forward. She was crowned with a blossom of a headdress, chin tipped up, and robes flowing around her. Dread curled in Maleda's stomach as she recognized Ramonda.

"What are you doing in this facility?"

Firm and cold. She stood just at Maleda's height, but Maleda still felt like she was beneath her. She fought to not tremble and to not hold her breath as Ramonda was inches from Maleda.

"Well." Ramonda's voice was too quiet.

Zaddae started, "Professor, I encouraged Maleda to come here so—"

Ramonda put a hand up to stop Zaddae from talking and he obeyed.

"I want her to answer." Maleda steeled herself to respond.

"I can explain," Maleda rushed, "We were trying to find something for Princess Clementina and we thought that it might be here. She left—"

"Ah!" Ramonda cut off Maleda, "Don't say anything else." She looked between Zaddae and Maleda, sizing them up.

"Come with me," she commanded beckoning them with her fingers. Maleda kept her eyes on the woman's back barely daring to glance at the masked guards that surrounded them. The march was silent through collections and Maleda registered when they passed their initial entrance only to approach a new opening in the floor. The woman went down first followed by a couple guards and the pattern repeated for Maleda and Zaddae. They proceeded through a new set of tunnels in much better condition than the previous ones, filled with terratech lights. Maleda jumped when she saw a group of people crossing at the end of the tunnel. They were clutching stacks of parchment, scrolls, and books. After an abrupt turn, they ascended a series of stairs and found themselves at a wall that spun in on itself to reveal a room littered with sunlight, books, and papers. The guards took positions on the walls encircling them, watching their every move. The woman sat down at a monument of a desk, its trim ornate in carvings and when she was settled, she sent the guards out. While she stared at her hands, Maleda and Zaddae exchanged glances.

"Now that we are alone and secure, please continue Maleda." She was still staring at her hands but gestured for Maleda and Zaddae to sit, so they obeyed. Maleda did not feel confident in her liberty to ask questions, but she just poured the fear into her shaking leg, and she told Ramonda about her dream regarding the Mariner Prince, as well as Zaddae asking her to follow Clementina's notes regarding finding something in collections.

"Do the emperor and empress know that you are here?" Ramonda looked between Maleda and Zaddae.

"Professor." Zaddae started and Ramonda silently turned toward him with a slow blink. "The empress and emperor are on the other shore to check its status. They've gone to meet with the King of the Whitlands."

"Zaddae," Ramonda sighed, "I would have preferred if you and Maleda didn't sneak into the museum."

"But you know that they would likely keep her in the castle for longer, no matter how much they talked about Maleda seeing the city." Zaddae countered.

"Please professor," Maleda interjected, "I don't think that I had that dream for no reason, and I think that I just need more time to look at what the princess made. More time to understand it." A warmth took over Ramonda's face as if she were smiling to herself. She chuckled as she closed her eyes and shook her head.

"Well, I will let you both in on something."

Ramonda walked up a set of stairs that winded up the wall and stopped before a grand window. She gestured for Zaddae and Maleda to follow and they proceeded up the stairs and met her at the top. Professor Ramonda pointed out the window at a magnificent structure with something like a tower attached to it and banners waving in the wind.

"That is where Princess Clementina used to study. She was an advanced student, and she had her own choice of private quarters. She chose that tower because it is attached to the arts building. It seemed that her soul ran on what she learned in that building," Ramonda said solemnly.

"What are those colorful banners on the outside of it?" Maleda inquired.

"It is our way of remembering her." Ramonda seemed to be holding herself tight, as if she were trying not to tremble. "The formal term would be mourning, but Clementina would want us to remember how much she loved color and how it was the stuff of life. Each one is a little different, sewn with different stories and different colors, but they all belong together." Professor Ramonda pulled out a scroll of paper from her robes and wordlessly placed it in Maleda's hand. Maleda questioned the professor with her eyes, but Ramonda nodded her head, encouraging her to read it.

Professor Ramonda,

If you see Maleda again, please give her the tower

and please have it draped in those beautiful colors.

I know she would love it. Please convince my parents

to let her stay there. She needs that freedom,

So that she can remember who she is and who she can be.

And I know that I never got to finish my work,

But I want her to have it and to finish it however she likes.

She should be able to find my notes and diagrams.

With all my love and Olodumare watching over me,

Clementina

By the time, Maleda had reached that name on the last line, she had already bit her tongue to keep her eyes from watering. She had heard about Olodumare so little now, but she could not help but question how this Olodumare could let Maleda disappear, forget everything, forget her best friend, and lose her best friend. Clementina was more kind that Maleda could imagine, and she did not know how to process how sweetly she spoke about her. At least, she had Zaddae and now professor Ramonda.

"She," Maleda started careful of the warble in her voice, "she wants me to have the tower and she said that she wants me to have her work. What does she mean her work?"

"I will show you," Ramonda said warmly and so Maleda and Zaddae followed her out of the office.

* * *

They left the way they came, but made a few different turns, running into some students on the way. They still had parchments on hand. Finally, they ascended some steps and came across a door. Once professor Ramonda entered it and walked through, they were surrounded by a garden of free-standing sculptures and even though they were walled in, they looked up and saw the sky. Maleda's eyes could not process all the works fast enough, but there was no time as Ramonda gestured for them to follow her through another door on the side of the garden. The inside of the tower was so familiar, safe. She remembered none of it, but there were multiple lounge areas and rooms for study. Once they reached the top of the stairs, Maleda knew they had reached the princesses' rooms. Once Ramonda pushed the door open, Maleda saw the apartment that the princess had kept. It was two levels, with the first level as open space and the second being her rooms. Zaddae's face flickered with something Maleda could not place.

"Even though there was public workspace downstairs, she would often haul her work up here. We didn't have the heart to clean the flecks of paint left over on the floor," Ramonda said, "and you'll see that this door leads you right to collections."

Sure enough, there was a door that opened onto an enclosed bridge, so she could see the sculpture garden below. Ramonda guided Maleda and Zaddae through it. They found themselves back in the dark room filled with art and artifacts. It didn't take them long to find themselves amongst the wall of mirrors.

"Each of these mirrors shows something beyond the reflection, but it seems like they have minds of their own. Sometimes, they guide us to the things that we need to see," Ramonda offered. Maleda looked into each frame, and she saw the light glinting behind her. The golden frame. She turned and went into the darkened space behind her, feeling for it.When Ramonda made that part of the room glow with terratech lights, she saw that the frame was a curling fusion of wood and gold. It was about twice her height, and it was around three times her height in length. The canvas itself was flourishing with color. Yet, it was unfinished.

"Her project was special. I barely got to see anything beyond sketches. I know you'll find a way to finish it," Ramonda smiled.

"Thank you, professor," Maleda said, looking from them to the canvas.

"But," Ramonda countered, "he's not allowed to stay here." Ramonda had a knowing look in her eye and Zaddae did his best to keep his face neutral, but Maleda could see the wrestling of his hands behind his back. "For one thing, boys and girls stay in separate wings. For another thing, this is an independent study building and the princess did not leave him anything to study. Besides, you can come visit Maleda, continue with your training, daily guarding, and when you're not here, the guards at the university will be more than excellent."

"Of course, professor. I wouldn't want to contradict policy," Zaddae offered.

"As for you, Maleda, an independent study means that you have no classes that you are obligated to, other than this. Well, *we* will leave you to your work and allow you to make yourself comfortable." Professor Ramonda was turning to leave, and it seemed to be on cue when two masked guards appeared out of nowhere ready to guide Zaddae out. They walked back into the princesses' apartment, leaving the door open to the collections.

Maleda was enveloped in things she could not understand, but her brows furrowed when she wondered how long—

"And don't worry about the emperor and the empress. I will inform them that you will be staying at the university."

There was a ringing and a light going brighter and darker up the stairs.

"I think you'll want to get that." Ramonda's smile did not reach her eyes as she turned from Maleda to Zaddae. Before he turned to leave, he gave Maleda a close-lipped smile and looked up towards the light that danced across the window. She understood and so she smiled back. As the door clicked shut behind her, Maleda bounded up the stairs and found a dark bedroom save for the raised platform glowing in the corner. Maleda did not know how to operate the thing, but once she touched it, Selene appeared in the room, nearly transparent and three dimensional.

Maleda jumped, but she quickly recognized the little fireball. Selene put her finger to her lips and looked around as if there were someone else in the space, but Maleda crouched to get eye-level with the girl's projection.

"What are you doing?" Maleda hissed.

"Shh!" Selene hissed back. "I wanted to see you." The little girl beamed up at Maleda.

"How did you know I would be here?"

"Well, Baba and Mama thought that you would miss University, so they thought you might end up staying in the tower. I wanted to see if you were there! I remember when I saw you in the desert and—"

"Wait, how did you see me in the desert?" Guilt crossed the child's face, but she still had a slightly cheeky look in her eye.

"Well, I snuck into you and Clem's tree room and there wasn't anything there, but there was this one time when stuff started showing up on the inside of the tree, like drawings, so I knew it was you! Like someone invisible was drawing a million things at once." Maleda's heart ached at that.

"Well, I'm here now, so how about I teach you what my teachers show me. Does that sound good?" Maleda smiled as Selene straightened up and vigorously shook her head while giggling. "Good and why are you sneaking to talk to me? Are you supposed to be doing this?"

"No." Selene said while looking off to the side.

"Well, I'll tell you what, it will be our little secret." Maleda smiled and as Selene smiled so big it revealed a missing tooth, she realized how much she loved that little girl.

CHAPTER 36 - MALEDA

After Maleda exchanged her goodbyes with Selene, she found herself smiling at everything in the room under the coming glow of evening. Her smile only broke when she heard a tap at the window. Rooted in place, she wanted to be sure that she wasn't hearing things, but as she saw a brown hand repeat the tapping again Maleda rushed to open the window for Zaddae, who was slightly winded when he landed inside the tower.

"How did you get in without anyone seeing?"

"Same way I got into the castle without anyone seeing." He quipped. Maleda raised a brow as she saw him brace himself on his knees.

"Are you alright?" She asked while crouching to get a look at his face. There was a fresh, dark mark beside his eye.

"Who did that to you?" Maleda demanded.

"Well, it's none of your concern. Lovely professor Buru was not pleased to learn that I moved you into the University ahead of time, so…" He gestured towards his eye. "He told me so, but I don't want you to get upset. Whatever comes is necessary, if it means we get to find and extinguish the source of the assassination plot and help you learn how to use your powers."

"At least let me do something about it. Did he beat all of you?" Maleda pushed him into a lounge chair. "At least sit down. I'll find something." His chest was heaving as if he'd been in a brawl. She turned and left him to go downstairs to find a rag. Luckily, there was already water drawn in a pitcher and bowl. She just had to find a rag amidst the cupboards. Is this what they did for the slightest misdemeanor? However, Maleda felt that

Buru handled things more roughly than anyone else anyway. She found a rag and soaked it.

When she returned upstairs, Zaddae was panting slightly less, and he was reclined with a hand over the bruised side of his face. She sat down on the chair facing him and pulled his hand down.

"Here, let me," she said as she made slow careful work of tending to his eye, "So what do you think about what professor Ramonda said?"

"It's interesting and troubling. From the message in the tunnels, it's almost as if the princess knew she was going to be killed." Zaddae winced.

"Yes, I was thinking about that after I spoke to Selene."

"Crystalgram?" He asked.

"Yeah." Maleda grinned as she recounted that girl's carefree smile.

"So, she must have contacted you from the palace. Princess Clementina worked on modifying that kind of technology for her project, but I didn't really get to see what she had in mind."

Maleda saw the veil of sadness cross over his eyes.

"The mirrors. They were pointed towards her artwork," he mused.

"Yes," Maleda offered, "it was mostly hidden in shadow, but the golden parts glinted in the light."

"The princess wanted you to finish her project for her, or at least use it to be here at the university."Zaddae pulled her hand from his face. "But I did want to tell you about something else. It looks safe here, but there's something that they're not telling us, not telling me, and I think it is beyond who killed the princess. Professor Ramonda never traveled with that many guards."

"Does that mean they are here, whoever it is?" Maleda was near to panic.

"I don't know, hopefully not, but we can't be too careful. I'm still training, so that means that I will visit you as often as possible so we can work through this."

"Could I convince you to stay with me now?" Maleda asked. Zaddae pulled her in for an embrace and she didn't realize that she was trembling until he held her close.

"If morning comes and they find me in here, I'm not sure I'll be allowed to be near you at all. I'll stay close by and when tomorrow comes I will be at that door, not to long after the sun rises. No one's going to hurt you."

Maleda nodded against his shoulder, and he released her enough, so that they could look into each other's faces. She convinced him to stay until she fell asleep, and he obliged her. Once she was asleep, the dream of the Mariner Prince continued.

CHAPTER 37 - THE MARINER PRINCE

His vision moved from the gray, stormy sky to the obsidian-like waters as he was thrown about. With his body constantly beaten and battered it was a miracle that he stayed conscious. Eventually, the water receded, and he found that his hands felt the grit of sand. He was too weak to open his eyes and death seemed like it was ready to cradle him. He felt his body being flipped to face the sky and didn't fight his convulsing as he coughed up the seawater.

The king laid on his side as the water vacated his lungs and he opened his eyes to see a sky blackened by storm. Maybe his men had survived. He rolled over to look into their faces because surely, they had found him, but he looked into the face of masked figures with spears. The kind of strength powered by fear rushed into his body and his eyes couldn't take in the scene fast enough. He backed away from his captors and clumsily tried to get to his feet. They slowly started to pursue him, as if they knew he was battered prey that would fall to them no matter the effort. The king turned his back on them and the sea, making his way to run into the forest. He pushed aside branches and dodged trees as he tried to get away. He had nothing on him, not his sword, no weapon at all! When he turned his back to see if he was still being followed, his foot met air instead of ground. He tumbled down what felt like a hillside and a few seconds felt like an eternity when he finally landed at the bottom. With quaking muscles, he struggled to rise only to fail as he fell back to the ground. He fought to turn to his side and look up to the spot where he fell. The king managed to back himself up against a rock shadowed by fronds. He struggled to retain consciousness, vision going from blackness to the figures watching him from the point that he fell. Blackness and one was directly in his face. He barely opened his eyes when he heard voices whispering above him. One of them took off their masks, but he couldn't focus on their face. A calmness washed over him probably fed by exhaustion. Black silhouettes hovered above him, and he faded into darkness.

CHAPTER 38 - MALEDA

Maleda woke when her room was cast in shadows and moonlight and felt a compulsion drawing her towards the collections room. At the top of the stairs, she saw that it had been closed, just like she left it after speaking to Selene when she went snooping around the apartment. She heard her footsteps as she proceeded down the stairs and into the collections room, but it was as if she was floating. A voice called her, but even though she knew it was a voice, she could not hear it. Rather, she felt it stir within her. Maleda proceeded past the mirrors that did not show her reflection, Princess Clementina's artwork, and the sculpture of the princess until she reached the entrance into the floor from which she and Zaddae came earlier that day. She lifted it without strain and went down the steps. The ancient terratech lights were somehow lit and they indicated a path for her to follow, but time blurred and she found herself already there. There, meaning a chamber she had never seen before, where the roof was made of glass, and she could see the stars. A huge, twisting tree was there too. Maleda was in someone's burial room.

Well, aren't you bright child?

Maleda staggered as she felt the voice dance through her chest, like a woodwind. A gentle light bloomed on the floor and Maleda was already backing into the wall, fighting the burning in her eyes. From that light, came a human figure, a woman wrinkled with time and onyx eyes glowing.

She seemed to be wrapped in colorful robes floating about her, with the moonlight dancing in her silver, kinky, hair and over her dark brown skin.

Hello, my child.

Maleda tried to speak, but it was like moving boulders to try and force her mouth to move.

I am Ayam Uolenga. I came before Princess Clementina and I need your help. The same evil that took her away still lurks this empire. It has even affected the animals, as if demons were cast into them.

Maleda's breath caught at the confirmation. The attackers were still out there.

We don't have much time. You will have to attend a class soon where you will be in the shade of the woods. When you see the shadow and hear the call, don't be afraid. She knows her.

How could this be happening? Her head looked towards the starry sky as she heard some sort of distant cry.

Pay attention to your professors and your dreams, every single one. Ramonda will know what you are looking for, but Buru can work the dark.

The sound came louder.

You must go now. Noslen cannot hold them. Tell no one of this.

Maleda felt time blur and she saw the bed, raced towards it.

She woke with a startled gasp and reached upwards as if she were falling. The room was still cast in shadow and moonlight. She found herself clutching her left hand closed and she opened it to reveal Cham. Zaddae must have disappeared into the night. Then, she remembered that unholy outcry. It was just a dream, just like everything before. She tried to reassure herself as she stared down at the ring, but the landscape on the inside of it had changed to show a room with a tree, a roof clearly built to see the sky, and something shrouded in light, but actively sparkling. She moved to lean out of her room and saw that the door to collections was closed, but she thought better than to go and investigate the noise. Her heart rattled in her chest, but she merely shut the door to the bedroom and silently raced until she was back in the bed. She kept repeating Zaddae's words that nothing was going to hurt her until she gave into exhaustion.

CHAPTER 39 - THE PRISONER

The prisoner barely remembered that he had been enslaved before, but to a spell. A spell that twisted time. He remembered a girl, her name. She'd perished and his heart ached for the pain that she must have gone through.

Some days, the prisoner felt sad and didn't know why. It was like he lost something incredibly precious, but he forgot what it was. Perhaps, he missed someone, but it was like it was someone he'd never met.

CHAPTER 40 - MALEDA

Maleda was a combination of slightly bleary-eyed and on edge, when Zaddae knocked on her door early the next day.

"What happened to you?" Zaddae asked quirking a brow.

"Oh, I just had a bad dream."

"Do you want to talk about it?"

"Well." Maleda paced the room and Zaddae stood by the door watching her. "I dreamt about the Mariner Prince again. He was drowning in the beginning, but then he was on land with these people in masks. He was afraid of them, like he'd never seen them before. He was running away from them, but he fell and then he passed out right as they were coming for them. I think I had another dream too, but I don't remember it. When I woke up, I just saw that I was holding on to Cham. I don't remember exactly, but I feel like something strange is going on in this tower." Zaddae was silent for a moment as Maleda continued to pace.

"You have gone through a whole lot recently. Maybe you need to slow down and really take a breath of fresh air, like walk through the city with me?"

Maleda stopped pacing and looked at Zaddae. Concern swam in his eyes, despite his smile.

"It could be an opportunity for us to get a better sense of our surroundings and you would finally get to see the city. I wouldn't let anything happen to you."

"Okay," Maleda agreed.

Mirriam

The emperor and empress asked for Mirriam to scout in the city, as the medium had informed them that the city would need watching today and that she would need to look for something.

"What is that even supposed to mean? What am I looking for?" Mirriam muttered to herself.

Mirriam was in a generally disagreeable mood as she sat on one of the rooftops in a merchant square. Not only had Maleda and Zuvan snuck off, but they had snuck off without her knowledge nor did they ask for her input about said sneaking off! It was definitely a proper moment to brood, mutter, and maybe even drink, at least in her eyes, but she only did the first two. She *could* only do the first two because she had a black mask obscuring her nose and mouth. However, wearing the black, snug, long-sleeve shirt in the beaming sun made her have to beat the idea of water out of her head. She had to focus. This was Maleda. She could only hope that nothing would potentially endanger Maleda, but in order to ensure that was the case Mirriam had posted herself in a hidden spot where she could see the tower that Maleda was staying in. That was until she spotted Maleda and Zaddae leave, and she decided to traverse rooftops to follow them. There was nothing particularly out of the ordinary as they dipped in and out of shops and dallied in front of aggressive salesmen. Yet, she couldn't be too sure.

Maleda

The city was nothing short of extraordinary. There was everything to see and everything to do in the Empire of Two Shores. It was a city of cities, divided by boroughs, decorated with a multitude of fountains and lakes, brightly colored tiles on the faces of carved buildings, skyscrapers, theaters, shops, and market squares. The sounds of music and varying languages filled the streets, along with a rainbow of faces. The markets that they saw hosted goods from merchants of the empire, as well as wares from far away continents. When they got to the sea that separated the shores, Maleda looked her fill from one of the many bridges strung between the southern and northern side. Both coastlines were lined with houses and mansions whose colors gleamed in the light of the sun. Docks—some covered by stone carved domes supported by pillars—hosted impressive looking ships both for air and sea, as well as smaller vessels too. Universities and libraries were peppered throughout the empire and she found that it didn't matter if a student was affluent or poor as education was available to everyone. Maleda learned that there were societies and congresses formed amongst scholars, scientists, and artists promoting research and knowledge. When Zaddae and Maleda weren't walking the paved streets, they took a train to get around the different boroughs of the empire. The train system ran above ground and below ground, connecting the parts of the city that were above ground along with the parts of the city below ground.

At one point, Maleda's heart started to race, but not in the way she would like. Her heart was moving too fast, and her lungs were too small. It was easy to suggest going back to the tower, to hide. No. She clenched a fist at her side. Her anxiety wasn't going to ruin this. She was determined. She just needed to breath for a second, to shake the feeling of restraints off her. Maleda swallowed as she tried to manifest the courage, so she turned to Zaddae to ask—. Zaddae was looking down at her with a small smile and silently offered his arm, so Maleda took it. He had read her mind. She exhaled feeling a bit more steadied. It seemed like he was a little more at ease too, but perhaps she was just imagining things. When Maleda looked back at the street ahead, she saw that they had come upon a theater, not one of the open-air ones, but a tall building decorated with terratech lights flashing in a pattern. There were letters between the lights, the title of a play, perhaps a musical. A light bloomed in her chest, and she gasped a little. Zaddae let out a chuckle.

"Oh, can we go see what it is?" Maleda's smile broke across her face as she looked up at Zaddae. He just half-smiled back at her, with a raised brow.

"Of course." He said simply.

When they walked closer, Maleda saw that someone stood outside the theater doors with a radiant smile and expressive arms, trying to usher people inside.

"Excuse me?" Maleda asked and the person turned that grin on her. "What is this?"

"Oh, it's a free show for the day dedicated to the long-lost princess." Their voice danced with enthusiasm.

"Really?" Maleda's brain swam with possibilities, and she looked back at Zaddae, his expression unreadable. Perhaps he was reading the opportunity, as well.

"Oh yes! There'll be an orchestra and dancers. You should definitely go in an see it."

"Oh well…" Maleda looked between the person selling them on the show and Zaddae, who still looked thoughtful. "I think we will. Thank you!"

Maleda gave a parting smile and Zaddae said his thanks as well. Once they proceeded inside, no one was waiting in the lush lobby, but once they walked through the next set of doors, there were people scattered in different seats. It seemed like Zaddae had shaken himself out of his trance.

"So, where would you like to sit?"

Maleda looked around the darkened theater to investigate.

"How about here?"

Zuvan agreed. She pointed out a couple seats in the middle aisle, but at the end of the row. Great for seeing the performance from the center and perfect in case they needed to make a quick escape without a fuss. The curtain was still drawn, but the orchestra was below the front of the stage, practicing and Maleda could hear the other patrons whispering among themselves. The cacophony of sounds was harmonious and familiar, somehow.

"So, were you thinking what I was thinking?" Maleda whispered to Zaddae.

Zaddae looked at her and seemed to consider. "Well, what were you thinking?"

"That this could be significant, a sign or a clue, or something. Honestly, it sounded exciting out in the street, but now I'm a little nervous."

Zaddae huffed a small laugh. "It's not like you'll be the one performing."

"Yes, but still. I don't know what we're going to see." It was Maleda's turn to consider as she looked at Zaddae's face, something illegible written there. "What were you thinking when they were telling us about the show?"

"Well, I was honestly caught off guard. I mean, there's nothing with a dedicating a show to her. It's just—" He faltered, searching the stage in front of them for words. "To have these official monuments and statues for her, just makes it that much more…irreversible. Permanent. It's one thing to try and get past it, deal with it. But then there are constant reminders making it fresh again."

Maleda's chest caved in. She did not think. Of course, this would be too much. He didn't speak because he really didn't want to be in this theater.

"Oh, we can go." Maleda started to rise, but Zaddae put a hand on her arm.

"No, no." Zaddae said quickly. "If there's one thing I've learned, you can't run from pain, at least not forever. It's unsustainable and besides all that running will make you hurt eventually anyway. I mean, it's not like I want to rehash it every day, but I'd like to get to a point where more often than not, her memory makes me smile and that'll only happen through exposure, I guess."

Worry still gnawed at Maleda. "Well, I understand that and agree, but I don't want you to force yourself."

"Maleda." Zaddae had slightly squeezed her arm then. "I want to be here with you. I want to see it. I'm just a little nervous, like you are."

As Maleda's vision adjusted to the dark, she could see the sincerity in Zaddae's eyes, his smile.

"Okay." Maleda whispered back with her own small smile. Zaddae withdrew his hand and they both looked ahead, just in time for silence to envelop the theater. A conductor had walked in through a side door and stood before the orchestra in a golden jacket, her presence beckoning them to be at attention. Something about the sight made Maleda tilt her head in recognition, but she'd never seen the woman before. She stroked her thumb over Cham, still a ring on her finger and decided to let it go. The conductor turned to face the audience.

"Everyone, the Arkestra."

The conductor turned back to the *Arkestra,* raised her hands, and the players raised their instruments. The music was so delicate at first, as if they were edging towards something. A hidden chorus sang, voices lilting through the air and she felt light against her skin. Maleda wasn't sure if she had imagined the lights that danced in the air, but when she looked to Zaddae and saw the glow dancing in his eyes, she knew she wasn't dreaming. The magic of the Arkestra allowed them to conjure up lights that sparkled around them. The lights flew towards the stage and created multicolored pillars of light above the Arkestra. They vaguely resembled figures and they seemed to gesture down to the curtain opening.

It all rushed by so fast, but it was elegant and thrilling all at once. No words were spoken, but there was a flurry of dancers and spinning skirts that told a generational story of adventure, love, and loss. It ended with a set of two girls and two boys. The girls ran down center stage and peeled off to either side, to reveal one girl posed on a platform and rolled downstage. She remained perfectly still as the two boys joined her downstage on either side facing her at the center. Applause erupted and Maleda jumped, still caught up in the trance of what she'd witnessed. Maleda applauded with the rest of the crowd and rose with Zaddae to exit the theater.

"That was amazing!" Maleda declared. She looked to Zaddae and there was a bit of a faraway look in his eye.

"Yeah, it was. She would have loved it." He looked to Maleda and smiled.

Once they strolled outside, they heard music coming from one of the streets behind the theater. Drums and strings beckoned Maleda to follow. When Maleda and Zaddae rounded the corner, she saw the performers and some of the Arkestra members outside dancing and making music in the streets. People from all around were joining and the crowd was just getting bigger, extending down the block. Some were hand in hand and others were spinning, jumping, or playfully grinding. Some newcomers even brought their own instruments. It was like a party. In all the excitement, Maleda and Zaddae got swept into the crowd. Her heart skipped a beat at the sudden push, but Zaddae held onto her hand and pressed her into his side, so as not to lose her in the crowd. He bowed his head to speak into her ear over all the joyful noise.

"Do you want to leave?"

He was so careful and considerate of her anxiety. But this time, she felt safe in spite of the heat radiating through her at the sight of the crowd. Life just exploded around her and she was not going to deny herself. She would partake.

She just smiled and held onto his arm. "I'd like to stay. What about you?"

"As you wish."

So, they stayed, and they danced with the crowd.

* * *

When Maleda and Zaddae ended their zealous stroll at one of the empire's beaches, Maleda had a sketchbook with an array of new depictions of the empire, especially sculptures peppered around the city of cities that depicted these magnificent figures of these beings called Orisha. It seemed that people had all different kinds of beliefs in the empire, but the Orisha seemed sacred whether the sculptures were just a mark of history or not.

They had danced, until their chests were heaving. When a particular song started, enclaves of people started to dance in lines, all their moves matching, until it seemed the whole block followed suit. Sidestepping, kicking, throwing their hands up, and turning. It took her a minute to get adjusted, but Zaddae held her hand, so she didn't trip over herself. Maleda swore she could still hear the music in the distance.

With a contented smile across her wind-kissed face, she decided she could die for a place like this. It was an alarming thought, but everything from the sight of the shoreline to the zealous shopkeepers made her fall deeply in love with this place. It was her home, and she wouldn't let anyone disrupt the harmony of a place like this, though those were tough words for the girl that had never been in a fight or couldn't get past why Buru was so discontented by her presence. She decided not to think on it any longer.

"I love this place and I know I haven't even seen half of it," Maleda declared.

"I can tell," Zaddae chuckled, "and it seems like you're feeling a little better than this morning?"

"I'd say so!" Cham chirped making both Zaddae and Maleda jump. Maleda pulled Cham from her bag and held her in the palm of her hand.

"You know, you have poor timing," Zaddae gritted out at Cham.

"I'm sorry about that, but I think that I'm getting fixed. Still, it feels so slow."

"What do you mean you're 'getting fixed'? I haven't done anything with you." Maleda said.

"You haven't," Cham chimed, "but *she* is."

Maleda's eyes widened, "Who? You mean the matriarch?"

"Still not her, but I can't tell exactly who it is. I've felt particularly more *myself* since we've gotten back to the empire."

"And what's that supposed to mean?"

"As your guide, I knew I was supposed to be with you, but lots of information escaped, but I can feel it coming back in sparse pockets, but I don't think it's anything helpful right now."

"Information such as?" Zaddae inquired with raised brows.

"Well, the fact that Maleda should be at the university." Zaddae huffed and looked back at the ocean as Cham rushed to continue, "I know that decision is already spoken for, but at least I have a definite indication that she should stick around."

If Maleda were to be honest, she was thankful that she had another voice confirming that she was going in the right direction.

"Well, thank you anyway." Maleda smiled. "Has anything else come back to you?

"Yes, some source tells me that you should pay close attention to your dreams."

As soon as Maleda heard the word 'dreams' the woman with the hair colored like moonlight came back to her along with a haunting echo. It shocked her so much that all she could do was nod and ask Zaddae to walk her back to her tower quarters at university.

CHAPTER 41 - THE PRISONER

The prisoner sang to himself about the brown-eyed girl he saw outside the window. Hummed as he remembered how she danced. The open smile on her face. What it would be like to walk with her, be with her. But he did not know her name.

He was so tired and it was still so dark. He barely gleaned any light in his confinement. And even then, the little glimpses of light he received, felt like a tantalizing punishment as if the captor knew how desperate and worn he was.

CHAPTER 42 - MIRRIAM

Maleda and Zaddae ended up at one of the empire's beaches sitting in the sand, while Mirriam spied on them from a rooftop. The two rose and headed in the direction of the tower. Well, that was that. Mirriam was ready to distantly escort them back and give a peaceful report to her majesties, but that was halted by a figure on an opposite rooftop that was watching Maleda and Zaddae as well. Mirriam cursed under her breath and rolled the shoulder on her trick arm. It didn't seem like he'd seen her as he was so intent on Maleda and Zaddae. Yet, when she shifted to rise, the figure turned their head towards Mirriam. She jumped to his rooftop to close the distance between them. Mirriam could see that the figure was a man a little taller than her and he too wore a mask that showed from the bridge of his nose up, along with dark-colored covert wear. The skin she could see was white, like porcelain and his dark hair was tied back. He definitely needed his garb more than she did.

"What are you doing here?" Mirriam loudly whispered. "Reveal yourself!" Yet, he just stared and tilted his head to the side, sizing her up, but ultimately decided to turn his head back in the direction of Maleda and rose as if to follow them. Mirriam rushed him and threw a punch, which he blocked. Actually, punch after punch, he continued to block, sidestepping her as if it were all a dance. While Mirriam grunted and gritted her teeth, her opponent barely let out any sounds of effort. Was he toying with her while something else happened to Maleda? Mirriam crouched and swiped the masked stranger's feet from under him, while she cheated a glance at Maleda as she walked with Zaddae. Positively unhurried and unaware of the fight happening on the roof. Yet, the stranger had never lost his footing and Mirriam quickly found herself on her backside. Her opponent looked down at her and he swayed like a snake and his arms hung limp. Mirriam bounded to her feet and grounded herself, fists raised. No weapons yet. The mission wouldn't exactly be covert if blood was spilled…or if she added a tally to her body count. They just stood feet away from each other, one staring the other down.

"You shouldn't have come." Mirriam narrowed her eyes at the stranger's voice. It was *layers* of voices, as if each one fought for dominance.

It was Mirriam's turn to tilt her head. "What do you mean? Who are you?"

"You should have stayed in the desert."

"I suspect friends of yours found us in the desert, stranger." Mirriam quipped.

The man just continued to stare, but he was more thoughtful and still, as if he considered her words. Mirriam glanced to where Maleda and Zaddae had walked, but they were out of her sight. Good. Hopefully, they had made good enough headway.

"My master grows impatient, and he calls me away. I will not be seeing you again, but the animals will."

Mirriam barely got out one word before the stranger sprinted across the rooftop and bounded away from her. With something short of a gasp, Mirriam started after him, desperation fueling each of her running steps and her leap onto the next rooftop. It was only a few moments later into her pursuit when she realized he was going in a completely different direction than Maleda, but by the time relief kicked in, the stranger had dropped. She rained in her gasp when she approached the edge of the roof where the man had fallen, but he was nowhere to be seen. Not on the streets below and not clinging to one of the walls. Mirriam cursed and her nostrils flared as she pulled out her mobile crystalgram device. She had to give a report to the empress, right away.

CHAPTER 43 - MALEDA

Once they returned to the tower, Maleda contemplated all the different brown faces that she saw and how she'd like to sketch them, paint them even. As she daydreamed, she searched the apartment more and she discovered layers of texts and notes that seemed to refer to Princess Clementina's artwork. She hauled the canvas into the princesses' apartment—dismissing Zaddae's help to his amusement—and stared at it while Zaddae worked on sharpening a blade. Maleda could only imagine where he kept it hidden.

The next day she found herself amongst other students milling about between classes. She heeded professor Ramonda's words and decided to explore other classes beyond her independent study. There were so many open classes and lectures that she could attend, as long as she was on time. The professors even encouraged her to ask questions. Amidst all the havoc around her, she needed to know what she left behind and she needed to know what world Clementina came from, so Maleda started with a history class, where she learned about the power of terratech and how terra stones had been used throughout history to help care for and protect the planet. Olodumare—again that name—designated this responsibility to people when the world Dziko was first created. There were other theories and studies that held their truth to them about how the world got its start, but they all seemed to leave out Olodumare as the author. She also learned that there were some people that had the ability to live 1,000 years as heightened beings, not purely immortal, but the closest to it. They had incredible relationships with the terra stones and were able to manipulate the elements if their essence naturally existed in one's body and spirit upon birth. Yet, pure mortals who were bound to 100 years instead of 1,000, had the ability to wield terratech, but with slightly handicapped abilities. They were also used for healing and the people in the department of sciences wanted to see how far they could extend those abilities. Before the professor could get into any more of the lesson, class was dismissed. Maleda could have stayed to ask questions, but Zaddae was waiting outside the classroom to escort her to her next class, Ramonda's class.

* * *

Professor Ramonda's class actually started at various times, but this time it was in the evening. As the professor went on about the unusual behaviors of animals outside the empire, Maleda was contemplating Princess Clementina's project. Clementina was trying to incorporate movement with projected terratech imagery. Maleda needed to study her notes further in order to understand what allowed for the projection of specific imagery. A shadow loomed over her mind, though, and she realized that Ramonda stood before her as she was lecturing, so Maleda slipped her notes into the pack strapped at her hip. The classroom was the forest, not too far from the edge of the wall.

"The animals appear to be behaving strangely and we think that it may have to do with some terra stone abnormalities. There are even reports that some have seen terratech attached to some animals. Some even swear that there is a strange glint in some of their eyes."

"Professor, how could the animals have terra stones as a part of them? They can't grow on animals, can they?"

"Olodumare-willing, they could, but no one has gotten close enough to an animal to be able to note that. The animals range from elusive to hostile and we don't want to irritate the populations. As long as we maintain a proper distance, we should be safe. Today, I want you to see these animals, as close as we can, so that you can understand what lies beyond the walls of the empire."

Rather than stroll into the woods, the class went onto an airship, but unlike the one that Maleda used to flee the desert. It was a more modest vessel constructed with and powered by terratech. The ship had an underbelly complete with a lab, seating, and windows. The observation deck was peppered with students watching the empire shrink behind them and other students gaping at the forest below them. Maleda's fingers ached from gripping the railing and she shoved down the memory of running for her life. She reminded herself that things were different now. She wished Buru did not call Zaddae to work and because nighttime was approaching with this class, she would not be able to see him until the next day as the punishment for being caught out of place at night would be severe.

"Some say that we need to get rid of the troublesome animals." Ramonda had silently approached her side and stared out at the forest. "What do you say to that my student?"

"Well, I'm sorry professor," Maleda began, "but I haven't seen an animal yet."

"Do you think that it would be any better if they could be seen?"

"Well, if we saw them all the time, we would know that they had nothing to hide and nothing to fear. It would be easy to get rid of something that is always a constant threat that never disappears. The fact that they are actively avoiding us makes me wonder if they are hiding for a reason that we cannot see."

"Hmm." Ramonda mused. "There was a time when humans and animals were fierce companions. Well, I hope that you are not left with that choice."

"What choice?"

"To lose your life in getting lost over what once was. To remember what it was like and hesitate."

As the ship settled to land in a clearing, Maleda could still see the empire before they cleared the treetops. Strange, even in the tinted glow of the sun getting ready to set, Maleda did not even hear a bug chirp. Was professor Ramonda sure it was safe? They all departed the ship and strolled into the forest, but it seemed like there were faint lights ahead to guide them.

"Bioluminescence was common among the life here, but it's power has dimmed and again, we cannot trace the exact cause, but suspect that there is a disruption in the terra stones."

"Excuse me, professor?" Maleda wanted a clarification. "Did you mean just plant life?"

"No, my student. From the animals to the plants."

"How could that be?"

"Olodumare flows all around us. The light is what shows that connection and the piece of Olodumare within. The light glows stronger in some than others. It can be because they are more connected or because they are powerful. The problem is understanding why that light has become... malicious."

Could someone try to hurt her with the powers she had inside? Despite the beads of sweat forming on her head, she shivered. They stopped at a modest river where they noted a small group of antelope drinking from the stream. They seemed to be quiet, undisturbed. The antelope milled about themselves either unaware or not caring about the presence of the class gawking at them. Maleda twirled Cham in ring form on her finger as she studied the elegant creatures. She wanted to draw them, so she pulled out her stick and kept dipping it in ink as she scratched line after line onto a page in her sketchbook. Once she had gotten the gesture of them down, she started to distinguish them from each other. Maleda only stopped when she heard a small cry.

"Dik dik dik." A small quiet cry, but she could not see the source.

"Do you all hear that?" Maleda whispered. It felt like she was talking more to herself than the other students. "Professor, what is that sound?"

"Probably one of the baby antelopes. We may have startled them and it's probably best for us to move on to another area." Ramonda smiled and started to lead the class away, but Maleda lingered until she was at the back of the group, still confused. The source of the sound did not seem like it was across the river. Maleda darted to get back to the river's edge and she saw it, not that much farther down. A baby antelope curled in on itself as it made weak cries looking across the river. Perhaps they accidentally left it behind or they expected the infant to follow. Professor Ramonda was not too far away, but she was gesturing towards a tree and discussed something to do with bioluminescence. As Maleda creeped toward the baby antelope, she did not know what she would do to get it across the river, especially without angering the parents. She noticed the antelope following her from across the river. The water went down as Maleda kept walking and she eventually led the group of antelope so that they were right across from the whimpering babe. It looked so delicate, so easily broken, and vulnerable. Maleda kept a yard's distance as they approached, barely disturbing the water as they stalked across the river towards her and the baby. The males had their heads high with horns near shining. They could easily gore her for thinking that she was going to endanger the infant, but a doe just looked her in the eye, tilted its head, and nudged the baby antelope until it stood on quaking legs. They continued by the riverside and Maleda watched them stroll through the sunlight filtered forest. She turned around to find professor Ramonda staring at her with calm eyes that seemed to contain a menace. The students were cowering behind her.

"Professor, I know we were supposed to stay with the group, but I couldn't just let the baby be separated."

Professor Ramonda did not respond, but she moved her hands behind her back, probably ready to lecture. Maleda wasn't sure if she was ready to discover the full force of her temper or how severe she would be with punishment.

"Professor, I'm—" Ramonda lifted a hand and her eyes had a new glare to them. As Ramonda stalked closer, she saw that it was a knife. Maleda's heart ratcheted.

Maleda started, "What are you—"

"Don't move." Maleda realized that Ramonda was not looking at her. She could barely hear its breath. Would it be better to not know what it was? The notion lingered as Maleda slowly turned around to see a beast lurking in the shadows close to the ground. She had a terrible inkling that even though it already looked huge, that it was not standing at its full height. Red eyes glowed and glared at her through the dark. The creature looked like it was hesitating, turning its head at them, at her, and like that something tugged on Maleda's mind, but she could not identify the thought, the feeling, the name. Maleda had no time to ponder the new gray cloud in her mind when the creature bellowed with a primal screech and barreled after her.

* * *

Maleda bolted for Ramonda, but the creature was already there. Had already bounded over but landed with a fierce elegance between them. Maleda skidded to a stop and ran the other direction. She could hear Ramonda calling her name almost as fiercely as the creature, but the calling faded and Maleda continued to run. It was an amalgamation of a beak, four legs, talons, and wings. She careened through branches, trying to steer the thing away from a clear line of sight, but it was on her tail. Maybe she could lose the animal under the cover of darkness. Another fierce roar pierced Maleda's heart and she could see some dark blur running alongside her. Maleda tried her best to let go of the aches in her body and the labor in her breath, so that she could become a machine bent on speed. The roar of the second beast disturbed Maleda. Somehow, it sounded wrong, sending a shudder down her spine. She slid under a fallen tree and looked back to see the creature leap over it with impossible ease. The thing on her side was still on the opposite side of the river concealed by darkness. The beast behind her was starting to whimper, but it pursued her relentlessly. It only broke its huffing and groans to roar at the thing across the river, as if it was fighting for its kill.

There came a voice, rather felt than heard.

It beckoned her to follow it. She did not know how to interpret its direction, but somehow, she felt like she was approaching something. As she rounded a tree, there was a bright light and a man with cascading robes strapped with fierce weapons hovering in the air. He already had a sword extended and without moving his lips Maleda knew it was him who said *run child, quick!* The creature behind her peeled off, but the one on the opposite side of the river sped through the trees covering it and bounded across with the help of wings like a bat. The membrane glistened even as the sky was tinged with the colors of evening. It shot for Maleda, but the man got there first. In moments the creature was pinned by a sword through one of its wings. It shrieked in agony, but only trembled so as not to tear the wing any further. The man made the creature unfurl itself from the cocoon of the undamaged wing and Maleda saw the stuff of terror. One large eye, a body like a human but skin of pale gray, knife-like teeth, taloned fingers, and taloned feet. The man bowed his head, only a foot away from the creature's face.

Why have you come here, Bowa? It seemed like the creature mimicked the man in responding without moving his mouth and hissed with spit driveling from between its gray teeth. Yet, it's voice was distorted and Maleda could not here what it said. It seemed that the creature was going to open its mouth to speak, but the man swiftly ended the creature by putting a staff full of light in the creature's face, making it disappear. The man put away the sword and leaned on the walking stick even though he seemed to be hovering in the air. He still did not move his mouth, but Maleda felt him speak. He gestured towards his chest.

"Noslen?" Maleda said aloud. A crunch came from the woods and Maleda thought the creature had brought a gang to avenge it, but it was a woman slightly glowing in the night.

"Ayam?" Maleda had felt her voice too. How did she know their names and why did she look so familiar? *Because my child, I spoke to you in between being asleep and awake.* The woman had spoken.

"Who are you and what was that thing?" Maleda managed to keep her voice level. She flicked her head about, flinching at the silence in the woods. The man spoke. *I am afraid that the first is forbidden and the second is, as well. We cannot answer you child. We need phrasing that can be bent.*

"I saw you back at the tower at the University, yes?" She felt their answer. "You were in a dream of mine. You told me you came before Princess Clementina." She gestured towards Ayam. "And she said you were holding someone off. Was it that?"

My child, Noslen began, *there were creatures that I cannot speak of, but I was holding off one of those.* A shudder ran through Maleda.

"What keeps you from telling me?" It was almost like a physical pain wracked him when he spoke.

A force from long ago that still seeks to poach his prize. He thought that he found all he wanted long ago, but he did not count on you.

Was it the person who killed Clementina? It must have been. He knew where she was. Maleda's heart began to thump in her chest.

Calm yourself child, Ayam put out a reassuring hand, *we do not think he knows where you are exactly, but he sends out allies and servants to change that.*

"Why does the creature fear the light?"

It is its end, Ayam said. Then, they spoke simultaneously, holding hands as if it strengthened them.

My child, we grow weak being far from the tower, but we will escort you back. The darkness is not safe for anyone, especially you. They barely hovered across the ground towards the University, towards the wall that guarded the empire. Yet, Maleda had more questions. "What about that other winged creature?" Something shifted when she mentioned the animal, as if it made Noslen and Ayam sad, but they did not want to show it.

Ayam answered. *Well, the one Noslen took care of operates on its own will. Hopefully, the other creature can too. Having to fight for your own will is hardest at night.* When Maleda looked up from the crunching leaves, she saw the wall approaching.

They spoke simultaneously again. *Remember what we said exactly and look for answers. Tell no one what you have seen.* They gestured towards a barely there emblem in the wall. Maleda ran her fingers over the mark and a passage opened in the wall. When Maleda turned to face them again, Noslen and Ayam had vanished and Maleda was left alone to traverse the passage. She still had Cham in her possession and converted her from the ring form into the holographic map, so she could see where she was going. She followed something she could not name, but somehow found herself back up a familiar set of stairs. This time the box had already been moved, so she easily pushed aside the door and bounded up the stairs. After she had laid the door back in place, Maleda strolled through Collections and back into her room across the passageway. She shut the door and turned to see Ramonda waiting for her. Her shoulders had even slumped at her arrival and she took Maleda's hands. Once Ramonda had spun her around to make sure Maleda was not hurt, it began.

"Thank Olodumare you weren't killed." She turned to one of the guards behind her. "Call off the search. We've got her." The guard merely nodded and proceeded out of the room and Ramonda looked back at her. "We looked for you but could not find you. I feared that the beast had—" Ramonda paused, glowering at the ground. "Never mind. Maleda, even though this is all new to you, you must trust when we say that there is danger. It did not infect the minds of those antelope, but it certainly got to that thing chasing you."

Maleda was ready to explain how she got away, but as she opened her mouth, Ramonda put out a hand.

"I don't want you stepping foot out in that forest. As a matter of fact, classes will no longer be permitted to venture beyond the walls of the empire. The hostility of the animals has grown exponentially. I think you should learn a thing or two about them. Although I can't keep you from venturing to other classes or elsewhere, I would advise you to stay in the tower and work on the project."

Overwhelm and shame washed over Maleda as she said, "I'm sorry that I worried you professor. I was just trying to help that little antelope be reunited with their family. I didn't expect *that* to come chasing me." It seemed a little unfair to have this lecture as Ramonda was the one who decided to have class outside the walls.

Ramonda let go of Maleda's hand, spun around, and walked toward the door, but before she exited, she turned back. "I am glad you're alright, Maleda." Ramonda's voice took on a firm, yet softer tone, "We already lost the Princess. I couldn't bear to lose you too. Not again." Maleda pressed her lips into something shy of a smile. When the door clicked behind Ramonda, Maleda tilted her head down and laced her fingers behind her neck. A pit had developed in her. It was filling with anxiety over disappointing Ramonda, fear of the second creature, and curiosity of the first. Maleda grabbed at the hurting place in her chest, and she reluctantly went to study the project that sat in the middle of the apartment, trying to make sense of the amalgamation of images strung together. It was like she recognized the images on the canvas, but from another life. The imagery of forest and shade is what particularly bothered her, and it stayed on her mind until she crawled into bed, still staring at the painting through the door. Maleda would have fallen asleep, but she felt a voice.

CHAPTER 44 - MALEDA

She felt it pulling her from the sheets. Somehow, she knew she would not be able to rest unless she followed it, so she picked up her belt of tools, including her sketchbook, ink, quill, and two daggers, as she followed the feeling into the Collections room. Earlier she had felt the voice of Ayam and Noslen. Maybe they wished to speak with her again. The voice brought her all the way to the secret hatch, and she lifted it silently and pulled it behind her. The dirt thickened under her feet as she silently padded down the stairs. There was no logic, no reason that told her where to go. It was as if she had followed this path in a dream. After a long corridor, she found herself climbing a near hidden set of stairs. Maleda feared that something would leap out of the darkness, like the creatures from before. She was tempted to run back. Her fear rattled her chest and just when it seemed like she could not take it anymore, the stairs lit with a light colored like the evening. Dominated by purple and streaked with patterns of pink, yellow, and orange. Thank whoever had mercy on her. With the walls cast in the ethereal glow, she proceeded up the stairs with more confidence until she was stopped by a door, ornately carved. Maleda pushed the door inwards and saw the familiar sight of a tree, almost like her own in the desert, like in the palace. This is where she first met Ayam and as if she were summoned, Ayam was sitting on a great root, smiling at Maleda. Noslen leaned onto the root next to her, smiling also. Even though their bodies seemed aged, they also seemed infinite, like they could draw on strength beyond what Maleda's mortal eyes could see.

Both were in an amalgamation of brightly colored armor, accented with swaths of fabric, but where Ayam's coily hair was silver and long, Noslen had a silver afro that haloed his face.

"Hello, my child," Ayam said and this time her mouth moved. Her voice was warm and mellow, like honey pouring, but it also sounded like time passing on an easy afternoon. The moonlight filtered a blue light through her silver hair, as if it were a crown.

Maleda just stood staring at them. She was simultaneously afraid to approach, but she also never felt safer.

"Well, come now." Noslen put a hand on his hip and a smile bloomed on his face. "I know you're shocked, but you should not be rude to your elders." He spoke rhythmically with aspiring between his words. In spite of herself, Maleda let out a laugh and she approached them. The light that they emitted was not blinding, but she had a feeling that it could be if they wished it.

"I wish I could embrace you child." Ayam said as her hand passed through Maleda's. "You were very brave today, but I know that you must have lots of questions."

Maleda realized that they waited for her to speak as Noslen and Ayam waited in silence with warm eyes.

"Oh, yes. Umm." Maleda tried to decide what to start with. "You said you came before Princess Clementina. What do you mean? Is she a descendant of yours?"

Noslen answered, "She is our great-grandchild, and we love her so." Maleda started again, but Ayam halted her with a hand, "Also, my child. We cannot tell you everything because the one who sent the creature after you has willed it so."

"With the curse of Masks and Memory." Maleda realized and Ayam nodded.

"Have you wondered why your eyes sometimes burn and why color once danced in your skin? If we tell you anything beyond what he has forbade and cursed, it will light you up like a beacon and they will find you. It would be much harder to protect you then. For you to know everything, it would be best if you learned it all yourself. Then, you may be more prepared to handle what comes."

"So, whenever I truly understand everything around her death, somehow the person who killed her will know? Would they be able to find me?"

"Not exactly," Noslen said, "but we do know that if we told you, that the evil one would smell the terratech in you like a jackal. As for how that jackal hunts, we do not know. For now, as long as you do not know the whole story, you are hidden, but barely. So, ask what you like, but be mindful that we may not be able to give you the answer that you want. Additionally, we are weak in this state, so our time with you may be short."

"I heard the empress bring up the Spirit World before. Is that where you're from?"

They nodded.

"Is Clementina there with you?" The hope that bloomed in Maleda's chest shriveled when she saw the tortured expressions pass over their faces and the way Ayam wrung out her fingers. Yet, she spoke.

"The princess's soul is not resting as it should in the Spirit World. Her soul is trapped somewhere."

"Trapped? How?"

"We're not sure, but there's no other place a spirit can go. We have to assume that somehow her spirit is being held captive in this world."

"How could I find her?" Maleda's eyes flicked between the two of them.

"Child, I don't know," Ayam confessed, "but the sooner you figure out the reason, the true story behind her death, it should become that much clearer.

"Oh, by Olodumare! Why me? Why can't I just know? Why can't I just help her?" Maleda sank onto one of the large tree roots as she felt Ayam and Noslen watch her, bewildered. That was the first time she'd used a god's name. It had always been 'by the sands.' Perhaps they were stunned at her for being crass. Maleda considered how she expressed her exasperation and she also considered how she owed her friend freedom and a resting place. Yet, Maleda was not prepared to see Ayam's silvery luminescence float in front of her nor was she prepared for Ayam's hands to attempt to cup her face, attempt to coax her to look up as if she were not restricted to the boundaries of the Spirit World.

"You could say that you and Clementina were like sisters. You could even say that you were like our own. Clementina was like a butterfly who tried so hard to find herself and get off the ground." Something deepened in Ayam's eyes. "But she didn't know how strong her wings were. She probably wouldn't believe you if you told her how beautiful they are. I believe you are sharing that trait with her right now. Maleda, you have power within, and we didn't come to you on a half chance. We believe that you can do this, can help her. It'll just take time for you to feel out your wings." Wait, wings. In the forest…

"Today when we were in the forest…" Maleda began as she attempted and failed to grasp Ayam's wrists, remembering their barrier. "Why did those creatures attack me? Did the evil one send them?"

"As a matter of fact, the evil one did send them. However, I think one was in allegiance, while one was harder to control. You must understand that the evil one brings corrupted creatures to its side, as well as manipulates the ones that people have come to love and appreciate."

"Where did the evil one come from and what do they want?"

"My child, you are too direct. The evil one fell into jealousy and what do jealous people want?"

"What they do not have and for some reason they want what is inside me. Some foreign person wants what has kept me alive." Maleda deduced. Ayam only closed her eyes and nodded.

"Do you think I have a chance?" Maleda was afraid to hear the answer.

Noslen spoke this time, "You most certainly do in our eyes, but you must believe that. For if there are no enemies inside you, then the enemies outside you cannot hurt you. If you do not confine yourself to the darkness, then you will be able to stand in the light and let out your light."

Although Maleda could not feel Noslen's hand going through hers, she felt the strength he tried to encourage.

"Well, then I have another question. Is there a way to save the creatures that have been manipulated and corrupted? It sounded like one of the creatures after me was in pain, like it was fighting whatever controlled it."

"Hmm," Ayam sighed, "I know that if we were to stay here and focus on one creature, perhaps we could shield it from that perverted power." Maleda kept that kernel of information for later.

"Well, my child," Noslen said warmly, "we will have to rest now and after what we expelled today, we may not be able to accompany you for a while. However, we will be with you." They walked towards the tree bridge with warm smiles as they faded away. As Maleda lightly stepped back to Clementina's room, lights still guided her and for the first time she felt watched over, felt an inexplicable kind of warmth. The only thing that her mind wrestled with as she fell off to sleep looking at Clementina's painting was the notion of how to help the creatures that fell victim to the evil one.

CHAPTER 45 - MALEDA

Days later Maleda had not seen Clementina's grandparents and Zaddae showed up for the first time since the incident in the woods, promptly standing in the corridor as she was leaving the tower. His eyes were laced with worry and Maleda could see a tinge of darkness under his eyes.

"Are you alright?" Zaddae made her stop, so he could examine her, almost practically spinning her around.

"Yes, I'm fine," Maleda rooted herself to the spot. She was starting her commute to class early, so she had time to speak with him.

"Where were you?" Maleda searched his face. Zaddae's shoulders sank.

"I was trying to find my way back into the school beyond the restrictions I have been given. Really, I can only be here during the day, as you know, to help you to your classes. But there have been meetings among the professors, ones that I was required to attend and ones that Buru would not have me miss, lest he knock me around again."

"What have the meetings been about?"

"They have been talking about how hostile the animals have been getting and creatures that humans should not tangle with, yet they will not mention them by name but by description. It's almost like the professors themselves were spooked. I mean, I know that we face an unknown, mysterious threat, but the looks in their eyes have changed. Even Professor Ramonda discussed the thing that she saw run after you, even though it was mostly hidden in shadow."

"Well," Maleda began, "after what I saw after me, I think they have the right to be afraid."

"Speaking of that," Zaddae redirected, "how did you get away from the creature?" Maleda pulled him along, so they could start walking.

"I just ran, Zaddae and I think it got caught off guard by something else. I was running alongside a lake and there was this other creature on the opposite side. It *flew* over and was about to have me, but I think it got caught in a trap. I wouldn't turn around to check for fear of losing my pace, but I heard unearthly shrieks."

"You didn't see it at all." Zaddae pressed.

"Well, I saw flashes of them in the beginning as I was twisting and turning, trying to get away. One had feathers, wings, and powerful legs, and felt much bigger than I was, like a giant. Yet, the other was like the size of a human. From the way of its shadow, it looked misshapen, but it surely had wings."

Silent alarm flared in Zaddae's eyes and he was staring at nothing in particular for a moment as she spoke of the second creature.

"I need to find a way to be here both day and night." Zaddae looked back at her with a new fury. "I don't care what Ramonda says. It is not safe."

"Well, it came in the evening, only staying in shadow. When I was in the sunlight, it did not touch me. I've got a feeling that it needs the cover of darkness, somehow." They stopped in the garden of sculptures at the base of the tower. "I'm learning about this world, here but there are some things they won't teach us in class. Could you help me to do some research once my classes are over?"

"Research?" Zaddae quirked a brow.

"Yes, research. We need to find what attacked me, so I can understand. Just meet me in the tunnels, later."

Zaddae had arms crossed, but he nodded in agreement. They could not fight their way out of this. Well, maybe Zaddae could, but the best skill that Maleda could employ at the moment was to run. Before she could stand and fight, she needed to know her enemy.

* * *

When Maleda's classes ended for the day, she found that the sun was still high, and something pulled her towards the creature from the other day. The one who chased her, but who also seemed to be in pain. Hopefully, she could find her answers in books, but maybe distant observation or going back to the scene could give her clues. Maleda found her way through the tunnels easily and found herself greeted by the shady trees of the forest's edge beyond the gate. Maleda knew she was being irrevocably stupid in going out in the forest by herself, but something that she could not explain continued to pull at her. Nothing made sense and it felt like everything was closing in on her. Despite her horrid first experience, she felt a sense of calm when she went into the forest, so she followed it. It was quite possible that this evil one could have allies that did not fear the darkness, but she was going to believe that it was not true, just this once. It was almost like one of her peaceful walks through the desert oasis as her feet crunched over small twigs and wet dirt from last night's rain, just bigger. If only the rain could wash away everything else. The pained cries of that one creature that followed her so ferociously made her heart ache in a way that she could not understand. Even in the calm stillness under the trees, she felt the wails of that creature.

Like a meerkat, Maleda was erect, head flitting from one side to the other. What was that sound? Her hand twitched as she kept herself from going for her dagger. As she flitted around, she saw that there was nothing in the shadows. She was tempted to turn and run back into the walls of the empire, but something stopped her as she started to turn. It was that cry again, but it sounded pained. What if she left someone out there hurt, or dying? Maleda didn't know if she could live with that choice on her conscious, so she retrieved the dagger from her belt and slowly proceeded forward, while keeping off the main path, but she kept it in sight. As far as stealth, Maleda knew that she needed to be quiet and watchful, so she looked around and above herself, careful to avoid bundles of branches. Yet, she did not account for false ground as she tumbled through the earth. It was flashes of darkness and light from above as she rolled down and down some more. The earth went from wet and muddy to dusty and hard. She finally came to a stop and felt the thud of her dagger slide against her thigh. She recovered it slowly as she tested out her newly sore muscles. A string of groans escaped her throat as she felt the new stings of pain across her skin. She couldn't imagine all the cuts induced by her fall, but when she opened her eyes, her field of vision was encapsulated by colored light. Crystals. From the ground and from the ceiling. How they glowed. She gripped a large green one and pulled herself up. It was terra stones, large and small littered throughout a cave. Maleda looked up to where she fell from. It was too steep to climb back up, but there was a crack of light. As Maleda pulled herself up from the ground, her eyes widened at that same suffering call. She knew she couldn't stay in one place for long, so her only choice was to find a way out by moving forward. The crystals made a labyrinth of the cave, but somehow, they provided their own light. The place seemed ancient and somehow life found a way in those caverns as Maleda noticed vines scrawled across the walls. Even trees and grass were sprinkled about the place. She still kept her guard up as best she could, but after her tumble, she did feel a little ridiculous and embarrassed in spite of her being alone.

However, the cave seemed to be barren save for the crystals, sparse vegetation, and that awful moaning. Maleda followed the cavern as it rounded a corner and she saw a mass of white with a beam of sunlight shining down on it. Maleda had to reign in her gasp as she ducked behind a rock. Her heart wanted to hammer its way out, but she forced herself to breathe slowly and silently as her eyes began to sting. With dagger still in hand, she barely leaned out, just so she could clearly see the creature. If it was not the thing that had attacked her, it was most certainly kin to it.

By the sands.

Where did it go?

A sickening feeling gathered inside Maleda as she felt a titan-like presence behind her. She didn't dare turn around. If she saw that thing looming over her, she would lose all of her will, so she ran for the now abandoned light, silently hysterical. Maleda backed herself against the wall of the cave trying to stop herself from shaking. She looked up from the ground to see two stony eyes staring back at her on the other side of the spotlight. The creature stalked forward one, two steps. It was still a good distance away. She did not know what she would do, but she wasn't dying yet. The creature half cast in shadow made a sound that Maleda could not quite make out to be exactly menacing, but even in the stony eyes of that creature, she could see that those same eyes were also laced with pain. Maleda did not know how she knew. It was like something ancient that she felt.

"Are you hurt?" Maleda hesitantly asked the creature. It almost seemed like the beast was offended as it pulled its head back and hissed with caution at her. The cries of pain returned and were followed by the creature charging into the light and at Maleda with a furious screech. Maleda shut her eyes then and shielded herself with arms outstretched and palms to the beast. They would not even know what happened to her this time. The evil one had won. There was a flash of white and something like a rush of voices.

Yet, she was still there. Not crushed. Still breathing.

Maleda opened her eyes and turned to see the creature wide-eyed with head resting in Maleda's quivering hand. The creature looked just as surprised as she was, with wide brown eyes staring back at her.The beast had the nerve to look confused, as if it wasn't sure what to do with its kill. The creature backed up slightly and sat on its hind quarters. For the first time, Maleda could take in the entirety of the creature. She was like an owl, at least the head, but with four legs and wings that could challenge the sails of the ship Maleda flew in to get to the empire. Maleda remembered the sculptures outside the library, and she heard about these creatures mentioned in passing in her history class. It was a griffin, an owl griffin to be exact. Magnificent beasts that flourished in the continent of Alfajiri and a little to the northeast in the more northern continents.

Maleda started to slowly walk toward the creature, but it tensed a little letting out a warning screech. Maleda quickly sidestepped and the griffin followed her example tilting her head at Maleda as they circled each other. The eyes of the griffin became less menacing somehow and Maleda watched her slowly move her wings into different formations. It took a moment for Maleda to realize that she was following the movements of Maleda's arms. It was something on the edge of her mind, a dance. Somehow, her body remembered, and she didn't. It was like she was back at the tree only this time she met her invisible partner. Maleda followed the memory in her bones and let herself be led into a tighter circle orbiting with the griffin, until her hand was hovering above the griffin's head again. They stood inches from each other, and the griffin nodded its head but still kept its eyes on her. Maleda felt like she needed to respect the creature somehow, so she bowed her head and laid a hand on the griffin's head. A flash of images, too fast to see, but each a memory. Flying. She was flying, but she couldn't tell if it was Bami's wings or someone else's wings. Maleda was heaving to get air into her lungs when she opened her eyes.

Bami.

Her name was Bamidele.

Maleda tested the name out loud, "Bami?"

The griffin bowled Maleda over and of all things, she chirped with undeniable joy. Then, Maleda was swept off the ground and was being held in Bami's arms as if she were the griffin's favorite doll. Somehow, she knew this creature and somehow, she could see into her mind as if her memory was her voice. Maleda laughed in spite of herself and squeezed the creature back as she cooed over Maleda's head. Finally, Bami let Maleda down and she laid on her belly with Maleda sitting on Bami's front legs. Maleda studied the newly warm eyes of Bami as she stroked the side of her head.

"Why don't you just fly away Bami? You've got a set of wings on you."

As if Bami understood her word for word, she squawked and lowered her head for Maleda to touch again. Maleda braced herself as best as she could for the breathlessness.

Light turned to golden waves, an ocean of sand and airships of metal. The ocean of sand turned to forest and light turned to shadow. The growling and gnashing of teeth as she was being followed. Running with the darkness because it made her. Running after a girl trying to help some antelope, until someone struck her out of it. When she peeled away, she saw a man with a disdainful look facing off with some creature sheathed in shadow. A man that was so familiar, glinting in the sunlight.

Maleda was gasping when she came out of the vision.

"You were there in the desert. You distracted the people in the ships. You saved my life." Maleda hugged Bami's head and pressed her face into her feathers. "You know me from before and someone tried to use you to kill me."

Bami cooed and nestled closer to Maleda. She couldn't risk her attempted killers hurting Bami again. They could send Bami after her again if they found her, or worse they could send her after the rest of the people in the empire, maybe even the empress and emperor if the killers were bold enough. Maleda had to go get help. She rose from her spot and stroked Bami's head one last time.

"I have to go, but I'll be back." Maleda tried to soothe her, but as she was turning to walk away Bami grabbed a corner of her clothes and yanked her back.

"Bami, I need to get someone to help me." Bami squeaked in protest. "Bami, I need to ask someone what to do." Maleda admitted, her voice raising with fear and frustration. "I don't know what to do." Bami let go of Maleda and tilted her head at her, with pupils dilating to the point of Maleda's will. She didn't know what to do with her. Even though Bami was a force of nature, she certainly could not stay in the caves. That would mean risking her killers finding them both and maybe even mind controlling Bami again, only this time Bami would not snap out of the trance. Maleda paced with her hands squeezing her twists and Bami watched her, tilting her head back and forth. She had to think. There had to be something.

Wait.

Ayam and Noslen.

CHAPTER 46 - MALEDA

Ayam said that they could possibly protect one of the creatures from being manipulated by the killers, so the best option was to lead Bami through the dilapidated tunnels, get her back into the school, and into Ayam and Noslen's burial room. They wouldn't have been able to make it out to her anyway having spent themselves communicating with her. So that's how Maleda found herself scurrying through the cave to find connections to tunnels, like the others. She trusted that they would lead her back into the empire's walls and back into the tunnels of the university. Miraculously, the far reaches of her memory gave her some ancient sense to know where she was going, and she found herself guiding Bami through the barren parts of the school tunnels. Maleda doubted that anyone got a good look at Bami, but there was no explaining away her leading a giant—once malicious—creature through the school. Maleda kept a hand on Bami's head to keep her hushed. For as huge as she was, she knew how to be light on her feet. If Maleda could just get Bami to Ayam and Noslen, she would have an effective place to hide. Upon rounding the corner that led to her room in the tower, they came across a hooded figure who was facing away from them down the corridor. Bami growled and seemed like she was ready to bound in front of Maleda, but Maleda's heartbeat slowed when Zaddae turned around, eyes about to leap from his skull. He had drawn his swords.

"Maleda, what are you doing with that thing?!" Bami rumbled under Maleda's hand as she shifted her shoulders up and down, as if ready to pounce.

Maleda ran and stood in between them, hands held out to either side.

"Wait! Stop! This is Bami! I think she knows me from before." Maleda urged trying to soothe Bami and stop Zaddae.

"Bami?" Zaddae cocked his head at her, swords still drawn.

"Yes, it's short for Bamidele. If she knew me from before, then maybe you may remember her too." Maleda smiled nervously as her head darted from one to the other. As she looked between the two of them, Bami settled a little at Maleda's command, but still looked agitated, while Zaddae stared at the creature in near disbelief.

"Bami." He repeated quietly.

"Yes, so you do remember." Maleda ran to him, but then she saw the veil over his eyes, "Don't you?" His swords were limp in his hands, and he looked from the ground to Bami and finally to Maleda.

"You don't remember, do you?" Maleda realized. "I mean, it's all right if you don't. I just thought maybe there was a chance."

"I honestly thought that I remembered as most as I could, but now I'm out of my mind because I know I've seen this creature before. I've heard that name, but I don't know where," he put the swords away and rubbed his temple, "It doesn't make sense."

"Is there anything you remember about griffins?" Maleda's tone softened.

"I just know that they were respected, elegant creatures. They were part of the coat of arms for the empire and there are statues of them in front of the library in the castle. Some of the rulers even had them as companions.," Zaddae's voice faded to quiet, and his face went gaunt.

They could not continue this conversation here. Someone could catch them, so Maleda dragged the now silent and haunted Zaddae and the still ruffled Bami up to her room. Zaddae looked at Bami as if she were a ghost and stood in place as she stood by a wall, still glaring at him. He seemed nearly weightless as Maleda pulled him to sit down in a chair.

"What's gotten you so spooked?" Maleda asked him.

"I don't know what it is, but I feel like I should know her, and I think that she may have been Princess Clementina's companion. If she has been following you through the tunnels all this time, then I suspect that she must remember you being close to her. You and the Princess may have treated her like she belonged with both of you. She would be desperate to protect whoever is left alive." Maleda put a hand over her mouth. This was Princess Clementina's griffin. No wonder Bami remembered her. Yet, Maleda could not let herself dwell on that. She still had to take Bami to Ayam and Noslen, without alerting Zaddae to where she was going.

"I'm going to hide Bami here, in the tunnels—" Zaddae barely shook himself out of his trance.

"Okay, I'll come with—"

"No." Maleda cut him off. "I need you to go to the university library. We need to get some books about the animals in the area." Maleda was shoving Bami towards the door that led to collections.

He didn't look like he could be broken from his trance or maybe he was just suspicious of why she wanted to usher him away so quickly.

"What are you going to do with her?" Zaddae gestured at Bami. Maleda looked back and spoke.

"That's not your concern and I'll take care of her."

"How on earth you going to take care of—." However, Zaddae could not finish his sentence because Maleda was already shoving him out the door.

When the door clicked shut, Maleda sighed and nearly slid down exasperated as she stared back at Bami who was wide-eyed and staring at her. Maleda navigated the barren parts of the tunnels and brought Bami up to the burial room that was at the top of the tower. It didn't take long for Ayam and Noslen to appear. They raised their brows at Bami's rambunctious bounding. Maleda spoke to them quickly.

"I found her in the forest, and she was wailing. She was hiding out in an old cave littered in crystals. I think she snapped out of whatever was controlling her."

"That would be my handiwork," Noslen said. Bami seemed to be unnaturally comfortable around these two.

"You all know each other, right?"

"That we do." Ayam responded.

"But you can't tell me?"

Ayam shook her head with a thin smile. Evening had eclipsed the empire and Maleda looked out over the city of cities.

Maleda spoke, "I don't know what's going happen. The people need to be protected and now they're these creatures running around."

"I believe that somehow everything will work itself out in the end. It has to." Noslen responded.

"But don't you worry." Ayam reaffirmed. "We will keep her safe and you can come and visit her as much as you like. You seemed to be in a rush, so go on. We got her."

Maleda smiled at them and said her goodbyes while she rushed back to the tunnels to go meet Zaddae at the library.

* * *

Zaddae was waiting dutifully outside the university library, stiff and silent. He seemed to still be in that trance when Maleda showed up, but he was at immediate attention when he looked into her face. The university library was similar to that of the castle, albeit only a little smaller and crowded with students. Some were huddled off to themselves, intensely studying while others did their best to quietly enjoy study time with their friends without getting kicked out. Yet, there were still plenty of archives, parchment, and books to pour through. Maleda had scrambled to bring her trusty satchel equipped with journal, ink, and pen. They both had stacks of books nearly up to their chin with everything Maleda thought they would need. The table was treated with golden light as the sun set beyond the window they sat by. Various books were open and laid on top of each other.

Some books were on creatures, while others were on the power and history of terra stones and the more recent advancements of terratech. She had scrawled notes into her journal, at least what she thought was relevant, but when she came across the image that beheld the gray skin and membranous wings, she could only stare. She did not know how long she had been like that, recounting the sounds of that wretched thing coming after her. She didn't need to say anything to Zaddae as she looked up because it looked like he was already reading the silent terror on her face.

"What is it?" He urged.

"That," Maleda began, "That is what I saw. That is what chased after me. I'm sure of it." She took a breath and tried to collect herself as she turned the book, so Zaddae could properly see. "It says it's a Popobowa. It says that they are *demons* that walk around as people by day, but winged, one-eyed monsters in the night."

"But didn't it attack you in the evening, when there was still sunlight?"

"Yes, it doesn't make any sense." Maleda remembered every horrible moment of how that beast made disturbing noises. "It did stay in shadow though. Maybe they have learned to just stick to darkness in general terms, not just the night."

"If that were the case, there would be more of them out there, unless they are testing the waters. It's like someone kept the horde hostage and only let a few out of their cage."

Maleda wanted to keep the terror at bay, but she had so many questions. The idea that there could be more creatures like that out there? The idea that the evil one who was behind this was holding them back while they were chomping at the bit? It was too much. Her spine straightened with the wave of realization. Her eyes flitted from the books in front of her to the ones around her as her theory ran free in her mind, as if she could catch pieces of it with her eyes, string it together, and slow it down enough to come out of her mouth. Zaddae seemed to glimpse the gears turning in her mind.

"Do you have an idea?"

"I paid attention in class, to what the emperor and empress said, and to the statues in the city, but I guess everything rushed by so quick that I didn't really take the time to think."

"Think about what?"

Maleda leaned in and Zaddae did the same. "Some of the teachers say that the beginnings of terra stones, of the world itself are inexplicable, but people like Ramonda say Olodumare willing." Maleda yanked a book out of the stack wildly flipping to find it. "This is the only explanation."

"What are you looking for?" Zaddae was puzzled at her frantic searching.

"You'll see. There is a story that says why these stones exist on our plane of existence. The god Olorun—people also call him Olodumare—is the creator of world order among the Orisha. He acts as their father. It is said that Olorun lived in this world before he went to the skies, lived here with his children. Whenever they wanted to do something beyond their own abilities, they asked Olorun for power. One day, one of his children—Oko—asked Olorun to just give them each power once and for all, so that they did not need to ask Olorun every time they wanted to do something. Olorun was conflicted and felt unsure about how he would distribute power amongst his children equally. So, he sought advice and spoke to a chameleon and—"

"A chameleon? So, what, he just had a chat with it?"

"Yes, there was a time when the bond between animals and people were strong enough that they could converse, some by mouth and some by the mind." The significance of what Maleda and Bamidele shared struck her. "Maybe both." Zaddae raised a brow, but she continued on. "Anyway, the chameleon told him that he should leave it up to chance. He said that Olorun should go up to the skies and send messengers down here to tell his children that powers would rain down. If his children wanted to gain any power, they had to get it themselves, chase it down, that way whatever rained on them was left up to chance and their abilities. Power must have been in the form of terra stones and he rained them down for his children to catch."

"Well, that doesn't explain how people after that would receive powers," Zaddae quipped.

"Well, he left the stones down here, for anyone to grab I suppose. If you insert it into the skin, it may just make you stronger or you may get powers. Yet, he wanted people to remember the importance of seeking that connection to Olorun in that power. Beyond the empire, there are nations dedicated to the four elements. The Orisha could act like patrons to each of the nations, deciding who is to receive power. I don't think it's as simple as this stuff just always being here."

"Okay, besides the creation story, what exactly are you saying?"

Maleda brushed aside the slight hurt at Zaddae's curtness and continued.

"What if Clementina called on one of the patron Orisha to the city? To protect her?" Beneath the mask of disbelief, Maleda could see a flicker of something in Zaddae's eyes. Maybe hope, so she let the theories tumble out further. "What if she's not trapped, just hiding and safe in the spirit world? Or maybe something happened and the Orisha couldn't protect her in the Spirit World? Who knows? She could have asked them to split and store her soul all over the city? It could make it harder for the evil one to find her. Maybe the Orisha couldn't tell them? Couldn't tell us?"

Zaddae looked out of the window, "Do you even believe in that? The Orisha? It could just be random. Also, what do you mean them?" *Them* meant Ayam and Noslen, but Maleda just said, "Y'know Clementina's family." Not entirely a lie. Ayam and Noslen did not just come from nowhere. Maleda knew that, but it was a little terrifying to admit that there was someone much bigger than her, who may have bestowed powers, but created a rival in the process with this anonymous evil one.

"I don't know what to believe, but it's the only thing I can go on. You say that there are people who say that this string of events is nothing more than random anomalies, but they forget that every story has its author. On top of that, it couldn't hurt to believe it's true. It at least would give us something to investigate closer."

"And what would make you possibly believe that? For sure?" He really wouldn't let this go. Maleda considered betraying Ayam and Noslen's wish to not make anyone aware of their appearances to Maleda, but she just took a breath and asked, "Why do you find it so hard to believe that there was someone who gave us what we have?"

"I loved her, and they took her away," Zaddae hissed. He didn't need to say it. It was written in how his jaw worked when he spoke of her, saw the colors of her banner outside the tower, or when he passed that statue of her being swept into euphoria by an ocean wind. The venom in his whisper was not for Maleda and she just hurt for him. Maleda remained quiet as he continued. "If they are there, then why did they let her die?!"

"I don't know," Maleda's voice lowered, "but I believe there is a world parallel to this one and I believe there is a reason why Olodumare cannot confer with us. I'm sure of it. We both don't remember what tangled with our minds before, but we will figure it out. You will see."

* * *

Maleda brought her books out of the library and Zaddae helped her carry them in silence. When they made it back to her tower chambers the purple and orange glow of evening had struck through the windows of the tower. Maleda decided not to bring up Orisha again, so as not to torture Zaddae about Clementina's memory any further. Maleda's ache for Clementina was foreign as she did not really remember her at all, but rather it felt like a strange sadness.

Zaddae's anger was simmering and present, but that anger was just a bodyguard for something else, even if he did not want to admit it. Maleda was surprised when Zaddae requested to stay in the tower with her, whilst they were pouring through information on terra stones.

"I just feel antsy for some reason," Zaddae said as he laid a blanket out on one of the lounge chairs. "Maybe it's because I got to finally see what attacked you or because you're hiding that griffin somewhere around here. And how do you know that it's not going to turn on you again?"

She could not tell Zaddae about Ayam and Noslen. She couldn't tell anyone. For all she knew, when she said something, they could disappear.

"Just know that she is safe now." Maleda stared at the ceiling as she untwisted and retwisted her hair. "I'm actually happy that you are here with me because even though nothing has come for me in this tower, I still feel uneasy like every bad thing is waiting outside the window and I just can't see it. If the assassin that came after Clementina is still out there and used creatures, is still using creatures, then I don't know what to do. And you said you would train me in my terratech—granted I know that meant a lot of reading and sneaking out of the castle—but I'm still unable to call on it willingly. It only flares up, like it's leashed by someone other than me. Despite what Ramonda said, I don't feel like I'm going crazy even though I can't decide when to let it out. It just seems like everything—" Instantly,

held her there. "Do you want to talk about it?" he whispered gently. Maleda just shook her head and looked down at his hand holding hers. "Maybe tomorrow."

CHAPTER 48 - MALEDA

I t took a while for Maleda to fall back to sleep, but when she woke, she felt the warmth of sunlight curl around her like a hand. She opened her eyes and faced Zaddae who was also sleeping on his side. One hand held hers, while the other was draped over her back. She did not want to disturb him. He never looked this peaceful, with knees drawn up and coils falling carelessly over his face. For once, he didn't look like he was in some restrained pain over losing Clementina. Somehow, even in the absence of memory, she felt like she was betraying Clementina. Maleda stared up at the ceiling wondering if she should just close her eyes or if she could attempt to remove herself without waking him, but she felt his hand sweep to her shoulder blade and she looked back into his sunlit eyes staring right back at her. Yet, his hands did not retreat and Maleda continued to quietly consider his face, unable to say anything.

"Good morning." The timbre of Zaddae's voice was lower in the morning. "You need to dampen the rainbow in your eyes. It's much safer as a brown eyed girl for you."

All Maleda could manage was, "What?"

Zaddae's hand left her back to reach for a mirror on a nightstand not far from the bed and she saw the rainbow eyes that last appeared at the castle in that mirror. It was so strange being around mirrors and seeing herself in them, like a permanent twin. Maleda willed them to be brown with a deep breath and somehow, the rainbow was flooded out with the cover of her brown eyes. Thankfully, the colors in her skin had not deigned an appearance. She took the mirror from Zaddae and sat up.

"Do you think that they'll be after us soon, because of that just now?"

"It was not an aggressive display of terratech, so I'm sure you'll be safe." He smiled at her, and she smiled back, but she had no idea how to address the fact that he had held her through the night, so she quietly pulled herself to the edge of the bed and looked out of a window. An airship roamed about the sky donning the colors of the Princesses' tower. "What's that for?" Maleda asked shyly looking back at Zaddae.

"This is the month that the princess was killed, and you disappeared. The emperor and empress wanted to remember you both. Mourning is more than just the day one is lost." Zaddae looked at Maleda with a shaky curiosity and maybe even questioning. He seemed like he was going to reach for her but must have thought better of it and gently squeezed her hand.

"I'll let you get dressed," he said quietly and with a shy, hesitant smile, he left the room and Maleda heard him descend the stairs. As he waited in the larger space with Clementina's unfinished painting, Maleda quickly changed into a tunic and pants, lacing on her barely-there sandals. As she strung herself together, she couldn't help but memorize where he had touched her and the gentle warmth of his hand, his smile. Maleda's heart still pounded, but she was unsure of the true reason for its rapid beating.

CHAPTER 49 - MALEDA

Professor Buru had told Maleda that he wanted her project to be used for an important event to welcome a foreign ally, a means to show what they had to offer so the pressure to do well increased. Days had gone by and Maleda continued to work diligently on Clementina's painting, while having conversations with projections of Selene in the evenings. Cham even let Maleda use her to paint in her brush form. She drew inspiration from the empire, sometimes walking the streets with Zaddae. They particularly liked to frequent galleries and bookstores. On one of those walks, Maleda and Zaddae walked into an unsuspecting shop, bell cheerily ringing at their entrance. The woman there sold art supplies. Some of the paint was laced with magic, while others were just normal pigment. Brushes, fabric, inks, thick sticks of graphite. The potential to make so many different things. It was all so wonderful. Upon noting Maleda's wide-eyed enthusiasm, she guided Maleda and Zaddae to the back of the store, revealing an airy room filled with painters, scattered about the room. So, she joined a society to paint with artists of the city. This particular society was one that submitted artwork to the royal court and even restored work in royal estates. Maleda even joined the emperor as an apprentice when he and his wife returned from their trip, traveling between the university and the castle to help him work on research. Maleda had never called herself an artist. She just knew that she loved to create, but it warmed her soul to have the society members around her. They were also an entertaining group, debating techniques, daily news, or even local lore. Maleda just listened and sometimes stifled laughter from behind her canvas.

"Did you all hear about the animal they found outside the walls?" A fellow painter named Safina asked. She had dark brown dreads that tumbled from underneath her yellow turban and onto her cacao-colored shoulders.

"Yes, my daughter told me about it yesterday. It sounds like it wasn't an animal of this realm if you ask me." An older man named Malik Mutarrif responded. "This subtle chaos has persisted ever since the Forgotten War." He stroked his beard which was peppered with flecks of silver.

"But doesn't it seem more intense somehow?"

"Yes, and that's what worries me. I would feel a little better if I were able to summon my hydrokinesis."

The turn in conversation made Maleda's heart sink to her feet, but thankfully the day's painting session was concluding, and she was on her way to the castle to prepare to work with the emperor, or as she liked to call him, uncle Olmec.

Maleda and her uncle were in a large lab room with sunlight pouring in from glassless windows near the ceiling, like a training room or gymnasium. Maleda had three panels of Clementina's. The longest elaborate one was a collage of paintings, while the other two were blank and turned slightly to face each other. As Maleda's guard, Zaddae was given permission to witness Maleda's project and he stood some distance away observing the experiment. The professors were also in the lab as well, quietly doing research and looking over to Maleda's setup. Buru, of course, seemed to be looking down his nose at her, but she tried not to worry about that.

Maleda's shoulders rose with a deep breath, and she readied herself. When she exhaled, she danced in front of the panels, almost like she did in the desert, and the panels came to life. In mirrors staged yards away, she could see how the panels reacted behind her. The largest one that contained the collage seemed to move with an energy and life that could only be explained by terratech.

Scenes from land and sea moved behind her, but Maleda did not understand it all, only that this was the world she had left behind. In trying to understand Clementina's project, she knew she would not be able to dive into that understanding, yet. All she could do was follow the steps that Clementina had laid out for her and practice them until this moment. With each movement, she somehow summoned projections of figures from the images. Women danced and spun from the canvas followed by men, all different colors and sometimes the colors alternated. Despite how lively these projections were, their faces were not clear, and they eerily made Maleda think of her dreams. It all depended on harmony, a connection, so Maleda would oblige that notion. At one point, she faced a glassless window and held a pose waiting expectantly. When the fwoosh was followed by Bamidele's perching in the window, she knew her wish was granted.

There were murmurs of fear, and she could hear the professors readying weapons. Even uncle Olmec, had his hand on the hilt of a sword and beckoned. "Get away from that griffin, Maleda! It's not safe!"

Bami started to look agitated, so Maleda spoke, "No, it's okay. This is what Clementina wanted. We don't have to fight them." As if her words calmed both the spectators and Bami, the griffin flew on swift near silent wings until she was beak to nose with Maleda. Much like their first meeting, they circled each other while holding each other's gaze and Maleda spoke again, "We can help them. We can be one again."

Once they were close enough, Bami closed her eyes and bowed her head as Maleda mimicked the motion. Maleda kept her eyes on the floor as she readied to lay her hand on Bami's head, but just as her hand grazed Bami's feathers, she heard someone command. "Bami attack!" Then, Bami reared up and screeched into the air.

That was not according to plan. Maleda stumbled back as she tried to calm Bami, but it seemed like Bami was after something that was not there, spinning around as if she were chasing something on her back. Everyone was in full panic now, but Bami was only part of the reason. A display that Maleda had never seen in the program came to life. All the projected images of the men and women dancing in a circle around them bound themselves together to form one being. A man. A titan with no clear face, but he was a silhouette of red and black. The giant went on one knee in front of Maleda and she stumbled back. Its voice was a layer of voices that grated against her ears, "You will bow down and give me what lies beneath." The display retained an alarming red glow as the man disappeared and Maleda lost all sense of will as she scrambled backward and turned to see Buru with eyes locked on the giant man in front of her. He had a fire in his eyes, a fire that made her blood run cold. When Maleda looked back to where the titan stood, he had disappeared and was replaced by a shadow that stretched from one of the high windows Bami descended from. There was a figure, a man attached to that shadow. How long had he been standing there? He was too far away to see clearly, but Maleda could see that he was masked and wore black.

The figure made a distinct flick of his fingers and then curtains flew from the windows to wrap around her body, like a python. The emperor, Zaddae, and the professors ran to help her, but the free ends of the curtain snapped at them like a snake, not allowing them to get closer. As Maleda struggled, she looked back up at the man in the window and it seemed like he was struggling as well. It was like he was resisting trying to double over and even with the distance between them, she could see him tremble. He shouted as if through clenched teeth, "Bami!" A red glow tainted Bami's eyes and she hissed at Maleda briefly, but she shook her head violently and charged at Maleda.

He had sicked Bami on her and Maleda shut her eyes, unable to defend herself. She felt tugging and ripping at the silk and Maleda opened her eyes to see Bami attempting to free her. Maleda looked back up to the window and the stranger was gone. The sudden squeezing had nearly numbed Maleda's limbs and she struggled to push herself up with quaking arms. She did her best to wave Bami off as soldiers sounded like they would start to seize her.

"Go Bami." Maleda commanded as the soldiers drew closer. Bami would not budge and started screeching anew when Zaddae rushed over to help her. Bami charged Zaddae and knocked him over and he failed to rise. Maleda could barely breathe. This was not Bami. It was the man in the display or even the one who was in the window possessing Bami. She kept this in mind as she tried to keep Bami from charging Zaddae or anyone else. Maleda grabbed Bami by the beak and drew her face down until they were eye to eye.

"Go to the tower. I'll be fine. You'll be safe there." Bami stumbled backward and squawked as if she were questioning, but she obeyed and flew out the glassless window. She allowed herself a breath of relief before she turned and ran back to Zaddae. She nearly skidded to a stop and tried to squeeze in amongst the people crowding his body. Emperor Olmec spoke to a set of guards and was giving orders about tightening security, but he was swiftly by Maleda's side, gently holding her shoulders. One of the soldiers addressed her. "He's still breathing, just knocked out. He'll have a nasty headache when he wakes up."

As they readied to move him, Maleda noticed Buru standing off to the side, staring down his nose at Zaddae and then at Maleda. Before Buru or anyone else could speak a medic announced, "Take him to a private room." The soldiers moved Zaddae over to a hovering gurney, one of the experimental benefits of terratech in the castle. As they passed Buru, she noticed an odd and alarming glare in his eye. He seemed to be looking at nothing in particular until he briefly brought his glare and smile to Maleda, but as quickly as she saw the smile, it vanished. She kept the terror to her rapidly beating heart and away from her face as Buru watched the soldiers inspect her project, like he was admiring some handiwork.

* * *

Nothing abnormal was found in the inspection, making things more curious and worrisome. Worry was the thing that Maleda was trying to push away as she looked at the patch of Zaddae's forehead that had started to turn purple as time went by, but he remained still, save for the rising and falling of his chest in sleep. After examination, they noted that he should avoid any rigorous movement, namely leaving the bed. As evening edged into night, Maleda remained at Zaddae's bedside. It was not safe for either of them to be alone, not after that display. Mirriam had ran into the lab with the empress, both of them fussing over Maleda as she insisted, she wasn't hurt. When they deigned to stop, Mirriam pulled Maleda into a hug and whispered that she would find who was doing this and keep her safe. Once one of the guards briefed her, she nodded at the rulers of the empire and ran out of the room and that was that. Maleda hadn't seen her since the castle. She didn't really have the time nor headspace to miss her given everything going on and Mirriam would have probably tried to keep her out of the city anyway, while Zaddae encouraged her. Was that what she's been doing this whole time? Buru had not made his way over to visit Zaddae yet. He was the only one in the room that had that distinct look on his face. Was he in league with that titan? Were they scheming how to attack next? Why would he do this? Maleda was furiously twisting and untwisting one strand of hair, reminding herself that she had daggers in her cloak. There were times she swore she heard that seething voice, but she knew that her head was just torturing her with a new memory. The exhaustion extended from her mind to her whole being and she released her twist when she finished wrapping it back together. She slumped in her chair and held her head in her hand.

"What's gotten you so scared?" Maleda jumped at Zaddae's voice, and she looked over at him. He was smiling of all things, weakly, but still a smile.

"How are you feeling?" Maleda leaned closer and furrowed her brows in worry. His golden eyes looked confused and wobbly in the candlelight, with his eyelids threatening to close. "Zaddae?" She questioned. His head lolled around the pillow with his eyes half open.

"I don't want you to get hurt." He muttered under his breath. "You should leave me."

Maleda shook her head and laid a hand on Zaddae's. "No, I'm going to stay with you, just like you were there for me." It was as if that made him come to and his bleary eyes opened wider.

"Maleda?"

"Yes, I'm here. I'm alright, but you got hit in the head."

"How?"

"The display turned against me somehow, like someone entered another program into the canvas. A projection of a red titan spoke to me, threatened me. Then, there was this masked man in the window, and it was like he was trying to possess Bami. She hit you in the head while she was still under, but she shook herself out of it this time though and I sent her back to the tower to protect herself."

"Wait, so Bami hit me?"

Maleda raised her brows and scoffed. "So that's what you're worried about right now? That's what you got from that?"

"Well, I'm a little disoriented and now that I know the perpetrator, I can dole out proper punishment." He was toying with her, even while bleary-eyed and surely in pain.

"Well, I don't know if you'd be the one to win." Maleda quipped.

Zaddae had the nerve to look hurt, mouth agape and all. "Maleda, you'd really kick a man while he's down?" Maleda just tilted her head and grinned, but the corners of her lips fell as Zaddae schooled his features. "Regardless of my current state, it seems like someone had to have planned an attack."

"But the artwork has been in the tower the whole time and I'm the only one that has had access to it. No one could have tampered with it."

"But what about before you were even at the tower? Someone may have thought that you returned." Zaddae winced a little as he rubbed his head.

"But no one made a big announcement of it."

"Then another option is that someone knew you got away." Pain seized Zaddae's head, and he sunk deep into the pillow.

Maleda laid a hand on his shoulder, the best thing she could think of to coax him through it. She considered before she mentioned her next suspicion, but then she remembered that Ayam told her that Buru could work the dark and barreled ahead.

"There's another thing. I think Buru had something to do with it. When we were being attacked, I turned away from the display and he looked like he had a fire in his eyes like he was…*reverent* to the arrival of the titan and the man in the window. He may have just been scared, but something just seemed off and he gave you and I strange looks. Ramonda needs to know."

"No."

"What do you mean 'no'? She's been my ally and I may be wrong but—"

"No, I second your suspicion. But Buru is a professor *and* so is she."

"You're not suggesting they're in league with each other, are you?"

"I would really love it if they weren't, but we don't know that. We also don't know the hysteria that Buru could cause. Do you think he realized that you knew?"

"No, I believe I looked more panicked than anything. I just don't understand why he would do this, get in league with whoever is trying to kill me?"

"I don't know, but we will have to find out. No one can know. Not Ramonda, not anyone. We will investigate Buru ourselves."

"But you're injured. If he had something to do with Bami's possession, who's to say he wouldn't do something worse than make her ram into you? He's beaten you up before!"

"First, I had one black eye and second, that's a chance that we'll have to take. Besides, I'll just sleep it off." Zaddae tried to settle more into his pillow.

"I have a feeling that when you wake, it will feel like he beat you all over again." He grinned with closed eyes, but he spoke into the darkness. "Thank you for staying with me." Speechless, Maleda hugged him, and he squeezed her right back. It was so strange to feel needed.

CHAPTER 50 - MALEDA

After a few days of rest and planning, Zaddae and Maleda readied themselves to follow Buru. The emperor and empress had to go on another trip across the shore to meet with their ally. They asked Maleda if they wanted her to stay but she reassured them that she was okay. Maleda had already made sure that Bami was safe and hidden away in the tower, so she could be kept from possession and possibly hurting anyone else. Ayam and Noslen did not appear this time, but she trusted that they were hovering in their invisibility, silently watching over Bamidele. Zaddae had gone with Buru to outposts a little beyond the city in the deserts. They were far enough away that transportation was needed to get there. Ramonda had encouraged Maleda to move back into the castle and abandon the tower at university, but Maleda chose to stay. Maleda believed that Ramonda proposed the idea out of hopes for her safety, but she seemed to be happy that Maleda would still be around. She wanted to believe that was the only intention she had. After forgetting everything and trying to rebuild a new life, she wasn't sure if she could take any more lies. Cloaked and bejeweled in hidden weapons, Zaddae and Maleda left through the floor in Collections to venture into the tunnels.

Since Cham was able to fill in more gaps, they followed her projected map and the sound of an ancient rumbling. It was a tunnel for the trains. The vessels ran on terratech carrying people to places in the city that would take too long to walk to. She and Zaddae slipped into the crowd of people waiting for their scheduled train. Zaddae knew which train Buru usually took and to which station, so Maleda dutifully followed him. Buru entered one car and they were two cars behind. The train rocketed through the underground and Maleda was initially startled by its ferocity, but she secretly enjoyed its rush, like the train was alive. They were mostly silent through the operation save for when Zaddae indicated for them to shift patterns and directions. When they got off the train, Buru was already on the move. Zaddae was on the edge of breaking into a run and Maleda was nearly jogging after him.

Once they cleared the crowded station, Maleda was fascinated to see that they were still underground.

"An underground city." She spoke with pure fascination. No matter how much she and Zaddae talked about it after their first stroll, she was still astounded.

"It is a marvel." Zaddae responded without looking back at her. "Inspiration from the people of the Ardhi nation. Homes and businesses all under our feet."

Zaddae halted and Maleda nearly ran into him.

"What's wrong?"

"I lost him."

"You lost him!?" Maleda tried not to let her voice rise into a panic.

"There's only one outpost around here. There is an abandoned station nearby, so he might try to keep people

off his trail. Just follow me." With that Zaddae took Maleda's hand and they strolled down the underground

avenue. Maleda was too overwhelmed by the gesture, but she squeezed back.

"Better for people to think that we're just innocent city goers." He smiled down at Maleda and his face

became a little harder when he focused on the streets in front of him. As they got further away from the station,

the streets stayed busy, but shadow seemed to lurk about the people around her."

"Not every place is as safe as others. Just stay close." Maleda did as advised and kept her environment in mind. Everything was illuminated by terratech lamps hung from doors or atop posts. She noticed clothing lines strung across tight alleyways, as well as decrepit signs hanging from iron work protruding above some doors.

Everything was coated in a layer of dust as all the buildings were made of the clay deep in the earth, the pillars that held up the city it seemed. Above them was a ceiling of clay and rock still in its natural rough form for the most part. They kept walking and Maleda felt a sudden burst of light from above. It was bright white but after her eyes adjusted, she saw that it was the sky. An entrance into the caverns of the underground parts of the empire. Pillars held up the broad opening with people filtering about the place as if it were a busy market. Zaddae and Maleda walked past the bustle until they came across a desolate and still dusty corridor. The traffic had stopped, and all was silent. Farther down the corridor, sunlight flooded the ground and then there was no more corridor. It was like they stepped into a bowl. The sky was above them and the bowl had layers each with dozens of open archways that led into darkened walkways. Zaddae looked at her in earnest. This was the abandoned station. Where would they start to look for Bu—

"Hello there, loves." A voice crooned. Zaddae's hand let go of hers, so he could draw his weapon. Maleda kept her hand near her dagger at her hip and they orbited around each other trying to find the source of the voice. The crooning came again. "It seems like you are a bit lost."

"Zaddae?" Maleda's face hardened as she sought the voice out, but her insides were screaming for her to run.

Then, someone walked out from one of the archways, a level above them. Their robes were blowing in the wind, but Maleda could still see the glimmer of something metal at his side.

"Welcome!" He announced with head tilted toward the sky. When he looked back down, Maleda could see his face was covered save for his eyes.

"A young couple like you should be out and about the empire." Maleda spun around to find a woman leaning in the archway behind them. She was dressed a little differently sporting bright striped leggings. She circled them widely like a predator sizing up its game. "You wouldn't happen to have any money would you?" Her venomous smile was coated with a thick layer of sweet innocence.

"Afraid not," Zaddae answered firmly, "but as pirates, you should be able to find it on your own."

"Pirates?" The man above laughed. "I always felt that we deserved a more sophisticated sort of title." He leaped from his perch and was on level with them. "We're something more like artists. What we do takes skill, motivation."

"Well, we have nothing on us save for our weapons and they are humbly made, wouldn't catch the price you'd be looking for."

"I'm sure." The woman laughed. Then, they just stood looking at them both.Something was off. Why hadn't they gutted them yet? They should be dead by now, unless they were wanted alive.

Maleda dared to ask, "What is your motivation?"

The woman released her sword swiftly and the metal sang, "A price."

CHAPTER 51 - MALEDA

"Ahh!" The woman charged at Maleda, but Zaddae shoved her out of the way. "Run!" he bellowed. Maleda obeyed, but she wasn't going to leave him, so she stayed as close as she could after she entered one of the corridors. The woman was gaining behind her, and her light footfall sounded efficiently treacherous. Zaddae was fending off the man as best he could, swords slashing against each other with grunts of resistance. A sharp slice of pain burned at Maleda's leg, and something ricocheted off a pillar. Throwing knives! She had throwing knives. Maleda was forced to dive deeper into the corridors. She couldn't afford to lose where she had been, but more than that she could not afford to hesitate. She stilled and dust lifted into the air. Maybe she lost her. Maleda spun around on herself studying the repeated columns that seemed to pattern her vision infinitely. Sunlight filtered onto the ground, except where she stood and she bolted just in time before the woman slammed into the ground, right where she would have been. Maleda ran back for the corridor that led toward the open arena. She sprinted until she skidded to a stop. There was no time to recover as the woman had already pounced on top of her. Maleda hadn't used her sword in combat yet, but she already had it across her chest ready to push against the sword slicing towards her. Her arms quaked underneath the weight of the woman, and she gritted her teeth willing herself to hold her off. She didn't dare take her eyes of the mad woman in front of her, not even when she heard Zaddae scream her name.

She would not back down, no matter what.

"Well, it looks like the end for you, love." The woman gave a cruel smile as she beared even more weight down and tried to jab Maleda's side with a kick. Breath was sucked from Maleda's body, and her eyes began to burn.

Her vision seemed to go dark for a moment, but she heard a screech and just like that Bamidele landed with a fury. She was immediately on Maleda and ripped the woman off her, throwing her onto the level above. Before the man could properly react, Bami had sprinted over and threw him up to where the woman was sprawled across the dirt. She let out a wretched screech that assaulted even Maleda's ears, but she was glad for it as their attackers scrambled to pick themselves up and run into one of the darkened archways.

Maleda let herself fall back onto the ground and squinted up at the sky, hand on her surely bruised side. She heard Bami purring as she stood over her, nuzzling her face into Maleda's, but Maleda just wanted space to breathe. She patted Bami's head while trying to get her to inch away.

"Yes, yes, thank you. Oof!" Instead, Bami collapsed onto Maleda's stomach staring at her with pleased eyes and tail swinging happily through the air. Zaddae came to the rescue and snapped his fingers, but he was still breathing heavily.

"Come on now. Get off her."

Bami looked back at him and obeyed, but she grumbled to herself. Maleda sat up on her elbows and Zaddae knelt to be eye level with her.

"Are you okay?"

"Yes, all things considered. Do you think he's still there?"

"Yes," Zaddae started, "but it might take us too long to get to him on foot. Buru is efficient. He does what he needs to do and is on his way. Around this time, he's usually still there, but he might be gone by the time we arrive."

Bami seemed to squawk in answer to their forming question.

"We could fly there." Maleda suggested, brows rising.

"Pardon, but I am not getting on that thing. It doesn't seem like she cares for me."

As if Bami understood him clearly, she let out a daring hiss, feathers raised slightly. Zaddae seemed to itch to grab for his sword.

"Wait!" Maleda got to her feet and stood in between them looking from one to the other. "I don't know why you don't like each other so much, but this is not the time. When we catch Buru doing whatever he's doing and we've confirmed he's part of the plot to kill the princess and me, you can chase each other to your heart's content. Deal?"

Bami raised a brow at them both as if considering her words.

"I'll judge the matches." Maleda offered, but then she stepped to Bami's side and mounted her. It was awkward to rise as there was no stirrup or saddle, so she attempted to jump and slide herself up. However, she was inches from success, but before she could slide back down, Zaddae was their holding her legs and heaving her up. Bami grumbled a little.

"Bami..." Maleda warned. The griffin sounded like she was muttering of all things. Maleda offered Zaddae a hand and heaved him up as best she could. There was nothing to hold onto, save for wrapping their arms around her body, gripping her feathers, and leaning into her back.

"Is she even trained?" Zaddae questioned.

"Possibly..." Maleda responded. She whispered to Bami while she placed a hand on her head. "Let's try this."

They were instantly connected and Maleda reflected back to the drawing of the desert outpost that Zaddae had shown her. With a squawk, Bami was shooting up into the air. Maleda peered over Bami's side to see nothing but sand and the bowl they had once stood in was shrinking to the size of a divot.

Zaddae was leaning into Maleda's back and bellowed against the wind. Maleda let out her own scream and her stomach flipped, but at the same time she never felt more alive. She laughed trying to bring out some bravery. "I guess she knows where she's going!"

"She better!" Zaddae howled back.

The rapid ascent gradually slackened into a horizontal glide. Bami continued with her shadow sweeping across the sand and mountains beneath her. She was completely aware that they only stayed aloft for as long as Bami would allow. For all Maleda knew, someone could shoot them down, but she felt herself let go as she accepted the risk for this freedom. What would the ocean look like underneath her if Bami flew over it? She was drawn from her thoughts when she noticed Zaddae's arms wrapped around her waist. She did her best to look down without tilting her head. She did not want to think about anything to do with that, so she turned to him and the quiet awe in his face made something bloom in her chest.

"It's amazing, isn't it?" She gestured to the world below. "This freedom. So, when do we get to the outpost?"

"It's a little ways ahead. Part of it is nestled into the wall of a mountain, while another part of it stands above the dunes. I'll let you know when. It will shimmer like a lone gem in the distance."

There was quiet for a moment and the both of them just took in the wind and the open air.

"You'd think that being able to scale a building would make this a little easier for me." He chuckled arms still firm around her waist.

"Well." Maleda started. "You're able to control your pace and you're holding onto something that's still attached to the ground. Look, I'm scared but this feels so…" She couldn't put words to it, but she sucked in a breath, tilted her head to the sky, and let it go as emphasis for her non-verbal point. "You know," she said looking back at Zaddae. Her chest seized when she saw the softness in his eyes, the same softness from the time she had that nightmare and woke up to that same stare. His gaze shifted to what lay in front of them and he pointed. "There, she can take us down. Hide your face."

CHAPTER 52 - MALEDA

L ike Zaddae, Maleda pulled up the cloth over her face and turned to see something that indeed looked like a glimmer in the distance. Maleda beckoned for Bami to descend, and she obeyed. They were still a distance from the part of the outpost that jutted out of the sand and lay in the face of a lone mountain of red rock. The building was stark white against the red, but it was nearly encased by a crevice-like passage of the same red rock, like a gateway. Maleda spotted dots patrolling various points of the structure. If this was a research outpost, then what sort of research prompted security? They crept closer and closer, keeping out of sight.

"How do we get in?" Maleda asked.

"Well." Zaddae began. "To get in, we will use a back entrance. These things were built to withstand emergencies, so there should be a cave in the recesses of the mountain that leads into the outpost. Like for an evacuation. One leads out on the other side of the mountain."

"All right." Maleda nodded, but not two steps into the start of their new direction, Bami was pawing at her face. She still followed, but she started to squawk. Zaddae and Maleda's eyes widened, and they scanned Bami, but saw no sign of injury. Zaddae even laid his hands on her head, but that just made her buck him off. Maleda put hands on either side of Bami's skull and cooed. "What's wrong? You have to be quiet." She moved her hand to the center of her head and Maleda saw something wrapped in darkness with a poisoned smile. "I see you there. Now where are you? If you tell me a story, I'll make it painless" it sang. Maleda let go and nearly fell on her back. They still had to round the corner to get to Zaddae's intended entrance. Bami still whined and swatted around her head.

"What's going on?" Zaddae said as he tried to help her up.

"Who goes there?!" A voice bellowed from around the corner. Zaddae cursed under his breath. He looked about frantically, feeling the wall of red and when he found a satisfying spot, he started to kick it in until he successfully created a hole, large enough to fit Bami. "Time to improvise," he said as he shoved Maleda into the hole with the sounds of Bami close behind followed by a great boom. She closed her eyes as she tumbled, afraid of what she would fall into. When they finally stopped, Maleda was dazed, head still spinning in her skull and her surroundings were dark. And soft? Bami's wings unfurled from around her and she could see the crystals that lit up the cavern. She looked back up the slope, messy from the fall and saw that their way had been sealed shut. Her body would not allow her to sit up yet, so she merely rolled over to see Zaddae facing away from her, also under Bami's wing. Maleda crawled over to him and shook him. When he didn't respond, she pulled him until he rolled over. There was a small cut on his head, but he still slept.

"Zaddae?" She whispered unsure of their company, even though they had just disturbed a mountainside. Maleda found the strength to sit up then and drew her knees in, not sure what to do. She lightly slapped his face, but he remained unresponsive. She turned away looking to Bami and then at the field of crystals surrounding them. Panic rose in her system and then Bami seemed to quirk a brow and let out a short and efficient bellow, causing Maleda to scream.

"Aah, Bami!" Maleda stopped herself realizing they were in private territory, but then Maleda heard a groan and her eyes went wide. She turned to see Zaddae pushing himself up.

"Zaddae!" She cried and embraced him.

"Ah! Let go, let go!" He said between his teeth. Maleda pulled back and saw him bent over, holding his side.

"I'm sorry!" She realized.

"It's fine. My side just got smacked around. Well, that was improvising." He gritted out pointing up to where they had fallen from. "They will think some poor creature got crushed in a landslide."

"So, we can still move on after you've recovered of course?" She beckoned Bami over, so he could lean on her.

"Not exactly. I knew about that one cave system around the other side. This one is connected to it, I know, but I've never seen it other than on a map."

"So, you know where we are in theory?"

Zaddae nodded. Maleda looked about the space trying to get a sense of the giant cavern littered in crystals growing out of the ground. There were tunnels high above them, but no stairs led to them. Light filtered through the walls of the cavern opposite them in thin beams.

"What's that?"

"Light from the inside. We are just outside the walls and under them."

"Do you think we could navigate with them?"

"Quite possible." He said while heaving himself up. Maleda assisted him. "Thanks. Let's climb those crystals."

So, they began their ascent with some difficulty, mostly trying to get over aches and pains from their fall. One after another they grabbed onto crystals that jutted out of the ground like forgotten spears on a battlefield until they heaved themselves up to the grates that let in the thin slivers of light. At first, it was so bright that nothing was truly recognizable, but as their eyes adjusted, Maleda made note of the pillars of darkness that interceded the light for brief moments. People walking. Yet, it did not seem like anyone was patrolling this space. Some had bundles of scrolls under their arms, while others had books. Each person was draped in some range of armor and robes, but they seemed to be more comfortable with the cargo that they carried than the clothes they wore to aid them in a fight.

"Do you think we could follow the light from the halls to find Buru?"

"Yes." Zaddae shook his head. "We could try that."

So, Maleda and Zaddae climbed atop Bami with Zaddae closest to Bami's head, so he could direct her. Bami was slightly ruffled, but she obeyed Zaddae's command. They drew deeper into the cave, away from where they had fallen, but after they got their bearings, it became easy to understand how the raw, jagged caves flowed with the building. The light from the grates danced between the crystals, creating a glowing field. As they silently crept over the crystals studying the halls, Maleda could not silence her mind.

"I never did say thank you, did I?"

Zaddae craned his neck to look at her. "For what?"

"For…well…everything. I can't imagine what it was like to endure Buru's beating when I first came to the university. In spite of that and threat towards your position, you have still done your best to not just be my guide in all this, but my friend."

His shoulders seemed to slacken even though he fisted Bami's feathers.

Maleda continued. "I just can't get over the fact that so much has happened and I may not ever remember it. It's hard to know what to feel. It's amazing that I haven't gone forgotten to everyone."

Zaddae laid a hand on hers briefly but kept his eyes on the inside of the building.

"I would never forget you." A heat lingered on Maleda's hand, but she did not have time to contemplate it because she saw Buru striding down the hall, making a sharp turn to the right. Zaddae coaxed Bami in Buru's direction. They were so close. As the walls of the cave changed between light filtering from the building and the crystal embedded walls, Maleda was afraid they would lose him. It was like Buru was hurrying towards something. They stopped when Buru reached an enclosed room. It had the makings of an office with papers thrown everywhere, scrolls of all sizes on shelves, and other oddities. He paced and kept turning about himself as if he were thinking. Was he deciding what to do with Maleda's suspicion of his betrayal? She noticed a collection of different-sized glass containers on a counter on the wall opposite them. Each one had some sort of ingredient in it, some solid, some liquid. Maleda looked to Zaddae, and his eyes widened. She whispered, "What do you think he's doing?"

Zaddae's voice was a lethal whisper, "It could be a number of things, but given recent events and the ingredients, I would guess that he's making a poison. He could even be preparing a spell, using the objects as a conduit, which is as good as a poison anyway."

Maleda did not have to ask who it was for. Did Buru want to keep his betrayal under wraps at such a treasonous degree? Suddenly, he stopped pacing and stood in front of the beakers, facing away from them, releasing an exhale. It seemed like all sound was sucked from the room and Maleda wasn't sure if she needed to hold her breath.

Maleda's heart pounded. He did not see them, could not have seen them. Perhaps, he suspected someone would follow him and he did not want an audience. He looked off to the side but turned away just as quickly. His shoulders rose and Maleda could see his hands balled up into fists on the counter. He muttered, but although she could not hear the words, the rhythm of it sounded like a spell. Maleda grabbed Zaddae's shoulder, but he already put Bami into action.

Miraculously, she stayed silent, and she was speeding across the field of crystals in a glide. There was some grumble that followed close behind, but Maleda wouldn't dare to see what it was. She squeezed Zaddae from behind at the memory of the one-eyed creature that came after her in the forest. The sound grew more intense, like an approaching wave about to swallow them up.

"Just hold on!" Zaddae yelled over the beasts behind them. Bami continued to shoot forward through the tangle of darkness, light, and crystal that bounced around the cave. They got to a more open part of the cavern where the glittering ceiling seemed to be a mile away and Maleda saw their reflection bounced back at them from stagnant water below. Bami was flying low enough to disturb the water beneath them, so when Maleda turned her gaze towards the reflections behind them, all she could see was a fury of blurred movement and all she could hear was the gnashing of teeth. *No, don't run away. We have so much to discuss.* Maleda shook her head trying to rid herself of the voice, but it seemed to fade off on its own. When she looked ahead, they were headed for a thin pass, too thin to fly through. Maleda could feel her stomach shift upwards as Bami dropped to the ground and began to sprint for it. There had to be an unfathomable number of possibilities for directions to go in the cave system and only the people skilled in its secrets knew how to get out. Maleda hoped that Zaddae knew what he was doing.

The roaring grew louder and Bami kept true to her speed, splashing through the water. Maleda's heart seized when she saw that there was a wall of rubble before them with nowhere else to turn only a hundred yards away, but Zaddae kept kicking Bami's side urging her to go on.

Maleda yelped into Zaddae's ear. "What are you doing!? There's nowhere to go!" They were halfway there.

He gripped her hands banded around his waist, "Just trust me!" He went back to burying his hand in Bami's fur and leaned even farther into Bami's back with Maleda following along. They were going to careen into the wall, leaving their scattered bodies to be picked off by whatever was behind them. They were almost upon it, when Bami shot upward to a spotlight that Maleda had not noticed before. As the sunlight and shadow of the forest rippled across their faces, the sound of the shrieks and roars faded behind them.

Then, it grew silent save for their blustering through the trees, until Bami failed to dodge a branch and tumbled to the ground. She let out a growl, while Maleda and Zaddae were bucked into the air. Just after they grabbed onto each other, they were enveloped in black, tumbled, and then Bami opened her feathers and released them from her grasp. Maleda was still trembling as she continued to hold onto Zaddae. She could have sworn he was shaking too.

"Oh, by the sands! What was that?!"

Zaddae helped her sit up and they saw that they had broken past the edge of the forest with the mountain in the distance containing the post on the other side. Zaddae took too long to answer, sitting in silence staring at the mountain dungeon they had just escaped.

"I don't know what he did." Zaddae's voice was clouded in fear. It seemed like a struggle for him to hold it all together, but he kept his voice level. "All the sounds. I can't tell if it was one big creature or a collection of many.Either way, we can't stay here." He helped Maleda to her feet. "It would be best if we stayed to the ground." So, they started walking.

"I don't understand what's happening. Buru has always been our ally. What could he gain from joining with creatures, like the Popobowa and whatever else was in there? Who's he in league with?"

Ayam and Noslen warned her about keeping the occurrences that took place as private as possible. The less people who knew, the less danger she would be in, but it didn't seem to matter anymore. Buru helped find her in the desert. Buru likely triggered the warning animation and helped whoever the titan was make the curtains nearly squeeze her to death. Buru knew someone was watching him and sent monsters after them. Maleda hoped Ayam and Noslen could forgive her, but she could not keep everything to herself anymore.

"Zaddae." She grabbed his arm and he looked at her, concern knitting his brows. "I need to tell you something."

So, she told him everything. She told him about Ayam and Noslen, how they knew the princess and that her simply making the information surrounding Clementina known aloud could endanger her more. She described how Noslen defeated the Bowa and how they promised to keep Bami safe from the thing possessing her. She explained the dreams she had where she visited a purple-toned landscape and the voice she heard almost an hour ago, which was the same voice she heard in her dreams heard from the display.

Grief struck Zaddae's face and something like…heartbreak.

"How could Buru do this? He was always tough on me, but I looked up to him in some ways. I never thought that he would have killed the princess, would have tried to kill you. Why has he waited so long though? You're back and clearly not dead."

"He wanted someone to perform when the emperor and empress return with a foreign ally. I think he intends to use the moment as a demonstration. The other day, you could chalk that up to the 'other side' showing their discontent, but the idea is that we shouldn't let that scare us. We should still show the spirit of this nation and show our pride to our leaders. Then, the day of the performance, another account happens. Another murder, chaos ensues, and these creatures could help him rule the country and whoever he's working with."

"Why would he do that?"

"I don't know. Power is such a base excuse, but it is the most common one.I don't know how he gets in my head and frankly I don't want to know."

"We need to seriously consider our next move."

"I think we need to perform." Zaddae's brows shot upwards, but Maleda held up her hands to stop his incoming argument. "Just hear me out. We don't know what's going to happen if I run. Last time, we lost our memories of the war and the face of our enemy. Who knows what could happen this time? We need to stand and fight. He thinks that we are helpless and can't do anything against this. He's taking this time to make fear a slow burn, but if he's making something in that outpost to poison me, perhaps we can make something as a countermove."

Zaddae let out an exasperated sigh. "I'm listening."

CHAPTER 53 - MALEDA

As they walked back to the university through the forest and then through the underground tunnels where Maleda once found Bami, they decided that they would make a counteracting agent, one that would out Buru once and for all. As for the performance, it would be revolutionary in the face of all that was lost. They stayed in the dusty ancient tunnels until they reached the stairs that led up to Collections in the museum. Maleda went first to check that no one was patrolling the area. As she peered through the crack in the door, she only observed the tapestries, pottery, and other art still in its place, save for the giant statue of the princess. The block that it stood on was still there, but the statue had been moved, probably restoration for celebrating the princesses' birthday coming up. She dismissed it and stepped up into the room, but before she could announce that the coast was clear, professor Ramonda was strolling down one of the aisles.

She panicked but moved to shut the floor door.

"Hey, w—" Zaddae started, but Maleda shook her head. He recognized the warning and backed down.

"Go towards the room at the top and just stay there." Ayam and Noslen would have to forgive her for telling Zaddae everything, but hopefully they would protect him. They protected Bami, anyway.

Maleda feigned interest in one of the tapestries when she heard Ramonda call her from behind.

"Maleda." Maleda turned around and saw Ramonda standing at the edge of an aisle. "Maleda, did anything *exciting* happen today?" She felt

Ramonda's eyes scoping her clothing.

"I was just out in the city, but I came back to look at some of the artifacts. I noticed that the Princess's statue is moved. Is it in preparation for the princess's birthday?"

"Well, yes, much preparation is needed at this time. The emperor and empress died in a way the day they lost Clementina. Everyone did, actually. But this time is meant to remember what she meant to us." Ramonda guided Maleda until they reached the wall of mirrors adjacent to where Clementina's painting used to be. "I know that a complex rests in you because part of you doesn't remember her, while another feels this ancient connection. It may feel like you'll never know, but I think that you can. Maybe what you want to find about yourself is buried deep, in a darkened place that requires some light."

Maleda nodded. "I hope so, because everything does seem like I should know it. I should know her, but I don't." Ramonda laid a hand on Maleda's shoulder.

"But you better get ready. The emperor and empress are back and want to see you at the castle." Ramonda left Maleda with a smile and proceeded out of Collections. Maleda's shoulders sank, and her mind was spinning, not with a particular thought, but as if it was a light that was too bright. She remained that way as she walked to the tunnel that led to the space above the tower with Ayam and Noslen. When she entered the room, she saw Zaddae sitting on a raised root at a notable distance from Bamidele, but Ayam and Noslen were nowhere to be seen.

"Are you sure that they were here? When we entered, there was no sign of them," Zaddae said waving a hand at the empty room.

"They were," Maleda started, "Maybe the events as of late have made them weak and they are resting beyond where we can see."

She hoped that they would come back soon. Maleda actually wanted them to meet Zaddae. "What did Ramonda say?"

"Just that the emperor and empress are back and wish to see me at the castle as soon as possible."

"Well, then you will need an escort." Zaddae smiled. Maleda smiled back, but her smile was brittle recounting all that she had lost and what they were about to do to fight to get it back. Zaddae saw her anguish and strolled over, taking Maleda into a comforting embrace. She hugged him back and Bami purred, cocking her head at them. Maleda stared over Zaddae's shoulder, past the tree and the glass to look out over the city. This place would not be subject to the tyranny and underhandedness of Buru.

CHAPTER 54 - THE PRISONER

The prisoner found himself looking through two windows, but somehow it didn't bring in anymore light. He'd already seen different things through his one window. What circumstance was granted that allowed him to have two windows in this world of mist and gray? As curled in on himself, he saw two different places at once through the windows.

CHAPTER 55 - MALEDA

Maleda changed into something that was still travel-worthy, but had a more cheery, innocent look to it as opposed to her all-black garb from earlier. The sun was on the verge of starting its pathway down as they went through the city. Ramonda would have preferred a more discreet route, but Maleda insisted that they walk through the city. They couldn't go so far as the coast to get a look at the ocean, but the thought of golden sand turned watery, and blue was still on her mind. She and Zaddae ventured to the castle, while surrounded by guards who kept their distance, per Maleda's request. Some guards were inconspicuous posing as citizens, while others were close by, proudly striding in their armor. The city bustled with activity and colors were strewn throughout the city while people honored the princess' memory. Maleda had never been through the front gates of the castle, even when she worked in the lab with the emperor or empress. She was always sneaking around with Zaddae and using the tunnels, so it was nothing short of special for her to see the garden verging on jungle that bloomed in front of the gorgeous castle, which stood like a terracotta titan, proud to be a part of the colorful earth around it. Zaddae escorted her quietly to the throne room, but when Maleda started to quiver he put a hand on her shoulder and gave a reassuring smile. She nervously smiled back. She hadn't even realized she'd been shaking and Maleda could not understand it. She had met the emperor and empress before and after a series of unfortunate events, they practically declared their adoptive love for her. They were her aunt and uncle after all. Maleda nodded that she was ready to enter the throne room and Zaddae signaled the guards standing on either side, so that they swung the doors open. Maleda had never found a time to enter this room either.

The throne room was…communal with chairs arranged in a circle to face inward, with a gap towards the door. There were two distinct chairs that stood out above the rest. The backs of them fanned out like that of a peacock, a bird that Maleda had seen roaming and posing in the streets. Yet, the emperor and empress did not appear to be there. Maleda's shoulders immediately slackened as she looked around for them, but when she turned to Zaddae, he was already gesturing towards the balcony. Once Maleda dodged the view of the peacock chairs, she saw the emperor and empress facing away, looking out over the balcony at the two shores. Where one city ended at the sea, another began at the shore just across from it. Mirriam was standing off to the side and noticed Maleda immediately with one side of her mouth pulling up to a grin. She looked to the emperor and empress, who turned to greet Maleda with a warm, almost melancholy pair of smiles. She wanted to break into a run, but instead briskly walked over and they immediately took her into an embrace. They were silent for a moment and Zaddae held back by the door, but Maleda could see his smile, a bit melancholic too. Once they loosened their grip, Maleda asked, "How was your trip?"

"Fruitful." The emperor answered. "There were many great discussions to be had about collaboration between the empire and the lands of the north. The King from the Whitlands is caught up in affairs at the moment, but he is sending his son ahead of him to come to your performance." The emperor looked between Zaddae and Maleda. "It's a show of good faith, that they care about…everything that's happened, and I appreciate them for it."

"Well." The empress declared. "We wanted to take you somewhere before all the real business begins. It's a place that you and Clementina both loved to visit. We thought it might calm your nerves before everything starts to rush."

So, they turned on their heels and proceeded through the throne room doors, with Zaddae and Mirriam tailing them. Mirriam had not spoken once, upholding the duties of an ever-silent guard, but she reached for Maleda's hand from behind and squeezed.

* * *

They met up with the royal children along the way and they greeted Maleda with a barrage of hugs, smiles, and hurried talking. Selene had her arms wrapped around Maleda as they continued onto their mystery destination and whenever she looked up at Maleda and smiled it seemed like her brown eyes captured all the light around her. Maleda caught Zaddae grinning sweetly at them and he looked back to the floor. After they walked through the castle they found themselves exiting onto the mountain it rested in. The wind greeted them by whipping up their robes and dresses and there was a golden glow over the grass as it danced. The empire was an array of lights and busy streets filled with buildings of all shapes and sizes, but Maleda's breath caught when she saw the blue dunes. That's all she could think to call them. She had desperately wished to see the sands move around her, like a golden ocean, but this was the real thing, and she couldn't get enough of it. It was like she was in the desert again, but everything was so fluid as if it could carry her anywhere. White light glistened on the surface on account of the setting sun and her heart sang with each crash it made against the distant rocks as well as the lull of waves rolling on the shore far below. The burning in the back of her eyes had returned, but she didn't care. This rolling majesty was the most beautiful thing she had ever witnessed.

Maleda gently pulled the still clutching Selene off her leg and laid a hand on her shoulder instead. Selene seemed to be content with letting go as she started to jump and dance around in the flowers that decorated the mountain. She even got the two youngest brothers to indulge her, while Akande kept them from becoming little menaces. Zaddae silently approached and stood by Maleda's side, while the emperor and empress were trying to tame their herd of children.

"May I ask what you're thinking?"

Maleda turned her head from the ocean and looked at Zaddae, who gave her a reassuring smile. For a second, Maleda noticed an odd shimmer about Zaddae. Maybe it was a glow of real joy, probably for the first time in the face of all this horror. Maleda could feel whatever was on his face in her heart and she felt weightless.

"Honestly, I'm taken with the ocean, and I wish I could just stay here and not do what we have to do tonight, but I can't imagine letting this city fall to war again either."She looked from the golden city to Zaddae's face. His eyes were still locked onto the breathtaking view, but something in his eyes had shifted. It was almost as if something in him was dying and he did not have time to mourn it, only time to appreciate what was in front of him, maybe who was next to him. Maleda had tried to dismiss her thoughts ever since she suspected what he and Clementina were, but she could not deny that her friendship with him felt inwardly complicated and on the verge of something new. "What are you thinking?"

Zaddae looked at her, the glint in his eye passing over in the light of the setting sun, "I'm thinking that you are a warrior. Don't be fooled by all the running and the sword fight. Your books and paints back at the tower are your weapons. Your strongest fight is in your mind. You fought to get back here even when you could only understand a fraction of the remains you found. Before this evening goes on, I just want you to know that I will find a way to help you fight and I want you to know that I'm sorry that I couldn't be there for you."

"There's nothing to apologize for. How could you know where I was and what I needed? I don't know what any of this means for the future, but I do know that you are the only one trying to help me figure this out. We will figure this out together. We will remember together, and I promise you that." There would be no declarations, not yet. That would be unfair.

"I hope so, because guests are arriving." Zaddae's eyes flitted over to the ships both in the air and in the sea arriving onto their side of the shore. The emperor and empress went and looked out too. "We better get ready for the performance." Zaddae smiled and guided Maleda back into the castle with the royal family and a grim Mirriam tailing them.

CHAPTER 56 - MALEDA

Maleda changed in her old castle quarters, so that she donned a blue dress with yellow detailing, subtle and sparkling. Zaddae had gone off to change but promised to meet her by the tree room where Clementina's memory was stored. Maleda wrapped herself in lightweight robes, so as not to damage or stain her performance wear. Additionally, her face was marked in illustrative lines and dots of white paint, what felt like a painted mask of sorts. As Maleda walked to the tree room, she realized that she had not seen Buru since they spied on him in the desert outpost. She was sure that he was still ignorant of their suspicions, but there was no doubt he would show up that night to finish what he started when he killed Clementina. The tree room glowed with orange light that filtered through the glass dome ceiling. Maleda stepped onto the root bridge and entered the archway. She was careful to not brush up against the art on the walls. She had been so lonely in the desert, but it was nice to see that her suspicions and dreams scrawled onto the wall finally came to mean something. She found herself staring at the signal of the blended mural she created and almost got lost in a trance when she heard the room doors open. She exited the tree and stood atop the bridge to see two pale males at the door. One was tall and had an unsettling curl of a smile atop a squat face with bone straight hair that flared out and down from his head, stopping at his shoulders. The other male was another matter entirely. Taller than Maleda at least by a head with hair cascading to his shoulders in inky waves. His eyes were jet black and seemed to be full of something like sorrow, but he looked at the floor in front of him as if it were too painful to voice. Something familiar lied in his face, but with Maleda's cursed memory she could not properly sort it out. The man with the Cheshire smile stood closer to the door and announced, "Hello, we had a feeling that we would find you here. My name is Calhoon, advisor to the King of the Whitlands, and this is Prince Zuvan. He is an acquaintance of the royal family and an acquaintance to Princess Clementina."

An acquaintance. Maybe Calhoon was just being formal because Zuvan's face looked like it was clouded with grief.

She bowed and stood back up. "I'm so sorry. I'm Maleda, cousin to Princess Clementina."

"I'm grateful that you made it." He spoke with a sweet, sad smile, but his charcoal eyes seemed to burn.

Just then, Mirriam burst through the door.

"Maleda, your presence is requested," she said staff in one hand. Why hadn't Zaddae come yet? She would find out later. She bowed again to the both of them as she hurried out of the room.

He smiled as she passed and said, "I hope that your performance is successful."

She looked back to see Zuvan standing bone straight, staring at the tree, shoulders sinking and head nodding towards the floor and then she was on her way to get ready for her part in the ceremony.

CHAPTER 57 - MIRRIAM

Mirriam had slipped out of the ceremony shortly after she had fetched Maleda. There was gaiety amongst the somber remembrance. The ceremony was for the dwellers of the city itself, but the Whitland King was to come and pay his respects. She knew that Maleda was set to perform and was sorry that she was going to miss it, but the lead she found was worth the guilt. It could save Maleda's life after all. After Maleda and Zaddae had been attacked, she did her best to hunt after the pale figure in black, searching for clues listening to whispers in the streets. At one point, she decided to go to the high window to see if the man in black left anything behind and Mirriam also tried to follow his most likely escape path. She traded the mind of a guard for that of an assassin. It was upon channeling that role that she found a scrap of parchment forgotten on a rooftop. She almost passed by it but she skidded to a stop. The marks left in the corner of that rooftop made it look like someone had been in a brawl. Someone had clawed the ground, the wall. The parchment itself was shoved in a crack as if the person did not want their attacker to see, but the map noted a desert outpost, so Mirriam followed it. She had seen Maleda and Zaddae coming back from the outpost and they looked shaken. Yet, Mirriam was told not to disturb their ventures. They didn't look injured and she was too far to hear them, but she knew the source of their panic was in that outpost, so that's how she ended up running for it. Perhaps this is where the assassin resided or maybe this was where the rumored beasts were hidden. Upon her arrival, she didn't see any activity and it looked everyone had cleared out to attend the princess's remembrance ceremony, even the guards that would be patrolling. It was eerily quiet with dusk approaching, but she steeled her spine and went forward. According to the map, there was a back entrance. She would be able to use it, unlike Zaddae and Maleda who lost that chance because of that humongous creature. Mirriam was a little nervous to meet it. That is if that time came. The entrance itself was nondescript, a hatch hidden in dust along with the handle. She started to lift it…

"Would you mind if I tagged along?"

Mirriam dropped the handle and in an instant drew her sword out to clash with that of the opponents. Her eyes widened as she recognized her opponent.

"Puzo!" Mirriam hissed. "What are you doing here?"

"Well, you didn't think that the emperor and empress just had you go out on covert missions without someone to watch your back?"

Mirriam raised a brow.

"Just to watch my back? Or to make sure that I wasn't a traitor?"

"Okay, a little bit of both." Puzo confessed, shrugging his shoulders.

They both still held their swords against each other's.

"So, why give yourself away?"

"Well, after what I've seen, I believe that you have no ill harm towards Maleda. On top of that, I don't know what you'll find in there, so I'd like for us to approach this together…if that's alright?"

Mirriam narrowed her eyes and lowered her sword.

"Agreed." Puzo nodded and Mirriam continued. "As you said, we don't know what's in here, so we must be prepared."

Mirriam turned back to the handle and lifted it to reveal a descent into a cave and they continued on.

Outside, the silence was tolerable, but once they were inside, it was suffocating. They soundlessly padded through the cave's field of crystals, but something surely waited for them. Puzo had felt it too. Mirriam could tell when she heard the whisper of him knocking an arrow. She already had her sword drawn.

She and Puzo went rigid as a low growl echoed off the walls of the cave.

A distant glow flashed in time with a thunderous shake.

Then another and another.

It was too quick for them to see what it was until the field of crystals lit up in the face of a creature made of innumerable spectrums of light.

CHAPTER 58 - MALEDA

It was tradition to hail the bright memory of someone in the empire. They remembered the princess by lighting lanterns and allowing them to be carried away by the warm wind under cover of twilight. Some were made of terratech lights sculpted into winged forms that flew over Maleda's head, only to settle and gently come apart in the water below as if they were blooming lilies. It was like a returning of sorts. No words were said as the masses turned away from the water and towards the castle once the lanterns had all flown away. Maleda could not believe that her performance with Zaddae would be the thing to bring up a positive memory of this princess, but it was chosen for a reason, and she would do her best to remember a friend that seemed so foreign. If not for her own peace of mind, then it would be for the peace of mind of the people who had loved her, still loved her. The royal family stood on an elevated platform with a crowd staring up at them. The paintings were each colorful stroke projected into the air, lit by firelight. Maleda spotted the emperor coming out of the castle with Zuvan, surely exchanging condolences as both of their faces seemed to be glazed with something sad.

She closed her eyes and her shoulders rose as she sucked in a breath, but when she opened her eyes and released the breath, she saw Zaddae on the other side of the platform nodding at her and giving a small smile. In crafting their new plan, Maleda realized that Clementina's spirit would likely have witnessed who her killer was and since she was surely watching from the ancestral lands, she'd be able to provide even more condemning evidence. That is why they painted their faces in lieu of ceremonial masks to hide their identity and help encourage Clementina to show herself. This remembrance ceremony would last days and there was to be feasting, more dancing, and sharing of memories of Clementina. After all the fuss of having Buru arrested, Maleda hoped that they could still do some of that. She wanted to properly remember Clementina and she had so much time to do it with her family, with Zaddae too. The orchestra started up behind them with the delicate dance of strings being carried in the wind and so the performance, the reveal, began.

Maleda and Zaddae walked towards each other, steady with the rhythm of the drums. They walked around each other in a tight circle, eyes locked onto one another. That was the moment that Bamidele would have come, but it was replaced with Maleda and Zaddae.

They had what seemed to be cloaks attached to each of their outfits, but they pulled the cloths over their heads to shield their faces, until the cloths reached their waists. They were each able to see through a square hole in the cloth stringed over with rows of cowrie shells. They spun around each other, making waves with the cloth and strutting around the stage. She could hear the gasps and murmurs bubbling up over the crowd, but she tried not to pay attention to them. As a girl, she was not supposed to be a dancer in an Egungun masquerade, but—besides Clementina's parents and siblings—she and Zaddae were closest to her and Maleda wasn't sure if they would encourage her to enact a summoning. The orchestra had crescendoed as they broadly circled each other and the drumbeats became more intense as they echoed through Maleda's bones. Maleda had read about what it's like for a spirit to possess someone but there was nothing like the present moment of it. That was the most that elders and scholars could agree on.

A now familiar burning sensation started behind Maleda's eyes, as if she had been crying. However, the pain faded as quickly as it came and Maleda's sight transitioned from the crowd in front of her. She was looking at her own body dance on the stage and her eyes were shining white, but the light encapsulated her whole body, and she heard a voice coming from where her body stood.

"She is my carrier and I'm her guardian just as I have chosen her to be a guardian," a feminine voice echoed.

CHAPTER 59 - MIRRIAM

A translucent marvel of a beast without a face, that contained an infinite spectrum of colors. Colors that she hadn't seen before. It stood before them like a cresting wave, continuously folding on itself. The growl that left it was wrong somehow. As the ripple of it resounded against Mirriam, she recoiled at the sound. Puzo let arrow after arrow fly, but the creature was left unaffected. Mirriam swore that she heard them clatter as if they just went through the creature. Mirriam rose her sword to the creature, but it was too far away.

It was hard to stamp down her awe of something that looked so otherworldly.

That was until Mirriam had to jump out of the way when it slapped a taloned hand down and scraped through the earth, leaving crystal rubble in its wake.

Side by side, she and Puzo faced down the creature.

"Any idea what this is!?" Mirriam shouted.

"No clue!"

The creature swiped again and they jumped back, only to be awarded by the creature's roar.

As Mirriam stared it down with its innumerable spectrums of light, she swore that each color had a mind of its own, moving inside the beast.

One of those colors crashed into the translucent skin that kept it leashed inside the creature and that line of color was directly in front of Mirriam.

The creature became manic then. Throwing itself into the walls as if it were going insane, causing Mirriam and Puzo to lose their footing.

Mirriam gasped as she was about to go down, but Puzo grabbed her and held her upright. It was just enough time for her to see that same line of color creep out through a hairline fracture of the creature and beeline for her. She tried to avoid it, but it crashed into her.

Her name was on Puzo's lips, but his hand was ripped from her arm as a spectral of light collided with him too.

She didn't know what Puzo felt, but Mirriam couldn't rise from her knees. She couldn't help the tears that streaked down her face. The creature in front of her wasn't exactly a soul-eater, but it kept half of hers inside it. The memory of Puzo threatened to drag her further into the earth. She couldn't stand to look at him. She remembered, not just her princess, but she remembered the wave of Maleda's power and what she saw. In a different sort of cave, when her spirit had first been flung across the continent. She remembered her homeland and…her family. Gods, were they alright? Were they still there? Later, she'd find out later. For now, Maleda had found a way to break the curse and Mirriam had to rescue her princess.

CHAPTER 60 - THE PRISONER

They were all in a prison of shadows, murky and gray with the fabric of reality undulating like a wave. Yet, he couldn't see anyone else. It was like his captor wanted to keep him separated and alone, but he could sense them there, could feel their light, the colors of their spirits all trapped here. Still, there was one spirit he couldn't sense, and he believed it was because she was not there. Somehow, she got away and he was grateful for it. He held onto that kernel of hope and let it be a reason for him to keep breathing. Maybe he should have let it be a reason for him to stop breathing. It wasn't safe, no matter how much he wanted to see her again.

CHAPTER 61 - MALEDA

This was not in the books.

Before Maleda could properly panic or figure out how to get back into her body, she felt herself being pulled as if she were attached to something by a thread and she was flying. With the sound of the drums still present in her ears, she flew past the crowd and over the castle towards the university, the world now tinged purple. It was like her vision was split because she could still see her body surrounded by light.

"Just as I took the form of a bird and flew to the beyond, I have kept her split, one half safe in an inanimate form. Like a butterfly in a chrysalis."

It seemed like there was no obstruction to her as she passed through the walls of the tower all the way through to a hidden room in Collections, where Clementina's statue was waiting. On this side of existence, Maleda could see the golden light glowing within the statue. A light that slowly seemed to shift and move through a spiderweb of cracks. Maleda laid a hand on the statue and Clementina had awoken. In a flash of light across the sky she flew to Maleda's body, but Maleda was still outside of herself, still looking back at her body, but the voice remained the same.

"The attempted killer will reveal himself and the souls that he split." The feminine voice continued.

It was only then that her vision snapped back into her own body, but she didn't see Clementina's spirit leave hers…Maleda almost didn't notice Zaddae and that he was also stuck in place. Zaddae had fallen to the ground, just as the red crystalgram stirred itself from the painting again. *I SEE YOU!* The voice shrieked in her head, but Maleda saw the mouth moving on the crystalgram too. Her split vision was above the panicking crowd and from her body now. Maleda fell to her knees to help Zaddae, but the air seemed like it became thinner, and she could barely feel Zaddae underneath her fingertips. She turned to Buru, but when he made his move, it was not at her, but the crystalgram. He was trying to weaken it, but either his powers were failing him, or the true nature of that crystalgram had finally unleashed itself. She would have scrambled to Buru, but Zaddae was too weak, and his breathing was too labored. Maleda looked to the crowd and saw someone stalking slowly to the stage amongst all the frantic runners.

"You will find that another spirit has been split as well." Zuvan's voice carried through the crowd as a layered whisper. Zuvan's eyes were pinned on her as he stalked closer and Maleda looked down too Zaddae who was no longer opening his eyes and in a matter of seconds the essence of him seemed to fade in her hands. She shrieked and tried to find some remnant of him, but he had just disappeared. In her panic, the headache returned, but it was more splitting than ever. Tears streamed down her face as she scrambled away from the crystalgram. She found herself closer to Zuvan only to see him fall and convulse on the ground, but as suddenly as he fell, he was on his knees. His expression was strained, and charcoal eyes had gone to a mixture of topaz and red.

Mirriam was already there and caught Maleda as she struggled to stay on her feet. She swore that she could hear the whooshing of flames. Everything was fading in and out then. Maleda found herself trapped in an expanse of darkness, like a cave, and she heard shrieking like before, but it had faded. Lights bloomed in front of her in the darkness, all of different colors, and they molded themselves into people. All the people, whose souls had been split. Each one had its own thoughts, voice, feelings, and fear. Each one had its own body too. She saw faces that she recognized, as well as those that were to far away to remember. They were flying away from the cave in the outpost to reunite themselves with their bodies, to be full souls again. One familiar professor stopped in front of her and Ramonda took Maleda's face in her hands and said, "Thank you." With the flight of the spirits, Maleda found herself in darkness that suddenly became a hazy purple-blue light, and she was in that land of her dreams again. She was surrounded by new pillars of light blooming in front of her. The pillars died down until the glow was reserved to just their eyes. There was a pantheon of bodies that surrounded her, the Orisha. She was remembering.

CHAPTER 62 - MALEDA

A woman stared at her, and she never spoke, never made a sound, but the look on her face told Maleda exactly what was about to happen. Maleda was running backwards. Time was undoing itself as she retreated from the dunes. Time seemed to move forward again when she was back at the castle, in the Empire of Two Shores. The emperor and empress doted on a young girl, who had not yet hit her years that led to the thousand. There were other children like her, people she once knew. Cherika, Jassiem, Jasmine, Dunia, and Girani. They ran along the shoreline on the other side of the empire, closest to the Whitlands. Free, young children.

Then, one day those children wrestled with an incomprehensible fever, a poison. Only the terra stones provided by Olodumare could save them and only if it were sewn into their very bodies. They had started the ritual, so those terra stones unleashed powers that had laid dormant, but Clementina needed more. She needed all the elemental terra stones and they saved her while she quivered in a cold sweat. When she opened her eyes, they danced with rainbows and faded to brown again, as it would do off and on. But the king, Clementina remembered the king who looked at her power with jealousy and lust. The secret conversations she heard. His eyes burned with an orange fire. The Empire had helped them, traded with them, helped build them up, but he wanted more. The Princess knew she would have to run and made a plan with her friend, the Prince Zuvan. She knew the attempt on her life was certainly coming, as he let her know every word of it. People were disappearing and there was talk of creatures that did not walk this world.

Clementina knew that she would die and so she left clues to be found, unraveled, and hopefully understood. She did not know the attack would come so soon. She had not been able to get letters to the other kingdoms. There was no time for anything but to run. She and Mirriam ran through long tunnels and the oasis had still been standing at that time, but fire rained down and blew it apart. They were running, but Maleda got hurt and Mirriam disappeared. She sent a prayer to a child of Sky Father wrapped in golden yellow, a bargain really, but once her masked opponent broke it, she was flung across the great beyond. Once she knew she'd be lost, she sent another prayer for someone to hold her memories and the knowing half of her spirit. A prayer to save Zuvan too. When she fell, it was not clear if she would wake, and she didn't. Maleda did.

As she stood on that purple plain, no one spoke. Everything flooded back to her, but it was like she remembered the life of someone else, as if this body did not belong to her. There was a hum thrumming in her that she did not hear, but rather felt. It was more than a simple kinesis mentioned in her books. It was her magic. She couldn't stand, so she fell to her knees. There was no uncle and aunt, no cousins. Only a mother, father, brothers, and a sister. She was no friend to Clementina.

"Princess Clementina Maleda?"

Her mother handed her name down to her, but she always preferred her second one. She was Clementina, but Maleda could not accept it. It was her great-grandparents radiating with the purple light of the land.

"We were hoping you would return." She looked at them and she tried to calm the shaking that rattled her insides. They were radiant in comparison to the faded light they emitted before. She spun on herself looking at the circle of pillars of personified strength around her, all robed in their different colors. But one of them was missing.

"Where is Oshun?" Her voice didn't sound like it did before like her accent had morphed in the time that she was gone. The words fell from her mouth before she felt sure enough to ask them, but she received her answer when a woman draped in silky yellow appeared and silently approached her.

Her smile was soft and refreshing like water and her skin was brown like the walls of the castle in the empire. She pointed two fingers at Maleda's collarbone.

"I am in you." Oshun spoke with a voice that moved like honey. She gestured to the other Orishas. "We all are in you."

She could feel them all in her, almost like they were all breathing the same breath, except it wasn't burdensome. It was *right* somehow. Maleda couldn't bring herself to think it was true, but she asked anyway.

"Why?" Oshun tilted her head at Maleda as if to say *you know why*, but she answered her anyway.

"In the beginning days of this world, we all lived down here together, one and the same. Over time, our Father gave us powers to care for this planet—"

"It was at my advice that Sky Father rained down the powers." Cham chimed in, still on Maleda's finger. "And he granted me the ability to remain and shapeshift beyond my colors."

So, Cham was the chameleon.

Oshun continued. "And then humans came along to protect this planet too and to seek our wisdom. Many years ago, there was a fight in the heavens for someone became jealous of what Father could give, what he possessed. They kept their face hidden when they revolted, but after a trying war that rattled the stars, they were struck down here, along with their followers. Since they had chosen the dark path, they would not be able to properly see the light without unspeakable pain and destruction to themselves, so they hid in the darkness, until they found bodies that they could possess or people who would join their side."

Maleda's hands were shaking, and she clutched them to her chest, right next to her rattling heart.

"And just as those who had chosen the dark path were locked into the world of the living, we were also locked out from the otherworld. You were sent to watch that planet because it was safest, as there was little to no magic and the magic that was there was *warped*. It was unlikely that you would be found. The bargain had to be that strong to keep them at bay. But we saw that they would not stop. The leader would not stop. So, the only way we could make sure this world was protected was to bind ourselves and our powers to souls throughout time, so that we could keep an eye on the world without actually stepping foot on it. You were so young when I chose you to be the ultimate, the one to have all of us in you. Something had been done to you, and by the dark ones, I could sense it. Your father and mother labored over your broken body and prayed for your survival, so I and the others filled the stones with our power and brought you back to a full life. *You* are the only one that has all of us."

Maleda looked between Oshun, the other Orisha, and her own hands trying to parse through the information that she was submerged in as well as the things they did not say. She barely broke the surface of her thoughts to ask a question. "But what about everything that I saw? The suffering and the people working so hard to reclaim and maintain their magic?"

"Well, I wanted you to see what you'd be fighting for, but I suppose some of us would argue that the inspiration was a bonus." Oshun offered a half-smile, but she had a knowing look in her eyes. Maleda felt as if she was saying *I know you want to fall apart, that you need to, but not yet...not yet.*

There was a poisoned smile and a metal face she could barely remember. All the memories that went by felt like they didn't belong to her. They were like her dreams painted clearly, but they were hanging in the halls of a home that didn't feel quite like her own. Maleda tried to brush this aside, especially when she saw the simultaneous flinch that went through each Orisha.

"What's happened since I've been here?" Maleda asked quietly.

"The empire was under attack, and we believe the leader has made their intentions clear. The power that was used to save you is the same power that lies in you, that you are learning to control. They want it, but you cannot let that happen for if they have your power, then they have access to ours."

There was an undeniable, yet unnameable change in the air.

"Remember, we are not here for placating and begging, but for manifesting. We've been inside you all along and we will be with you. Just concentrate and you will find us within you again." Oshun put a hand to Maleda's face, the way a mother would and she saw the Mariner Prince again.

CHAPTER 63 - THE MARINER PRINCE

Maleda was disembodied again, watching the scene unfold in front of her. The king fought his closing eyelids as the girl paused to look back at him and he drifted off as she walked out of the room. Once he was deep in his slumber, the king woke to find the world toned purple around him. He looked out the window cut into the wall and he saw that the sky was toned purple and blue, with lights moving through it like gentle spirits dancing in the wind. He looked back into the room and saw that there was a group of people standing at the foot of the bed, decked in the regalia that made him think of royalty, but he recognized these people from stories passed down and illustrated scrolls. These were not mere women and men, but the Orisha.

The king went into a cold sweat as he stared at them and they just looked back at him.

"Why do you quake, King?" the woman in yellow asked.

The king did not know how to answer her, but he tried anyway.

"I'm in a strange land and the people here speak a tongue that I don't understand...and you're here."

"We're always here," the woman in yellow walked over to him, "You know that very well."

"Yes, but I converted-"

"You and I know both know that was only for alliances and royal courts. It never truly happened inside. Even with the name of another on your lips, you still placate Sky Father for help."

The king was still astonished that they stood there, but he managed to ask a question.

"What has happened outside?"

"We are in the ancestral land. It seemed best to talk on this side of the realm."

"I don't know what I'm supposed to-"

The King stopped short when Oshun was inches from his eyes. He heard a scoff from one of them, but Oshun paid them no mind.

"You know that I guide love and sweet water. Pay no attention to the ignorance and aggression from iron and war." She briefly glanced back at Ogun and then focused back on the king. "There is more worth in alliance here, more for your future, more for the harmony of the world."

"What do you mean?"

Oshun retreated a few inches and maintained eye contact with the king.

"In a time coming, one of your descendants will have all the Orisha. She will go against all odds to save the world as you know it, just as I did when I took the form of a bird and flew to Sky Father in the beyond. But unlike my solo trip, she will need allies."

"What am I supposed to do?"

"Nothing. Not yet, anyway. Just continue as you are, King Noslen. Bring people together and build an empire."

Maleda's eyes widened and her mouth hung open. All this time...

Oshun smiled as she rose from his bed and stalked away back to the others. It seemed like she briefly looked at Maleda's intangible form, before her eyes went back to the Orisha.

"What about my men?"

"In due time."

"How do I know that they won't interrogate me and want me killed?"

With back still turned, Oshun chuckled and spun to face the king with an amused smile on her face.

"My king, they may just regard you as a God."

The king was confused and found that his body was too heavy to lift from the bed, too heavy to follow the Orisha. He found that his vision blurred and the Orishas were getting farther and farther away. Still, he called after them "wait…wait," until his world faded into darkness. It was like Maleda and the king mirrored each other as her body became impossibly heavy and she beckoned to them as well, but Oshun merely touched Maleda's face again. Maleda closed her eyes and then she opened them to find herself encapsulated by a starry night sky.

V

Part Five

MOURNING

CHAPTER 64 - MALEDA

They were in the desert again. It was hard for her to sit up, but Maleda managed to turn her head and the white walls stained red that surrounded her were unfamiliar. There was a mountain there too. Bamidele was curled behind her, supporting her head. Were they back at the oasis? No, these walls were different and still standing. White walls against red rock. It was the desert outpost. The evil one and their legion had destroyed it. That beautiful repository of knowledge had been decimated. Hopefully, they had all gotten out by the time they sensed danger. Maleda's power flared like heat with her anxiety. Mirriam was crouching with her sword out and her eyes flicked this way and that, until she caught sight of Maleda waking. She rushed over, sword gone limp in her hand and her shoulders slumped a little, as if she'd been holding her breath.

"Are you all right?" Mirriam tried to hold back the panic in her voice.Maleda nodded and looked down. Apparently, that wasn't enough for Mirriam and she put a hand on Maleda's shoulder encouraging her to look up again.

"Maleda, you need to tell me if you're hurt or if something's not right. We can go back to the oasis. It will be alright. I just—"

"I know Mirriam!" Maleda raised her voice just shy of a yell, as she was not aware who lurked in the darkness. Then, those words sparked the treacherous wobbling in her voice. "I know that I have the elemental powers of the Orisha and that the Orishas can speak to me and that I am the princess to the empire! I know that Clementina and I are one and the same, that my soul was split, like everyone else." Her powers were warm under her skin, but it felt wrong this time and her stomach gave her pains in protest. "Where are they? Where are the emperor and empress?" It was strange even then to refer to them as mother and father. Mirriam opened her mouth, but then she immediately cast her eyes down to the ground. Was Maleda supposed to demand it of her as the princess? Before Maleda could decide on how to get it out of her, Mirriam helped Maleda to stand, and they stood on some prominent rocks jutting out of the side of the mountain and Maleda saw it all from a distance.

Smoke was rising from the city. There was an orange glow that darted around the city. No. Everyone was in desperate need.

"I don't know where they've gone." That wasn't good enough.

"Take me to them!" Maleda demanded, voice not free of its shake. "Take me back to the castle, I have to see. We can't run again! They'll just find us and do something even worse."

Mirriam looked from Maleda back to the ground again. "I cannot and will not risk your life."

"Well, whether you lead me or not, I'm going!" The fear registered in Maleda's mind, but she couldn't consider it, not now. She would have to be scared later. Bami seemed to squawk in agreement. For a second, Maleda wasn't sure if Mirriam would truly hold her ground, but she huffed and shook Bami to get her up. Maleda boarded her first and then Mirriam saddled up behind her. Then, Bami launched herself into the sky, a silent and speeding shadow in the night.

* * *

Bami tried to stick to the outskirts as best as she could for the sake of safety in the shadows, but Maleda still felt the warmth of the fires. The whole city was not overtaken, but there were certain spots that looked like they were ravaged, as if they were targeted, like someone was searching. The school, the tower specifically and the castle in the distance. They sped towards the castle, and it didn't take long to find a makeshift entrance of a hole in the roof. The hallways were trashed with glass, wood, holes in the wall, and other debris. The silence was the loudest thing that Maleda had ever heard. In spite of all the bodies of guards and others running around the halls, she walked slowly trying to ignore the crimson that crept along the walls and the sheets with hands and feet sticking out.

Innocents who had been hurt, killed because she was revealed. Maleda walked slowly to the last place they had all had a quiet moment together. The door to the throne room was ajar and the golden light of torches was shining through. When Maleda entered it took all she had not to fall to her knees. She saw the sword of her father stuck into his throne, just as her mother's sword was. Twin swords each with a message on paper smeared with blood. It started with the paper on her mother's throne. In order to read it clearly, she had to relieve it from the sword that pinned it down, so she held her mother's sword in one hand and the note trembled in the other. The crackling of the fire and the distant shouts faded. Maleda simply looked to the empty strap on her belt, where those swords were always supposed to be. She put her mother's at her side first. Then, she grabbed her father's sword and read the continuation of the note as she strapped it into her belt. She had to steady herself. She was breaking down on the inside, but she couldn't give up. Not yet. She could not allow herself to fall apart, not yet. Mirriam silently appeared at her side with Bami in tow. Maleda handed Mirriam the notes and waited for Mirriam to read them as she gripped the hilts of her parents' swords. Swords that she didn't know how to use. Mirriam's face made near imperceptible shifts as she went from the first note to the next, but she noticeably adopted the features of a soldier. She looked back up with a fire in her eyes. Maleda steeled herself and tried to hold onto the Orishas that had held onto her. She could sort through her memories later. She could find who she was later, but at that crucial moment, she had to save her family.

The trains had stopped running in the tunnels, but it was the most incognito way for them to reach the Whitlands, speeding along thanks to Bami's strong legs. As Maleda stared ahead into the fractured tunnel, her mind ran through the letter she read and the conversation she had with Mirriam. She had fought to keep herself steady even as her true state threatened to rip itself out of her with each warble of her voice.

"He's taken them, not just the emperor and empress, but Apara, Folu,… Akande, and…Selene." Maleda wanted to wash the world away in a flood.

"He's got to be planning to take them back to the Whitlands, under the bidding of the evil one. He plays a dangerous game making him his ally. I don't know what the evil one promised him." Mirriam continued. "An elite squadron must be sent after them. The professors helped rescue you. They will surely get your parents." Mirriam stopped a guard to find Puzo.

Maleda remained quiet for a moment, and she felt Mirriam's eyes on her. "Maleda, I know that this is beyond…" She seemed to falter for words. "You can't shut down on me now." She reached for Maleda's shoulder. Her hand found its way there and it took all Maleda had not to shake off her hand. Maleda knew she deserved to be punished. If only she had figured everything out sooner, the fog of her ignorance would have lifted and maybe they would not have been ambushed like this. Maleda looked Mirriam in the eyes.

"We can't send anyone after him, not unless that squadron includes me."

"You know that's all he wants! I will not let you put yourself at risk. You'll all die that way." Mirriam looked over the damaged throne room as fury and frustration passed over her face.

"I've read as much as I could to understand this world," Maleda said while looking to Mirriam. "From what it says on the paper, he will not just kill me right away. Some bargain called for that and that means that there is a chance."

"For what!" Mirriam bellowed. "Even though you know your true name, you're as good as a stranger to your own home! You barely know how to fight or remember!" Maleda swallowed her blunt circumstances.

"The Orisha are with me! I may not know how to fight, but they have risen up in my being to protect me before!" Rapid footfall sounded and stopped by the doorway. The guard that was there took a knee, for the long-lost princess.

"Puzo could not be found, and the professors are rumored to be missing." Mirriam nodded and the guard rose and ran back to repairing the mess they were all in. They didn't have time to seek them out. For all they knew, they were either hiding or dead. There was no time, so Maleda looked back to Mirriam. She braced a look of steel even though her insides felt like they were wilting, a skill she had acquired long ago.

"It has to be me, and I don't care how you feel about it, but I am going to rescue them." *My family.* That's what she should have said, but those words tasted like something she didn't deserve. Mirriam gave her a long heavy look before she agreed, but they decided that sneaking through the tunnels underground would be the best way. Maleda wondered if the king would be obliged to wait to hurt them until she got there or if he had already begun torturing them. She wasn't sure what would wreck her more, but Maleda didn't have time to wonder as Bami careened through the tunnels. When they arrived at a stop, Bami slowed on near silent, predatory feet. The terra stones dimly lit up the walls still. They creeped up the stairs and through the passageways until they reached the surface. The other shore of the empire was not as badly ravaged. Actually, it looked mostly unscathed, as if it was meant to be separated from the other shore, like they should never belong together. She couldn't tell if the inhabitants were silently eliminated or if they were shielding themselves quietly in their homes. The Whitlands were just beyond the mountains at the edge of the city, the border that cradled them in. She could see it in the distance over the rooftops and between buildings that scraped the sky. Mirriam leading, Maleda following, and Bami tailing them from the shadows snaked along the sides of buildings and silently paced themselves through the streets, so they could try to get out of the city.

Maleda should have known something was wrong when she sensed the sudden chill behind her. When she turned, she did not see Bami lurking in the shadows behind them. She was simply gone. Bami wouldn't just pursue someone. She would have remained at their back to guard them. The king's dark allies were more devious than she thought. When Maleda looked ahead, Mirriam was looking back as well. Her eyes widened with alert, and she put a finger to her own lips. If they had snatched Bami, then they were already here. By the Orisha, they could be on a rooftop watching over them at that moment.

Bami's fighting. She has to be. If Maleda didn't focus, then they would surely be doomed by her rising panic. Maleda briefly noted the mansions and smaller castles peppered around the shore and some near the interior of the city, closest to the mountains. They loomed over her like giants who could see her undoing before she could. Then, she realized that they housed her undoing when she felt Zaddae's voice. It did not ring in her ears, but throughout her being. She felt his essence reaching for her and it was laced in panic. Mirriam had no reaction and Maleda knew she could hear nothing. It was coming from her left, in the direction of that house from years ago. As she heard his voice again, she saw his crumpled form on the stage as they were finishing their performance. In her panic and focus on the royal family, she forgot to think about what had become of him. A small gasp escaped her. Mirriam turned away from scouting her surroundings to give Maleda an inquiring look just as she was knocked out and Maleda was dragged off. One moment she was screaming and the next, she was bleary-eyed after something hard collided with her head. Darkness threatened to consume her vision. She still heard Zaddae echoing along with a sickening laugh as she faded into unconsciousness.

CHAPTER 65 - MALEDA

Maleda didn't know how long she had been floating in that see of blackness, but she found herself twitching until she pulled herself fully from the dark waves into the light. The stickiness of unconsciousness somehow felt like she was falling. Oshun was not there to comfort her now. None of the Orisha were. Maleda found herself uncomfortably hoisted under each arm and the tops of her feet were sliding along the floor as she was dragged forward. She was in a room filled with dazzling light that bounced around the space due to mirrors at her left and right, even in the ceiling. She saw the men that dragged her forward, hulking, and rough creatures, but somehow inhuman. She couldn't see beyond their frame to look into the mirrors at her current state, so she looked ahead at the golden throne and the king who sat atop it.

His eyes were what caught her first. They were like a fire that burned black they were locked on her. His mouth held no expression. A thin line that could not even be pegged with portraying disgust, but when she was tossed to his feet, he smiled then. It was the way a father would. He was feline in his subtle movements barely jostling his dark wavy hair that ran over his shoulders. His skin was unnervingly pale, paler than he ever was. What happened to him? No matter her questions, he was her enemy now.

"Well, it's good to see that you are alright. I was so worried after that little display at the princesses' remembrance ceremony, or should I say your ceremony."

She remained on her knees and looked up at the king.

"Where are the emperor and empress?" She asked with a slight shake in her voice. "Where is my family?" There. She admitted it and was near to breaking down in front of the enemy.

"Oh, don't you worry. They are most definitely safe." The king chuckled and put a hand to his face. "Oh, my goodness. I must have forgotten myself. We haven't been properly introduced. Everyone knows who you are, the missing Princess of the Empire of Two Shores: Clementina Maleda Kianira Layla Lesedi, but after your unfortunate bump..." He pointed towards his own head. "You may not remember me. I am King Alexander of the Whitlands. It was some time ago when you were poisoned along with the others." He began to pace around her, a predator watching its prey falter. "In order for you to be saved, terra stones needed to be sewn right into your nerves, right into your bones. Your very blood runs on the stuff. That kind of power could be harnessed to free my power in a way that couldn't be imagined."

"So, you also have powers by the terra stone?"

"No, I'm afraid. But because of your father, I've learned that it can be implanted. It was his feverish work, along with your mother's, that kept you alive, but they are coded to you specifically after implantation. They only obey the song of your body, but if you pass permission over to me, then I can use them."

"I would never give them over to you."

"Well, I can also force them to work in a tool independent of me. I don't know what I'll choose yet."

"Why are you doing this?"

The king stared her down and something shifted in his gaze as he averted her eyes and a smile bloomed on his face. He began to speak with a quiet, sweet venom, "I remember when I first met your father. He came from the west and we were meeting strictly on diplomatic principles, strictly for our own arranged marriages. I was to wed one sister and he was to wed the other, Taraji and Rehema. Well, you know how that turned out, as he ended up choosing your mother instead. It was my brother that ended up marrying Rehema, but miraculously I married Taraji."

He said the queen's name with such reverence, but his expression hardened. "And one day she was gone. Whether it was by her own plot, or whether she was victim to someone else's, is no matter. I thought that if I married one of the royals from Alfajiri, there would be a cooler political climate, but you all have brought squalor and discord to my shores. Our daughter was not born brown, but white. She has been threatened, attacked even because her skin is whiter than the palm of your hand. Thank goodness for that, after seeing what your kind can do. She is innocent and it is no fault of hers that she is her mother's daughter. She is to inherit this land and she will not be tested by the likes of people from your continent."

He started to pace around her then. Maleda knew the people he spoke of. There were some witch doctors who abandoned all sense of ethics and would experiment on the people who were born with skin whiter than the sun. Maleda's mind just stuck on 'your kind' and she understood his poison all too well after watching that planet, so long ago. It was like the longest nightmare she'd ever had.

"In spite of these events and circumstances, my kingdom is experiencing the greatest prosperity in its history. A higher standard of living and a better system of order, no crime unpunished. I intend to expand this good fortune, build an empire. As a show of good faith, the Empire of Two Shores can be the first partner in our expansion and to top it off we ask that you provide us with your power source." The terratech. "If you simply hand over your terratech, then we will not harm you or your family." But they would decimate the rest of the continent. Dread coiled in Maleda's gut. Was it mere grief that had caused the king to become this power-hungry? He was cold, unfeeling, so different than the man who laughed and joked with her father. As retribution for the queen being gone, did he want to scramble to take all the land and parse through it looking for her? If he actually found her and her reasons were deemed unsavory, would he have her imprisoned, killed? Maleda could not do anything but shake her head to deny the King.

"Oh? No?" He chuckled. "You will not be saying the same thing once I show you the pain you have inflicted on others. I may not have been born with powers, but I have made an ally that has given me only a fraction of what I desire. With my ally, the sun will never set on the Whitland Empire."

He turned from her and ascended the throne. She had to appeal to him.

"Please." Maleda began. "I am sorry that she was lost that day, but you and I both know she was honorable. There must be a reason—"

"Oh, foolish girl." The king spoke through his teeth like he was fighting the emotions he reigned in and rested. "They took her away from me."

Maleda was so focused on the war in the king's face and what *they* could mean that she almost didn't register the blow. Her cheek stung and her vision went starry in one eye. It surprised her so much that she just blinked. The hard mirror-like floor bit into her face as she went down. She turned to glare at the guard, but the shock of the figure standing in her way sucked all words from her being.

"You may recognize this face better than the one you've familiarized yourself with for the past few weeks."

She looked at a combination of two people squeezed into one. She saw Zaddae's warm eyes and someone else's black pools of sorrow. The brief look she had gotten of Zuvan's eyes. This wasn't the boy she remembered. This person was broken. He was impossibly pale all traces of his brown gone from his skin and his hair was straighter and retained a different kind of curly bounce. Yet, it was him. What had the King done to him? The guard standing at his side readied to hit Maleda again, but he remained impassive and said nothing.

"So, son, this was the girl you coddled all this time. And to think that I thought you hadn't found anything." The King chuckled.

Zaddae—no, Zuvan—didn't say anything. He just watched silently as the guard was joined by two others who shoved her around with blows hard enough to send her hurling in another direction. Maleda's panic and pain were fighting each other, but eventually it was only the guards throwing her around that kept her upright. It seemed like an eternity when they stopped and even then, they dragged her roughly across the floor, but not before the King offered a parting message.

"Trust, princess, I will coax it out of you." A chuckle sealed his promise and the last thing she saw was Zaddae's impassive face before she passed into unconsciousness.

"Wait!" Her head was yanked back out of the pool of inky black as she was taken back to the presence of the king. He descended his throne again, with even more venom in his smile.

"Have you ever wondered about time and how it has felt so ancient and odd to you?" Maleda was silent in the face of the tyrant.

"I did not poison you. My father's father did, 200 years ago." Maleda's heartbeat ratcheted faster. Even though her memories came back to her full force, she didn't want to accept it, believe it. 200 years. Although Oshun didn't say it, Maleda knew, but she would not admit it out loud. It was too much to confess what was stolen from her, the time stolen from her. She didn't feel old. Her body felt the same, but her memories, the Orisha, and this man kept telling her she was older. "Congratulations, you are a heightened being."

"That's not true. It's only been two years—"

"No, you see. That's a trick that my friend has orchestrated. You believed that only two years have passed, but you missed your wretched city for two mortal lifetimes. Your family believed it too. As a matter of fact, the whole empire was cloaked in that belief and time was slowed so that they would remain as they are. And the ones who fought it were forbidden to say otherwise." Maleda couldn't even croak. Her soul was lead and it threatened to drag her to the floor. She was frozen in place. "Enjoy your night."

* * *

Maleda wished that unconsciousness had stayed with her. Maleda stared into nothing as she was dragged through the castle and slammed into a stinking cell, layered with hay on one side and a bucket on the other side. She was shaking in a way that she could not control. All she heard was that cursed number. 200 years. So, she was a heightened being. Absent from her family. Absent from her city. Absent from her culture, from her life. A sickening heaviness took over her, but her stomach wanted to purge itself. Yet, she just sat there shaking, making soundless cries as her eyes blurred.

Metal bars kept her in, and a defiled stone wall was at her side. A barred window was beyond her reach, and it let in the fading orange evening light. As she sat curled in on herself, her mind was flooded with the people like her on the parallel planet. How they lived, wondered, and dreamed. How they tried to fill in the blanks of their ancestors who had been rendered nameless and whose stories were swept into an abyss with an impossible descent, hidden in a desert with ever-shifting sand. Yet, she had seen the depths of that abyss only to crawl out of it and she had thirsted for her memories that were scattered across that desert. Would it have been better if she just stayed down or if her curiosity wasn't satiated? She knew the answer, but all she could think was bless her people and curse the invention that threatened to damn them. Bless her people but curse the pain she was going to face. Maleda almost didn't hear the faraway clang, but somehow, she snapped back into her body and looked about frantically, making sure the guards weren't coming for her. She locked onto those fire eyes, and she shoved herself into a corner of the cell. At first, she thought that two soul-split Zuvan bodies had shown up again and a gasp escaped her throat. The cell door remained closed, and she curled into herself quaking, awaiting the first blow.

"Maleda." his voice sounded strained. "Please look at me."

She refused.

"Was any of it real?"

No. She *should* have said 'none of it was real.' Declarative and cold. Yet. She could not perform and pretend. Pathetic, that's what she thought of herself. A low rumble of a laugh came from him all semblance of the strain gone. She turned to look at him and she was breathing fire.

"Silly girl, did you actually think I loved you? Do you think that just because you've forgotten, you don't have to be responsible for what you've done? We don't have the luxury of forgetting. You took something from us, and you will give it back."

"What could I have possibly taken?"

"I'm surprised you haven't figured it out yet, but it's no matter. Once we have your powers, it will be returned."

Zaddae's words swirled in Maleda's mind, but she just tried to focus on getting more information.

"Why do you look so pale?"

"The King's ally gave him wishes before you disappeared. He split me into two beings. I could change into another person in the same body, or I could walk in two bodies. At the performance, I was assimilated back into one body. This is my true form."

Well, at least he was still the talkative type, even if he didn't answer her question.

Maleda hesitated. "Zuvan" The name felt strange coming from her mouth, but he looked at her intently all the same. "All this time and it meant nothing to you?"

There were warring emotions on his face and remarkably he seemed to be going paler, until he fell to the floor, clutching one of the bars. Maleda gasped when a muscled figure emerged from the shadows and crouched beside him.

"Are you alright Zuvan?" The figure asked. The voice was anciently familiar, yet she couldn't place it.

Zuvan did his best to wave him off, but the figure remained there as Zuvan's face was full of strain. Yet, with one breath the strain in his face passed and his face again became expressionless. He chuckled again as he rose.

"Forgive me, that's a little infarction passed down from my father. I'd like to think that I'm stronger than him though." He was turning to walk away.

"Wait, you said that the king's ally wished for you to be split *before* I disappeared. How could you have been there? And how could the king have been there?" He couldn't have accidentally let that information slip. Was he mistaken?

"Magic does strange things."

Maleda eyes widened with the realization, and she watched as Zuvan and the shadowed stranger walked away. Even with this new information, she made herself give in to sleep. The gruesome guards who had their faces masked came back the next morning and threw the cell door open.

CHAPTER 66 - MALEDA

They dragged her from her cell and shoved her along, making her injuries sing out in protest. There was no one else in the room save for another man at the king's side who was not there the previous day and the king's brother, arms crossed over his barrel chest. The daughter that the king spoke so strongly of wasn't even there. Wouldn't the king want her there to witness Maleda's torture or did he secretly think that she was too dangerous? Zuvan was at his side as well, but his face was impassive, not even a twitch in his jaw. Yet, there was something that shifted in his eyes as if he fought to stand there. Perhaps she was just imagining things.

"Did you sleep well?" The king crooned as he reclined in his throne.

"You were there 200 years ago, weren't you? Not your ancestor?"

He completely ignored her comment.

"Well, I hope you slept well because you're going to have to put up a fight."

"Why not just tell me that? Why try to confuse me? All these secrets—"

"Because!" He hissed cutting her off. "It's more fun that way." By the sands, what was he talking about? Maybe 200 years had robbed him of his sense.

"This ally has helped you use magic to keep you and Zuvan alive for all this time. Surely, they can give you what you're looking for." The king rose and threw off his cape, glistening in gold, white and red royal dressings. One of the masked guards drew something from behind the throne. Maleda's breath caught when she realized it was the chest at the foot of her bed. She wished that somehow it was empty, but those enchanting bottles with that magical paint glistened and clinked when he threw the lid open. He picked one up and uncorked it and looked thoughtfully at the red paint as it slid around in its bottle.

"Hm." He hummed simply before he threw the bottle down on the floor. Maleda jumped and the guards held her back, but she didn't think she could move as he grabbed one bottle after another and threw them at her feet. In shock, Maleda begged him to stop, but he continued and looked at her with disinterest and back to the bottles as he continued to destroy them. Maleda didn't expect herself to scream, but she did, and it was a wonder how she didn't shatter every cursed mirror in that throne room. The memory clambered back over her. She remembered her father, Emperor Olmec, presenting them to her, explaining how these paints worked. How they could store memories, be programmed, and how they modified the substance together. All of the love stored in those bottles was shattered and spewed across the floor. Tears broke their way from Maleda's face as the king looked at her and raised his eyebrows.

"Oh, nothing to say now?" Maleda looked at him with an ancient sorrow in her eyes as she breathed through her tears, but her words were filled with a different ancient malice.

"Stop. This."

"Or what? As I've been told, your terratech is less than desired as you lack the ability to even call on it." Maleda kept her chin up and her eyes burned as she stared down the king, even though her being was filled with shame. "I hear that you are an artist and an engineer of sorts." As he said it, a guard shoved her down into the paint and she felt the shock of it go through her. It was responding to her terratech, but something felt wrong. Something felt twisted. The paint somehow shifted to the blurs of images that crossed her mind. She couldn't tell if the paint wouldn't let go of her hands or if she was just too stunned to move.

The king sneered down at the shifting pool of paint. "Oh, looks like your mind's a little messy." Maleda looked from the king to Zuvan's placid expression becoming hard. Then, a memory came across the splatter of paint. It was through her own eyes. She was peering around the corner, and she heard her eldest brother arguing with her father and mother. *Why would the Orisha choose her? She wasn't born with this power! You only sewed them into her bones! All she does is go off on her own. She doesn't care about this kingdom the way I do!* He stormed away and Maleda retreated in her hiding place as she watched her brother bolt down the hall. She hadn't believed that she could do it then, be the chosen one. She wasn't even chosen. She had struggled to train for that short time before the attack on the castle, although she tried her best. The paint wanted to show her more, twist her back into the time where she felt her original insufficiency. Her vision seemed frayed when she fell back into the throne room and the room swayed as she was on her knees. The paint stayed on the image but swam as if it was its own body of water. Maleda had used her art to escape to another world, but now the memories and criticism she found in it threatened to swallow her up.

"Don't think you're getting off that easy artist." He casually strolled to her side skirting around the paint that had mixed together on the floor. Then, his hand had fisted her hair and his foot shoved her back down. Her hands were locked in the paint again and there was no way to break free. "A story, a story. An artist always tells one whether they want to or not."

She was sucked in again and she remembered the king even more. They thought she'd forget, but she remembered everything. She felt her blood boil from the poison that had been unknowingly slipped to her and the other children, but a venomous voice whispered to her while her body convulsed. Even on that glassy throne room floor, she relived it and convulsed all the same. It was not the king, but his ally who she heard.

"If you could understand where exactly I come from, you would be even more terrified of me." Maleda mouthed for silent calls for help and her vision flashed from the other children's bodies around her to the sneering king.

"One day, you will grow older with terratech sewn into your bones and I will ask for it. If you do not give it to me, I will destroy all you love. You can hide and your allies will have to fight, but either way I will find you." That voice slithered across her entire being and its chuckle sank into her. Maleda tried to shake off the memory, but another started up. This time the paint slid away from her fingers and drew itself up into forms of people. Mirriam and Maleda in those hoods, back at the castle in the empire. They were arguing and Maleda had tried to set up hints for herself around the city as best as she could in case she ever returned. Whoever threatened her long ago claimed that everyone would forget her, save for him. Maybe it was better this way. If she could just disappear and everyone was cursed to forget her there would be no one to look for, no one to connect to. But the king and his ally had other plans. The door bolted open just like she remembered, but it was Zuvan who came through, ready to apprehend her. The son of his father. The fierce anger and fire in his eyes faded when he saw her. He kept his iron swords aloft and Mirriam was ready to take him out, but the chaos distracted him and he moved to slow to kill them. Maleda bolted into the passage hidden in her room, the one she never got to try upon her return. She tried to revive the memory of where the passages went, but she never stopped running. No one could know that it was the kingdom across the water and beyond the Empire that committed these acts. They didn't want war. They wanted annihilation. Maleda heard Mirriam chasing after her screaming *Run Maleda!* She didn't know how far she ran, but the pain ricocheted between different parts of her legs, lungs, and sides and even if she was going to hurl her guts up, she couldn't stop. Her terratech flared in her, but she didn't know how to release it. It threatened to burn her down, but Bamidele already felt her distress and found her way into the tunnels. She was a thing of glory, but she swept Maleda and Mirriam up, continuing to bolt faster than Maleda could comprehend.

Maleda was jolted out of inky blackness with a bucket of water as she sprawled on the floor of her cell. She was barely aware of the snickering guards whose laughs echoed down the hallways. She shook and could not manage a sound from her ravaged throat. She was reliving it, every second of it. Maleda could feel the terratech's power pulsating under skin, could swear that it whooshed out of her fingers. He probably saw that and was glad of it, satisfied that some power could be extracted at the expense of her pain. It was probably the only reason he stopped and was preparing something else. She barely clung to the parallel memory of her convulsing and being absorbed back into the pain of that three-dimensional memory made by the paint she had once loved. She remembered Mirriam being taken away and waking up to Mirriam crouching over her. Mirriam could not have betrayed her. Someone had to have helped her heal after that. And Zuvan. What was she to think of him? He was choosing that night whether to strike them down or let them go, but he hesitated, and it was that hesitation that made Maleda shudder along with those iron swords. It pulled on her mind, but the scholar in her was tired. No one came for her that evening or in the night. She had no weapons and possessions on her, except Cham who remained on her finger and blended into her skin, invisible to everyone but her. Did the king already slaughter her parents?

No allies. No hope. No courage. If only she had not run away, maybe she could have found a way out of her curse, but she was rotting in a cell waiting for a punishment that could only be unimaginably worse than the last.

CHAPTER 67 - MALEDA

They waited days before they dragged Maleda out of her cell again, sliding miserable trays of something that resembled food. She tried to ignore the echoes of screams and accompanying laughter as she backed herself into the corner of her cell, but they eventually came. Zuvan was not with the guards this time either and for that she was severely grateful. She didn't know if she could look at him now. Unlike the throne room of the previous two visits, this one was in a room full of columns. The throne was flush against the wall as if it had been carved out of the wall itself and the columns, she passed were wider than she was. She walked with the guards, each gripping and arm way tighter than necessary. The king's smile the other day had been near chipper in comparison to the one he had at this moment. It was dark and twisted as if he just discovered something that he didn't like.

"I've had enough of this. Waiting for your powers to surface. A wisp of it showed itself the other day, but I am not satisfied with menial tests to try and coax it out." The guards threw her at his feet. No one else was there but the man at the king's side with a deadly sneer on his face. "So, I've decided not to wait any longer." From some dark corner, an array of hooded people with hands bound behind their backs were shoved into the room. Maleda couldn't feel her heart beating, felt like the air was being stolen from her lungs. Zuvan, their escort, brought each of them to their knees and removed the bags from their head. Maleda stared at the royal family, her family. "Nothing to say again? Well, aren't we crafting a story to tell?" The king sneered at them.

They looked unharmed, more than unharmed. They looked completely untouched.

"Confused about the difference in appearance?" He forced her father's chin up to look at Maleda, "See, while I had you all staying with me after the dreadful attack, I was looking for your daughter like I promised. Found her, like I promised. The only difference is back at the castle you did not agree to supply the terratech I required and she had no choice. But what difference does it make now? She knows how little you think of her. All of you for watching her run like a frightened dog, a mixed beast that doesn't even know what it is."

"Maleda, don't you listen—" The emperor's words were cut off by a blow to his side and he doubled over, recovering with wheezing breaths. Maleda looked from him to the rest of them. Selene's tear-streaked face almost broke Maleda and kept her focused on finding a way to get them out.

"Mabow, I'm sorry—" Her eldest brother got out before he too was kicked in the side. Sorry. Not a denial, but a confession to his prior disbelief in her. She did not have time to think on it now, only time to think of how to get them out.

"So, what do you want? You want me to produce some form of terratech or I watch them die?!" Maleda bellowed at the pale king.

"Oh, no. That would be far too easy. I want them to witness your failure, your downfall. In front of me. Right here, right now." Then, Zuvan walked forward with Mirriam. There was a strange glow about his eyes now. The guards had even back away. Maleda had never seen that glow before. Mirriam on the other hand was sweating and struggling against an invisible grip. Her right arm then converted into a whip that buzzed with terratech currents. So, the king had her body modded out in the desert. Trick shoulder indeed. Every time she rolled it, that discomfort must have been from the unfamiliar tech in her system. Zuvan looked even more blanched then normal.

"Either you give me ownership over your terratech or your family will watch you die inch by inch." Zuvan growled at Maleda in a way that made her stumble back a step.

"Run!" Mirriam bellowed before her arm whipped itself about against her will. Somehow, he had a hold of what replaced her real arm and fractions of the rest of her. Mirriam ran after her, trying to resist, but Zuvan bolted. The room seemed endless and Maleda did well to avoid the balcony at the edge of the room. She ducked into the maze of columns and stayed silent. Not a shadow to be seen and not a footstep to be heard, but she ducked as his blade sliced into the column that she stood behind moments ago. Even though she timed the dodge just right, she still found herself on her knees but scrambled to run away from him. Maleda didn't know how to fight, wasn't trained in it and now she had to brawl with him. Maleda grasped at anything, absolutely anything to get him to stop.

"Zaddae, stop!" She dodged another blow and backed up in the direction of her parents, the throne. "You told me that you cared for the princess before this all happened. Not the figment of Clementina, but me! Don't do this!" He was coming in fast with a speeding walk, both swords out.

"Foolish girl." He crooned with fire swimming in his eyes. "I would never care for you."

"You told me you did!" Maleda barely dodged a swipe and felt the sting on her arm, the new warmth spreading down her arm. "Please, I don't want to hurt you!"

"Oh, you will!" The king cut in. Maleda looked to him as she was keeping her distance from Zuvan, who was slashing his sword across the ground. Every thought eddied out of her head. The king had Selene's hair fisted and she was doing her best to fight him, but her little fists were feeble punches against the might of the king. "The prince has forgotten where his allegiance lies, so today of all days he needed a little encouragement. Something tells me that you could use a little of the same."

Zuvan barely missed Maleda again and the sword grazed her side, ripping her shirt and revealing bloodied skin to the air.

"No, don't hurt her! Please!" Maleda begged keeping her tear-streaked eyes between Selene, the king, and Zuvan. "I will do what you ask!" She bellowed past the sobs that near drowned her. "I promise. Just let her go!"

"No! My patience is thin. You will show me now!" But Maleda couldn't.

There was no reserve to draw from, no connection. Even as she screamed Oshun's name in her being, there was nothing that resounded in her. She had no idea what to concentrate on except for Selene's face and that made something fizzle at her fingertips, but apparently that was not what the king wanted.

"Not enough." That was what he said with lethal calm, like a loud whisper, before he unsheathed a hidden knife and thrashed across Selene's side. Maleda's vision went white, and she couldn't hear her own scream over the blinding bolts of lights and she called on every Orisha known, to annihilate this pale invader. She was trapped inside some spinning energy and she tried to break free of it, fought the outstretched position she was thrown into. Water spun at her left hand, earth at her right, air at her right foot, and fire at her left. The sheer force of it rattled the king out of his control and everyone fell onto their backs in the face of Maleda's might. Around her, columns of light sprang up each colored as an element and each shaped like an older version of the children who were poisoned just like her. She felt their awakening and could see through their eyes for a brief moment. They were out there and alive, hidden like she was, but alive.

Maleda's felt her control slipping. The warmth of the light made her heartbeat quicken, but an overwhelming sense of calm washed over her. Maleda found herself sitting on the ground further away from the room, like she was looking through a window and she found herself standing behind a female figure adorned in golden fabric. Oshun had taken the forefront control of her body and Maleda took in gasping breaths as she let her.

Oshun called on all the Orishas that saved Maleda's life and continued to reside in her soul. They shot out of Maleda in bolts of multicolored light and she could see each of them flying to points that encircled the empire, both shores. They hovered like small stars until they grew to the size of titans and stretched out their hands. A golden light spread out from each of their hands growing and connecting to form the shape of a dome buzzing with golden light, protecting the empire. Beneath the dome created by the Orisha, the empire's own dome had risen as well, with a similar golden color, another layer of protection but from the mortal world.

It was then that she felt the arrow pierce her side and she snapped back inside herself. The power still flurried inside her, but the figures disappeared into the floor. Maleda heard Bami's screech long before she broke through the glass that separated them from the balcony outside. She attempted to attack the king, but Zuvan warded her off with arrows. In spite of the pain at her side, Maleda ran for Selene who was already in Akande's arms. He somehow freed himself, their parents, and her other brothers from their holdings. He passed her onto Maleda before he turned to end Zuvan, but Zuvan had already taken him down with one blow, unmoving. Mirriam was somehow broken of her bonds, but Zuvan was still reined in by the king.

The three youngest siblings piled onto Bami and Mirriam shielded them as best as she could while she did so. Maleda squeezed Selene's hand as Bami howled.

"Get them to the castle!" Bami broke back out onto the balcony and was airborne. Another arrow sliced Maleda's leg and Mirriam pulled her along screaming at her to run. Her parents screamed at her to go and Zuvan had nothing but murder in his eyes. Mirriam was at Maleda's side as she ran. Her tree had to be long destroyed and those desert dunes would forever be stained with the blood of those killed in the fire. She had to call on that memory that was buried deep within her, the symbol of how she would live. As she sprinted for it, she asked for that power to do one thing for her in her escape. She could feel what she sought rising from the floor, no longer dry, but flowing towards her at lightning speed. She tried to let the muscles of her back breathe as she bolted for that impossible fall. Maleda didn't need to turn around to see the paint rushing in from the throne room and feel it rushing up her pants, her skin. They were only feet away, but she could feel herself unfolding. They jumped and Mirriam held onto her and Maleda's wings unfolded and she became the Black Butterfly. Thankful that she lived, her parents gave her a motion tattoo that paid homage to the Orisha that saved the world, the same one that flew in the form of a peacock to the otherworld to save the planet. She felt the paint seal itself over her golden wings. Her metal rainbow, gilded wings broke free from that tattoo at her back and she and Mirriam dived for the waters below. There was an ancient passage that led to one of the flooded, damaged tunnels. When they had finished running back to the castle, she learned that the royal children had been taken by Puzo to her father's home country and Selene would be tended to there. That was if she lived. Bami was still there waiting as Maleda had the arrows swiftly pulled from Bami and her wounds tended to. Mirriam hoisted Maleda onto Bami's back after hurried bandages were applied. They had to run past the city, past the dunes. Although her potential power was great, she had a lot to learn before she could save anyone, but she had to believe that she could save her family, the empire, and the continent. There was no time nor mercy that allowed them to mourn. The skies were no longer safe. Her wildest dreams on parchment and ink had come true and burned behind her along with the screams as creatures from the night pillaged their way to the city. They had to find safety and sanctuary across the dunes that rolled like water, until they reached the waters and could disappear like their Igbo brothers and sisters in the civilizations of the deep.

CHAPTER 68 - ZUVAN

Zuvan screamed inside himself, screamed against what he had done. His spirit was imprisoned by one of the ally's aides. Maleda had been brilliant with those lines and dots glowing on her brown skin. Her rainbow-colored wings. If it was the last he was to see of her, he would take it. If he were to see her again, he wanted her to kill him because that meant she would get to walk away. What he had chosen to do and now been forced to do... It had been foolish to try and seek her out. Look at what he'd done, what he'd unleashed. Yet, his face was placid as he knelt before the king.

"Now, you disgrace. There will be no more funny business." Zuvan knew he made sure to say it in front of Maleda's parents, in front of the limp body of her eldest brother. It was a means of sealing the performance. "You will bring me back that lost black princess with all of her terratech flowing through her or my second will bring me your head."

Zuvan nodded.

"Yes, your majesty." No matter how he may have wanted her before, he was too far gone to consider it now or consider it good. Now, Zuvan was after that black girl and the terratech laced in her body, so they could claim the rest of the continent.

Acknowledgments

Thank you to everyone who has been part of my writing and publishing journey:

To God: I don't know how I got here, but no matter how high I was or how discouraged I was, you were there. There was a part of me that believed I wouldn't get here, but here I am. Thank you for your presence and for clearing the way for me.

To my tenth-grade English teacher, Ms. Susan Watson-Bell: I remember that you had us do quarterly assignments where he had to submit a poem as part of our portfolio. You kept writing 'submit' at the bottom of each of my poems, but I didn't know what you meant. I waited until the fourth and final poem submission to ask you and you told me that I should submit my poems to writing contests. I was so surprised and the possibilities seemed that much bigger. Thank you for being one of the first people to encourage me to share my writing.

To my English Teacher, Ms. Susan Jones: Thank you so much for being an amazing teacher and for being wildly encouraging. I loved being in your class and I loved learning from you. You've definitely earned your retirement!

To my AP Euro and History teacher, Mr. Larry Schirling: Thank you for teaching me that history is a big story! I would come home to my parents reciting the stories that you told us about rulers, movements, and governments. You were such a joy and I didn't know how much I loved diving into history until I experienced your way of teaching. You've had more impact on me than you can understand.

To my Honors Academic Writing professor, Ms. Cynthia J. Lowenthal: Thank you so much for indulging my story ideas and giving me advice during your office hours. It was always so fun and enriching talking to you. You also helped up my writing abilities and gave great feedback for my class assignments!

To my Poetry Writing I professor, Mr. Gary Jackson: I'd never experienced as much creative freedom as I did in your Poetry class. Your assignments allowed me to dive into what drives me as well as what haunts me. It was great talking to you about my work during our office hours. You provided solid guidance and encouragement.

To my Afrofuturism professor, Dr. Lisa Young: Thank you so much for existing, like straight up. I'd barely dived into Afrofuturism before your class, but you helped me understand it so much more. You helped me connect the dots and really understand the significance of Nnedi Okorafor (Africanjujuism and Africanfuturism), Octavia Butler, Janelle Monae, Sun Ra, Ntozake Shange, etc. There was never a dull moment in your class and thank you for blowing my mind.

To Drisana McDaniel and Sara Makeba: It was so great to talk with you both and Lisa in that coffee shop about Afrofuturism and everything else. It felt like we were destined to meet. It was so amazing to do the Come On In the Room presentation with you and meet like-minded ladies of color. Just like I told Lisa, you both blew my mind and I'm blessed to know you.

To my Civil Rights professor, Dr. Jon Hale: I was afraid to take your class because I was expecting to feel depressed every day, but it was the opposite. It was liberating for all of us to talk about the past and how we can shape the future. Your passion for the Freedom School was so inspiring to take in and it was always cool to talk to you about the day's topic after class. Thank you for affirming my ideas and giving me advice.

To my Honors advisor, Dr. Trisha Folds-Bennett: I remember our very first conversation at the Honors interest meeting about the travel program to Latvia and Lithuania. Thank you for encouraging me and being there for me through the years as we went over my class schedule or talked about my business ideas.

To Dr. Jason White: Thank you for being my professor and for your office hours! You were always so helpful and encouraging! All the way from Arts Management to Arts Entrepreneurship, you have inspired me and encouraged me to take control of my journey.

To Dr. Karen Chandler: Thank you for being inspirational, motivating, and overall amazing. Your high standards in Arts Management class helped me to elevate my own and you are such a visionary!

To my Mom, Dad, and brother Josh: Thank you so much for riding the waves of my dreams with me and encouraging me to chase them. We have been through and overcome so much through the years and I'm glad that you've been here with me through the journey.

To my readers (especially my black girls): I hope that you feel seen. I hope that you are encouraged to tell your stories, make your art, do your science, do your dance, and do whatever else you want. The possibilities are endless for you and you are worth it, no matter what anyone says. Thank you for existing and thank you for reading my story.

About the Author

Jessica Mack grew up in Ladson, South Carolina, where she spent her childhood bouncing between libraries and bookstores. Jessica started telling stories because she was jealous of magical beings called storytellers who could breathe life into their universes with just their words, so of course, she decided to get some magic and make her own worlds too. In renaissance-like fashion, she is also an artist, poet, blogger, youtuber, and is working on telling stories in other media as well.

You can connect with me on:
- https://bio.link/ebonyxscape
- https://twitter.com/ebonyxscape
- https://www.facebook.com/ebonyxscape
- https://ebonyxscape.com